Gods of Aberdeen

MICAH NATHAN

SIMON & SCHUSTER
New York   London   Toronto   Sydney

SIMON & SCHUSTER
Rockefeller Center
1230 Avenue of the Americas
New York, NY 10020

For information about special discounts for bulk purchases,
please contact Simon & Schuster Special Sales at
1-800-456-6798 or business@simonandschuster.com

Designed by Julie Schroeder
Manufactured in the United States of America

1   3   5   7   9   10   8   6   4   2

Library of Congress Cataloging-in-Publication Data
Nathan, Micah.
Gods of Aberdeen: a novel / Micah Nathan.
p.   cm.
1. Young men—Fiction. 2. College students—Fiction.
3. New England—Fiction. I. Title.
PS3614.A86G63 2005
813'.6—dc22   2005042514

The author gratefully acknowledges permission to reprint lyrics from
"Please Don't Talk About Me When I'm Gone"
Words by Sidney Clare, music by Sam H. Stept
© Copyright 1927 (Copyright Renewed) and
assigned to Bourne Co. and Remick Music Corp. in USA
All Rights Reserved   International Copyright Secured

ISBN 0-7432-5082-6

Acknowledgments

This book exists because of my parents' belief in the value of creativity, and because of my sister's love for stories.

Thanks to Marly Rusoff, agent extraordinaire, and the incomparable Marysue Rucci, my editor at Simon & Schuster. I am indebted to Henry Morrison, Larry Block, Arthur Phillips, Chuck Adams, and Pat Withrow, all of whom played pivotal roles in this book's genesis. I am also indebted to Tara Parsons, the Nathans, the Kanes, the Cohens, the Bickoffs, and to my three brothers: Jake Halpern, Brian Smith, and Jonah Dayan. Thank you all for your support and optimism. It helped more than you know.

My deepest debt is to my wife, who believed when I did not, and who nurtured this dream as her own.

To Rachel, who holds my heart

Gods of Aberdeen

Grounded in the natural philosophy of the Middle Ages, alchemy formed a bridge, on the one hand into the past . . . on the other into the future, to the modern psychology of the unconscious.

—CARL JUNG

A man may be born, but in order to be born he must first die, and in order to die he must first awake.

—GEORGE GURDJIEFF

Prologue

I remember Aberdeen College well—even now I could tell you what it looks like, on any particular day, at any particular time. I could tell you how the air tastes and how long the shadows are that run from the silver maples in the Quad, streaming over the grass like rivers of ink. I could tell you about winter in Aberdeen, sloping ice-sheathed drifts, tall, naked trees painting the snow black. How the wind sounds when it darts through the forest, how the sky looks at night, white dots spattered across a shadowy canvas.

Not too long ago I returned to Aberdeen, to Dr. Cade's house, walking to the back, to the pond, which I expected to see as I remembered it most fondly: jagged reeds along its edge; kites of gnats looping endlessly above a mirrored surface crinkled by the wind; nets of hornwort and duckweed hugging the shores. But despite the years the flash of memories was still too vivid, and I couldn't dip my fingers into the cool water for fear of seeing something bubble up from the unknown depths and greet me with hollow eyes and bared teeth. And as for Dr. Cade's house, the house that had seduced me away from my freshman year at Aberdeen, it now looked abandoned. Its windows were covered in grime, the paint was peeling, and the driveway didn't wind through the eons of time, as I'd once imagined, but ended where it always did, at a small walkway where the grass poked between the flagstones.

I drove into town and saw that Aberdeen itself had also withered;

time diminished it into what it always was—a stately old college nec-
essarily blind to the outside world. The H. F. Mores Library, where
mysterious forces once loomed, was now only a stuffy crypt of books.
The hills and forests surrounding the campus, where we'd spent those
bitter winter mornings searching for our lost friend, had regained
their anonymity, towering copses of spindly trees dissolving into a
dark blur. There were a few students milling about the Quad, those
who'd returned early from summer break, and I glided among them,
unseen, under Garringer's spire-tipped shadow, to the black oak at the
edge of campus. On its trunk, amid puckered scars and cracked bark
and an obsidian trail of ants, I looked for the remains of the initials
Dan and I had carved into the wood, many years ago on a warm
October day. I knew where Dan was, but the other friends I'd made
during those days had long disappeared within the folds of time,
swallowed like old wounds on the trunk of that black oak.

I went back to Aberdeen because I hoped it could return something of mine it had taken long ago. But I realized such places never
give back what they take. It's a toll they exact, and when the debt has
been paid, you know your time is done not by the clang of any bell,
but by the soft rustle of apathy. Nostalgia becomes a dark lens, the
promise of immortality sheds its skin, and you find yourself gliding,
unseen, under the shadows of the giants in your life, who have grown
too tired to take notice.

PART I

—

Aberdeen

Chapter 1

I arrived in Fairwich at dusk, and with my arrival came the rain. The clouds had been threatening all day, from New Jersey to Connecticut, and when I stepped off the bus there was a gust of cool wind, the clouds rumbled softly, and the rain began. I called for a cab from a payphone booth and waited in the booth, watching the sidewalk darken and the leaves drip. Down the street a little boy dropped his bright yellow bike on his front lawn and ran into his house.

The storm had worsened by the time the cab arrived. The cabby wore a green baseball cap, frayed around the edges, the plastic backing of the cap dug into the tanned, black-hair-bristled rolls on the back of his neck. A limp cigarette hung from the corner of his mouth. I asked him to take me to Aberdeen, and he asked me if it was my first year. I said it was. He nodded, one hand on the wheel, the other draped over the top of the passenger seat.

"Where you from?" he said.

"New Jersey."

"I used to date a Jersey girl," he said.

I leaned my head against the window and stared at the trees, letting them whip by in a brown and green blur. The road didn't have any shoulder, just a thin line where the blacktop ended and spiky weeds began. It reminded me of my old home in West Falls, riding into town with my mom, staring at the road edged with dusty, dark earth.

"First time in the country?" The cabby eyed me in his rearview.

"I'm an American," I said.

He looked at me in the rearview again. "You serious?" He laughed. "I mean out *here*. In the country. Farms . . . forests . . ."

"Oh," I said, "I haven't been in the country since I was ten."

"Parents don't take you camping anymore?"

"I'm an orphan," I said.

"No shit?"

I nodded.

The cabby took the cigarette out of his mouth, stared at it a moment, and flicked it out the window.

As the cab rounded the bend of the brick entranceway, behind the thinning maples and pines, there stood Garringer Hall. It looked less like a student union than a medieval castle, and I imagined a dragon, with green scales and membranous wings and eyes like glistening rubies, circling down from the gray sky and perching on the largest of the three spires. I pulled out the tri-fold map that had been sent to me in my acceptance package. Two smaller structures flanked the hall, with a covered brick and wood causeway joined to the western-most building. This was the H. F. Mores Library—where I would be spending two mornings per week, according to my work-study assignment—not as tall as Garringer but longer, made of the same rough-cut granite blocks and topped with mullioned dormers. The easternmost building was all ivy-covered dark stone with a turreted roof, a massive clock sitting atop the center turret, and I recognized this structure as Thorren Hall, the main classroom center on campus. We drove slowly up the gradually sloping hill, students hurrying around us with their gray umbrellas and brown book bags and black shoes shiny from the rain.

I don't remember exactly what I expected of my housing, though I imagined it would be similar to every image I'd seen on TV of college dorms: small, carpeted, and a bed with a sagging, stained mattress. I was surprised, however, when I opened the heavy wooden door to my room in Paderborne Hall. Inside was a gracious space, with an eleven-foot peaked ceiling, a scarred parquet floor, and a dark-stained desk, set against bookshelves still showing the litter of students past—gum wrappers, pens, and paper clips. Ivory-colored drapes fluttered in the breeze from an open window. I dropped my bag and sat on the floor, listened to the soft thunder, watched the sable-colored clouds rolling over the swaying trees with their pale leaves turned up against the storm.

Affinity for open spaces is in my blood; I was born and spent the first ten years of my life in West Falls, Minnesota, in a small house on a farm. My father left when I was five, and my mother died of cancer when I was ten, and I was sent to live with her second cousin Nana, in a two-bedroom apartment in one of Stulton, New Jersey's "urban renewal" zones. It was a prison sentence. Nana didn't seem too fond of me, and her husband Leon and their two sons were downright hostile. My classmates at my new school didn't like me because I was too young, having skipped a grade in grammar school.

There was something suffocating about Stulton, like a wet, gray blanket had been dropped over the city and we were all trapped underneath. Summers were the worst—the squall of dripping air conditioners, hot bus exhaust, heat shimmering off the sidewalks. During summer I missed my childhood home the most. I felt if I could just return to West Falls and sneak back into my house and live like a stowaway in the crawlspace or under the attic eaves, that everything would be okay again, that I'd slip back into my former life and it would be as if my dad had never left and my mom had never died. But going back home was just as impossible as my mom's resurrection. West Falls had died with her, and Stulton was all I had left.

But eventually I adjusted, and I made the high school into my sanctuary, the only place where I could read in peace and not have to listen to the blaring TV or the barking dogs or the arguing neighbors. I'd stay in the school library after hours, reading my books until the janitor noticed and sent me home. Sympathetic teachers gave me paper and pens, notebooks and a calculator, and I won academic awards every year up until graduation. I displayed an affinity for languages, especially Latin. By senior year I'd made some good friends, and even though I missed West Falls, I'd developed a sort of hardened loyalty to where I was. It was misery, but it was a misery I knew well.

After graduation my friends scattered like seeds in the wind. I was the only one who stayed. I took a job as a stock boy at a convenience mart across the street from our apartment. Every month college brochures arrived, and every month Nana told me I was too poor to afford college. Slowly I felt myself catching her apathy and resignation about life. My friends were gone. My sanctuary—high school—was gone. So I lowered my head and kept working and stashed the money from my paychecks in a hole in our bathroom floor. And then one Sunday night, while taking out the trash, I saw the dark outline of a brochure with ABERDEEN COLLEGE printed across the front in gleaming white, peering at me through the garbage bag's translucent plastic. I ripped open the bag, took out the brochure, and read it while sitting in the dim light of the stairwell.

Aberdeen College. Located in Fairwich, Connecticut. Established 1902. Its motto, printed beneath:

Ex Ungue Leonem

From the part we may judge of the whole. Literal translation: from the claw we may judge of the lion. The glossy brochure photos promised it all: gently sloping hills, lush trees, a shadow-speckled country field. Centered on the front of the brochure was Garringer Hall, looking like a Gothic cathedral with students standing on its front steps. The blonde women were smartly dressed with plaid bows in their hair, and the men had leather book bags and preternaturally confident smiles. *Ex Ungue Leonem.* Every student a representative of Aberdeen College, for now and the rest of their days. The tang of New England countryside will seep into your skin, snake its way into your bones, and there it will remain, tendrils of ivy forever enshrouding your limbs.

The seduction was brief and complete. Everything else was a formality—the application, the pleas for financial aid and scholarships, the letters of recommendation from my teachers and my boss at the convenience mart. The day I received my acceptance letter I took my money from the bathroom floor hole and bought a bus ticket and a leather book bag. Three months after reading that brochure in the dirty stairwell of my Stulton tenement, I finally escaped. Aberdeen College was my deliverance.

◆ ◆ ◆

A day after I arrived, as I walked past the H. F. Mores Library on the way to meet with my advisor, the library's front door banged open and a tall student stumbled down the stairs. His light brown hair was a tumble of cowlicks and his blue shirt was half-tucked-in. He stopped on the path, adjusted the pile of books under his arm, took off his glasses, and held them to the sky. He was taller than I, a little over six feet, with broad shoulders and a small, symmetrical face.

"Do you have the time?" he said.

I didn't say anything, not sure if he was speaking to me because he was still looking at his glasses.

"The time," he said patiently. "Do you have it?"

"Quarter past."

"Past what?"

"Nine."

He put his glasses back on. "You ever get insomnia?" he said.

I nodded.

"It's like a dream," he said. "Staying up all night. The day comes and everything feels like a dream."

I just stood there.

"What's your remedy?" he asked me.

"I read," I said.

He laughed. "There's the problem," he said. "Reading keeps me up." He turned and walked away, clinging to his books. I watched as he disappeared down the path.

My academic counselor, Dr. Henry Lang, was a bald, thin-lipped, portly man, awkward as a horse fitted into a chair. His office in Thorren Hall was small and meticulous; everything had a holder—his pens, his glasses, his pencils with separate erasers, and even his umbrella, snugly confined to a wooden tube near the coatrack.

Dr. Lang took off his glasses, placed them in their brown leather case, and looked at me, papers in hand. "You've done quite well on your placement examinations." He took a thick gold pen from its holder. "Although I didn't find any record of Latin classes on your transcript."

"They weren't offered," I said. "I taught myself. Mr. Suarez the Spanish teacher helped me out sometimes after school."

Dr. Lang raised his eyebrows. "Well, then, I'm sure Mr. Suarez would be happy to know I'm recommending you start in Latin 301. Dr. Tindley is an excellent instructor. You've chosen history as your major, correct?"

"I have, sir."

Dr. Lang almost smiled—his upper lip struggled to curve itself, but the weight of his forehead and his flat, broad nose pushed it back down. "As you may already know, our history department is one of the finest in the nation. I, myself, am an esteemed member of the faculty . . ."

At the conclusion of his exegesis he leaned back, the chair creaking under his weight.

"So you see, Mr. Dunne, while you may have done well in high school, let me caution you against hubris. For someone of your economic standing, such opportunities should not be squandered. As for your work-study position"—he glanced at the papers on his desk—"you will be working for Mr. Graves, the head librarian."

Dr. Lang lowered his voice, leaning forward against his desk. "Most of the students at Aberdeen find Mr. Graves a bit *difficult*. I assure you he is eccentric, nothing else. A normal consequence of the aging process."

He leaned back in his chair and rested his hands on his stomach.

"We had a boy like you, a few years ago," he said. "Came from a broken home in the city. Father was a drug user, mother had gone to prison for something awful, I can't recall what it was." He pursed his lips as if he'd tasted something bad. "I told that boy if he needed anything at all, to please just let me know. You may find this hard to believe but I *do* appreciate the difficulties of adjusting to a new culture."

Dr. Lang shook his head. "The boy dropped out, nevertheless. I believe drugs had something to do with it. You grew up in the city, correct?"

I nodded.

"Tell me," he said. "Were illicit drugs readily available to you?"

"No," I said. "My foster parents weren't junkies, if that's what you mean."

"Goodness, no. I wasn't implying that at all." Dr. Lang shifted uncomfortably in his chair. "I'm just concerned with the consequences of raising one's children in an urban environment. My niece lives in New York, and I worry about her constantly. She told me a classmate of hers is *pregnant*. Can you imagine?"

I heard some people in the hallway complaining about the student parking on campus. Dr. Lang sighed deeply and plucked his gold pen from its holder. "Adjustments are difficult. There's no shame in admitting that, and I'll tell you the same thing I told that poor boy: Should you find yourself feeling overwhelmed, please do not hesitate to let me know."

◆　◆　◆

At 7 A.M. the following Tuesday I walked alone across the Quad, toward the H. F. Mores for my first day of work study. The Quad was a large square of lightly wooded land left between the triad of buildings—Garringer, H. F. Mores, and Thorren—and the paved road that wound through campus.

The library smelled like old, cracked leather and antique wood. Its vestibule was carpeted in threadbare Persian rugs, framed by an ornately carved archway, leading into the main room with fifteen-foot corniced ceilings, and couches and chairs scattered about. A massive desk sat about ten feet from the entrance against the wall on my left. Tall rows of books, narrowly spaced apart from one end of the room to the other, dissolved into darkness. I walked to the desk, boards creaking under my feet.

An open book lay atop the scratched and faded surface of the desk, flat by virtue of its own weight, the pages thick as if made of linen. The text was written in Latin, in beautiful Cyrillic script, illuminations framing the page: green vines, blood-red roses, a maze of thorns curling around a small man in the upper left corner. He was entwined, every limb trapped, his mouth open, his one free hand clutching a stone from which beamed golden lines. The text contained only a formula, some chemistry experiment involving acids and minerals. It was the last line, however, that caught my attention:

"*Experto credite, sic itur ad astra. Sed facilis descensus Averni.*"

Believe one who has had experience, it read. Such is the way to immortality, though the road to evil is easy.

I turned to the next page, smooth rustling of the paper breaking the silence. There was a piece of yellowed paper inserted in the spine, like a bookmark. Someone had written on it in shaky, uneven script, and the ink was faded, as if very old:

"*Fiat experimentum in corpore vili.*" Let experiment be made on a worthless body.

A metal gate screeched like the cry of some monstrous bird. I straightened up, startled, and turned my head toward the dim recess of the bookshelves that lined the wall. I only saw the faint outlines of books fading back into unlit rows.

"Hello?"

I felt ridiculous, shouting a greeting in a vast, silent room. A cloud passed over the sun and the library became dimmer still, outlines becoming ghostly and blurred. I put my work-study papers on the desk and hurried back to the entrance, glancing behind me. Before I closed the door I heard something tapping from within the darkened building, like a cane rapping on the wooden floors.

My first class later that morning was in Thorren. Dr. Tindley's room was a medium-sized lecture hall, the seats arranged in an ascending semicircle with a podium at the front and center. The colors of the room were brown and orange with gray carpeting, and when Dr. Tindley walked in he blended with the surroundings, in both voice and dress. He spoke with a clipped British accent, and had a sparse reddish beard, little round glasses, and a patch of white curly hair. His suit had probably been expensive at one time, but now it was a dated dark yellow and brown plaid print. His knit tie was flipped over, and a coffee stain marked the thigh of his wool pants. He picked up the black mug he had carried in and slurped at it.

"For those of you who had Dr. Rupprecht last year, I'm Dr. Tindley . . ." He sounded bored by his own voice. "As is my policy, I will be distributing an assessment examination today. It is not only for new students, who may have been placed into this section prematurely"—he glanced at me, then looked away—"but for all of you, who may not have kept up on summer readings. Please consider that today's exam is not a part of your course grade. I issue it for your benefit alone."

I finished the exam ahead of everyone else, and handed it to Dr. Tindley, who read my name on the sheet and beckoned me to follow him toward the door.

"I don't believe I've seen you before," he said in a dramatic whisper. "Are you a freshman?"

"Yes," I whispered back.

He nodded, as if all was understood. "I see, well, Eric is it? Yes, well then, I have some space available in both my 101 and 201 class. Would you like me to reserve a seat for you?"

"I think I'll be fine here, Dr. Tindley," I said, still whispering.

His mouth formed into a small *o*, then he straightened up and pulled the bottom hem of his jacket. "Very well. We shall see by tomorrow."

On Wednesday, Dr. Tindley introduced us to his student assistant, Arthur Fitch, whom I recognized as the student I'd seen last week stumbling out of the library. Art handed out our placement exams, and two words were written at the top of mine: *Excellent work.* Halfway through the hour Dr. Tindley called upon me to translate a particularly tough passage from Virgil. Two other students had tried and failed, but I had little problem with it. For the remainder of the class Art kept looking at me. When the hour ended I quickly left.

That night I ate dinner in the Paderborne dining room with two freshmen who lived across the hall from me: Kenny Hauseman, a skinny, soft-spoken kid with a wandering eye that made me uncertain which one to look at while he was talking, and Josh Briggs, whose pimply forehead was hidden behind blond curly hair. Josh's brother Paul was a senior at Aberdeen. I'd heard the entire Briggs family were Aberdeen alumni.

I asked Josh if he knew of Art Fitch. "Of course," Josh said, snapping off a celery stick in his mouth. "Everyone knows Art. He's like a genius. My brother was in a chem class with him last year. He said Art was *hilarious*. Always arguing with the teacher, bringing weird books into class. I guess one time Art stole all this shit from the chem lab and the teacher thought he was using it to make drugs in his bathtub."

"Was he?" I said.

Josh chewed loudly. "Who knows. He ended up paying for all the stuff he took. No one really cared. Art's folks are loaded, so you know how *that* goes. Speaking of money"—Josh liked to tease me about being poor—"how's that work-study thing going?"

"I'm in the library," I said. "Working for Mr. Graves."

"Mr. Graves is a devil-worshipper, you know," said Kenny.

"It's true," Josh said. "There's a grave of sacrificed pigeons in the woods behind Kellner."

I had only been at Aberdeen a week, and already I'd heard the rumors about the thousand acres of heavily forested land owned by the school. There was supposedly a marijuana farm of epic proportions hidden somewhere among the towering pines and dense thicket, genetically engineered marijuana stolen from a government lab. Some tales were more believable than others—midnight professor/student trysts, fraternity orgies, druidic rites performed on summer solstice.

Josh picked at one of the pimples on his forehead. He winced and withdrew his hand. "Newell Nichols saw the grave," he said.

"That's right," Kenny said. "During freshman orientation Newell went hiking with a couple of his buddies, and they found it."

"Maybe Newell lied," I said.

Josh shook his head. Kenny glanced up at Josh's forehead, then turned to me.

"Come with us," Kenny said.

. . .

We walked past the H. F. Mores and toward Kellner, the honors and graduate student housing on the edge of campus. Its tall, rectangular shape was like a sentry outpost on the border of some village. Lit rooms speckled the dark brick, outlines moving around inside. I thought briefly of Art, whether he lived on campus, or if, like those impossibly cool upperclassmen and graduate students I eyed from afar, he had taken a place in downtown Fairwich.

Josh stopped at the edge of the woods, hands on his hips. Kenny and I looked back at him, his round head lit from behind by the half-moon. A gust of wind rustled through the knee-high weeds we were all standing in.

"I don't think this is a good idea," Kenny said. He had his hands stuffed into his pockets and his shoulders hunched up. His hair blew in the cool wind.

Josh turned to me, as if I was suddenly in charge.

"Are you guys scared?" I said.

They both shook their heads. "We're just cold," Josh said. "But whatever."

"Yeah," said Kenny. "Whatever."

We walked about a hundred yards into the woods, our shoes threshing through thick weeds until trees towered overhead, and where their limbs spread nothing lived beneath, so that the forest floor was soon a soft bed of rotting pine needles and the furled remains of old leaves. The forest canopy was broken in some spots, through which moonlight trickled, barely lighting the dark floor. We walked on, and Josh suddenly stopped and pointed ahead.

"That's it," he said.

I walked forward and bent down, and there they were: dead pigeons, piled into a shallow trench lit by moonlight, blanketed with sticks and leaves.

"What do you think?" Kenny said, whispering, standing near me.

"Disgusting," I said. I could smell their little plump gray bodies rotting. The smell reminded me of the Dumpster behind the Stulton tenement, especially during the summer, when the odor was so bad you could almost see it.

"It's satanic," Josh said. He bent down and picked up what looked like an old crumpled beer can.

"Why would Mr. Graves sacrifice pigeons?" I said.

Josh chucked the can. It clattered off a tree trunk. "I don't know," he said. "To conjure up the Devil, I guess. What else do Satanists do?"

I stared at the grave and shuddered. "What should I do?" I said.

"About what?" Kenny said.

"About my job at the library," I said. "I can't work for a Satanist."

"Quit," Josh said. "My brother can get you a job at Edna's Coffee Shop as a busboy. He's best friends with the cook."

"But it's work-study," I said. "If I quit I lose my scholarship."

"Well, what do they expect," Josh said. The wind gusted and he shivered. "There's got to be something in the school charter about not having to work for a fucking devil-worshipper."

I didn't sleep that night. Instead I sat at my desk and read my textbooks straight through until morning, until the rain that had been perched over campus for three days straight started again, and then I headed for the library.

When I saw Cornelius Graves for the first time, he wasn't the villain I'd imagined, but a hunched, decrepit old man with a sprig of white hair. He held a large stack of books in one arm and a cane in the other, shambling out from the rows of bookshelves. He moved toward me, yellowed eyes staring blankly, cane rapping in front like a blind man's. His mouth hung open. I couldn't see his legs or his feet, because his robe dragged along the floor.

He moved so close to me I could feel his breath, and then he craned his head up and squinted. White hair sprung from his nostrils and his ears. His wrinkled skin was draped over his bones like an old sheet over antique furniture. He looked like he was melting.

He pointed to a sign posted on the wall above the desk. It showed the library hours.

"Come back in an hour," he said.

I found my voice. "I'm Eric Dunne, sir," I said, backing away slowly. "I left my papers for you on Monday."

He put his hand to my chest and I stopped.

"Did you get my papers?" I said.

He unloaded the pile of books on his desk. "Your papers," he said. His voice was dry and weak. "Eric Dunne."

He sat down, rested his head on his hand, and clutched the green copper pommel of his cane. A pendulous, tarnished silver cross hung from a chain around his reedy neck. The library was silent except for the patter of rain hitting the slate roof, and outside I saw thick storm clouds hanging low, just above the treetops. A gust of wind spattered raindrops against the windows.

"My books interest you?" he said, tapping a closed book lying on top of the pile on the desk. I recognized it as the one I had looked at Tuesday.

"I'm sorry, sir?"

"This one, here . . . you read from it. Tuesday."

"Oh, that," I said. "It just caught my eye. I apologize."

"For what?"

"I don't know," I said.

Mr. Graves sat there, wheezing. He looked like he could die at any moment. Instead, he licked his lips and cleared his throat. "My mother had a saying," he began. *"Si jeunesse savait, si vieillesse pouvait.* A favorite maxim of Claude-Henri de Rouvroy, Comte de Saint-Simon . . . Mother said he whispered it to her during dinner one night, at that time when General Lafayette was a brash boy wearing the cap of a revolutionary." He cleared his throat again. "Do you speak French?"

"A little. I took a year in high school."

He looked deeply disappointed. He leaned forward. "Who sent you?"

"I'm here for work study. The papers I left you—"

"I threw them away. I was not consulted."

"I'm sorry."

"Eh? Sorry again? Why are you always apologizing? Who sent you here?"

"Dr. Lang," I said, stammering.

"Henry tell you to watch me?" Cornelius rapped his cane on the floor. "I do as I please."

A clap of thunder rumbled close by. Cornelius opened a book and made as if he were reading. He terrified me, but I couldn't leave. How could I tell Dr. Lang I'd already been fired?

"I need this job," I said.

Cornelius looked up, hands resting on the open book.

"You need this, eh? Not *want*, but *need*, is that it? I hear the children talking of *need* all day. All their actions spring from these phantom needs, so why should you be any different?"

He waved his hand at me as if he couldn't care any less. "Shelve these books and stay out of my sight." He motioned to the stack on his desk, and then turned away.

I took the books and ducked into the first row of shelving, trying to calm myself, my face hot with anger and embarrassment.

I met with Dr. Lang later in the afternoon, at the usual spot, seated across from his wide desk while he reclined awkwardly in his chair. He had a cup of coffee and a half-eaten croissant spread onto a napkin, which was on top of a neatly stacked pile of papers. Dr. Lang had offered me a job as an assistant, and we agreed on a schedule of two days per week, any days of my choosing. I don't know what exactly I was supposed to do, and even now, years later, as a professor myself I can't say what I actually *did* for Dr. Lang. It all fell under the category "administrative" but other than stuffing faculty mailboxes with letters and making photocopies of syllabi, I don't remember doing much work.

"You must go back," Dr. Lang said, when I told him about my encounter with Mr. Graves. "If the bursar discovers you have reneged on your scholarship conditions, it will affect your ability to attend Aberdeen. I suppose I could intervene on your behalf, but I really don't see the need."

"But Mr. Graves doesn't want me there."

"All the same, you must go back."

"Maybe you could say something to him . . ."

His withering look provided my answer. The other half of the croissant disappeared within the pit of his mouth.

That night I looked up Claude-Henri de Rouvroy, Comte de Saint-Simon. He was a French philosopher who had advocated a society governed by technocrats, one in which poverty would be abolished and replaced by rationalism. He published several books, including *De la réorganisation de la société européenne.* He was considered a radical in his time, and he died in Paris at age sixty-five from a burst appendix.

Cornelius said his mother had spoken with him at dinner. *If youth only knew, if age only could,* Claude had said to her, speaking of Lafayette, the same Marquis de Lafayette who had kept company with Thomas Jefferson and La Rochefoucauld. Cornelius was, if nothing else, senile; Claude-Henri died in 1825. For what Cornelius said to be true, he would have to be more than one hundred and fifty years old.

◆ ◆ ◆

Over the next week my days and nights fell into a routine. My insomnia returned but I didn't care. Because I was on academic scholarship I was already obsessing about my grades, and I was convinced that if I got anything less than an A, Dr. Lang would ship me back to Stulton. So I studied almost all the time. I studied and I slept, and when I couldn't sleep I'd study some more.

Once my classwork was finished, I'd go for long walks around campus, exploring the buildings. There was Kellner Hall, beautiful Romanesque done in red brick, and at the edge of campus I found the Waithe Center, the athletic facility, built almost entirely of glass. I learned that Garringer Hall had been a Catholic church before Aberdeen converted to a four-year school, and a janitor told me the rest: the church was the first building on the land, later owned by a priest, Father Garringer, who deeded the building to Aberdeen's founder, Ephraim Hauser, in 1901. Remnants of Garringer Hall's old form still existed, however; the first ten rows of pews served as seating during presentations, held on a raised stage where the transept and altar used to be. Student organizations placed their tables along the sides of the nave, where the chapels had been. In midday multicolored light filled the hall, filtering through the original stained-glass windows, and local legend claimed the spirit of Father Garringer roamed the halls at night, angered that his church was no longer.

At dusk I'd leave my room and sit by a tree in the Quad and listen to the comforting noise of students milling around, tossing Frisbees and footballs, making plans for the weekend. Sometimes I'd see Art striding across the Quad with a short kid who looked my age, and Art would be talking excitedly the whole time while the kid listened with his head down and his hands clasped behind his back. Once I saw Art walking with a beautiful woman in a long gray skirt. He was talking and talking, as he did every time I saw him, oblivious to the stares and head-turns the woman left in her wake.

Wednesday Latin class had Art filling in for an absent Dr. Tindley. Art stood at the podium and ruffled a stack of papers. "Dr. Tindley told me to inform you that Friday's quiz is postponed until Monday," he said. Murmurs of relief rippled through the classroom. "And so we'll begin where Dr. Tindley left off last time. Please open your *Aeneid* to Book Six. Arnold . . . I believe it was your turn to read."

Arnold Ewen was a short, pudgy junior with a patchy goatee and drug-reddened eyes. He sat in the back row and fell asleep often, and I didn't understand how he'd made it into Latin 301. He looked up at Art and held his notebook close to his chest.

"I had some trouble with mine," he said.

"This is a particularly hard section," Art said. "I'm sure everyone found it difficult."

Arnold sighed and shifted in his seat. Someone snapped their gum.

"Okay, starting with line one?"

Art nodded.

Arnold struggled through the section. At the end he slumped in his chair, the back of his shirt darkened with sweat.

Art looked at me, and, giving no sign of recognition, asked me to pick up where Arnold had left off.

I pulled myself closer to the desk and opened my notebook:

Those you see here are pauper souls,
The souls of unburied men.
Charon takes the buried across these dark waters
While all others remain until their bones find the grave
Or til they fret and wander this shore a hundred years.

It was, in my opinion, an excellent translation, one I had worked at especially hard. Art looked unimpressed.

We moved onto Aeneas's emotional meeting with Dido, Art asking me again to read.

I left your land against my will.
The gods commanded me to their bidding,
As they now spur me through this world of darkness and
    shadow,
These rotting lands and their endless nights.

"Eric's passage is a good place for us to start," Art said. "Here we have Aeneas pleading his case to Dido. *Aeneas with such pleas tried to placate / The burning soul,* Virgil writes. Our hero has learned—too late, it seems—that his duty is the calling to end all callings. It demands much from him at the expense of everything else: his happiness, his love, his hope for free will. Dido knows she cannot stand in his way, that his obligation to the empire of Rome is far greater than his love for her, or for anyone. Drop a few lines down, where it reads *At length she flung away from him and fled / His enemy still, into the shadowy grove.* Dido leaves him, her heart broken, and even though Aeneas is visibly moved . . . *Aeneas still gazed after her in tears* . . . look what the next line says: *Shaken by her ill fate and pitying her.*"

Art nodded, his eyes wide with excitement. He jabbed his finger against the open book lying before him on the podium. "Read that again. *Shaken by her ill fate and pitying her.* It's not that he simply feels guilt. He's actually *shaken.* Aeneas sees his actions as coming from somewhere outside himself, and of course he's upset that Dido's been hurt, but this doesn't weaken his resolve. In fact, he doesn't even see himself as directly causing her pain. She's caught in the path of his unyielding destiny, which is why Aeneas *pities* Dido. There's the dichotomy—her loss is emotionally devastating, and yet in the midst of his terrible sorrow Aeneas has no doubts, no regrets. He's prepared to sacrifice anything for the greater good, even the ideal that we, in our modern times, hold so sacred: *Love.* With this sacrifice, Aeneas becomes one of the great heroes in literature. And what is Aeneas's reward for his unfailing pursuit of destiny?"

I looked around the class. No one appeared the least bit interested. Someone snapped their gum again. I heard a kid chuckling in the back of the class.

"Aeneas's reward is a life of misery," Art said, clearly exasperated. "Now if that isn't heroic, I don't know what is."

Art approached me after class, as I packed my books. Up close he was taller than I first thought, a few inches above six feet, and his light brown hair was slicked back behind his ears. He had small features: a short nose, small chin, small mouth, but large blue eyes that were bright and intense, even behind his glasses. The mouthpiece of a pipe stuck out from his jacket pocket.

"Your translation was excellent," he said.

"Thanks," I said. "I really liked your lecture."

"I think you were the only one." He looked at his watch. "Do you have a class after this?"

I shook my head.

"Great," he said, and he flashed a smile. "Would you mind joining me for a quick coffee at Campus Bean?"

The Campus Bean coffee shop was in the student union basement, which had been expanded to also include the campus bookstore and the Commons—Aberdeen's all-purpose eatery. Art and I sat at a small table in the corner. He drank an espresso, I ordered nothing. He asked me how I was enjoying school.

"I love it," I said. "I feel like I've been here my whole life."

Art sipped from the tiny white cup. "You think you're among the elite, is that it?" He smiled. "I'd be wary of confusing your surroundings with the inhabitants. Half these kids are here because their parents didn't know what else to do with them. They just want their sons and daughters going to a college where the brick is covered in ivy and the dorms all have leaded windows. Take that kid in our class, Arnold Ewen. He's a miserable student, and he's been on behavioral probation since day one."

"What for?"

"A prank his freshman year. They decided to run a kid up the flagpole, some poor little fellow who got stuck with Arnold and his cohorts in their dorm suite. Halfway up the flagpole the rope snaps and the kid falls. Busts his head wide open on the pavement."

"That's horrible," I said.

"No kidding. But do you think Arnold got punished? His dad is some big-time international lawyer, paid for Aberdeen's new boathouse. He bought off the kid's family, got the school to give Arnold a slap on the wrist, and that's all."

The boathouse was a monstrous wooden structure sitting on the edge of campus, jutting out into the Quinnipiac, with the legend FRANCIS J. EWEN BOATHOUSE emblazoned in white block letters on its face.

"Of course not everyone here comes from money," said Arthur. "Take me, for example. My family's not starving, mind you, but no summer homes in Ibiza. And then there's you," he said.

"Me?"

"Oh, yeah. One glance tells me what I need to know. Your shoes, your clothes. Hand-me-downs, am I right?"

I was mortified. "Is it that obvious?"

"Of course, but that's not the point. Don't think for a second that half the rich sots strutting about don't look at you and think: 'There's a kid who doesn't want his father's damn money. Good for him. Wish I had the courage to tell the old man to piss off.' The funny thing is that you're obviously on scholarship, so they don't know the half of it. You know how people say the rich can afford to be charitable? Well, the poor can afford to be noble."

Art stuck his pipe in his mouth, and then struck a match and sucked in his cheeks, puffing out a sweet-smelling plume of milky smoke that floated above our table. He sat back and rocked on the rear two legs of his chair, and looked around, watching students pass by.

"Tell me more," he said.

"About what?"

"I don't know . . . anything. Where you're from, what your folks do. The usual."

I gave him my story in brief—both parents gone, relocation to Stulton, the cramped tenement apartment, and my fight for survival.

"How did your mom die?" he said.

"Ovarian cancer," I said.

Art whistled, impressed. He set his pipe down and pulled his chair in, facing me with both hands on the table. "What are you doing for money?"

"I'm working at the library," I said. "And Professor Lang offered me a position in his office."

"What do you think about that crazy old bird?" Art said.

"Dr. Lang?"

"No. Cornelius Graves."

I lowered my voice. "I heard he was a devil-worshipper," I said. "Did you hear about the pigeons he kills?"

"*Pigeons?*"

I nodded. "I saw where he dumps the bodies."

"Where?"

"In the woods behind Kellner," I said.

"How many?"

"I don't know," I said. "A bunch. In a shallow grave."

Art looked skeptical. "Did you see anything else? Any black candles at this supposed grave?"

"No, but—"

"Makeshift altar? Defiled crucifix? Maybe a ceremonial knife?"

"I don't know what a defiled crucifix looks like," I said.

Art sighed. "My point is, the woods around here are filled with coyote and fox. Maybe you saw a coyote den. Like the scorched bones marking the entrance to the dragon in *Beowulf.*" He smiled. "Dr.

Lang on the other hand . . . now there's a world-class prick. If anyone worships the Devil it's that pompous bastard. I did a translation and analysis of the 16th-century Benedictine poet Teofilo Folengo's work for Dr. Lang's historiography course last year, and he gave me a C. I protested to the board but they protect their own so I was just wasting my time . . ."

He faded off. He looked like he was getting mad. He rubbed his pipe and the anger slipped off his face.

"Have you met Dr. Cade yet?" he said.

I hadn't, but I'd heard about Dr. Cade—he was conducting a lecture series on the Crusades for the history honors students. Posters were stapled onto the corkboards in the Paderborne lobby, flyers had been taped to the hallway walls in Thorren. Dr. Cade was reputedly a scholar of international renown, and his classes were always filled to capacity after only the first day of preregistration. He had invited Professor Randolph M. Cavendish, professor emeritus from Oxford and host of his own PBS show *The Wonders of Antiquity,* to deliver a guest lecture during the series, which had become a big deal within Aberdeen's academic circles. One afternoon at work I overheard Professor Lang and Professor Grunebaum engaging in an excited, hushed discussion about arranging accommodations for Professor Cavendish. They had all offered their homes for use during his stay, and there was a certain cattiness to their tones when they discussed how he was, in fact, staying with Dr. Cade.

Thorren's freshman library (a small room in the basement with outdated, used copies of classroom texts filling its shelves) had a copy of Dr. Cade's Pulitzer Prize–winning novel, *This Too Must Pass,* encased in a glass box atop a marble pillar, displayed prominently in the middle of the library. Below the book there was a quote, etched into the marble: *If there is one thing to dread, let it not be death, let it be stagnation of the mind.* The first time I saw Dr. Cade was from afar. I had watched him walk from Thorren across the Quad, carrying a small briefcase and wearing a dark, well-fitted suit. He was smaller than I had imagined he'd be, about my height and slimly built, but his form cut an impressive spectacle, confident and serene, a monk striding placidly across the lawn while all around undergraduates bustled and fumbled, sometimes stopping to stare and point at the dark susurrus in their midst.

Art relit his pipe. The coal flared and oozed smoke. "Dr. Cade recently secured a hefty advance for a three-book series on the Middle Ages," he said. "It's still in the developmental stage, outlining the chapters and such, but he already has some idea of where he wants to go with it, what sections to focus on, et cetera. A majority of the prewrite process is research, and tons of it, but Dr. Cade doesn't have the time to spend his days in the library. So I've been working as his research assistant for the past two years, myself and two others. He provides us with room and board, and a pretty nice monthly stipend—"

"He pays for your apartment?" I said.

"We live in his home. It may sound strange, but logistically it makes sense. We're a team, and being able to share and compare notes is crucial. Researching enough material for three volumes requires a lot of work, especially a work that's going to be competing for the Pendleton. Are you familiar with the Pendleton Prize? It's academia's most coveted honor. Judged by a secret panel, awarded once every ten years at some exotic location, and never in the same place twice. I think last time they held the award ceremony in Khartoum . . ."

One of the students at a nearby table—a thick-necked kid with a crew cut, dressed in jeans, work boots, and a sweatshirt—leaned back in his chair and stared at Art, but Art ignored him. "Anyway, I'm the project coordinator," Art continued, "and as you can imagine I'm under the gun. I'm always looking for additional help. Especially with translations and some of the prewrites. Your translations have a nice rhythm. I'm certain you could—"

The thick-necked kid cleared his throat. He was built like a bear. His green sweatshirt had ABERDEEN RUGBY stenciled across the front.

"You're not allowed to smoke in here," he said.

Art puffed away. The rugby player cocked his head to the side. He looked at Art's pipe, then at Art.

"Didn't you hear what I said?"

"I heard you," Art said.

"Then put the pipe out."

"I will when I'm finished."

The rugby player sighed. "Don't be an asshole," he said.

Art turned back to me. The rugby player stared a moment longer, then returned to his lunch.

"That's what I'm talking about," Art said, and he drew on his pipe and blew a smoke ring. "Rich kids. No mettle."

I didn't know what to say. Art tapped the pipe tobacco onto the floor and crushed it with his shoe. "It must be liberating, knowing you're the last one," Arthur said to me, tucking his pipe away.

I smiled, confused.

"The orphan thing," he said. "You're all that's left. No siblings, I gather."

"How did you know?"

"Educated guess. You like Chaucer?"

"I don't dislike him," I said. To this day I've never read anything by Chaucer.

Art laughed. "Chaucer said it best: *Over grete homlynesse engendreth dispreisynge*. Familiarity breeds contempt. Spend enough time around death and it stops being scary, and becomes something you hate. Know what I mean?"

"No," I said. "I don't. I wasn't really scared of death until my mom died."

Arthur shrugged and looked at me sympathetically. "You should go see Dr. Cade and tell him I spoke with you. Tell him I think you'd be a good addition to our little club."

He gave me a quick salute and then walked away, briefcase in hand, while I remained at the table wondering why he had any interest in me at all.

Chapter 2

Friday morning I found Dr. Cade's office in Thorren Hall. The corridors were silent, with just my footsteps breaking the solemness of the hallowed sixth floor, which held all the offices of Aberdeen's most senior professors. Dr. Cade's office was the last room at the end of the hallway. I quickly walked by it, hoping to hear a voice from within, but there was nothing.

Under his nameplate a cartoon was taped to the door, its edges crinkled and yellowed. It was a black-and-white drawing of a man sitting on a couch in a living room, face buried in his hands. A woman wearing an apron, her hair in curlers, was standing over him, pointing a finger in his face, her mouth open in mid-yell. A poodle was at his feet, lifting its leg and urinating on him, and through the living room window you could see a policeman knocking on the door, holding a boy by the collar. The caption below the comic had been cut out, and written in its place was a single sentence in red ink:

Quos deus vult perdere prius dementat. Those whom a god wishes to destroy he first drives mad.

I knocked gently. Moments later the door opened, and an eye stared out at me.

"Can I help you?" The eye blinked.

"Dr. Cade?"

The eye closed, slowly, as if tired. "Yes?"

"I'm Eric Dunne. Arthur Fitch spoke with me yesterday."

The eye remained shut.

"He mentioned something about your project needing help . . ." My voice trailed off.

The eye opened. "And?"

"Art said I'd be a good addition."

The eye looked down. "Is there anything else I can help you with, Eric?"

It was strange, to hear him use my first name. It had a contrary effect, sounding even more formal and distant than if he had addressed me as "Mr. Dunne."

"No . . . I just wanted to see if—"

"I'm terribly busy," the eye said. "If you'll excuse me."

Click. The door shut, and I turned and walked away, angry at myself for having gone there in the first place.

Art wasn't in Dr. Tindley's class, and so I sat distracted, unable to concentrate on the lecture. Cornelius's little story kept repeating in my mind. His mother had dined with a contemporary of General Lafayette. *Impossible.* I thought back to the open book I had seen on Cornelius's desk, with the entangled, blissful man, holding a golden stone, drawn as if light glowed from within.

"Mr. Dunne?"

I looked up, and Dr. Tindley was staring at me from behind his podium, his long nose pointed down and his lips pursed. He tapped his index finger on the wooden lectern like a metronome.

"Book Six of Aeneid? Shall I translate for you or just say the page number?"

I turned to my text and began to read aloud of Aeneas's descent into the underworld.

That evening at dinner I sat with Nicole Jennings. She was an art major from New York, the kind of girl who laughed at sitcoms and liked to wear hot-pink nail polish and little-boy T-shirts, showing off her taut, tanned stomach. She had changed her hair color at least three times since school started, wearing outfits to match, and most recently she had chosen blond, which went with the ivory-colored sweater she now wore. Its bottom hem stopped just short of her pant line and her navel peeked out. We had very little in common, our friendship one of those sociological phenomena exclusive to college and small office settings—enough exposure and you can befriend nearly anyone.

We were eating grapes and talking nonsense—dorm drama, how the semester was going. She asked me about my job, and I told her about Cornelius, and what Josh and Kenny had shown me in the woods.

"I heard," she said, plucking a grape from my plate, and holding it between her blood-red nails. "That devil-worshipping shit freaks me out . . ." She shuddered dramatically. "Did you know last year they found some girl's bones in those woods? You know what I think, I think that Cornelius guy is a sicko."

"He might be crazy," I said. "And I think he's dying. He coughs up blood."

"Well, he's so *old,* anyway. He probably has cancer or something. He has to be like, ninety years old. At least."

"He said he was older. He said his mother dined with the Marquis de Lafayette."

"Who's that? The guy who liked to torture women?"

"No," I said, staring as she rubbed her hand across her stomach. She was a flirt, no doubt about that. "Lafayette fought with the colonialists during the Revolutionary War. He died in 1834. If Cornelius's mother dined with him—and let's even assume she was a little girl when this happened—that would still make Cornelius over one hundred and fifty years old."

She seemed unimpressed. "My dog lived until he was twenty. What about that old guy in the Bible . . ." She stretched her arms over her head, another mannerism of hers, perfect for showing off her large breasts. The sweater hugged their curves nicely. "Methuselah, wasn't it? He was something like a thousand years old when he died."

"That's just a fable," I said.

"No it's not. It's in the Bible." Nicole crossed her arms. "You don't believe in the Bible?"

"Absolutely not."

"Why? Are you Jewish? You don't look Jewish."

"I'm not Jewish," I said. I wasn't exactly sure of this—supposedly I had some great-aunt whose last name was Levine, but that knowledge had died with my mother.

Nicole let out an exasperated sigh. "Then why don't you believe in the Bible?"

"You're not making any sense," I said. "Jews believe in the Bible."

"Not according to what I've heard. Anyway," she smiled at me, flashing perfect white teeth, "maybe you should just ask Cornelius how old he is, point-blank," she said. "Unless you're afraid of what he might say."

Friday night I found myself sitting at my desk in my room, finishing the last section of Book Six. Nicole had slipped a note under my door. It was an artfully decorated piece of homemade paper with her handwriting across the front:

Eric—There's a Kubrik (sp?) film festival at Campus Bean. Sounds like your kind of thing. Stop by if you want. I've never seen Clockwork Orange.

Nicole seemed to be the natural entryway into college sexuality, but her aggressiveness was misplaced, in my case. I was inexperienced with the opposite sex—having kissed a girl just once in high school, my junior year, during the one party I attended in all four years. The girl was an exchange student from Thessalonica and she'd been crying on my shoulder the entire night, talking about how much she missed home, and how cold New Jersey was, and how she hated the cars and the blacktop streets and the buildings that all looked alike. I felt horribly for her, because I too felt homesick.

We had talked for hours, and toward the end I bent my head down and kissed her full lips, catching her in mid-sentence. It was part sexual experimentation and part pity, because I thought her English wasn't good enough to express the depth of her feelings, and my only Greek was Attic, learned from two years of studying Balme and Lawall on my own, which must have sounded archaic and bizarre to her modern ears. I could taste beer on her lips, and then she pulled me closer and shoved her tongue in my mouth, eager and hard, probing like a dental instrument. I pushed her away and got up off the floor and walked home, feeling ashamed for no particular reason.

I was two years younger than Nicole Jennings, sixteen to her eighteen, and the thought of doing anything sexual with her was an exercise in frustration and fantasy. I imagined all manner of scenarios, outlandish masturbation visions of heroic rescues—Nicole chained to the wall, dressed in leather straps and knee-high boots, I rushing in, guns drawn, spraying bullets at her captors—followed by sex, all sorts of positions, her mouth half-open, eyes fluttering in ecstasy, beads of sweat pooling between her firm breasts. I viewed sex at that time as nothing more than a naked athletic event, filled with sweat and physical exertion. And I knew very little about how to get it, an event so momentous that broaching the subject seemed impossible. Even if Nicole was practically lighting a flare trail to the nether regions of her anatomy, I still cowered in the corner, the dog that barks behind the fence and runs away when the gate opens.

My phone rang at eight, and I picked it up, expecting Nicole's raspy voice. I was holding her letter and thinking about her stomach.

"Hey Eric. It's Art."

There was a brief, but fierce battle. Lust vs. curiosity. I had wanted it to be Nicole. I had also been thinking about Art.

"What are you doing tonight?" he said.

I glanced at Nicole's note. The dots over the *i*'s were like bubbles. "Nothing," I said. "Just some reading."

He laughed. "Big shocker. Listen, Dr. Cade's having a dinner in celebration of a little coup of mine. I picked up a copy of Bracton's *De legibus et consuetudinibus Angliae* for two thousand U.S. dollars from some old lady in Bucharest. You familiar with the work?"

No, I told him. Why would I be?

"Come on," Art said. He sounded drunk. "Bracton . . . author of landmark work on English common law . . ." I heard someone in the background yell "Show-off!"

"Have you been thinking about our talk the other day?" Art said.

"A bit," I lied. I had thought about it a lot.

"And?"

"I'm interested," I said. "It seems cool."

I heard the clink of a glass. "I suppose it is cool," Art said. He sounded like he was smiling.

"Cool as a fucking cucumber," said the voice in the background.

"You eat yet?" Art asked me.

No, I told him.

"Then join us for dinner," Art said. "I insist. We're having lamb and some fantastic wine. I'll be at your place in twenty. And if you have it, wear something nice."

◆　◆　◆

Art's car was a late-'70s station wagon, with cracks in the dashboard and duct tape wrapped around the seats. Receipts littered the floor, along with coins, matches, and empty tobacco pouches. The backseat was completely covered with books—mostly paperbacks with torn pages and missing covers, but a few books bound in leather with brass clasps stood out.

Art wore small, gold-colored, wire-rimmed glasses this time, and he took out his pipe and began to pack it, propping his knees against the steering wheel. The overcast sky blocked out any moonlight, leaving us enveloped within the narrow circle of the car's headlights, slicing through the darkness.

"I understand you and Cornelius take turns reading your Latin passages backwards," Art said. "Rumors are spreading that you've been seen slaughtering lambs at midnight, in Garringer Hall where the altar used to be."

I stared out the window. "Cornelius told me the weirdest story," I said. "The first time I met him."

The car's interior briefly glowed red from a match. Art lit his pipe. "Let me guess," he said. "Cornelius told you that story about his mom having dinner with a Frenchman who died in 1825."

"Claude-Henri de Rouvroy, Comte de Saint-Simon," I said.

Art puffed and held the smoke. He let it trickle out of his mouth as he inhaled it through his nose. He completed the trick by firing out several smoke rings in rapid succession, each one passing through the other. "Wouldn't that be something," he said. "That would make Cornelius well over a hundred years old."

"One hundred and fifty," I said.

"Do you believe him?"

"I guess not," I said.

"You don't sound too sure."

I could only see the faintest of dark outlines outside my window, black trees against a black sky.

"Of course I'm sure," I said. "It's a ridiculous story."

"Have you said anything to anyone else about this?"

"I talked to my advisor, Dr. Lang. He told me to just ignore it."

"Then there's your answer."

Art slowed the car, made a sharp right, and turned into a gated driveway, tires crunching on the gravel. He rolled down his window and entered a number into the keypad. The gate opened slowly, and we drove in.

In spite of everything that happened later, during those dark days when the house was enshrouded in a cloak of snow and the orchard trees stood like skeletons in a winter graveyard, I still remember Dr. Cade's house as I first saw it that evening. A forest of stately trees on my left and right, rising like ghostly pillars in the darkness, a row of tightly manicured hedges lining the way, and the grand effect, about fifty yards from the entrance, at the end of a gently twisting brick driveway: his house. It was a two-story Greek Revival made of wood painted a gleaming white, lit by spotlights that gave it the appearance of a massive marble structure. Every window in the house was lit, and a chandelier, suspended by a long iron chain from the top of the vaulted ceiling in the main foyer, shone brilliantly out the windows nearest the door. Pumpkins sat on the front step, carved with the smiling and frowning faces of the Greek theater.

Art parked his station wagon next to two other cars. One was a small foreign car, and the other a Jaguar, jet-black with sleek low lines. Art turned off the engine and we sat there, listening to the tick and creak. "What do you think?" he said.

"It's beautiful."

"It is, isn't it? Dr. Cade owns ten acres of land; the woods all around us go quite a ways back. He says he wants this to be our sanctuary." Art unclasped his seat belt, talking out the side of his mouth and puffing on his pipe. "It's just us and God's handiwork out here, if you consider the two things separate."

I stepped out of the car. I don't believe in destiny or reincarnation, but for whatever reason—maybe something locked deep within my genetic code—I felt like I'd finally arrived at a place I'd once been taken from, and as Art and I walked to the front door, all was as hushed as in a place of worship, in veneration of my return home.

The inside of Dr. Cade's house was just as impressive. Hardwood floors, thick Oriental rugs tossed about in splashes of deep reds and blues. The living room had a large fireplace against the far wall, with three couches surrounding a huge copper-topped coffee table. Towering houseplants that nearly reached the ceiling framed the archway. A Flemish tapestry of a battle hung in thick folds behind one of the sofas; a large marble bust of Charlemagne sat in a corner. Over the carved mantle hung an expansive ancient map, framed in dark wood, lit from above by track lights. Beyond the living room were a set of French doors, and through their leaded glass I could see a smaller room—the study—with built-in bookshelves lining the walls, and a brown chair-and-a-half sitting in the corner, white crease lines spidering out from its seat buttons. Beyond the study was another set of French doors that opened to a dimly lit back porch.

A dog came bounding from the living room, big, black, and clumsy, his tail held high. He looked like a Labrador. He bumped against me, leaning his weight into mine, and snuffled and licked my hand.

"Nilus," Art said, bending down to scratch behind the dog's ears. "He's officially Howie's, but we've all adopted him."

Ahead of me were a set of ascending stairs, wide and deep, an off-white runner cascading down like a stream. To my right was the dining room, and the table was covered in white linen, set for six, with white china plates and bowls and tall, delicate glasses. A bouquet of autumn flowers was the centerpiece, flowers colored in deep orange and russet brown in a slim white vase. A swinging door separated the dining room from what I guessed was the kitchen, from the sounds—running water and clanging pots and the whir of a blender. I heard female laughter, high and lilting, followed by a metallic crash and a cursing male voice.

The door swung open and a bleary-eyed man walked in, holding his right hand as if in pain. He was barefoot, dressed in wrinkled khakis and an untucked button-down shirt. He had a full, round face, the type that foreshadows jowls in middle age. His body was a solid mass, broad-shouldered, with short, thick arms and a torso that dropped straight into his legs. Dark red hair lay atop his head.

"About time you made it back," he said to Art, and then he looked at his right hand and sucked air in between his clenched teeth. "Burned my fingers on the rack of lamb. *Your* rack of lamb."

Nilus remained at my side, nudging my leg every time I stopped petting him.

Howie looked at the dog and frowned. *"Nilus.* Cut it out. Go." The dog put his head down and went back into the living room.

I stood there, hands in my pockets, waiting for Art to introduce me. The kitchen door opened again and a woman emerged, smiling and shaking her head, holding a washcloth. She had honey-colored hair pulled back into a ponytail, almond-shaped eyes colored a deep green, a short, straight nose and thin lips. Her forehead was prominent and smooth. She had on jeans and a gray roll-neck sweater. I'd seen her before, on campus. She'd been the beautiful woman walking with Art, across the Quad.

"Put this on your hand, Howie," she said, giving him the washcloth, "and next time listen when I tell you to use a pot holder."

Howie took the washcloth and sat down on one of the dining room chairs. He cradled his hand in his lap and looked at me.

"I suppose this is Eric."

"Hi," I said, making my voice lower.

He nodded, unsmiling. "Howie Spacks."

"And I'm Ellen . . ." She shook my hand. Her fingers were soft and strong.

I folded my hands behind my back and tried to regain my composure. It was as if characters in a movie I'd been watching suddenly addressed me. Howie stared unsteadily, and Ellen turned to Art, rose to the tips of her toes, and kissed him on the cheek. He gave her a brief hug and motioned toward the kitchen.

"Is dinner ready? I'm famished," he said.

Ellen held his hand and led him toward the kitchen door. Art turned to look at me and slapped Howie on the shoulder. "He'll keep you entertained," Art said. "Would you like something to drink? Dr. Cade and Dan should be returning with the wine any minute now."

"I'm fine, thanks."

Howie sat back and crossed his legs. "Bring me the rest of my cocktail, would you?"

"That cocktail is the reason you burned yourself," Ellen said, pausing in the doorway. Art continued past her.

"So what?" Howie narrowed his eyes. "So you're not going to get it for me?"

"I didn't say that." She walked into the kitchen, and Howie let out an exaggerated sigh.

"You'd think a man could get a drink in his own home when he asks for it." His expression went blank and he motioned for me to sit down. I sat at the end of the table.

Howie tapped his fingers on the table and hummed to himself.

"So what's your story," he said.

"What story?"

"You're not much of a conversationalist, are you?"

"I don't know," I said. It was a stupid response but I couldn't think of anything else.

"You're very young," Howie said. "Art told me you skipped a couple of grades. Not the best idea, was it?"

"I only skipped one grade. And it wasn't my decision."

"What if you'd said no? Told the headmaster you didn't want to."

I shrugged. "I've never thought about that."

"Well, *Christ*. Take control of your destiny, kid." He leaned forward and with each word rapped a long finger on the tablecloth. *"Take control of your life or someone else will.* Best advice I ever got from the old man. About the only advice I ever got from him." He stared at me, his mouth set in a straight line. Red hair fell over one eyebrow. He looked back at the kitchen door. "Where the hell is my drink?" he shouted.

Howie looked at me again. "I gotta get my drink. Take a seat in the living room. Keep Nilus company."

Minutes later Howie sat across from me on an olive-colored couch, grunting like an old man as he fell back into the cushions, martini glass held precariously in one hand. The dog sat between us, head down on his paws, watching my movements.

"You like dogs, or are you a cat man?"

I shrugged and placed my hands on my lap. "I've never had a pet."

He nodded, looking disappointed. "What are your plans once you get out of school?"

"I don't know."

"You must have some idea."

"I don't."

"Well, I do. I'm looking forward to the business world," he said, sipping his drink. "The old man is vice president of a domestic shipping firm, out of the Midwest. They're thinking about going international, which means he'll need someone to jump-start the overseas operation. I'm graduating this spring, and after that I'm getting the hell out of Connecticut and back to Chicago. This New England shit gets old, fast."

"Are you a business major?"

Howie gulped the rest of his drink and let out a satisfied groan. "Are you kidding? And sit in class with those idiots? *Please.* Business is a learn-as-you-go enterprise. The old man doesn't even have his high school diploma. He's a self-made millionaire, honest to God."

"What are you studying, then?"

"History, just like everyone else here. Don't ask why. It's pretty much wars and kings—boring as anything. I didn't even want to go to college, you know, but my father said I had to before he'd let me get in on his company. Said I needed to see what else was out there before I made any adult decisions. Well, I've seen what's out there, and I'll tell you, Eric. It's a lot of shit."

"I can see your point."

"How can you? You're sixteen fucking years old. Christ, can you even *drive* yet? Hold on a second." He stood up and left the living room, then returned about a minute later with a refilled glass. "No olives left," he said, holding up his martini glass. "A man can't get an olive for his martini in his own goddamn house. What was it Hemingway said about a martini without an olive? Like a whore without tits . . . maybe I made that up. Who knows."

I nodded and opened a book that was lying on the coffee table. It was a large, full-color book on English gardens. Tall hollyhocks leaning over pathways, wild hedges brushing against a low fence. Order out of chaos. Howie sat forward on the edge of the couch and sipped from his glass. I wanted to say something, desperately, but couldn't think of a topic innocuous enough. He tapped his foot and drank, and when he finished he set the glass down and stretched his arms overhead.

"That's better," he said. "You sure you don't want something to drink?"

"Thanks, really. I'm fine."

"Suit yourself. Where were we?"

"You asked if I could drive."

"Rhetorical, rhetorical," he said, waving me away. "Did I offend you? Art mentioned you were a bit touchy."

"I'm really not," I said. I doubted Art had said that. "This is all just a little intimidating."

He raised his eyebrows in a look of genuine surprise.

"An honest man. I like that." He winked and picked up his glass.

"Looks like you need a refill," I said, pointing to it.

Howie tipped it upside down and we watched as two drops spilled out. "Why, I do think you're right," he said, smiling.

◆　◆　◆

My foster father was a drinker, and as a consequence I have some understanding of the culture of alcohol, and the idiosyncrasies of the average alcoholic. Most of all such people require patience—drunks are perfectly aware when they're inebriated, and few things make them angrier than someone who treats them as if they think the drinker doesn't know he's drunk. I also know they are, as a whole, incredibly self-absorbed; ask them enough about themselves and you're halfway to making a good impression. Join them in whatever mood they happen to be in, be the symbol of the sober counterpart validating the drunken opinion, and the other half is taken care of. Some actor I'd seen on TV said that alcoholics were egomaniacs with low self-esteem, and Howie was no exception, and so I rolled with his thinly veiled insults and eventually, thirty minutes later, when the door opened and Dan walked in, Howie and I had gained a mutual understanding of each other.

When I first saw Dan I thought I had a foxhole companion—someone who looked about my age but had been accepted into this clique of upperclassmen. He was holding a cardboard crate and wearing a black suit, with a matching overcoat.

"We got a case," he said, passing me over with a glance and talking to Howie. He set the box down on the hardwood floor in the foyer. "Paul struck gold . . . Vega Sicilia. Just in last week."

Howie rubbed his hands together and walked over to the box, peering inside.

I stood as Dan hung his overcoat on a rack near the door. He was shorter than me, with parted brown hair and a plain face. A mole sat on the upper ridge of a cheekbone. He checked his shirt collar and smoothed his tie, then looked at me and smiled courteously.

"Good evening. I'm Dan. Eric, right?"

We shook hands.

Howie appeared at my side and slapped a long hand on my shoulder and held a bottle of wine in front of my face. "You drink wine?"

"Actually, yes."

"Good for you."

Dan grabbed the bottle from Howie. "For safekeeping," he said, and he walked toward the kitchen, holding the bottle delicately by its neck. Howie stood in thought for a moment, then jogged to catch the kitchen door before it swung shut.

I stood alone, before the open front door, wondering where I was and what I was doing. Nilus loped over and butted his head against my hand. I looked out into the darkness, past the point where the light from the foyer faded and dissolved into the grass. The headlights of a car flashed by at the far edge of the lawn. Country silence, nothing but the chirping of crickets and the rush of wind through tree limbs.

I reached down to scratch Nilus's throat, and then he barked and I looked up and saw an older man with silver, swept-back hair, standing on the front step. He returned my stare with intense interest.

"It's only me, Nilus," he said in a calm voice. He extended a gloved hand and Nilus sniffed it.

It was Dr. Cade—I recognized his voice—and even in the dim light the blue of his eyes still gleamed. He looked over my shoulder, blinked once, and then smiled. "May I come in?"

"Oh . . ." I blushed and moved aside.

He stepped inside and closed the door. "Something smells absolutely delicious," he said, as he took off his overcoat and hung it on the rack next to Dan's. "They must be making lamb, my favorite." He stared at me, mouth held in a half smile.

"Eric, isn't it?"

"Yes, sir."

We shook hands. His grip lingered a moment longer, and then slid out of my hand.

"I hope I wasn't too brusque with you this morning," he said. "We're on deadline with my publisher, and I haven't had time for much else. You are in David Tindley's class, correct?"

I nodded, at a loss for words. I felt like I was in the presence of a celebrity. I suppose I was. Dr. Cade was dressed impeccably and simply, in a dark gray suit. His skin was tanned and lightly wrinkled, like the skin of a yachtsman, and his cheeks had a slight ruddiness to them. He could've been in his late fifties or early sixties but there was a vitality to him that made him seem much younger. He wore no jewelry, not even a watch.

Art walked through the kitchen door, wearing an apron covered in brown spatters. He walked up to Dr. Cade and smiled, and then motioned to me.

"This is Eric, Dr. Cade. The one I told you about."

"Yes, we have been introduced." Dr. Cade smiled back, and Art fidgeted, seeming unsure of where to put his hands. He looked nervous, as if introducing two mutual friends at the beginning of their blind date.

"If you'll excuse me," Dr. Cade said, pulling his gloves off. He said he had to change for dinner, and then he left, walking upstairs. Art clapped his hands together and walked back to the kitchen, leaving me alone, with Nilus.

Fifteen minutes later the dining room table, earlier a sterile picture of white linens, empty glasses, and cold silverware, was transformed. On it now sat a tureen of steaming seafood bisque, compliments of Art; a basket of French bread; a ceramic bowl filled with salad Niçoise, courtesy of Dan; finally, three racks of lamb, cooked to perfection by Howie, despite his war wounds.

Dr. Cade was the last to sit, and he closed the dining room off from the rest of the house by pulling shut a set of pocket doors that had remained hidden in the archway. He was wearing a thick cable-knit sweater and a pair of gray wool pants, the look of a relaxed, wealthy patriarch. The overhead light was dimmed, throwing a caramel sheen over everything.

They started their conversation as if I wasn't there, or as if I had been there from the beginning and knew everything they spoke of. I felt completely overwhelmed, in spite of Art's efforts to include me in the banter, and I spent most of the time trying to stomach the taste of the wine, which wasn't as sweet as I was accustomed to. I even made the mistake of asking for an ice cube, and there was a brief but poignant silence when I plopped the cube into my glass. Howie asked if I wanted any ketchup with my lamb and then everyone—except for Dr. Cade, I noted—broke into subdued laughter. I didn't get it at the time. I longed for my dorm, for the simplicity of the friends I had made there.

I had been seated between Art and Ellen. She smelled of lilac, subtle and lingering. I wanted to smell more of her, lean my head into her the way I would a sweet flower. At one point during the meal she noticed I had picked the capers out my salad, and she impaled one with her fork and made as if to feed it to me.

"They're quite good," she said, smiling, pushing the caper-tipped tines past my lips. Her eyes sparkled, glistening under lids dabbed with gray eye shadow. "Go on . . ."

I ate it from her fork, and that simple motion gave me an immediate, screaming erection. The etiology of desire is often a muddled search; we insert meaning into the accidental brush of a hand, or in the fleeting sidelong glance of our coveted, and yet I'm able to trace the exact moment when lust sprung forth and everything about Ellen—her lips, her chin, the curve of the back of her neck, the way her hand rested on her hip, delicate fingers dangling over the ridge of bone—was burned into my mind like a glowing brand, and even now, years later, I can still smell traces of its smoke, whispering her name in my ear. The etiology of my desire, then, however unglamorous, was marked by the insertion of her fork into my mouth, and I have forever associated the iodine pungency of capers with the most intense hard-on of my life.

Once the meal was finished there was that collective pause unique to big dinners. The racks of lamb were nearly picked clean and they sat in a messy jumble in the center of the table.

Conversation finally turned to me. They had exhausted all other topics. Dan spoke first:

"Arthur tells me you went to school in New Jersey."

I nodded.

"I went to Elm Hill," Dan said. "Home of the 'Camden Eight.' We raced crew against Polk in the nationals, three years in a row."

I had no idea what he was talking about. "I played intramural soccer at my school," I said.

Dan looked confused. "What school was that?"

"Thirty-Two," I said.

"Thirty-Two what?" Dan said.

I shrugged. "Just Thirty-Two."

"A number?" Dan looked shocked. Howie laughed.

"Was there a school Thirty-One?" Dan asked.

"I don't know," I said.

"But you must have heard about the Elm Hill–Polk rivalry," Dan said. "Polk's the most prestigious academy in New Jersey. They make it to nationals every year."

I didn't know what to say.

Mercifully, Art cut in. "Eric skipped two grades. He wasn't in high school that long."

"I only skipped one grade," I said, but no one was listening to me.

"Goodness," Dr. Cade said. He poured himself more wine. "Two grades seems a bit much. I'm surprised your parents agreed."

"I was in foster care," I said.

This grabbed their attention. There was an abrupt pause.

"You are an orphan?" Dr. Cade said.

That word again. *Orphan.* I guess I was. What is it called when the one parent you do have isn't a part of your life? Strictly speaking I wasn't an orphan—although I couldn't know for certain if my father was alive or dead. And he hadn't been a parent, at least not during the difficult part. He was a sperm donor who stuck around long enough to see that his child was going to be healthy, and then he left.

"That sucks." Howie shook his head. "My grandfather died last year . . ." He made a *whoosh* sound, his cheeks puffed up like a bullfrog. "*That* was no picnic. I've never seen the old man so upset. He'd cry for no reason—one night we were all watching TV and this commercial came on with this sad music . . ."

"I'm sorry to hear about your parents," Dr. Cade said. He motioned to Ellen, who rose and took his plate.

"You are an admirable boy," he continued, folding his napkin and dropping it on the tablecloth. Dan stood and began to help Ellen clear the table, while Howie teased her with his plate—handing it to her, taking it away, waving an admonishing finger and then ordering her to get him a shot of Hennessey.

Ellen and Howie began to argue, but Dr. Cade seemed oblivious of anything other than our conversation. I had difficulty concentrating, as Ellen had let her hair down, and it had fallen to one side, catching the light. It reminded me of a Byron poem I studied for an English class my senior year . . . *These locks, which fondly thus entwine, in firmer chains our hearts confine* . . .

Dr. Cade stopped talking, and in that pause I realized I was still staring at Ellen. She and Howie were now arguing about a woman's place in the home. I quickly looked away as Ellen smacked the top of Howie's head and left him with his plate, and Howie laughed and shouted something at her as she walked to the kitchen.

"She doesn't play that role well," Art said to Howie.

"She needs to loosen up . . . It's not like I'm antifeminist. You know, I think she needs a good—"

"Just shut up," Art said.

They stared at each other and then Howie pushed himself away from the table and stood up. He stretched his arms, yawned, and rubbed his eyes. "I'm going upstairs," he said, to no one in particular, and he gave a quick salute and walked toward the kitchen, holding on to the doorway for balance as he exited the dining room.

"Howie is an excellent artist," Dr. Cade said. "He's illustrating the maps for my books." He had directed the comment toward me but he was watching Art. Tension passed through the room like a hot gust of wind.

A minute passed. I heard Dan and Ellen talking in the kitchen, running water, the clink of dishware. Dr. Cade cleared his throat.

"Would you care to join me for a cordial in my upstairs study?"

I had imagined he'd be finished with me, after my pathetic dinner performance.

"Of course," I said, stammering. "I mean, if it's not too much trouble for you."

"If it were trouble," Dr. Cade said, standing, "I wouldn't have asked."

I followed him as he made his way up the grand staircase, my gaze fixed upon his back, trying to mirror the way he moved, a cool, Apollonian figure, as tranquil as the ocean under a clear sky.

Dr. Cade led me down a narrow hallway with a parquet floor. Portraits hung at eye level on the parchment-colored walls. Past two doors on my left, one door on my right, and then he took a key from his pocket and opened the last door before a smaller staircase at the end of the hall. From the bottom of the stairwell I could hear Dan and Ellen talking, along with the sounds of dishes being stacked.

His study was small and warm, carpeted with a single Oriental rug. There was a fireplace with a red-and-gray-swirled marble mantle, and above the fireplace a painting of a woman in a white dress in a golden field being dragged by a chariot with black steeds into a cave.

Bookshelves lined the far wall, behind a desk. They held delicate-looking bibelots and bijoux, tiny antiques like a museum display. They, in turn, were dwarfed by large leather tomes with tarnished brass clasps and tattered edges. The far wall had one small window, and through it I saw a clutter of thick boughs and branches, swaying and rubbing against each other in the wind.

Dr. Cade walked to his desk and uncapped a crystal decanter filled with a clear liquid. He motioned for me to sit as he filled two brandy snifters from the decanter.

"Grappa," he said, handing me my glass. He lowered his nose to the edge of his snifter. His profile was strong and simple; a patrician nose, thick eyebrows, a small, delicate jaw. He inhaled deeply.

The grappa was worse than the wine—it left a fire trail down my throat, exploding into a burning plume at the bottom of my stomach. My eyes teared and I turned away, embarrassed. Dr. Cade sipped from his and then put it down. He stood still for a moment, and then walked to the fireplace and removed the fire screen.

I took another taste of the brandy. It cooled fiercely on my lips.

"First fire of the season," he said. He took quartered logs and stacked them neatly against the soot-blackened reredos, and then he replaced the fire screen and pressed a button on the wall; after three clicks a tongue of fire shot up from under the piled wood.

"We had a fireplace," I said, "at my house in West Falls. It was a huge iron stove that sat in the corner of our living room. I remember bringing snow inside and plopping it on the iron top, and watching it melt and sizzle."

"This was with your foster parents?"

"No," I said. I took another drink; this time the grappa wasn't as biting, leaving a numbing sensation when it washed over my tongue. "My real family lived in West Falls, Minnesota. I lived there until I was ten, and then my mom died and I was moved to Stulton."

It still made me sad to talk about it. Talking about sad events requires preparation, like weathering a storm. You have to check if everything is sealed and latched. Otherwise your mind can leak; memories seep in, emotions seep out.

I gulped another mouthful of brandy.

"And your father?"

"He left," I said. "When I was five."

His face softened. "And your mother passed away five years later . . . how traumatic." He shook his head and stared at the fire. "Do you have any contact with your father?"

I really didn't feel like talking about it. I didn't say anything, just sat there, holding my glass with two hands.

"It's a difficult subject, I'm sure," Dr. Cade said.

I shrugged. I was scared I'd start crying.

"Freud believed a child's greatest need is his father's protection," Dr. Cade said.

"I remember the day he left," I said. *"Be right back,'* he said, just like that. *Be right back.* Everything seemed okay. I remember seeing his spoon sticking out of his coffee, and his plate of scrambled eggs with the steam still rising up."

I slouched in my chair. A tree branch tapped against the window. Orange flames coiled around the edges of the firewood. "I don't think about it anymore," I said. "He didn't even come to my mom's funeral."

Dr. Cade didn't say anything. We sat there for a few moments.

"I started having nightmares in seventh grade," I said. "After reading *Huck Finn.* The part where Huck's father sneaks in through the window, and Huck comes in the room and his pap is there, with his greasy hair hanging down over his face. I had a recurring nightmare of my father's face in the window, looking in at me, his hands pressed against the pane . . ." I shuddered.

My head buzzed and I blinked to clear my vision. I looked around his office, at the jade plant sitting in a Grecian urn by the door, at his framed diplomas adorning the wall closest to me—one from Merton College, Oxford, the other from Cambridge—and from downstairs I heard someone playing jazz piano. A log in the fire crackled and spurted a stream of sparks.

"Now, about your mother," Dr. Cade said, gently. His face had a pinched, uncomfortable look to it, as if he were asking a necessary question, but knew how unpleasant it was. "How did she pass away?"

"Cancer."

He nodded solemnly and sat back, rotating the glass in his hand.

"They gave her chemo for six months but it didn't help," I said. "And radiation for the last month, which did nothing except make the last of her hair fall out."

"Do you know the exact diagnosis? Was it non-Hodgkin's lymphoma?"

"A malignant tumor in her ovaries," I said. "The surgeon tried to remove it all but missed some pieces, and it metastasized and spread everywhere."

Silence between us, again. I scanned the room for a clock. There was one on the wall opposite the desk, a glass and brass work of art, with filigreed hands and an ivory-colored face. It was almost eleven. By now, I thought, Nicole would be returning from the film festival.

Dr. Cade broke the silence, finally. He filled his glass again, motioning to me with the decanter. I nodded, more out of courtesy, and he refilled my glass.

"Arthur highly recommended you as a research assistant, citing your expertise in Latin. I haven't had the chance to look through your file but Art's word is enough, for now. You are aware of the time constraints we're under, correct?"

"Art told me a little."

"Yes, well . . . every day is precious. And because we don't have the luxury of time, I would expect you to work quickly."

"I understand," I said.

"And you feel you would be able to balance the two—your schoolwork and my project?"

"I think so," I said.

Dr. Cade took a sip and set his glass down. He looked at me and smiled.

"It's getting late," he said. "However much I'd like to continue our conversation, I still have some work to do before bed."

I stood up, unsure if I should leave my full glass of grappa or down it in one gulp.

"I realize that talking about the death of a parent can be very unsettling," he said, standing up. "*To most men the death of his father is a new lease on life.'* Wise words, I believe. Perhaps they'll provide some comfort."

He continued as if to interrupt me, but I wasn't going to say anything anyway. I took a final sip, shuddered, and set my glass on his desk, mumbling *thank you*.

"I believe Howie will be taking you home," he said, and he shook my hand and asked me to please close his door on the way out.

◆ ◆ ◆

Howie was the only one in the living room, slumped on the couch, head back, mouth open, eyes shut. There were papers scattered across the coffee table, covered with sketches, and a jumble of pencils sat in an empty tumbler atop the English garden book. The dining room table was cleared except for Howie's place setting. Crumbs were scattered around his plate; his napkin was a crumpled ball shoved into a smeared wine glass.

The floor creaked under my foot and Howie jerked his head up.

"Shit." He squinted at me. "I'm supposed to take you home."

He looked in no condition to drive. "I'll call a cab," I said, probing my pockets to make sure I had my keys. "Don't worry about it."

Howie looked at his watch.

"It's pretty late." He looked over his shoulder, to the stairway. "You were up there with Dr. Cade?"

I nodded.

Howie lowered his voice. "How did it go?"

A door shut from upstairs, followed by the creak of footsteps.

"I don't think I made a good impression," I said.

Howie shrugged and yawned and sat up. He stared at the sketches on the coffee table.

"I'm so far behind," he said. "I'm supposed to have the initial inking done by the end of this month."

I took a closer look at his sketches. The largest one was a map of the world. Six wind-heads framed the continents, their cherubic faces puffed and blowing little fountains of wind; ships sailed in the direction of marked routes; snakelike monsters menaced the open seas;

elaborate strap work, like illuminations lining the text of ancient Bibles, framed the map in intricate latticework and clusters of fruit. The bottom right corner of the map had a decorative box with Howie's name in Cyrillic calligraphy.

"This is amazing," I said.

Howie looked unimpressed. "Once I'm done with the ink," he said, "I have to finish smoothing the copper plate, which is god-awful work. But you don't have to worry about any of that. Dr. Cade will have you doing the easy stuff, burying yourself in books like Art and Dan do, all day."

He rubbed his eyes and shook his head, like a boxer hit with a knockout punch trying to clear the cobwebs.

"Phone's in the kitchen," he said. "There's some cash in the cookie jar if you need it."

He faded off, and that's how I left him, staring at his sketches.

Chapter 3

The following month I didn't hear any news from Dr. Cade or Art. In fact, Art had seemingly lost interest, not avoiding my stare but simply ignoring it, taking his time after class to collect his book and papers, not noticing if I hesitated while walking past his desk. I thought back to the dinner, and searched for anything I may have done to offend my hosts, but I couldn't think of anything, and so I blamed it on general inadequacies on my part, and eventually, like all college freshmen, I became distracted by the fantastical existence of dorm life.

Fall was now firmly entrenched, bundling itself up in crackling leaves and stiff branches like an old ogre, trudging forward inevitably toward winter. The students had also changed, from whites and blues to grays and blacks; shorts and sandals gave way to pants and oxfords. The women I used to watch from my window as they jogged along the main strip now wore sweatshirts over their sports bras. My first round of exams went very well; I scored A's on every one, and likewise on my papers. This sparked a period of indolence, and I even got stoned for the first time, sharing a joint with Nicole during a small party in her room, in the last week of September. Later that night we kissed, while I clumsily groped her breasts under her white blouse, and it may have gone further but I fell asleep with my head on her shoulder, and when I awoke she had covered me with a blanket and tucked a pillow under my head.

I found her sitting on the bed, knees drawn close to her chest and glasses placed low on her nose. She wore red ABERDEEN ATHLETICS shorts and a gray sweatshirt. Her hair was twisted into a swirl and held in place with a pencil. She had a notebook propped open atop her knees.

She looked angry, her full lips pouty and pushed together, as if she were holding something bad-tasting in her mouth.

"What's going on?" I said.

She shrugged. "You tell me."

I looked around. My pants were lying under the nightstand. I felt foolish, sitting there in my boxers with a baby-blue blanket draped over my legs.

"Is something wrong?" I said.

"No." She turned the page of her notebook. "Who's Helen?"

"I don't know."

She looked at me, over the top of her glasses. "You don't *know?*"

"No," I said, pulling my pants under the blanket. "I don't know anyone named Helen."

Saying the name made it suddenly clear. *Ellen.* She had meant Ellen. I pulled my pants up, arching my back off the floor. *Ellen.* I had thought about her almost every night since the dinner, masturbating into oblivion, seeing her face pressed to my stomach, her lips resting against my skin. I had been piecing her together from women I saw every day on campus—her hair from the blonde down my hall, her lips from Nicole, her leaf-green eyes from some tall redhead I had spotted in line at Campus Bean.

"Not Helen," I said, *"Ellen.* She's a friend of Art's. His girlfriend, okay?"

"Art?"

"Art Fitch," I said. "He's a senior."

"I don't know him," she said.

"Well, he's kind of famous," I said.

"I'm sure if he were famous I would've heard of him," Nicole said. "Anyway, you were saying her name in your sleep. Over and over again. *Ellen, Ellen . . .*" She closed her notebook with a sharp *thwap.* "You know, if you're seeing someone you should've just told me—"

I stood up and ran my hand through my hair. "I'm not seeing anyone," I said. I turned and walked to the door.

"Then who is she?" Nicole said. I guessed that not many men had left her room so hastily. I looked back at her.

"I don't know, yet," I said, and I left.

Later that morning I made my way to the library. The sky was a dull wash of grays and blues, like silt at the bottom of a puddle. A crow glided to the ground in front of me and cocked its head, blinking shiny black eyes. I thought of Stulton's pigeons, fat and graceless, and then this black crow, walking below me, like a preacher with his head down, hands clasped behind his back. It stopped and thrust at the dirt, a swift, killing stroke, and then unfolded its wings and flew away, toward the woods.

The H. F. Mores loomed, wooden doors closed to the world. I took a deep breath, then climbed the steps as the skeletal remains of leaves swirled at my feet.

Cornelius was seated at the front desk, swaddled in the endless folds of his robe. His cane was lying across his legs, and he picked it up and poked a large plastic pitcher sitting atop the desk, nearly toppling it.

"Fill it up—there is a faucet in the bathroom. The plants need watering."

I looked around. There was one plant, a leafless ficus, in the far corner.

"What are you studying?" Cornelius asked.

"History," I said.

"Of what?"

I fiddled with the pitcher and dropped it. It clattered noisily on the floor. I bent down and snatched it up. "I don't know," I said, my face burning. I always felt like a complete idiot around Cornelius.

"You haven't decided yet, is that it?" His voice hitched and he stifled a cough. "Why history? Why not something useful and practical, something like philosophy?"

It's proof of your age that you think philosophy is something useful and practical, I thought.

Cornelius coughed and a glob of blood flew from his mouth and landed on the desk. He dabbed his mouth with a handkerchief. "You're friends with Arthur," he said. "I have his books for him, you know. You should take them before you leave."

"You know Arthur?" I said.

Cornelius nodded. "I know everyone. Henry Lang had hair when he first came to Aberdeen. Don Grunebaum was still married to his second wife. Dean Richardson was still a vibrant young man." He smiled. "It's the students that never change. Eternal idiots. Of course there are the rare exceptions. Your friend Arthur, for example. But one day he'll leave and an idiot will take his place. Maybe that idiot will be you."

"I'm no idiot," I said.

"Of course you aren't. Youth is never idiotic—only ill-informed." Cornelius grabbed his cane and pointed to the pile of books on his desk. "Will you bring Arthur's books to him?"

I nodded and looked out one of the windows. On its sill sat a pigeon, staring inside the library with its stupid, blinking eyes.

Thirty days had been the grace period—now, entering the fifth week after my strange evening at Dr. Cade's with Art and company, I couldn't stop thinking about them. All of their defining elements— Howie's glassy gaze, Dan's ill-fitted suit, Art's lanky aggressiveness, and Ellen's terrifying beauty—replayed constantly in my mind. I still saw Art in class but he had become as remote as an actor on a screen, someone I could listen to and watch, but who was incapable of interacting with me. I still had his library books—three strange, old volumes: Abram Oslo's *Index Expurgatorius,* some other massive tome titled *Gilbert's Universal Compendium,* and a reprint of the 1898 edition of the *Index Librorum Prohibitorum.* I'd kept them in my room, like victims of a kidnap, in a pile on my desk, and I'd been waiting for Art to find out from Cornelius that I had them. But Art didn't say anything to me, and Cornelius seemed to forget he'd let me have them, and so I left them there, collecting dust and water rings from late-night study sessions.

I had been avoiding Nicole since my fumbling exit from her room, and when she finally broke the tension it was classic Nicole:

GODS OF ABERDEEN — 57

She crept up behind me, in the Paderborne lobby, and crushed me in a full-body embrace, her dark hair falling all around my shoulders. I tried to apologize for leaving her room so abruptly but she covered my mouth with her vanilla-lotioned hand. *Please,* she said. *Let's not be all dramatic about this, okay?*

There was a hand-painted banner strung across the doorway of the student union, advertising an athletic rally for Aberdeen's crew team, which Nicole had become the coordinator of.

"You really should consider getting more involved around here," she said to me. "Have you ever considered joining a sports team? Aren't you tired of not having any friends?"

"I do have friends."

"Name one."

I stopped and smiled at her.

"You."

Nicole laughed. "I mean *real* friends."

"You're not real?"

"You know what I mean . . ." She grabbed my hand and pulled me along. "Real friends don't fuck."

I stopped again. "We had sex?"

Nicole bit her lower lip. "Not yet."

I looked away, my face burning. *Say something cool, say something cool.*

We walked across the Quad, Nicole talking the entire time. She told me she wanted to move to New York City and get involved with an art gallery in SoHo owned by her aunt. I was half-listening, lost in my own thoughts, when I saw what I thought was a child walking across the grass ahead of us, dressed in a suit and carrying a leather briefcase. I looked again, and recognized him. It was Dan.

I grabbed Nicole's arm and walked in the opposite direction.

"Hey," she said, frowning and yanking her arm free. She read-justed the French cuffs of her blouse. "What's wrong with you?"

"I don't want him to see me," I said. "That's one of the guys I told you about."

Nicole glanced over her shoulder. "Oh." She dropped her voice into a whisper. *"The crazy one?"*

"No. Just wait a minute until he's farther away."

"You're being silly."

"I am not."

She cupped her hands around her mouth. "*Hey you,*" she shouted, yelling after Dan. I had a sudden urge to run, maybe to hide behind a tree or duck around the corner of a building.

"If you owe him money you better get out your wallet, because he's coming over."

"Why are you doing this? You know—"

I promptly shut up. Dan was standing before us, smiling politely, holding his briefcase handle with two hands in front of his body. His suit was crisply pressed but too large. The shoulders were boxy, the pants were bunched around his shoes, and he had to pull the sleeves back to fully expose his hands. His thin neck jutted out from the recesses of his dark gray shirt.

"Good to see you again," he said, nodding to me. I introduced him to Nicole and he delicately extended his hand toward her as if he were greeting a woman dressed in an evening gown at a black-tie affair. She took it, looking both amused and surprised.

Dan looked skyward, squinting. "Beautiful day. Cirrus clouds and nothing else."

"Sure is," I said. Nicole looked at me funny and I mouthed *What?*

"It's the altitude," Dan continued, still looking up. "Five miles is the cirrus domain. At two miles altostratus appears. Look, there's one . . . You can always tell altostratus by the bluish veil."

Nicole craned her neck and shielded her eyes from the sun.

"I can't see shit," she said.

"How are things at the house?" I said.

"Same as usual," Dan said. "Lots of work, not enough time. How were your exams?"

I shoved my hands into my pockets, going for some look—I don't know which, rakish scholar, or something. "Not bad," I said. "All A's."

"Congratulations," Dan said. I nodded dumbly.

Nicole remained remarkably quiet. She was inspecting her nails, spreading her fingers wide and wiggling them.

"Look." Dan put down his briefcase and held up his hands, palms outward, as if I were holding him at gunpoint. "I'm not good at this type of thing so I'll just say it: I think you're capable of handling the workload."

"What are you talking about?"

He blinked. "I was just surprised, that's all."

"Surprised at what?"

"At your decision. I think you would have been a great addition to the team."

"Dr. Cade wanted me?" I said, incredulous.

"Of course. Didn't you . . ." He faded off. "I've been trying to reach you for the last week," he said. "I had to leave messages with your RD because she wouldn't give me your phone number."

I looked at Nicole. She'd been filing her nails and stopped in mid-stroke to raise an eyebrow. Our Paderborne RD was Louise Hulse, a morbidly thin, spiteful woman who did little else but sit in her room and listen to the Cure at full volume. Her room was right next to mine, and on the rare occasion she wasn't in her room she was at the lobby desk, lording over the mail and checking student IDs even though she knew everyone's face. I could set my clock to her late-night bulimic retchings.

"Louise is so paranoid," Nicole said. "A friend of hers was sexually assaulted freshman year, and now she won't give out phone numbers to anyone. She wouldn't even give my *aunt* my number. Can you believe that?"

I looked at Dan. "I didn't get any of your messages," I said. "Honest."

"Simple miscommunication," he said, with a shrug. "We had a house meeting a few weeks ago. Everyone agreed you would be a tremendous asset to the project." He smiled at Nicole. "Art's girlfriend Ellen comes to the house all the time, you know."

Nicole put her file away and blew on her nails. "What?"

"Professor Cade's house. He doesn't mind girlfriends visiting."

"I'm not his girlfriend."

"Oh. I thought—"

"Eric couldn't handle me, anyway," she said, and she stuck out her tongue. I slapped her shoulder, and she laughed and backed away.

"*Any*how," Dan said, "we didn't hear from you and we just assumed you weren't interested. But I'm sure the offer still stands."

I know I should have given myself more time to think about it, moving out of my room and choosing, more or less, to enroll in Dr. Cade's home school. It was a glamorous proposition: working and living with upperclassmen, maybe hosting parties for faculty. I thought of Dr. Cade's land, imagining it in the daylight . . . lazy afternoons on the lawn, playing croquet, sipping drinks. Ellen on a lawn chair, wispy skirt coiled around her willowy legs, rippling in the warm breeze. Arthur patting me on the back and motioning to Ellen with a sly, knowing wink. *She fancies you, too, old sport. I don't mind sharing, to tell you the truth.* Even Howie had a role—the jovial drunk, swapping stories about big oil and industry, the sweet smell of scotch on his breath.

"I think it's weird," Nicole said. "How come he has to live in the house?"

"I don't think he *has* to," Dan said, "but Eric would have a big, private room, a pond in the back large enough for canoeing, about twenty acres of woods. And you should see it in the winter." He looked to me. "Besides, the project requires teamwork. It certainly makes things easier living with your co-workers."

"Freshmen aren't allowed to live off-campus." Nicole nodded as if she had made a final, indisputable point.

"I lived there last year," Dan said.

A squirrel chittered and bolted for the trees, chased by another squirrel. The two dashed for the trunk, twisting their way up.

"Dr. Cade can make arrangements," Dan said, and then he picked up his briefcase. "His name carries a lot of weight around here."

Say yes, I thought. *Accept before you lose your nerve.*

"Let me think about it," I said. "Can I call you tonight?"

"Sure. Here." He fumbled in his jacket pocket and took out a card. It was a calling card, embossed with his name, address, and phone number. Nicole leaned in and looked at the little white rectangle in the palm of my hand. *Cool,* she said.

Dan said goodbye, and we watched him walk across the Quad, carrying his briefcase.

"God, he's such a *nerd*," Nicole said.

We continued our walk, following the footpath into the rolling forests that stood just beyond Thorren, staying on the thin trail that snaked down a ravine and along its edges, pebbles and twigs falling off the narrow embankment and splashing into the creek below. Nicole told me that confining myself to a house was crazy, and that I'd become a snob, hanging out with rich kids in a mansion "with a professor for a sugar daddy." "We'd never see you anymore," she said, putting on a mock pout. I promised her I'd have her over for tea and biscuits, and we could sit in the ornamental garden off the back porch and discuss the apathy of the bourgeoisie. She said I was already becoming an elitist, and then she pinched my side and scurried away, bounding down the trail, laughing and screeching like a child.

I ran after her, ducking under branches, brushing by stiff leaves that scraped my face. The path cut sharply, making its way to the creek, where it continued on the other side and crawled back up the ravine. Nicole was standing on an algae-slicked stone, in the creek, water idly flowing past her sneakers. I leapt to her side but slipped on the rock, and she caught me with a surprisingly strong grip, her arm shooting out fast. My foot splashed into the water and I steadied myself.

"Now you're in trouble," I said, grabbing both her shoulders.

We stared at each other for a moment. I was aware of her breathing, and the wind exhaling through the treetops. Slats of speckled sun swept across her face. Her hands gently grazed against mine, and I could feel water filling my shoes.

"What kind of trouble," she whispered, bringing her lips closer to mine. There was a fleck of dirt stuck to her lower lip, embedded in the wax of her red lipstick. I saw us from above, standing on the water-smoothed rock, fallen leaves floating past. My attraction for her was purely sexual, almost autoerotic in its narrow scope.

"Nicole," I whispered. I inspected the ground on the other side of

the creek, searching for a flat, dry patch of land upon which I could lay her down. Taking her to my room seemed like an impossible journey, too far away. I groped her breasts, searching under the stiff rasp of her shirt. She put her hand down the front of my pants and I returned the favor.

Suddenly, Nicole took a step back and wrinkled her nose. "Jesus that *stinks,*" she said. She pulled her shirt down. "Do you smell that?"

Something smelled like rotting garbage. I looked upstream, downwind, bending over in an attempt to shift my eyes away from the sun sparkles darting across the water's surface. The creek sloped upward and broke into small steps, jutting slivers of shale and bedrock formed tiny waterfalls, crisscrossed with fallen limbs and brown vines. I walked toward the wind. Nicole scampered across the creek to the opposite bank, her clay-stained sneakers picking their way through brambles and leafy mud puddles.

Ahead I saw a limp tail, its fur dark and matted, dangling over the upper ridge of the creek. I scrambled up the slope.

There was a big golden cat, half-rotted, its guts burst open and spilling their greasy contents into the water. It had died in the middle of the stream. A small pool had gathered within the cat's stomach, and there it swirled in currents the color of broth, leaking back into the creek, dissolving into the clear water that bubbled and skipped over the layered shale.

Nicole moved to my side. "The poor thing," she said. "How do you think it died?"

"Probably rabies," I said. I found a stick and poked the cat. Its flesh gave like a rotten apple.

"Don't touch it. It'll give you rabies."

"I'm using a stick," I said.

"Still," Nicole said, wrinkling her nose again. "It's gross."

A greenbottle fly landed on the cat's naked eye and sat there, rubbing its forelegs together. The tip of the cat's tongue poked out from its mouth.

"*Memento mori,*" I said.

Nicole grabbed the stick from me and poked the cat, puncturing its side. She squealed and dropped the stick in the creek.

"'Remember that you must die,'" I said. "In medieval times, objects of art were decorated with a skull or some other symbol of mortality to remind the viewer of the frailty of his own existence. Like this." I pointed to the scenery around us. "The dead cat contrasts with the beautiful forest."

"Whatever," Nicole said. "I just think it's fucking gross." She picked a leaf off a tree branch near her head and held it up to the light, staring through its venous skin. I was waiting for her to say something typically Nicole—about my mother, maybe, or a quote taken from Carlos Castaneda (she was in the middle of his *Teachings*). I had told Nicole a little about my mother's death, one of those late-night confessionals the intimacy of dorm life seems to demand. But I didn't want her to think about me within the context of my loss; pity has a very short shelf life, especially for those on the receiving end. The irony of such tragic events is that you don't want people always taking into consideration what has happened to you, and you resent knowing they harbor the illusion of you living within the confines of bad memories, unable to escape. But you do live within those confines, shackled to them, some with longer chains than others. Every new tragedy puts another manacle around your wrist, and demands you build up the calluses to bear it.

"You're staring at me like you want me to say something," Nicole said, dropping the leaf. It landed in the stream and I noticed an ant trapped on it, scurrying frantically from one curled end to the other. A line from the *Aeneid* popped into my consciousness: *It breaks eternal law for the Stygian craft to carry living bodies.* I picked the leaf from the running water, shook off the ant, and dropped the leaf back into the creek. It floated and spun and got caught in the cat's stomach.

"This might sound weird," Nicole said. "But I'm really hungry."

The mood had passed. We left, in search of food and drink to satisfy the urges that had gone unheeded.

After eating I returned to my room and fell asleep. I hadn't slept in nearly forty-eight hours when the nap came unexpectedly, slamming into me just as I sat at my desk to finish my Latin readings. I awoke to darkness and disorientation—television blaring in the next room, music playing above, a woman laughing outside my door. I clicked on my desk lamp and saw 7:00 P.M. in green numbers glowing from the clock near my bed. I had slept for five hours. I pushed the curtains aside and peeked out over the Quad's edge, at three students sharing cigarettes, one of them kicking aimlessly at a bunch of leaves. The other two were gesticulating wildly, waving their cigarettes around, the glowing tips like orange fireflies.

The phone rang and I snatched it up.

"Hey, sexy." It was Nicole. She was yelling at me over the strained whine of a hair dryer. I got an image of her sitting on the floor, hair dryer in one hand, phone cradled between neck and ear, hunched over her freshly painted toenails separated by folds of toilet paper.

"I was just going to call Dan," I said.

"Who?"

Nicole had a habit of pretending not to remember anyone she had just met.

"That kid we saw in the Quad," I said, annoyed. "I'm calling to accept Professor Cade's offer. About having me stay in the house . . . remember?"

"Oh, *that*." She sounded as if it were old news. "Listen, I'm about to leave for a party. You want to go? It's in town; this girl Rebecca Malzone, in my design class, is throwing it. Nothing too crazy, just some cool people, drinks, maybe a joint or two."

"No thanks," I said.

The hair dryer clicked off. "Have you suddenly become a scotch-and-soda man, now that you're moving in with an older crowd?" Nicole sighed. "Don't make me beg," she said. "I'll do it because I'm fucking shameless, but I'll never forgive you."

The possibility that it would be my last college-type party injected just enough romanticism into the scene to make it appealing. I told her I'd be at her room in ten minutes, and then I called Professor Cade's house. I left a message on the machine, rambling and stuttering through my acceptance, and told them I was going to a party in town and that they could call me tomorrow. After I hung up I considered

calling again to say if it made it easier I could just call them, but I re-
sisted that compulsion and showered instead.

◆ ◆ ◆

"In town" usually meant one of two streets: the aptly named Main
Street, or the incongruously named Governor Lane. Main Street cut
straight through downtown Fairwich, and it had, at one time, been
entirely cobbled, but now it was mostly blacktop, patches of it laid
over the cobblestone like caps on rotting teeth. Main Street had the
Cellar—a small, dingy bar below a pizza place—and that was about it.
Governor Lane offered the only college housing outside of Aberdeen
proper, mostly massive old homes barely clinging to their respectful
pasts.

Rebecca lived on Governor Lane, on the second floor of one of
the bigger, well-maintained homes, a French provincial stuccoed gray
with dark windows overlooking the street. The party was exactly as
Nicole had promised: no more than ten of us, conversation kept to a
low rumble, with frenetic jazz playing in the background. No one
talked to me and I found myself sitting in the corner on an orange
chair that looked like something out of those "house of the future"
films from the 1950s. The walls were poorly painted, with streaks of
nonmatching white skidding across their surface, canvases painted
with geometric shapes hung crookedly, perhaps for effect. There were
photography books filled with nude photos stacked on the chrome
and glass coffee table. Nonpareils sat in a heavy cobalt bowl, whose
glass surface was covered in glued pictures cut from magazines. Dis-
embodied heads had been connected to animal bodies, bikini-clad
torsos had been stuck under the faces of old men. A crow and a baby
had switched heads, and a pacifier was glued over the crow's feet.

Nicole was across the room, standing in the corner with an upper-
classman. He had a shaved head and he wore tiny, black-rimmed
glasses, and every so often he'd give me a mean look. He no doubt
thought I was staring at him because he was talking to Nicole, but
that wasn't the case—I had smoked half a joint and was trying to keep
the room from swiveling out of control, and I had chosen him as my
shoreline, so to speak, trying to ignore the tilting floor beneath me.

"Are you a friend of Nicole's?"

I slowly looked to my left and saw an older-looking man sitting Indian-style near the coffee table, one of the photography books in his lap. It was opened to a scene of a skinny man bound in leather and gagged with what looked like an egg and black electrical tape.

"Are you okay?"

I smiled and laughed. I had tried to answer his first question telepathically, convinced that my thoughts had taken shape and substance, formed into small blots that I projected toward where I imagined his frontal lobe to be. I could see the wet contrails of my thoughts, and the tremor of his forehead skin when the blots hit and penetrated through.

"I'm doing fine," I said, and sat back. "It's just that this weed is *really* strong."

He nodded and closed the book on his lap. He appeared to be in his early thirties, dressed in all black, a turtleneck sweater swaddled around his skinny torso. His black hair was stretched back into a ponytail, glistening with oil, and a couple of strands, black as ink, had broken free and spilled down over his forehead. He was barefoot and his toes were incredibly white and very long, almost like fingers.

"I'm Peter," he said, extending his hand. "I'm Rebecca's yoga instructor."

"Are you Hindu?"

He looked taken aback at my question. "Not quite . . ." He straightened his shoulders. "Being a yogi does not require the acceptance of Hinduism. I have attained *kaivalya* through my own spiritual beliefs."

I had no idea what he was talking about. He sniffed and rubbed his nose. "Have you ever practiced yoga?" he said.

His eyes were red-rimmed but focused. I attacked an itch on my elbow, scratching it so intensely I thought it was bleeding, but when I looked I saw only a raised weal. "No," I said, "but is it true that yogis can slow their heart rate to undetectable levels?"

Peter shifted his posture and straightened his back, slowly, deliberately, and not without some showiness.

"Yoga can give one control over one's bodily sensations. Like a spigot." He mimed turning a faucet. "One can choose whether to ignore pain, or experience pleasure. And just like the spigot, one can adjust and manipulate the intensity of a given sensation."

"Peter is fucking *ama*-zing." Rebecca Malzone appeared at his side, standing over him with her hand on his head. She was a short, very thin girl, with long, curly red hair and dark blue eyes. She wore a lacy sweater, showing her black bra beneath its white filigree. "I've been his student for almost six months. Peter says I have excellent balance."

Rebecca took a hit from her joint, tapped the ash on the coffee table, then took another hit.

"Watch this," she said. She handed the joint to Peter and proceeded to stand on one leg, lifting her other leg straight behind her, bending forward and grabbing her supporting leg while lowering her head to her knee. Her lace top yawned and showed me the finer details of her bra. Its fabric was frayed at the top.

"Very good," Peter said. He put the joint on the coffee table, pinching it between the tips of his fingers as if it were something dirty. "Would you like to try?"

I held up my hand, watching Peter between my fingers. "Not now . . . I'd fall," I said. The top of my head felt like someone was pouring icy water over it, cascading into each follicle and probing to the center of my brain. I touched my head to assure myself it wasn't melting. The jazz had degraded into one long, frantic horn solo, buzzing inside my ears like a fly bouncing off my eardrum. I scanned the room for Nicole but couldn't find her—the kid she'd been talking to earlier was now on a gray leather couch, sprawled over some cushions with another girl. The both of them looked very stoned. My brain sat in a placental sac, surrounded by gray, silty water. *Swish swish*, it shifted inside its bag, pressing against the side, like soft white meat swimming in dirty soup.

"I think I'm going to throw up," I said.

Peter had stood and had his hand on my shoulder. "You don't look so well," he said. His gray eyes narrowed. "There is something we do in yoga called *dharana*. It means 'steadying of the mind.' It is preceded by restraint of the senses and regulation of the breath. I have used it myself for situations such as these, when it seems my mind has spun out of control."

Dharana. What a perfect name for a child, I thought.

"Come with me," Peter said, squeezing my shoulder. Rebecca was gone and the horn solo droned on. I banged my shin against the coffee table but felt nothing. *Dharana* was already at work, its name like an incantation, warding away pain. I saw myself following Peter toward a door with chipped white paint. The living room was closing in behind me, walls expanding like a membrane filling with water. Wall cracks became blood vessels, pulsing and straining. I wanted to tell Peter to hurry, that we must get through the door before the walls burst, but we had already escaped, and I breathed in the blessed silence of the dim room we were now in, while behind me the wall's stretched skin split with a wet *pop,* and the horn crescendo became a flood, spilling forth with thousands of bubbles clinking against one another like hollow metallic globes.

I rubbed my face and took a deep breath. Peter was sitting on a bed, hands folded across his lap and his face expressionless. We were in a small room, furnished with the single bed and a chest of drawers. The overhead light was dim. The room smelled unused, the odor of a guest bedroom, decorated sparsely—a vase with mummified flowers on the chest, above the bed a crooked print of some busy city street, everything captured in movement, streaky and blurred.

I could still hear voices from behind the door. Peter patted the bed.

"Come," he said softly. "Breathe with me."

I backed up against the door. "I have to go," I said. The lightbulb flickered and I spread my arms for balance. Peter stood and walked toward me, his arm outstretched, long fingers wiggling like antennas. I lost focus for a moment, and I couldn't remember which way I was facing or standing, and so I decided it would be best if I sat down.

"*Dharana,*" I said. Rebecca had said something about yoga and balance. She had been on one leg. *One leg,* I thought. *How amazing.*

There was a light shining above me, like a distant star long ago exploded, its energy still echoing around the universe but its body reduced to infinite bits of cosmic rubble, wisps of gas, and a wobbly core of primordial goo, still spinning in place. If a swirling pocket of gas one hundred million miles away can still be seen long after its demise, I wondered how many of the voices of dead people were bouncing off our ionosphere like radio waves, their transmission faded but still receivable. Perhaps that explained psychics, and why their communions with the deceased are always so mundane and trivial—rarely information such as what the afterlife is like, or whether divine retribution exists—but instead comments about someone's new shoes, or how the weather is in Florida. *Maybe psychics are just radio towers,* I thought, *attuned to a lower frequency, mistaking old thoughts and past conversations as current communication with the afterworld.* Was my mother's voice among the signals, just past the channel where JFK is delivering his speech to a West German crowd?

"Your shoes. Would you like me to take them off?"

Peter was smiling at me. I blinked and looked down. For a brief moment I thought I had somehow fallen through the floor, and that I was trapped in a space between the floorboards. Where I had been sitting, against the door, I was now lying down, on the bed. My pants were unbuttoned and unzipped and pushed down to my hips, catching on the ridge of bone.

"Always about the shoes," I said, and then giggled. "Tell me about the afterlife. Do they have trees?"

I wanted to pull up my pants but I couldn't stop giggling. My internal voice was muffled; judging by its tone it had something very important to tell me but I couldn't focus. I knew Peter was trying to get me naked but it was so much easier to just lie there. There was a knock on the door. Peter jumped. He whipped his head around, toward the door, and then turned back to me, holding a long finger to his thin lips.

What happened next will forever be one of the defining moments of my life, the one instance in which a superhero swooped down from the sky and charged into battle like a raging juggernaut, tossing evil minions aside with a flick of his hand. That I was nearly comatose from smoking (as I later found out) a potent mixture of marijuana and PCP only added to the imagery; the colors were more vivid, the sounds amplified, and the whole thing became like a comic book, zooming to a close-up of Peter's terrified face, then switching to my chest and panning down to my waistband bunched around my hips. And then a quick cut to our superhero, Arthur Fitch, banging open the door. His tall frame filled the doorway, shoulders brushing against the jamb, disgust sketched roughly across his face, his mouth a slash, his eyes diagonal pen strokes, square jaw outlined in charcoal lines, shadowy and severe.

Peter stood at the end of the bed, arms crossed, chin held high, everything from heel to spine in perfect alignment.

"You have no right," he said.

Arthur strode in and bent over me.

"Eric," he spoke slowly and clearly, "are you okay?"

I looked at Peter, and then at the light above.

"No," I said. And then I added *I like Ellen,* even as my mind screamed at me to not say anything more.

Art nodded and patted me on the shoulder. "Pull up your pants."

He closed in on Peter. A blur of movement, and Peter was thrown against the chest of drawers; the vase with withered flowers toppled over and rolled off the side, clunking onto the carpet. Art towered over him and grabbed him by the throat. I managed to get my pants zipped but not buttoned, and I sat up.

"What do you want me to do with him?" Art was talking to me but staring into Peter's eyes, teeth bared and jaw clenched. His tie was flipped over his shoulder and his shirt was popped open. Peter was flailing at him, eyes frantic, mouth opening and closing in choked-off cries.

I stood and buttoned my pants. "Let's just go," I said. I stared at Peter with little emotion—he was a character in the frame, held in the clutches of an arm jutting from the border of a panel.

Art whipped Peter to the side, careening him off the corner of the bed and onto the floor, where he crashed onto his back and let out a yelp. And then there came a scream, and Rebecca Malzone stood in the doorway, arms held straight at her sides, hands clenched into fists.

"*What did you do to him?*" she half-screamed, half-sobbed, and she ran across the room, pushing past Art and falling to her knees, comforting Peter.

Spectators filled the doorway: the guy with the shaved head and black-rimmed glasses, a statuesque brunette wearing knee-high red leather boots. Someone mentioned the police. Peter was sitting on the ground with his back against the wall, one hand stroking his neck, shouting obscenities while Rebecca tried to comfort him. Art grabbed my arm and pulled me away, pushing through the throng into the living room. I saw Nicole, passed out on the orange chair.

"They need *dharana*," I said, tottering on the edge of the staircase, Arthur one step down and propping me up with his arm. The walls swirled and my consciousness faded, slowly, reducing itself to a single lightbulb high above, which flickered and guttered like a dying star, and then I slipped into the drugged unconsciousness that beckoned me with a cool, soft hand.

Chapter 4

I awoke in a moving car, my head resting against the inside of the door, right cheek painfully pressed against the door's cracked vinyl. Art was drumming his fingers on the steering wheel. The lower half of his face was lit by the weak yellow glow of the console. I rubbed my eyes until they watered, digging my palm heels into the cups of my sockets. Images floated to me out of the darkness—a man in a black turtleneck, kissing my bare stomach, running his long, clammy fingers across my chest, pausing to pinch my nipple and roll it between thumb and forefinger. My own hands pushing his head away, becoming entangled in his thatch of black hair, and his every movement turning my gestures of protest into gestures of intimacy.

I sat up and scratched at my neck where the seat belt had been rubbing against the skin. Drool evaporated on my chin. The road's yellow divider lines snaked toward us under the beam of headlights.

"PCP," Art said. "The joints at that party were laced with it. What were you doing there?"

"My friend Nicole," I said. "She knows the girl who lives there."

"Nice friend. She should know her supplier."

Peter's pale face tumbled into my consciousness again. I put a hand to my stomach. He had touched me *there*. I went under my shirt and felt my chest, where he dragged his fingers across. *And there.* I thrust my hands down the front of my pants and brought my fingers to my nose. There was the faint scent of someone else, unfamiliar yet intimate, like a stranger's cologne on your pillow. *There, too.*

"How are you feeling?"

I crossed my arms. "Terrible," I said.

"And the whole situation with Peter . . ."

His tone indicated he was waiting for me to fill in the rest, but I shook my head. "Nothing happened."

"He's just a lonely old queen." Art took one hand off the steering wheel and cracked his knuckles against his thigh. "Don't take it personally. I've seen him around other parties . . . the *yoga guy,* yeah, whatever." He shook his head. "He should know better. Someone your age . . . that's statutory rape."

I thought about Art's face looming over me as I lay helpless on the bed. *Are you okay?*

No . . . I like Ellen.

"I could've killed him," Art said, cracking the knuckles of his other hand. "And who was that girl? The one who screamed and ran to his side?"

"That was Rebecca," I said. "She's friends with Nicole."

"Cute girl," Art said. "But *screaming?* Get real. She should've been applauding."

I like Ellen. He was going to remember what I had said, I was certain. I didn't want to think about it anymore. I stared out my window. Dark landscape blurred by, shadows leaping, rising, and falling.

"Peter—who knew," he said, shaking his head in disbelief. "I didn't think he'd be so desperate. I thought he only dated men his age."

I said nothing. The very name sickened me. *Peter.*

Art half-smiled. "I took a few classes at his school, years ago, when he first opened. He always talked about his girlfriend." Art laughed. "He wasn't a bad teacher, but I didn't know any better—I thought I needed a yogi."

"I don't want to talk about him," I said. I was getting dizzy again. "Just talk about something else. Anything. I don't care."

Art nodded and drummed his fingers on the steering wheel. We drove in silence for a few minutes, then Art said:

"Have you ever heard of George Gurdjieff?"

I closed my eyes. Art went on.

"He was a 19th-century Russian mage. He believed there are three false ways to enlightenment: the physical, the emotional, and the intellectual. We can call it the way of the fakir, the way of the monk, and the way of the yogi. All three fall short because they rely on the teachings of their masters, and while they may enjoy more freedom than most of us, they're still subject to their master's short-comings. Gurdjieff had a solution for this, what he called his 'fourth way.' The way of the cunning man.

"The cunning man has set out to test everything and experience it himself. Gurdjieff felt most people live within an accidental reality— that is, things *happen* to them, circumstance buffets them like a strong wind. They base their decisions upon fate. Gurdjieff's cunning man is the opposite. He takes nothing at face value, he sets *his* own rules, imposes *his* will upon the world. People react to him, not the other way around."

The car slowed. "Gurdjieff felt the best way to become this cunning man is through unending work. Immerse yourself in impossible toil, he said, until it adds weight to your soul, and only then will you be able to withstand the winds of circumstance."

Art stopped the car and switched it off. I opened my eyes. We were at Dr. Cade's house, parked next to the black Jaguar. The carved pumpkins on the front step had been replaced by a large ceramic jug, and there was a stack of half-covered firewood in front of the garage door.

Art reached into the backseat and picked up a jacket. "I got your message, by the way, and Dan told me he spoke with you. We're thrilled to have you on board. Dr. Cade especially—he's looking forward to your work."

I felt stupid. The drugs made me feel stupid. I felt like I should say something but I couldn't arrange my thoughts quickly enough. Another wave splashed across the flooded landscape of my consciousness, dissolving the solid lines of everything around me into molecules like smoky bubbles. The edges of the dashboard melted, dripping black stuff onto my legs, soaking into the cotton of my khakis like spilt ink. I reached forward and touched the dash, cool vinyl rubbing against my fingers, reassuringly solid even as it left a viscid smear across my hand.

"Are you okay?" Art put his hand on my shoulder, his face wrinkled with concern.

"I kidnapped your books," I said.

"My books?"

"Cornelius gave them to me. Last month. He told me to give them to you but I didn't. They're on my desk."

Art frowned for a moment. "The books . . ." he said, and I saw a sudden flash of recognition. "Oslo and Gilbert?" he said. "The *Index Librorum?*"

I nodded. "They're back in my dorm room."

"I've been asking Cornelius for a month," Art said, irritated. "He said he forgot what he did with them."

"I'm sorry," I said.

Art jabbed the key into the ignition and turned. "It's not your fault," he said. "If Dr. Cade's decision hadn't taken so goddamn long then I wouldn't have lost a month. You said you have three books, correct?"

I nodded. "Was the amount of time Dr. Cade took to decide *unusual?*"

"Not at all. We're gunning for the Pendleton Prize, so he had to be sure you were the right fit. He interviewed each of us, and talked with Dr. Tindley about your language aptitude, and blah blah blah." Art sounded like he was sick of the subject. "I have to get those books tonight," he said. "You want to come along?"

"You're going back *now?*"

Art nodded, and drummed his fingers impatiently on the steering wheel.

"I can't go," I said, pulling my thoughts together. "I'm still stoned. If Louise sees me like this she might call campus health." I'd heard about Josh Briggs, who one week earlier had come to class high on acid, and was escorted to the campus health center by a security guard.

Art gave me a skeptical look. "Who's Louise?"

"My RD," I said.

Art shook his head. "You're being paranoid. Your RD won't do shit."

"She's a harpy," I said.

"You can't even tell you're high," Art said. "If you want, you can give me your key and wait in the car."

I really didn't feel like going back to campus. "I think I'll wait here," I said.

"Round key opens the front door," Art said. "You have to jiggle it a few times. Wait for me in the living room and if Nilus starts barking just scratch him under his chin and he'll shut up."

We traded keys and Art tore down the driveway as soon as I closed the door. I stood there for a moment, in the dark, staring at Dr. Cade's house, before slowly making my way up the front walk.

Distraction is the best thing for someone suffering from the unpleasant effects of a psychedelic drug. I think that's why, when Art got back to the house with his three books tucked clumsily under his arm, he decided to give me an exhaustive tour. He started with the kitchen, which was smaller than I expected, a door to the backyard, a breakfast nook to the left, and a stairway against the back wall that led to the upstairs. Two windows sat above the sink, and they looked out over the pond and boathouse. The pond was more like a small lake, stretching about two hundred yards back, bending to the right where Art told me it continued into the Birchkill and then emptied into the Quinnipiac River. Cattails and tall reeds lined its edges, and there, almost lost in the dangling branches of the willow, stood a boathouse that Art told me he and Howie had built two summers ago. It was more like a shed, with vertical boards and a gabled shingled roof. A single light hung from one corner of the roof, and I could see the bright orange shape of a life vest hanging in one of the small windows and the straight line of an oar leaning within. A rowboat was tied to the base of the willow tree, where it floated gently on a slight current, a breeze sending dark ripples across the black surface of the pond.

We went into the study off the living room, and then onto the porch off the study, which led into a beautiful garden with two ornamental stone benches and a fountain. Art showed me the basement, which had a pantry filled with cans and jars stacked to the ceiling, and a huge bag of cat food that Art said had been there for years. Half of an old pipe organ stood covered in a blanket in the corner, next to a bicycle that looked like it was from the 1950s, its front wheel missing and twisted racing streamers hanging limply off the handlebars. During the tour Art told me about Dr. Cade's book project, describing its beginnings—it was originally planned as a single volume, to be used as a course textbook—and the genesis of its concept up to its current form, that of an exhaustive, definitive, and meticulously researched series about the medieval era. Art spoke with tremendous enthusiasm, as if the project were his own, and he talked about his long hours spent poring over ancient manuscripts and texts, researching, discovering, refuting old information and adding new. Dr. Cade, as far as Art was concerned, was one of the few pioneer scholars in existence, "a man of incomparable intellect and linguistic prowess, a former child prodigy on par with Champollion and Grotefend" (I had no idea who those men were but I didn't ask). Dr. Cade had been courted by the world's top universities, Art said, and yet he stood by Aberdeen, claiming it as his own, the way a father would a child, working tirelessly to bring his school recognition.

Art took me to my room on the second floor, the last door before the stairway heading down toward the kitchen. The bathroom was directly across the hall. "Your room has the best view," Art said, ushering me in. "The morning sun is spectacular, especially this time of the year. It shoots right through the treetops."

The walls were dark-stained wooden panels, and there was a simple desk, a chair, and a lowboy set against the wall. The bed had a carved maple headboard framed with engraved acorns and sheaves of wheat. The ceiling slanted down over the bed, cozying the space, covering it like an extra blanket.

"You can sleep here, if you want," Art said. "Or I can take you back home. Either way," he looked at his watch, "decide quickly. It's late and I'm beat."

I fell back on the bed. "I'll stay here tonight, and get my stuff tomorrow."

"You guys want to keep it down to a low *roar*?"

Howie was standing in the doorway, shirtless, in red boxers, one leg bunched up around the top of his thigh. His red hair was mashed flat against his forehead.

"Go back to sleep, Howie," Art said.

Howie stared at me. "You're moving in?"

I looked to Art.

"Yeah," I said.

"Great. Someone else to share the bathroom with." He looked at Art. "Ellen called you, by the way. *Twice*."

"Thanks," Art said. His tone sounded like he didn't want to hear about it.

"She seemed pissed. I told her I didn't know where you were." Howie dug a finger into his ear. "I don't think she believed me—"

"I got it. Go back to bed."

Howie walked in and plunked down beside me. He smelled of alcohol. Up close he was more solid than I remembered, possessing a denseness that seemed dangerous, like a truck with poor brakes. His body showed signs of booze and torpidity—the beginnings of fat rolls hung over the waistband of his boxers—but there was still muscle beneath it all. His shoulders and chest were thickly built. He had been a football player in high school, I guessed, the kind who drank all night with his buddies and then racked up stats the next day through the red haze of a hangover. His dad was probably at every game, shouting above the din of the crowd, proud of his son who is secretly the kind of son every dad wants: distracted by women and sports, oblivious to teenage angst, lacking just enough ambition to ensure his place in the family business. I've always admired such father-son relationships. They are marked by war stories and conquests, goals become linear, purpose and intent are clear. You are what you are, and the only thing that can ruin such arrangements is when the son is unwilling to cleave to his own birthright and instead does something unacceptable, like become an artist or announce he's gay. If there's any proof of predestination, it can be found within the biographies of the sons of fathers who own Midwest shipping firms.

Howie covered his eyes with his arm and yawned. "Any women in your life?"

If Art hadn't remembered my Ellen comment before, I thought, *he remembers it now.*

"Yeah . . . a girl in my dorm."

"Is it serious?" Howie pressed on.

Art remained standing, arms crossed, his expression betraying nothing.

"Not really," I said. My head was clearing, the drug haze burning off. "We just fool around."

Howie pulled at his boxers, unbunching the leg, his other arm still lying over his eyes. "That's what I like to hear," he said. "I keep my options *wide* open. I don't like to worry about returning calls, or buying cards for Valentine's Day, or that other bullshit holiday . . . what's it called . . . *Sweetest Day.* Just another way to keep us in line. Remember this: the things you own end up owning you." He nodded to himself and then repeated his last line slowly: *The things you own end up owning you.* "That's right," he said, obviously pleased.

Howie seemed completely unaware of the awkward silence that followed. He remained on his back, one arm behind his head, the other over his face. Art gave me a little shrug of his shoulders, as if to say *He's your problem, now.* I nudged Howie with my elbow.

"Get to your own bed," I said. "I'm going to sleep."

Howie stood up and yawned. "Welcome to the house," he said, and he walked out, brushing past Art. The belligerent smell of liquor lingered, rising off the mattress.

Art stared at the floor, mouth set in a tight, hard line, and then he left. Radiators clinked and the windowpane tremored under a gust of wind. I closed my eyes and quickly fell into nothingness.

Chapter 5

I officially moved into Dr. Cade's house during the following week, packing everything I owned into two bags and loading them into Art's station wagon. I decided to keep my mailing address at Paderborne Hall, since I saw no reason to inform housing I had left, seeing how I wasn't paying for it anyway. Nicole said she was heartbroken, and she batted her eyelashes and held her hands to her chest in mock sorrow. I told her it was an opportunity I couldn't pass up, that I'd be making more money than I had ever made in my life, and that the morning sun in my new room was spectacular. "It shoots right through the treetops," I said.

Dr. Cade was out of town for two weeks at some conference in Chicago, and I felt that if he were home my initiation would be going much smoother; as it was my entrance wasn't as celebrated as I thought it would be. I felt like an intruder. My housemates' patterns were already well established—they ate together, worked together, and shared rides to and from school. They talked about people and places I didn't know. I hadn't been told anything about the project—when I asked Art what my assignments were, he said it was up to Dr. Cade, and left it at that.

Because of my isolation I spent more time on campus. I stayed after work at the library, put in extra hours at Dr. Lang's office, spent a few days a week reading at Campus Bean over a cup of tea. I felt stuck between two worlds: The world I had abandoned seemed forever lost—my friends in Paderborne gave me passing smiles and then walked on—and the new reality I was trying to birth myself into seemed unwilling to accept me.

Nights were the worst. My identity seemed dwarfed by the house. After dinner I would hang out in the living room and wait for someone to start up a conversation, but nothing ever came, and I'd end up petting Nilus until he fell asleep and then I'd hole myself up in my room. After waiting for everyone else to go to sleep, I'd emerge and wander through the house like a specter, haunting the hallways.

My only lengthy interaction during those two weeks was a strange one. I had actually managed to fall asleep before midnight, and was awakened by someone on my bed. At first I thought I was back in my dorm room, and Nicole had slipped in, unannounced. But when I opened my eyes into the darkness there sat Art, on the edge of the bed, his body outlined in moonlight. He wore a sweatshirt and shorts.

He remained still for a moment after I sat up. Then his voice, raspy and urgent:

"Are you awake?"

"Yeah," I said, rubbing my eyes. The clock read 3 A.M. "What's going on?"

"I think I'm sick," he said, and then he reached over to my desk and clicked the lamp on. His face was drawn, and his eyes looked sunken. There was a thin layer of stubble across his cheeks and chin.

My eyes ached from the light and I squinted and motioned for him to shut the lamp off.

"We can talk in the dark," I said. "That light—"

"I need you to look at something," he said, and before I could answer he turned his back to me and pulled his sweatshirt off. I immediately thought of Peter, and for a moment I thought I was going to throw up. Art's back glared harsh white, dotted with a few freckles.

"Near my left shoulder blade . . . see that freckle there?"

A small brown dot lay inconspicuously under the shadow of his scapula.

"Do you *see* it?" His voice grew impatient.

I swallowed against the nausea. "Yes," I said.

"How does it look," Art said, reaching back and scratching at it with his index finger. "It itches. It's been itching me all night."

"I don't see anything strange. It's just a freckle."

He sighed. "You're sure?"

"Yes."

"The freckle under my left shoulder blade."

"*Yes.*"

"What color is it?"

What could I do? There was no denying him. "It's reddish-brown," I said, "like nutmeg."

"I've been up all goddamn night," he said. He clicked off the lamp, stood up, and put his sweatshirt back on. "But sometimes it's necessary. Cancer is number four on the list of leading deaths for our age bracket. You know what one and two are?"

I shrugged. I wasn't particularly interested, especially since I foresaw nightmares as the only product of this late-night meeting.

"Accidents and homicide," Art continued.

"Everyone has to die of something," I said, trying to find some end to the conversation. "My mom died of ovarian cancer."

"That's right, I remember you said that." He shook his head, looking genuinely saddened. "My grandfather had brain tumors that drove him crazy. It's whispered that by the end he was eating his own shit and having conversations with King Richard about the rising cost of gasoline. Stomach cancer killed my grandmother, and both her sisters."

"Death happens," I said. All my pain and that was the extent of my coping philosophy. *Death happens.* Like a bumper sticker for the Nihilism Society.

Art walked to the door and stopped in the threshold. "It doesn't have to," he said, his body a shadowy outline standing in my doorway. After a pause in which neither of us said anything, he gently closed the door, leaving me to face my nightmares alone.

I spent many cold nights walking along Dr. Cade's pond, Nilus sniffing the ground and lapping black water from its banks. Professor Cade's property was huge—under the cover of night it loomed even larger, deep woods impenetrable like a wall of thorns, and the pond was its heart, murky even in daylight. Just a black sheet, sometimes creasing in the wind, sometimes holding floating leaves and twigs, but ultimately its face was unchanging. *It was here first,* I wrote in my journal. *It's like the last remaining drop of an ancient sea. There could be primordial fish down there, or the petrified remains of a ship's hull . . . I imagine it goes miles down . . .*

I was becoming dangerously accustomed to solitude, and I found myself ducking into doorways whenever I heard the footsteps of an approaching housemate, or dreading the sound of a car engine, which meant someone had arrived home. Despite all of this I still didn't consider my decision to move in to be a mistake. I saw ostracism as self-imposed asceticism, necessary for my growth as a scholar. And at least in that area I was thriving; straight A's in the classroom, but also an insatiable curiosity outside of my immediate studies. I became obsessed with categorizing, walking in the woods surrounding the house. Hemlocks and mountain ashes, towering blue spruces and leggy maples, and an enormous willow leaning over the pond, its spindly branches swaying in the wind. I learned all their names: *Tsuga canadensis,* cinnamon-brown bark, thick, deeply furrowed into broad, scaly ridges. *Sorbus aucuparia,* the Scandinavian refugee with pinnate leaves and orange-red berries. *Picea pungens,* silvery-needled, its outline like a monk swaddled in robes raising his hands to the sky. *Acer saccharum,* dropping seeds like whirring helicopter blades. *Salix babylonica,* grizzled old man, long, green beard trailing lazily over the pond.

I tried to memorize every title on the shelves of the H. F. Mores, row by row, by author and call number. To show off, I'd name each book Cornelius touched as he shambled down the aisles, pointing with his cane and cackling at every correct answer I gave. Knowing everything around me gave some semblance of control, and I was determined to discover what my limits were—did thought have substance? Was there a limit to the amount of stuff my brain could hold? At what point would the facts and figures burst from their cells and leak out of my ears?

My second Friday at the house found me sitting in the first-floor study, Nilus sleeping at my feet. The house was empty—Art mentioned he was going out with Ellen (whom I hadn't seen since moving in, and once again my paranoia convinced me it was due to my stupid comment the night of Rebecca's party), and Dan and Howie were on a double date that Howie had arranged with two girls he'd met the weekend before.

The study was cool and smelled of old leather, and someone had left a book open on a side table. *Collectanea Chemica.* I turned to the first page.

Because many have written of the Philosopher's Stone without any knowledge of the art; and the few books extant, written by our learned predecessors and true masters hereupon, are either lost or concealed . . .

I looked out the second set of French doors, leading to the ornamental garden. The cement bench held a couple of leaves. I saw pines and the gently sloping lawn leading up to the forest edge. It was nearing dusk and I could see the sunset through the trees.

Nilus lifted his head, pricked up his ears, and whined. I walked into the living room and looked out the window toward the driveway. A taxi was pulling away, and carrying two bags up the brick path was Dr. Cade.

He handed me his bags as soon as I greeted him at the door, while Nilus jumped around excitedly, bashing his tail into the walls, licking Dr. Cade's hand, looking up at both of us as if we were about to take him outside for a game of fetch.

"Leave those at the foot of the stairs," Dr. Cade said, pointing to his luggage that he'd given me. "We can bring them up later. Come with me into the kitchen and tell me how everything has been."

I'd been, in my mind, a ghost the past few weeks, and I had forgotten how intense Dr. Cade's focus was. His eyes swallowed me with a quick glance.

"Join me for a glass of wine?"

I accepted, seated at the breakfast nook while Dr. Cade uncorked a bottle of Chardonnay. "Arthur tells me you've been eager to get started with the book." He handed me my glass and poured his own. "I apologize for the poor timing. I'd been planning to attend this conference for months. I figured it would be best for you to become acclimated to Art's management style, without my interfering. Arthur hasn't yet given me the revised chapter outlines, but I'm certain I know what sections he's going to assign you. Has Arthur explained the importance of making our deadlines?"

"He did say we're on a tight schedule."

"To put it mildly. We must have the initial manuscript completed by the end of next semester, which would mean the galley release occurs prior to June, which in turn qualifies us for the Pendleton."

I'd read an article about Professor Cade's upcoming book series in one of the academic journals in Dr. Lang's office, which detailed the simmering enmity between Professor Cade and his one-time collaborator, Stanford professor Dr. Linwood Thayers. Dr. Thayers had won a Pendleton ten years ago for his biography on Pope Gregory VII, a project that began as a joint venture with Dr. Cade, but there had been a falling-out before completion of the first draft and Dr. Cade had resigned.

Dr. Thayers was also in the process of writing a book series on the Middle Ages, but, according to his agent, his books cover "the High Middle Ages, as opposed to Professor Cade's more broad-based, mainstream approach in treating the Medieval Era as one historical epoch." This, of course, had been taken as a direct insult by Dr. Cade.

"The end of next semester," Dr. Cade narrowed his eyes, "will arrive sooner than you think. My publishers can be put off, but the Pendleton board cannot. This is why your work is so valuable. I'd suggest you start some reading on St. Benedict of Nursia. You may find Gasquet's translation in my study, or if you prefer the original, I'll leave it out for you later this evening. You may use either one for your commentary—obviously I'd rather you worked strictly from source material."

"When do you need it?"

"Last month," Dr. Cade said. He didn't sound like he was joking. "But tomorrow night will have to do."

Nilus barked from the other room and the front door banged

open. Howie's voice boomed like a loudspeaker. Dr. Cade put his glass down and left the kitchen. St. Benedict of Nursia awaited.

• • •

An hour later I heard Art's voice, Howie's, and then Dan's coming from downstairs. I was at my desk, my clock ticking past 7 P.M. and I had written two things that evening. A half-finished, overwrought letter to Ellen sat folded at my elbow, which I had no intention of sending, but writing it had been cathartic:

> *I'm in love with you, Ellen. I've loved you since the first time I saw you walking out of the kitchen with that wet rag in your hand. If it were a matter of will I'd rather fall for someone my age who isn't dating my best friend, but this is beyond my control.*

The work for Dr. Cade lay by itself in the corner of the desk, one edge curled up:

> . . . St. Benedict insisted his school was designed for the ordinary man who desired a pure Christian life—in his own words, St. Benedict wrote that "nothing harsh nor burdensome will be ordained," this being a direct refutation of earlier monastic orders, who showed their love for God by performing feats of endurance and asceticism. And yet St. Benedict's rules demanded a different sort of endurance, that of obedience and utter humility, insisting that the Benedictine monk "must know he has no power, even over his own body." A monk was not allowed to disobey either abbot or prior, even if he thought what he was being ordered to do was wrong. This applied *in extremis:* even if a monk were ordered to perform something impossible, he was only allowed to state the reason why he found his task impossible. If his superior still insisted, the monk had no option but to obey, and put his faith in God's infinite wisdom . . .

I folded the letter to Ellen, put it in my pocket, and slipped the page for Dr. Cade under the door of his study.

◆ ◆ ◆

I sat for dinner at 8, and by 9 P.M. Howie and I had shared a bottle of champagne and were now moving to postprandial glasses of pousse-café. With each sip of the liquored strata I felt my own brain undergoing excavation, digging past the sandy, shifting layers of my consciousness into the more stable bedrock below. There was a flippancy to Howie that I began to appreciate, a masculine roughness I have always found unattainable and eminently fascinating. He filled my glass, refilled it, and slapped me on the back every time I drained another cup. It was peer pressure in its finest form, unabashed, and it was, as it turned out, exactly what I needed to tear myself free of the shroud of seriousness that had recently enveloped my life. From behind the invisible wall of our drunkenness I watched Art and Dan, and they too looked relaxed, even inclusive, engaging me in the kind of mundane conversation I so deeply craved. I told them about my schoolwork, about Professor Schoelkopf in my English literature seminar, a man famed for coming to class high on coke, sweat beading on his forehead and his nose red and raw like he had a cold. The specter of Ellen hovered on the edges of my consciousness, and at times the note in my pocket grew heavy like a chunk of lead, but I sensed nothing awkward from Art, and as the evening continued I wondered if I'd been the source of all the tension. Maybe Art *was* as I had seen him in my Gatsby fantasy weeks earlier, the kind of man who doesn't mind sharing. Or maybe he saw me as no threat, and found my feelings for his girlfriend flattering in a roundabout way.

Dr. Cade talked about his conference in Chicago, how his state-of-the-union address on the current condition of small, liberal arts universities was well received, albeit begrudgingly, by his fellow patricians of academia. Dr. Cade felt funding should be focused on keeping such schools as "liberal and artistic and non-career-oriented as possible," so as to avoid what he saw as the trap of uniformity that state schools were falling into.

"Of course, the situation could be remedied by a mandatory course on critical thinking for every college freshman in every school, public or private," he said, pushing his plate away. "Some of my colleagues have said such remedies are fascist . . . I think it's the contrary. I would encourage freedom of thought, rather than force-feed impressionable young minds narrow doctrines and career-furthering dogma. Teach them *how* to think, and then let experience be their guide from then on."

We had eaten light but well—a cheese tray, sliced fruit, bruschetta, and finger sandwiches made from baguettes and fresh cold cuts. The white tablecloth was dotted with wine stains.

Dr. Cade continued, raising his glass and tipping it to his lips. "Students are no longer taught concepts. Only facts and snippets of knowledge that reveal nothing because they are looked at too closely, like a Seurat painting a nose length away. You cannot appreciate its beauty until you step farther back.

"Arthur, do you remember what we covered in class last week? The seven gifts of the Holy Spirit?"

"*Sapientia, intellectus, consilium, fortitudo, scientia, pietas* . . . and *timor,*" Art said. He rested his chin on his hand.

Dr. Cade nodded. "Wisdom, understanding, good counsel, spiritual strength, rational knowledge, piety, and fear of God. *Synergy,*" said Professor Cade. "True knowledge—if we choose to define that as the path to seeking intellectual perfection—is more than the sum of its parts. It is an awesome responsibility, and should not be undertaken lightly."

"But without knowledge," Art said, "how can man possibly go forward to experience? Knowledge provides us with a map, of where to venture next. Shouldn't knowledge and experience be gained simultaneously?"

Dr. Cade smiled. "But knowledge comes much faster than experience, and so the medieval mind would recommend rejection of such knowledge until what you currently know no longer helps you move farther along the path. Of course, by that point you may have already taken a wrong turn. And thus you have another example of the paradox in medieval thought."

"*Homo silvestris,*" Howie said. "The concept of all experience and no knowledge. The wild man in the forest, a lustful, aggressive being who honors no god and is outcast from society. I remember that woodcutting you had on loan from Professor Sewart, of the wild man accompanying two royal courtiers through the forest."

"Yes," Dr. Cade said. "Another paradox. The 'untamed man' is conversely seen as a beast and yet superior to the average man due to his sylvan, uncorrupted ways. An early example of the 'noble savage,' unbound by ethics or spiritual awareness. Interesting though—if we had to choose who has done more evil, would anyone disagree it is the civilized man?"

"You can't be advocating we return to primitive lifestyles," Art said. "The pursuit of knowledge is inherent in mankind. We can't go back."

"We may eventually not have a choice," said Dr. Cade. "This quest for truth has given rise to terrible things: subjugation of lesser peoples, environmental despoliation, the advent of nuclear weapons. Remember what the forbidden fruit represented—not evil, per se, but knowledge."

"I would go on," Art said, running his fork tines over his napkin. "I would keep searching for intellectual perfection even if it meant my downfall."

Dr. Cade was poised to say something, I think, in response, but there was a knock on the door.

"That's Ellen," Art said. "I told her to bring a 'welcome home' gift for you."

Dr. Cade smiled and quoted a Latin epigram about Eve bringing the apple to Adam, and how when a woman bears gifts it usually foreshadows ill fortune.

Art got the door while I downed the prunelle in one gulp. Dan cleared the table with Howie, who was whistling to himself and precariously balancing plates in one hand. Then suddenly they appeared, with Nilus following them both closely, begging at their heels. I waved my hand in front of my mouth, checking my breath and then chiding myself for doing so. My plan was simple: act completely normal around Ellen, maybe even a bit standoffish. Pay more attention to Art, flatter him whenever opportunity presents itself, listen intently to what he has to say, nod smile nod smile, and above all, *no more alcohol.*

She was radiant in a gray turtleneck and black pants. Blond hair cascading down her neck, curling upon itself at the tips. Small breasts cupped by her fitted shirt, the sheer wall of her torso sliding into her waist. She slipped her shoes off and stood on her tiptoes to kiss Art. *Ah, yes.* The arch of her white feet, skin creased at the bend between toes and instep, heels smooth and clean, Achilles tendon like a slender cord emerging from the shadows on either side. I knew how her feet would feel against mine, cool, dry skin rasping gently like a cat's tongue.

Her smile terrified me. I felt I had never seen a smile until that moment. *At the heart of all beauty lies something inhuman.* Camus. How perfect for the moment, I remember thinking, a man who understood the horrors of futility. The product of our hopes are geometric in relation to their origins, and I held on to such scraps of hope, that Ellen's smile would one day hold years of our memories within the arc of its perfect red crescent. I hoped it would become familiar instead of terrifying.

And suddenly she was walking closer, Art trailing behind. I panicked and reached for the bottle of prunelle.

"Hello Eric," she said, and she reached down and kissed me on the cheek. She smelled of plum. Or was it the prunelle. I didn't know. I was very drunk.

"Brownies, for God's sake," Art said, holding up a brownie-mix box for me to see. "She brought *brownies.*"

Ellen grabbed the box from him. "I haven't gone grocery shopping in weeks. It's all I had." She looked to me and smiled. I smiled back.

"Then brownies it is," Art said. "I'll start a fire." He shouted for Howie, who burst in through the kitchen door, ubiquitous drink in hand. "Let's get some wood, old sport," Art said, clapping his drunk friend on the back.

Did he just say "old sport"? I thought. Howie yawned and shook his head. "Too cold out there."

"Poor baby," Art said, "let's *go.*"

Ellen grabbed my hand and pulled me toward the kitchen. "Have you ever baked anything? A young man like yourself, just look at these hands." She turned my hand over and stared at it, eyes narrowed. Her index finger trailed along its lines. Her hair lingered dangerously close. "Baby soft. Not a day of manual labor."

"I grew up on a farm," I said. I thrust my other hand into my pocket in a desperate attempt to pull my sudden erection against my leg.

"I thought you grew up in Jersey. *Stulton.* Or was that just a fable? The boy genius clawing his way out of inner-city hell." She laughed and squeezed my hand, clasping it warmly between hers. "Let's crack some eggs."

Behind us, Howie continued his protests, until there was a sudden silence in the conversation. Art laughed, loud and wild.

"You're paying the fucking dry-cleaning bill," Howie said, looking down at his winter coat. He had spilled his drink all over himself, to which Art had responded by pointing and laughing, doubled over, and Nilus completed the picture by taking after his master and lapping the small puddle of booze at Howie's feet.

Outside, the pond was a lamina of glass under the half-moon. Reeds stood on the water's edge like broken scarecrows.

The black granite countertop was covered with pans, mixing bowls, and dishes. Oil and cream dotted the stove. Clear shrimp husks lay at the bottom of the sink. I stared at them, transfixed, until Ellen nudged my ribs and placed three eggs in my hand.

"Break these and put them in this bowl."

We worked in silence, and when the pan was in the oven, Ellen rested on the bench in the breakfast nook and rubbed her eyes. She crossed her legs and tossed her hair back, picking stray hairs off her forehead with one hand. I remained standing, trying to regain balance, leaning against the counter at an angle too severe even though I was trying my hardest to look suave. I couldn't stop looking at her.

Ellen laughed, "You're not much of a drinker, are you?"

I shook my head. "I'm terrible at it."

She laughed again. "You've picked a good thing to be terrible at."

I nodded, trying to steady myself. We said nothing for a minute, and then words came to me, torturously slow:

"So how long have you and Art been together?"

Her lips were slightly parted. Hidden in the darkness of her mouth I could see a faint trace of the pink of her tongue. "A few years. I don't know, 'together' is such a vague description of it. We enjoy each other's company. We're exclusive." She let her mouth drop into a sarcastic smile. "As far as I know."

"Oh," I said. It was all I could think of. "Do you go to Aberdeen?"

"I graduated last year," she said. "I'm an assistant to the VP of Fairwich Trust. Howie says I'm a glorified secretary. He may be right, but at least I'm financially independent, which is more than I can say for him."

We switched places. I sat on the bench while she got up and started to clean the kitchen. I wanted to help her, but I was incredibly dizzy and slightly nauseous, so I stayed seated, hoping she didn't think I was being chauvinistic. She didn't seem to mind, though, and I listened to stories about her family out West, letting the heat from the oven warm my bare feet. Her voice was soft and relaxed, that tone unique to women when they are busy in the kitchen.

Her story sounded like something out of a movie: Her father was a hand surgeon, her mother a former Miss Tennessee. They lived on the ocean, a towering coastal home in San Francisco Bay, four children, Ellen the only daughter and the youngest. She told me about the first time she swam in the sea, and that a jellyfish stung her when she was seven. She attended Brook College part-time, in New Hampshire, but she had met Art at NYU during a lecture series on Italian archaeology, when they were both freshmen. Art had lived with her for a summer their second year dating, and her parents adored him, but he became depressed. He hated the ocean, and his job at the coffeehouse was eroding his idealistic love for the proletariat.

She told me about the first time she saw Dr. Cade—not at Aberdeen but at Brook College, during her first week at school. He had given a guest lecture on monastery life in the 12th century and Ellen said when she met him the second time, this time through Art, he remembered her name, even though she hadn't asked a question and had only introduced herself and thanked him briefly at the end of the lecture. She told me Professor Cade was the most brilliant man she had ever met, and then she laughed and said that if Art was ever going to leave her, it was going to be for Dr. Cade.

Howie burst in through the swinging door, red hair falling over his forehead like he'd just awakened, copper eyes bloodshot, unfocused, and glassy. He looked at the two of us, letting his gaze shift from me to Ellen, and then he smiled slyly.

"Did I interrupt something?"

Ellen frowned. "Don't be an idiot," she said, walking to the oven and peering through the glass. "The brownies are almost done. Do you want any?"

He nodded and grabbed an open bottle of wine from the table and poured it into a flour-dusted measuring cup, letting the dark liquid splash out onto the counter. Flour surfaced, swirling in a white mass atop the wine, but Howie ignored it. I watched, incredulous, as he drank the cup dry, then, wiping his mouth with his sleeve, he leaned back against the counter and stared at me.

"She's fairly fucking gorgeous, wouldn't you say?"

"All right, Howie." Ellen stood up and rested her hand on her hip. "Cut it out."

"So gorgeous she ties your tongue. You get all *gnarled up* inside." Howie mimed twisting something with both his hands, in front of his stomach. "Can't think straight."

"Stop teasing him. *Quit it.* I'm serious." Ellen marched right up to Howie and poked her finger into his chest. He towered over her.

"You ever hear of the *De Secretis Mulierum?*" Howie looked at me. "'Women's Secrets,' written by Psuedo–Albertus Magnus in the 13th century. Said women's bodies are naturally polluting and corrupting, and are a danger to men. He advocated three things—avoidance, persecution, and execution."

Howie smiled and pointed to his temple. He was still staring at me. "*I* see what's going on. She's corrupting your impressionable young mind."

"What's going on is you're too drunk to know any better." Ellen's tone softened.

"Maybe I am," Howie admitted, and he rubbed his eyes.

"We're going for a row," he said.

"Tonight?" Ellen said. "I thought you said it was too cold."

He flicked a crumb across the countertop. "I'm too numb to feel cold," he said. "You want to go?" He looked at me.

"I've never rowed before."

"So. It's easy. You just grab a fucking paddle, and . . . *row.*"

"That does sound easy," I said.

"Smart-ass." He headed for the living room but stopped at the threshold, propping the kitchen door with his bare foot. "Come on, Eric, you'll ride with me. You're the first mate. *Land ho.*"

I looked to Ellen for help, but she was pulling the brownie tray out of the oven, and she paid me no attention. She'd made her point.

Chapter 6

Dan and Art took out the canoe, while Howie and I shared a "pram," as he called it, a small, open boat with an oar attached by oarlocks on either side. Howie insisted he use one oar while I use the other; as a result we went mostly in broad circles, while Art and Dan jetted toward the opposite shoreline, toward the mouth of the Birchkill, hidden in darkness behind the overhanging trees. I could hear the soft splash of their oars and the low lilt of their conversation.

Our boat stunk of liquor. Howie had brought a flask of something and it spilled almost immediately, and the booze now ran along the bottom of the boat, sloshing back and forth. I thought he was going to pass out, and at one point he dropped the oar and kind of slouched backward, but he braced himself with one arm and trailed the other into the water, cupping a handful and splashing it onto his face.

"Sure is nice out here," he said, barely intelligible.

The biting air had awakened me a little. I looked for Ellen in the lit windows of the house but couldn't find her. The second-floor windows were all dark. There was a single window on the third story, and yellow light shone from it, like a staring eye.

"Is that the attic?" I asked. I remembered the attic being on the other side of the house, with only one window, facing the driveway.

Howie turned his head—no easy task in his condition—and then turned back to me. "No. That's Cade's room."

I hadn't, up to that point, even thought about where Professor Cade slept. For whatever reason I thought he slept in his study.

"The stairwell leading to the attic, remember?" Howie said, as if sensing my confusion. "At the top you hang a left instead of a right and Cade's room is the only door on that side."

"Have you been in there?"

He pulled his head back. "Where, the attic? Of course. And you haven't? Wh—" He stopped himself and looked down. He sat there, silent.

"Howie?"

"Yeah," he said, still staring at the bottom of the boat.

A loon screamed, echoing hollowly across the water. I heard Art call back, and his voice cracked. I couldn't see them, but heard the splash of their paddles on the opposite side of the pond, hidden around the bend.

"What were you about to say?" I asked.

"Nothing," Howie said, grabbing the oar again. "Where are those guys?"

"Way over there." I waved in their general direction. I sensed my opportunity closing. "Is there something you were going to tell me?"

I can tell you now there was more to my alienation than the shyness of a sixteen-year-old trying to adjust to a new home. There was something else, something I felt I was missing, like trying to figure out the dim outline of an object behind a curtain. I can't quite put it into words; it was more of a sensation, an intuitive prescience of unexplained events and missing pieces of a puzzle so obscure that they stayed in my consciousness like remnants of a dream. But there was something. A week earlier Dan and Art had gotten into a big argument in the ornamental garden, and it ended with Dan storming off. A few days after that I'd found Art passed out on the living room couch in the middle of the day, with a baggie of mushrooms lying on the coffee table, and when I said his name he slowly opened his eyes and looked around the room, dazed. I asked him if he was okay, and he said he was fine, that the mushrooms were morels he'd picked in the woods, that he'd had insomnia for the past week and had finally fallen asleep and why the hell had I woken him up? I knew he was lying. I just didn't know why.

There was more. Art was often in a bad mood. I'd hear someone sneaking around the house late at night. I heard footsteps in the attic and doors opening and closing long after we'd all gone to bed. One night while I sat in the darkened kitchen, stupefied with insomnia, I saw Art walking to the pond with a bag slung over his shoulder. I couldn't see what he did with it but when he walked back the bag was gone. Taken separately these events were the odd rhythms of an admittedly eccentric household, but together it all started to resemble something ominous, a connect-the-dots picture with half the dots connected. I just couldn't figure out the rest.

"Don't worry about it," Howie said. "They'll tell you, if they want."

"Tell me what?"

"I really can't say. It's not up to me."

He grabbed both oars and pulled, propelling us forward, first sluggishly, then a bit faster, his shoulders churning. We headed toward the back of the pond, toward the darkness.

"Howie," I said, almost desperate with curiosity, "you can't just say something like that and not say anything else."

"Relax," he said, pulling faster. We were skimming along at a fairly good clip. The wind soughed in my ears. Cold air scraped at my cheeks. "Art likes you. You're almost too young, but that might work to your advantage. It makes you less cynical . . . unlike me." He laughed. In spite of his condition he was a good rower, pulling with his whole body, in clean, efficient strokes, the oar blade slicing into the water without a splash and skirting just above the surface on the backstroke. Moonlight skated by, glancing off the calm surface of the pond in a running beam.

"Howie," I said, louder.

"Shush," he said.

"Would you listen to me for a second? I need to know—"

I heard a surprised shout and turned my head to see Dan and Art in their canoe, not more than fifteen feet from us, both caught in midpaddle, Dan wearing his ridiculous ski hat with the orange pom-pom on top. Art's pipe trailed a stream of smoke, like the smokestack of a tiny train, lit by the moon. He jabbed his paddle into the water and yelled for Howie to stop, while Dan paddled furiously, splashing, turning the canoe away. I grabbed on to the sides of our dinghy and turned back to Howie, who looked oblivious to what was going on. The loon screamed again as I let go of the sides and lunged at Howie, trying to stop the oars, but I caught Howie's right fist on the backstroke, and it slammed into my cheek, knocking me down. I fell into the bottom of the boat just as we rammed into the canoe; Howie rocketed forward, the toe of his shoe bumping my back, and he tumbled into the water. Everyone was shouting, including me, though I can't remember what I was saying.

I lifted myself up and quickly surveyed the damage. The canoe had flipped over and was almost split in two. Art was holding on to its side, and Dan was treading water. There was something warm running down my cheek and I touched it there. Blood on my fingers. From Howie's fist.

Art swam to the side of my boat, spitting water.

"What the fuck is going on?" he shouted. "Didn't you guys see us?"

There were other shouts, far off, from shore. A woman's voice. Nilus barking. "I tried to stop him," I said. "He was so drunk, and I don't—"

Something big flopped into the boat, tilting my end up and sending me tumbling again. I righted myself and turned around.

It was Howie. He was on his back, on the bottom of our boat, staring at the sky with one hand on his forehead.

"Holy shit," he said, gasping. "I almost died down there."

"You goddamn drunk," Art said. He drew himself up over the side and glared at Howie. "Are you fucking *blind?*"

"They wanted me," Howie said, looking at me. "They wanted me down there. They were clawing at my ankles."

"Who was?" I said. I shivered violently.

Dan swam over and clutched at the side of the boat. Howie stared back up at the night sky. He had a gash on his forehead.

"The cats," said Howie. "They're all down there."

• • •

An hour later I was sitting on the living room floor, knees drawn to my chest. Our clothes were in the dryer and Professor Cade had made us cups of Darjeeling and patched up Howie's wound with some butterfly strips and gauze. Art and Ellen were in their usual spot: he, lying flat on the couch, and she at his feet, her legs pulled up and tucked under. Dan sat near me, a blanket draped over his shoulders, his cup of tea resting untouched on the coffee table. Howie was alone on the opposite couch.

"Are you certain you aren't feeling any dizziness or nausea?" Dr. Cade had already performed some kind of diagnostic test on Howie with a pen light, inspecting his pupils, making him follow his finger. He walked into the living room now, still visibly worried, and bent over to inspect Howie's forehead.

"I'm fine," Howie said. "Really."

Dr. Cade looked at me. "And how is your cheek, Eric?"

I touched the bandage on my cheek. I felt foolish from the attention. It had been a scratch, nothing more.

"I'm okay," I said.

Dr. Cade narrowed his eyes back at Howie. "You were unconscious for how long, again?"

"Maybe one or two seconds at the most."

"Watch for any nasal discharge. If you feel nauseated, or dizzy, please let me know immediately. No matter what time of night, understand?"

Howie nodded and sipped his tea.

Dr. Cade walked out. We hadn't said much since coming back inside, just a few attempts at small talk that quickly fizzled. There was an air of narrowly averted disaster, and unlike most times when such an event sparks excited conversation after the fact, there was no excitement among us. We just sat there, basking in the quiet, interrupted only by the pop-crackle of the fire, engaged in our own thoughts.

What were you thinking? Art had asked Howie as we dragged him indoors. Ellen was on the shore with Professor Cade, flashlight in hand, trying to figure out what had happened and who was in danger. She ran to us when we ditched the boat a few feet from shoreline, the three of us carrying Howie, his arms wrapped around our shoulders and his feet dragging. He was confused and bleeding, and we had to shove Nilus out of the way because he was trying to lick Howie's hands for whatever reason.

I swear I didn't see you guys, Howie said, as Dr. Cade pressed a gauze pad to his cut. We were all in the kitchen, Howie seated in the breakfast nook, the rest of us crowded around, standing in puddles of water. The table had been transformed into a medicine cabinet—hydrogen peroxide, iodine, sutures, gauze pads. *Eric was talking to me,* Howie said, and he winced. *I wasn't paying attention.*

Art pressed the issue. *Didn't you hear me yell?*

Dr. Cade shushed them. *Talk about it later,* he said. *Let's first make sure Howie's okay.*

I couldn't imagine, though, how Howie hadn't seen them, or heard Art's frantic shouts when he realized we were on course to ram them. I remembered Howie's eyes, the moment before impact, before I dove to try to stop him. They were blank. Or had that stoic stare been resolve? Drunken resolve, at that. Maybe some sort of deep-seated hostility unleashed by copious amounts of alcohol. I looked over my shoulder at Art, who was still on his back, staring straight up at the ceiling. Ellen was reading a magazine, and had pulled a blanket over her legs. There was nothing there, I thought, no sexual tension at all between Howie and Ellen. If anything he antagonized her along with everyone else, and it wasn't even flirtatious teasing, but outright bullying. Cracks about feminism. Jokes about the clothes she wore. Asking her in front of Art if they had started planning for the wedding. She handled Howie gently, however, recognizing, I think, the childish fears inherent in all bullies. And their earlier exchange in the kitchen—he seemed to be enjoying it, but there had been something else behind his smile. Was it vindication?

I shifted my gaze toward Dan, who was transfixed by the fire, his face tinted orange, eyes reflecting miniature flames. His brown hair was still wet at the nape. Nothing from him either, nothing awkward between him and Howie. If anything, they interacted the least. Dan seemed to exist under Howie's radar. *What then?* I thought. Perhaps Howie hadn't seen them in the canoe. Drunken drivers are capable of going down a one-way street for miles, driving into lakes, plowing into snowbanks in broad daylight. Maybe it was just bad luck. And I *had* been distracting him with my questions.

"How are your ankles?" I said, turning to Howie. He looked up at me.

"Fine. Why?"

"You said something about them being clawed."

Ellen put her magazine down.

"When did I say *that?*" Howie slurped his tea. He had a large square of gauze taped to his forehead.

"After you got back in the boat. You were lying on your back and you said 'they' were clawing your ankles."

"That's nuts." Howie put his cup down and settled back. He looked genuinely surprised. "I must have been out of it. A lot of water plants in that pond, always twisting around your feet."

"They are a problem," Dan added, nodding. "The hornworts exploded this past summer."

"We dredged some in July. Remember that?" Art stretched his arms back and shifted his legs. "Filled half the boat with them, and went back four more times. I got burned so bad on the back of my neck . . ."

"You peeled for weeks," Howie said, laughing. "Like a leper."

And there it was. The closing off I had detected before, the drawing in of the ranks. I looked to Ellen, wondering what she knew, if anything. She was staring at me, and we locked eyes for a moment.

"Have a good night, all," I said, standing up. I looked forward to an evening of masturbation, indifferent to the sinister plots the others were hatching in my absence. I was too tired to think anymore. Maybe it was easier that I remain oblivious. Maybe ignorance really is bliss and all that.

"Oh, about your pants," Ellen said, holding her magazine open again. She wouldn't look at me. "You had your wallet in the front pocket. Thank God it didn't fall out into the pond. I left it for you on top of the dryer."

"Thanks," I said, and then it struck me.

I headed straight for the basement door.

· · ·

She had read it. The paper was soaked through but the ink had held; the note I had written to her and stuffed in my pants now lay in a folded square atop the drying machine. The cement floor was cool beneath my bare feet, the air smelled of dry wood and old mildew. Someone had left the bicycle with the missing front wheel and limp racing streamers lying on its side, a collection of nuts and bolts scattered nearby.

I opened the note and reread it, and then spent another minute trying to convince myself that maybe she hadn't seen it. Maybe she started to read it and then stopped, thinking it was for some other girl. There was no greeting line, so it was possible that she could've mistaken it for a love letter to someone else.

I read it again, ripped it up, climbed atop an empty crate against the wall, and pushed a basement window open. Cold air rushed in, carrying old, brittle leaves over the sash. A long-neglected spiderweb traversed the opening, cocooned remains of insects twirling in the wind. I threw out the pieces of the letter, watched them land in the cups of fallen leaves. Another gust of wind carried some away into the darkness, and there I imagined a piece floating high up, riding air currents, skimming and scraping along the roof of the house, glancing off the rainspouts, skirting down a windowpane and swooping into Art's room, where it would land, the one damning piece that would survive, unmistakably in my handwriting, gliding to a stop on his desk. *Ellen.* A single word surrounded by a wet scrap of paper. The one time in the letter I had used her name.

I slammed the window shut, sat on the crate, and cursed myself until I felt better.

Chapter 7

Over the next month I settled in, concentrating on my schoolwork and the assignments Dr. Cade was finally giving me—massive, daunting reams of untranslated text that I tackled during the weekends. But it was work, something I could lose myself in, and so I stayed with it without complaint, and it seemed the more I did the more Professor Cade gave me. I'd leave a stack of papers outside the door of his study Monday morning, and by that Friday an even bigger stack would be placed outside mine.

In early November I became briefly involved with a red-haired girl named Tania, from my English literature class. I remember only two things about her: She loved Ezra Pound, and had tried to get me to drop acid with her. We stopped seeing each other after I'd brought her to meet my housemates, and Art had eyed her with cautious disapproval, especially after she made a comparison between Pound and Boethius as an example of English being a more appropriate medium for poetry than Latin.

My dating Tania was attempt number one to exorcise Ellen from my mind. Attempt number two was visiting Nicole, every night, for two weeks straight, having sex like a madman until my knees rubbed raw from her dorm-room carpet, and at last I was able to mostly confine Ellen to my dreams, where she reigned like Morpheus, coming and going as she pleased. My dreams vacillated between the sexual and the macabre. We'd be having sex and I'd look down to see my dick mangled and pulpy, her privates transformed into steel clamps. A deep kiss would quickly degenerate into suffocation, her naked legs wrapped around my waist, the inside of her thighs pressed tightly against my hips, pelvis grinding into mine even as she sucked the air out of me. Sometimes I'd wake up in the middle of the night, my back soaked with sweat and the front of my boxers sticky with semen.

We never spoke about the letter she found—not even later—and it simply went away, one of those strange shared moments that dissolves by virtue of it being ignored. But emotional homeostasis, I decided, was far too important to risk on a woman who, in all probability, had absolutely no interest in me. I considered my decision pretty mature for a sixteen-year-old. I even consider it pretty mature for someone my age now. Of course I was kidding myself; covetousness is the stickiest of threads, strong like spider silk. If there had been someone to talk to, perhaps I could have dealt with it better, but I had no one.

Medieval philosophers studied the phenomenon of love like they would any other science, and so, in desperation, I turned to those minds. The concept of *Amor de lonh,* love from afar, a poetic notion of affection ennobled by suffering, desire increased by deprivation, and the necessity of obstacles for the fragile ideal to exist, for if given the opportunity to flourish, such love may prove false. Maybe that's it, I thought, maybe I didn't truly love Ellen at all—how could I?—and if the opportunity ever presented itself my delusions would crumble and blow away.

I remember one night in particular. I was rummaging through the refrigerator when Ellen walked into the kitchen, wearing a pinstriped men's shirt, the tail of it barely covering her green silk panties. She smiled at me with her tired eyes and set about to making tea. "For my throat," she explained, stroking the front of her neck and wincing. "I'm allergic to dogs and with Nilus here . . . sometimes my throat swells up." She didn't turn the kitchen lights on, working instead under the cold light coming from the open refrigerator.

My stomach seized and I stood there, frozen in terror. I had a frighteningly powerful urge to grab her and pull her toward me, and shout *Have you no idea?* She stood on her toes, reaching up for a box of teabags, and I watched the thin striations of her calves rise in a gentle swell of muscle before sloping upward into the back of her knee, where they blended seamlessly into the soft sheen of her skin. The skin of her bare thighs was taut, unmarked and so perfect that I felt ashamed, as if I were gawking at the legs of a physically precocious twelve-year-old.

"Is something wrong?" she said, standing with teabag in hand. It swung like a hypnotist's watch, its string held between her thumb and forefinger.

I shook my head. There she was, Phoebe resplendent in silken green panties.

"You look older," she said, half-smiling. Her index finger trailed along the event horizon of her upper thighs, the point at which the shirt tail ended and her flesh began. She hooked her nail under the fabric and tugged it up, slightly. As if scratching an itch. "Perhaps it's just the lighting in here," she said. Her voice was husky, lower than usual.

"I'm still sixteen," I said, and then I immediately cursed myself. *Of course you are you fucking idiot.* The refrigerator door remained open, my hand resting atop its edge.

She smiled and let the shirt hem drop back down. A whisper of green silk lay within its shadows, underneath which I imagined lay all sorts of soft, wet delights.

The teapot began to whistle. Moonlight filtered from the window behind her, shining through her hair. She *was* Phoebe, goddess of the moon, at least at that moment.

"Your water is boiling."

"Thanks," she said. Her tone was ambiguous. She turned her back to me and took the pot off the stove.

I stood there for a few more excruciating moments, kept company by my optimistic erection, and then I retreated back to my room, my single-minded soldier straining at the front line, again bitter at having to withdraw.

The day before Halloween I'd come home in the afternoon and found Dan sitting on the couch, reading a book, dressed in a red wool hunter's cap and matching coat. I thought it was his costume—maybe he was supposed to be a low-budget version of Sherlock Holmes—but as I slipped off my shoes, he looked up and smiled.

"What are you doing for the next few hours?" he said.

I had planned to sit at my desk and study, maybe take Nilus for a walk before it got dark. Dan stood up and jingled keys from his hand. They were for Howie's Jag.

"I have it for the day. Howie took a ride with Art to school, to look at some maps in the library . . ." Dan tossed me the keys. "Want to go to Horsehead Hills?"

"I don't have a license, but what the hell," I said. I had driven a few times before, my friends' cars, late at night, down many of Stulton's dead-end streets.

Dan walked to the living room window and peered out. "There's this farm in Horsehead called Wiktor's Orchard. We went last year. Fifty acres of Macintosh and Cortland trees, sprawling hills, little ponds scattered about. It's like something out of the Welsh country-side. We can grab some lunch at the Whistle Stop, if you want." He looked ridiculous standing there in his old English hunting outfit, brown corduroys sagging around his ankles, thick-soled brown shoes crisscrossed with scratches and scrapes. He had a birthmark I hadn't noticed before, a small port-wine stain under his left ear, which lent some variety to his otherwise entirely unremarkable face. Standing there in Dr. Cade's living room, in the full light of an autumn sun, I felt as if I got my first good look at him. Every other time it seemed we were buffered by those around us: my first dinner at the house, that day in the Quad with Nicole, the time when Art, Dan, and I spent the afternoon raking Dr. Cade's front lawn and then burned the leaves in a frighteningly large fire that had threatened to immolate a nearby maple.

Dan, as I did, had good social camouflage. It wasn't that he was ignored, it was that his presence filled the blind spot, shoring up the sides while others—Howie, Dan, Dr. Cade—took front and center. He was the person in the photo you didn't notice until someone pointed him out. Sometimes, when I'm feeling particularly cynical, I think that's why it took so long to find his body. His uncanny ability to blend in with his surroundings extended even to his death.

Horsehead Hills was farther than I expected, an hour and a half from Dr. Cade's house heading west, into ski country that during the warm months lay fallow as a stripped field, only to explode with expensive cars and whooping college students after first snowfall. We were first going to the Whistle Stop Café, a posh little restaurant built into the side of a hill, famous for its cantilevered design that had it jutting out over a rushing stream. We drove until the glare of the sun began to dip below the swooping hills in the distance, passing the time playing twenty questions and a similar game that Dan liked called Smoke, involving metaphors and famous people. I told Dan more about my childhood, and about my parents' farm on the plains and the intensity of the storms that lashed at anything sticking out from the unending flatness of the Midwest. Dan was fascinated with the Midwest, he told me, having grown up in Ithaca, New York, where his father had been a tax attorney and his mother taught philology at Cornell University. He had always lived among lush hills and gorges with waterfalls spilling over ravines, and the concept of being surrounded by an infinite ocean of earth was terrifying, as he put it.

"So it doesn't stop," he repeated what I had just said. "It just stays flat, as far as you can see."

I nodded, staring ahead at the rising road.

"I think I'd develop agoraphobia. Didn't you ever feel insignificant? Maybe that's not the right word." He fingered his seat belt. "Vulnerable, maybe? All alone with nothing around you, and those clouds you described, like giant hands pressing down on your house . . ."

"I loved it," I said. This was true. I couldn't imagine any place more beautiful. For me, there's nothing more sublime than an unbroken vista, absolutely uniform despite all of nature's inclination toward chaos and variety. And while I agree that forests and streams and meadows are more traditionally beautiful, the scope of far-stretching plains is the equivalent of natural modern art: minimalist, brutalist, evoking uneasiness and uncertainty.

We talked about Aberdeen for a while, our classes and professors and so forth, and Dan told me he was a senior.

"But I thought you were only seventeen," I said.

"I am. I skipped two grades at Camden."

"Wow," I said. I felt an unexpected pang of envy. Grade-skipping, I had thought, was my household claim to fame. "No one told me."

"We didn't want to steal your thunder." He chuckled and started to play with the automatic door locks. Up, down, up, down. "It's nice having you in the house, though. Sometimes I feel too young around those guys."

I wanted to tell him I understood, but I said nothing.

"How long have you been at the house?" I said.

"About two years, now," Dan said. "My family's known Professor Cade for a long time. Mother met him about six years ago at some conference at Brown. She's had a crush on him ever since. After my dad died she wanted something more but it didn't work out. That's all I know . . ."

"I didn't know you lost your dad," I said.

Dan looked out his window. "When I was fourteen. He used to fly his Cessna from Ithaca to Buffalo, to visit some friends he had there, some law firm in downtown, old law school buddies, I think. One night something went wrong and that was that. They found the fuselage about six hundred yards from the crash site."

"That sucks," I said.

"Yeah . . ." Dan sighed and shrugged. "What can you do?"

We said nothing else for a few moments, to let the memories dissipate.

I had so many questions I didn't know where to start so I just blurted it out:

"Last month I found Art passed out on the couch. He claimed he was sleeping but I don't believe him. I think he was drugged."

Dan looked at his fingernails, seemingly unconcerned. "Probably had too much to drink," he said.

"I don't think so. I didn't smell any alcohol."

"Hmm." That's all Dan said.

"Don't you think that's strange?" I said.

He widened his eyes and looked at me, surprised, I think, at my continuation of the topic. "Do you?"

I looked away, toward the road. A yellow BUMP sign riddled with pellet holes rushed past.

"Art's not a druggie," Dan said. "If that's what you're worried about."

"I'm not worried about that," I said. I felt surprisingly nervous. "What was that big argument you guys got into?"

He looked like he didn't understand.

"Last month, in the ornamental garden," I said. "He was screaming at you and you stormed off. You guys didn't talk for a couple of days, and that's when I found him passed out on the couch."

Dan shrugged. "Who knows. I can't remember. It probably had to do with Dr. Cade's project. I don't always make my deadlines, and you know how Art can get really moody sometimes . . ."

"Is it because of Ellen?" I said.

"Is what because of Ellen?"

"Art's moods," I said. "Are he and Ellen having problems?"

Dan started to play with the locks again. "If he is you can't blame him. Art's under incredible pressure. He has his schoolwork, the project, and then there's the whole Ellen and Howie situation."

That hit me like a punch to the gut.

"Ellen and Howie have a situation?" I said. I couldn't imagine it. In some way I could see how Howie might be attractive to the right kind of girl. He was big, and loud, and brash, and charismatic in the way big loud brash men are. But Ellen seemed far too sophisticated for him. If anything she seemed amused by Howie, but that was as far as it went.

Dan popped the lock up, pushed it back down. "I have my suspicions about them," he said. "They drive each other crazy. Crazy in that grammar school kind of way. You know—the boy you tease is the boy you like."

"Does Art know about this?" I was incredulous.

"I think so. I don't know if he cares. Ellen and him . . . they're a strange couple."

"I know what you mean," I said. Actually, I didn't, but I wanted Dan to keep talking.

"I don't know if Art really cares about Ellen. I mean, he loves her and all, but she's certainly not a top priority. Sometimes I think Art forgets what he has. Ellen's one of the most beautiful women I've ever seen."

I nodded. *I know.*

"Art can be obsessive," Dan said. "When he sets his mind on something . . . he shuts everything else out."

"He came into my room one night," I said, excited at having something to contribute, "and asked me to check his back for skin cancer. He didn't believe me when I told him it was only a freckle."

Dan shook his head. "You should see when he gets a cold. He's always afraid it's something like the plague or tuberculosis."

The road curved sharply and Dan directed me up a narrow driveway, gravel crunching under our tires, toward a small white home with a screened, wraparound porch. I saw people on the porch, sitting at tables covered in white linen, and when I parked and turned off the ignition the sound of rushing water rose up, and I walked to the edge of the driveway and looked over the hill and saw a stream far below, cutting through dense pine trees and bubbling past water-smoothed boulders. We were surrounded by green hills and a blue, cloud-dotted sky. The air smelled like fresh, cold water.

Dan got out of the car and stretched his arms overhead. He took off his ridiculous hunting cap and smoothed his hair. He looked around, rocked back on his heels, and cleared his throat like he was about to make a speech.

"Would you do me a favor?" he said. He was wringing his cap in his hands.

"Depends on what it is," I said, smiling.

Dan didn't smile back. "Please don't tell Art what I said about him and Ellen. And definitely don't say a *thing* to Howie."

"I won't," I said.

"I'm serious," Dan said. He looked pretty nervous. "I don't think they'd appreciate it, know what I mean?"

"Don't worry about it," I said. "I'm very good at keeping secrets."

. . .

The maitre d' seated us on the porch, in the corner, next to an older couple who barely talked and instead just sat there and ate their food slowly and purposefully. The woman was wearing a floral dress and she looked very proper, and her husband had on a dark wool suit like he was dressed for a funeral, and when he dropped his napkin and bent down to pick it up he let out a fart that sounded like a buzz saw.

Dan and I shot each other looks, and then we burst out laughing. We couldn't help it. The waiter came over as I was wiping my eyes with my napkin.

"Maybe we should move," Dan said. He stared at me and threw a sidelong glance to the older couple. From the corner of my eye I could see the woman was glaring at us.

"We have another table inside," our waiter said. He looked Art's age, tall and lanky, with longish, black hair and a slow, easy manner that reminded me of the popular stoners in my Stulton high school. His eyes were soft and sleepy, and he looked like he was smiling even when he wasn't. I didn't know Connecticut had anybody like that.

"We're cool," I said. The waiter nodded and filled our glasses with water.

"You guys go to Horsehead East?" he said.

Dan took a sip of his water. "We're not in high school."

"We go to Aberdeen College," I said. "It's about two hours—"

"I know Aberdeen," the waiter said, sounding annoyed. "I used to go there."

Dan's eyebrows raised. "What year did you graduate?"

"I didn't." The waiter pushed his hair off his forehead. "I finished up at FCC," he said. He smiled, daring us to say something.

FCC was Fairwich Community College, also known as "Fucked" among the Aberdeen College snobs. It was like our boogeyman. *Flunk out of Aberdeen and you're Fucked.*

We ordered our food, and four drinks later we were acting like idiots, making toasts to everything from Art's cancerous freckle to St. Benedict of Nursia, whom Dan had been asked to rewrite because my work had been "unsatisfactory," according to Dr. Cade. I was too drunk to do anything but laugh.

The older couple next to us were long gone, and the early dinner crowd had thinned out, so it felt like Dan and I were the only ones in the restaurant, surrounded by an alcohol haze and plates and plates of food. Dan ordered another bottle of wine, and dessert and then after-dinner drinks, and I drank so much I threw up in the bathroom.

"Ubi est vomitorium?" Dan asked when I returned to the table. I pointed to the restrooms and buried my face in my hands. The room was spinning.

"Hey, man."

I looked up and there was our waiter. I'd forgotten about him. The Stultonesque Stoner. I sat up and tried to clear my thoughts.

"We're finished," I said. "Seriously. I think I left half my dinner in the toilet."

"I don't mean to be the bearer of bad news," he said, glancing over his shoulder. "But my manager would like you guys to leave."

Across the room I saw a short man standing at the bar, his arms crossed. The maitre d' was next to him, and they were both fixing me with a hard stare.

"Is something wrong?" I said.

The waiter glanced at our bottles of wine and empty glasses.

"No problem," I said, taking out my wallet. "No problem at all. You know, I'm normally not like this." I couldn't stop babbling. "I never drank in high school. Honest."

"Aberdeen will do that," the waiter said. He sounded completely uninterested in my impromptu confession. "Hey man," he looked over his shoulder again, then back to me. "Is that crazy old librarian still there?"

I looked up. "Cornelius?"

"That's the one. Crazy like a fox."

"I don't know if he's crazy," I said, feeling suddenly defensive. "He might be a little senile. He's really old."

"Yeah, well you didn't work for him," the waiter said.

"Actually, I do."

"No shit? Does he talk to you in Latin?"

"Yes. But I know Latin so I—"

"How about pigeons? He ask you to catch pigeons for him?"

I wasn't sure I'd heard him correctly. *Pigeons?* I said.

The waiter nodded. "Yep. He'd give me a bag of seed and have me sit in the Quad first thing in the morning and round them up in a little cage."

I couldn't believe it. *If he tells me he helped Cornelius sacrifice them to Satan, I'll run out of here screaming,* I thought.

"What did he do with the pigeons?" I said.

"I don't know," the waiter said. "I didn't want to know. I'd just give him the cage and that'd be it for the day. And the whole time I'm like, I'm supposed to be a library assistant for this old geezer, not a fucking pigeon poacher. So you know what I did? I said to hell with all of you. Take your elitist bullshit," he started counting off on his fingers, "and your social cronyism, and your institutionalized racism—you ever see an African-American on campus, other than the *help*?—and shove it up your gold-rimmed asses."

It clicked into place. Our waiter was the boy Professor Lang had told me about. The boy who'd dropped out.

The waiter smiled sarcastically at me. "No offense, man."

"None taken," I said. "I'm not rich."

Dan returned. His shirt was half-untucked and he looked flushed. He saluted our waiter and handed him a credit card.

"It's on me," Dan said, patting my shoulder. His sleeves were rolled up. "I insist."

The waiter glanced at the credit card—I could see it was a platinum card of some kind—then looked at me, raised his eyebrows, and walked away.

"You making friends with the locals?" Dan said. He put his hunting cap back on and tucked his shirt in.

The short man and the maitre d' were still staring at me. There was a young, well-dressed couple seated in the middle of the restaurant, and they were watching us also. I suddenly felt unbearably self-conscious.

"Hardly," I said.

· · ·

I drove like a madman to Wiktor's Orchard, Dan unsure if it was still open but both of us too drunk to come up with a better idea. Luckily it was close to the Whistle Stop, and we soon came upon a hand-painted sign nailed to a massive tree by the side of the road, with a smiling, cartoonish worm sticking out from an apple and pointing the way with one of its three fingers.

WIKTOR'S ORCHARD
50 CENTS A POUND FOR THE BEST APPLES AROUND!

The farmer—a surprisingly young, businesslike man dressed in a Yale sweatshirt, tan khakis, and work boots—was dragging a yellow chain across the road when I pulled into the entrance. He stood still for a moment, eyeing us through the cloud of dust the Jag had kicked up, and then walked over.

"We're closed," he said, leaning on his arm, which he had pressed against the roof rim over my window. He had a long face, short blond hair, and his skin was very tan, standing out against his white teeth.

"We drove a long way," Dan said. "From Fairwich."

"You two Aberdeen students?" He was talking to me, after glancing briefly at Dan and scanning his bizarre outfit with a troubled frown.

"Yes, sir," I said. I looked at my hands, wrapped around the leather steering wheel of Howie's Jag. *We must look like spoiled college kids,* I thought. *And we definitely smell like drunks.*

"Well," he looked away, and then back. "I'm sorry you made the drive all the way for nothing." His tone indicated the opposite. "But we're closing for the day. Come back tomorrow. You know," he stepped back and eyed his watch, "we do open early."

"We won't have the time tomorrow," Dan said. "We came last year, at this time. You let us stay after dark, and we got our flashlights out of the trunk and wandered around. We bought almost twenty pounds that night."

"Is that so?" He started for the chain again. "Must've been a slow day. I can't imagine keeping this—"

"My friend said he'd send you some seeds. Arthur Fitch, remember him? You told him about using Foxwhelp apples for cider."

The farmer stopped and looked up in thought. "Oh, the tall guy, right?" His face loosened a bit and he stood there, chain in hand. "He sent me some rootstock, actually. Awfully kind of him. *Claygate Pearmain.* It's still in the nursery, about this high now." He held his hand at chest height and smiled. "How'd that cider turn out?"

Because I was around Art so much, I often took his charisma for granted. There was a side to him so concerned with etiquette and protocol that at times he seemed prissy. Contrasted with his love of nonconformity the two appeared incompatible, until I realized both achieved the same end. Had Art promised to send that farmer exotic apple seeds and then not delivered, Art would've been just like any other punky Aberdeen kid. But he'd gone so far as to pay for *rootstock,* shipped from some nursery in California, and it was that extravagant, august behavior that made Art so unforgettable, and, if I thought more about it, so false as well. It should've been no surprise to me, then, that Art had adamantly refuted Kantian notions of intent being paramount over action. *Regardless of a man's intent,* he once told me, while we rode in his car en route to the store, *if his actions are virtuous then what's the problem? You mean you'd rather have good intent and evil actions than vice versa?*

The farmer dropped the chain and waved us in, telling us that if we needed them, there was a basket of burlap sacks up the road.

I realized I had never been in an orchard before. My idea of an orchard had been a perfect grid of well-worn dirt trails, a flat colony of trees lined up, each identical in height, with bright red shiny fruit dotting their perfectly rounded crowns.

But Wiktor's Orchard was the complete opposite—rolling, slanted land, tilting at angles like a ship pitched around on roiling waves, sometimes uphill, then, without warning, falling away in a loose scrabble of leaves, pebbles, and roots. Fading sun sliced through the leaves in dusty motes, gnats swirled and swooped from shaft to shaft, the piquant scent of apples hung heady in the warm, late-autumn air. I picked apples for a little while, stuffed the sack quarter-full, and then wandered away from Dan, following the footpath up and over a heavily forested hillock, walking tightrope-style over a mossy log that had fallen across a stream. The orchard dropped away behind me, obscured by a tangle of wild, gorgon-haired bushes and the massive outcropping of a towering boulder. I paused and listened. The drone of insects. The bubbling trickle of water. The muted whine of a plane somewhere far overhead.

"What do you think?"

Dan appeared at my side and bent over to pick up a stone. He set down his half-filled sack and threw the stone into the stream.

"I keep expecting Caliban to pop out from behind a rotting log," I said.

"It does have that feel." Dan kicked at a clod of leaves bundled with dirt. "There are probably Indian arrowheads around here." He turned around and faced the boulder looming over us. Pockets of old leaves sat in its crevices, stripped branches lay in mid-tumble down its side. A beetle crawled sluggishly into the shrinking spot of sun lit upon the boulder's crest. Dan pointed to the base of the giant rock.

"See those? Bear marks, I think. They sharpened their claws there."

There was a series of long, scraggly lines, scratched into the stone.

"Are you sure?" I said, uneasily.

"Oh, yeah. There are bears all over this place. Last year Art and I found a cave about a mile that way." He pointed across the stream and toward a thicker part of the woods. "He dared me to go in."

"Did you?"

"Me? No way. Art did, though."

Of course, I thought.

"He said there were some old bones and clumps of fur. And that it smelled like a zoo."

I peered into the woods. "You want to check it out?" I said.

"Seriously?"

"Yeah," I said. "Why not. I've never seen a bear before."

Dan was staring at me, hunting cap tipped rakishly on his head, hand in his pockets and a loose web of brown vines wrapped around one shoe. Something buzzed by my ear.

"What," I said.

He shrugged. "Nothing." He was almost smiling.

We both stopped, my excitement about the bear momentarily pushed aside. A bird twittered and skipped along a branch over my head.

"Is something funny?" I said.

"I just had an idea, that's all." He bent down and picked up the sack of apples.

"About what?"

"It's silly," Dan said.

"What is it?"

He did smile, then. Daring and excited. Then he laughed. I laughed too, more out of confusion than anything else.

Something cracked in the distance, like a snapping branch. We both jumped, startled, and looked in the direction of the noise. A deer was standing about fifty yards away, staring back at us with its large, black eyes, and then it darted away, white tail zigzagging into the thicket.

Dan leaned toward me and kissed me on the cheek. I pulled back and stared at him.

"What the hell was *that?*"

Dan shrugged. "We should be heading back," he said. "I don't know these country roads that well, especially in the dark." He turned and started to walk back to the orchard, sack slung over his shoulder.

Dan, I said, but he didn't hear me, or else he pretended he didn't, and with that, the matter was dropped. We never spoke of that day again.

◆   ◆   ◆

A hot spell rolled in from the coast the first week of November, spurring a nostalgic revival on campus of summer days—students got out their plastic lawn chairs and coolers, sunned themselves on the steps of Thorren between classes, played shirtless games of football in the Quad. I decided against an afternoon spent reading in the library, and instead came home. I wanted to take Nilus out into the pond, maybe wade in with him and feel the silky mud squish between my toes.

It was an unusually bright afternoon, a searing white light coming down as if from two suns, and even the sky's color seemed faded from the intensity, dulling into a muted blue. I walked to the back of the house, toward the pond. The damaged canoe still rested on the grass, and had piles of leaves bunched up around its sides. Dr. Cade was at the edge of the ornamental garden, on his knees, digging in the dirt with a handheld spade. His back was to me, a splotch of dark sweat in the middle of his tattered chambray button-down. His sleeves were rolled to his elbows and strands of his silver hair waved gently in the cool breeze. I could see the hair on his forearms dotted with dark soil, and hear him breathing heavily with exertion.

Dr. Cade was working on a short row of unfamiliar plants—small hedges, low to the ground, the tips of their branches heavy with what looked like yellow plums. Even from a distance their fruit smelled sickeningly sweet, almost rotten. He stuck the shovel in the ground and grasped a trunk with both hands. I stepped on a branch and it snapped and Dr. Cade turned and saw me.

"Do you recognize this plant?" He grunted and strained, shoulders tensed, and then yanked the plant from the earth, clods of dirt flying into the air. A forked, rugged brown root hung from his hands, the thickness and length of his forearm. "Mandrake," he said.

I saw Nilus bound along the edge of the pond. He was chasing a small, plump bird, hopelessly, as the bird took flight and swooped across the water.

Dr. Cade tossed the plant into a wicker basket. "Arthur has been impressed with your research, and he tells me you have a penchant for all things Byzantine. Do I assume that extends to all areas of your life?" He smiled at his joke. "I read your most recent work, the brief section on Benedictine monasticism. I expected something a bit longer—"

"I know—" I said, but Dr. Cade cleared his throat and continued.

"What you did submit showed promise, and my only criticisms are due to your inexperience more than anything else. Don't be afraid to write more, is what I'm trying to say. For example, you ignored St. Macarius of Alexandria and St. Daniel the Stylite, both of whom provide an excellent contrast to what St. Benedict deemed 'the ordinary people.' Can you imagine what St. Daniel endured, sitting atop that pillar for more than thirty years? One has to admire them, if not for their beliefs, then at least for their conviction." He clapped his hands free of dirt and shifted on his knees. "You know, five hundred years ago we would have used Nilus to harvest this mandrake. It was believed mandrake housed homunculi that would shriek if disturbed, killing whoever pulled out the root."

"Are you transplanting them?" I said.

"No . . . quite the opposite. I'm harvesting for Professor Tindley. He makes some sort of mandrake tea, claims it keeps him healthy through the winter, though I suspect he enjoys its mild narcotic effects." He braced himself and pulled another plant, jerking it once, twice. The root ripped free from the ground and a high-pitched yowl echoed across the yard.

I jumped back, half-expecting Professor Cade to topple over, motionless, eyes open, tongue lolling out. Another pitiful wail sounded.

Nilus was swimming toward shore, whimpering and crying. I ran to the pond, my shoes squelching into the mud and haircap moss, and Nilus limped from the water and rushed up to me, pushing his wet head against my thigh. Dark blood dripped from his left rear leg. I saw raw flesh beneath the matted fur, like someone had swung an axe at his leg and landed a glancing blow. Nilus whined and tried to set his foot down, but this set off another round of yelping.

Dr. Cade walked over, bent down at Nilus's rear, and lifted the injured leg tenderly. The wound was a small arc, bubbling blood. "Looks like a snapping turtle may have gotten him," he said, and he straightened up and wiped his hands on his stained pants.

"Get some gauze and medical tape from the bathroom." He

stroked Nilus's head. "He'll need to be anesthetized for sutures, but I don't have anything here. If you wouldn't mind bringing him to the vet, I'll call Dr. Magavaro. His office is only fifteen miles down the road. I don't mean to delegate, it's just that I have so much work to do." Dr. Cade held Nilus by the collar as the dog stood silent and let the blood from his wound drip and soak into the earth. I started for the house, jogging past the mandrake root, when something scurried from the wicker basket and scampered into the leaf-covered field.

I stopped suddenly and looked behind me. A breeze ruffled the fallen leaves, blowing them over where I could see their veined underbellies. The fetid stink of mandrake fruit hung heavy in the afternoon heat. Nilus whined briefly and then stopped.

"Is something the matter?"

I looked at Dr. Cade, who had gotten Nilus to lie down on his side. Behind them, the pond's surface rippled, its dark water wrinkling under a light wind.

"No," I said, kicking the basket. I was confused and a bit light-headed, whether from the heat or seeing Nilus's leg I didn't know. The mandrake root shifted; drying chunks of dirt broke off. Swollen fruit rolled lazily, fat with juice and flesh, baking in the sun.

"I just thought I saw a homunculus," I said, half-joking.

Dr. Cade wiped his forehead again. "You wouldn't be the first."

An old lady was sitting in the lobby of Dr. Magavaro's veterinary office, cradling a small cage on her lap and humming to herself. There was a cat staring at me from behind the thin wire mesh, its eyes wide and nervous, white whiskers poking out. I shortened Nilus's leash and sat across from the woman, watching as the cat flattened its ears and opened its mouth in a silent hiss. But Nilus was too exhausted to take notice, and he rested his head on his bandaged leg and watched the movements of the secretary behind the front desk.

A tall, older man with white hair walked in from the back, and when he saw me he smiled broadly and extended his hand. He wore a white lab coat, spotted with stains of various colors.

"You must be Eric. I'm Dr. Magavaro." He had a strong, gravelly Maine accent. "William said he thought it was a snapping turtle bite, and from the looks of it"—he knelt by Nilus's side and carefully lifted the leg—"I'd say William is right. Would you like to come back and wait with him, while I prep the anesthetic?"

"He's going under?"

Dr. Magavaro nodded slowly. "Yep. Nothing to worry about. Standard procedure. The general anesthetic keeps him still while we operate. We're just going to shave the area, suture and staple, and he'll be right as rain in no time. Are you the dog's owner?"

"No, sir," I said, "he's Howie's."

"Ah, yes. The redhead. Oh, another thing." The thin woman from behind the counter walked over, and Dr. Magavaro handed the leash to her automatically, his attention still focused on me. "Some of William's cats are about due for their shots. You might want to let him know there's a nasty strain of distemper floating around the county. Four cases this month, mostly strays, but still, an ounce of prevention . . ."

"I didn't know he had cats," I said.

Dr. Magavaro looked surprised. "Oh, sure." It came out *Oh, shaw*. "He's a cat lover, all right. What's that term . . ."

"An ailurophile," I said.

"Yes, that's exactly it. Very impressive." He smiled. "Do you go to Fairwich Central?"

"I'm at Aberdeen."

"Oh," he smiled again. "I'm not too good when it comes to guessing people's age. Bring me a gerbil and it's a different story," he laughed. "I'll have Lily call the house when Nilus is ready. Should be no later than five, five-thirty. And remember to tell William about the distemper. I know he'd be heartbroken if anything happened to his cats."

❖ ❖ ❖

When I got back to the house, Art's car was in the driveway with all of its doors open, and the radio was playing some news program. Piles of books and papers sat on the driveway, stacked on a cardboard box top. Dr. Cade was evidently finished in the garden, since the basket wasn't there and the three remaining mandrakes were missing from the ground.

Art walked out the front door of the house, a glass in his hand. He was barefoot and wearing jeans and a white T-shirt. A layer of stubble spread from his chin down to his neck. "I heard about Nilus," he said. "Everything all right?"

"Yeah. They're giving him general anesthesia before stitching him up." I leaned on the car. "What are you doing?"

"Fall cleaning. It's supposed to drop like twenty-five degrees tonight, so I figured this is going to be our last nice day for a while. I cannot *believe* how much crap I found in here." He set his glass on the car hood, then walked to the driver side. "I found an apple core that must have been under my seat for months."

"Does Professor Cade have any cats?"

Art sat behind the steering wheel and opened the glove compartment. He gave me a funny look, one of those pained, confused smiles. "Not that I know of. Why?"

"Dr. Magavaro said he did."

Art looked down for a moment. "Dr. Cade? I don't think so." He continued to rummage through the glovebox. Empty tobacco pouches, books of matches, a double-A battery. "Cats are filthy creatures. Do you know their mouths teem with Pasteurella?" Art pulled a pipe out of the compartment and held it up. It was a fine piece, carved from wood, resembling a gargoyle, its tail the mouthpiece, the top of its leering head hollowed out for the bowl. The tip of its wagging tongue had broken off. "I wondered where this was. I bought this in Prague, three years ago, from an Armenian vendor in Mala Strana Square."

"Well, Dr. Magavaro told me to tell Dr. Cade that his cats are due for their shots," I said.

Art polished the pipe with his shirttail. "Are you sure he's got the right professor? There are a bunch who live around here."

"He knew Dr. Cade well. He called him 'William.' He also knew who Howie was."

Art shrugged and held the pipe up for inspection. "He's got his patients mixed up. Hey, what are you doing tonight?"

The weekly Thursday night outing. Art and Howie went out practically every Thursday night and came back drunk and shushing each other, stomping upstairs, talking in loud whispers about the various women they'd seen that night.

"I don't know," I said. I crossed my arms as a gust of cold wind hit me. "I have some reading to do. And I have to finish a paper." I wasn't sure if I wanted to hang out with Art and Howie, ever since Dan told me about Ellen. I felt like the Ellen situation was a fault line that could go at any minute, and I didn't want to be anywhere near it when it did.

"That reminds me: Where are you with Dr. Cade's work?" Art slipped the pipe into his pocket. There was a crow somewhere close by, cawing loudly. A thick line of clouds amassed far off on the horizon.

"The Franks," I said. "Merovingians and Carolingians."

"Sounds good. Better pay attention because your next assignment is on Charlemagne. So, you interested in tonight or not?"

"I told you I don't know," I said.

Art smiled and got out of the car. "I hope you realize what an honor this is. We've never even taken Dan along on our Thursday night adventures."

"I'm not surprised."

Art stopped. "Why not?'"

"It just doesn't seem to be his style, that's all."

Art nodded. "The gay style, right?"

"I didn't say that."

"Well I did. He ever make a pass at you? Dan tends to get crushes on his friends."

"Everything's cool with Dan and me," I said.

"You sure?" Art smiled mischievously. "I don't believe you," he said.

"You don't believe anyone," I said.

Art laughed. "The only person who doesn't know Dan's gay is Dan. He should just fess up and it would make things a lot easier around here." He swept a pile of junk off his front seat, and into a box.

I hunched my shoulders up against the cold wind, and watched as the clouds rolled in. They were dark, the color of basalt, thick-bellied and vast.

◆ ◆ ◆

My memories of Minnesota winters are filled with nothing more than cold, cold wind and unrelenting ice. The last winter before my mother died I remember getting up early on a Saturday and staring out at the barren cornfields and it was like a frozen sea—water that settled in the tractor tracks had turned to shining ice overnight. There weren't any trees, anywhere, only the broken stalks of corn plants rising from the fields like splintered bones, and our tractors covered in green tarpaulin that flapped and fluttered like a trapped giant bird every time the wind blew.

By contrast, winters in New Jersey had been dirty and miserable. The snow quickly turned black, cars cut slushy trenches in the salt-laden streets. Cities become even more claustrophobic in the winter; you can feel them closing in around you.

My first snow at Aberdeen came that night—a storm that enveloped Connecticut from Short Beach to North Hollow. We took Howie's Jag into town, the black sky spitting fat white flakes that swooped and swirled all around us. Howie drove surprisingly slowly and carefully, like an old man.

Our destination was a small bar on the edge of town called Pete's Pub, famous for its ten-cent chicken wings (a local cuisine imported from Buffalo), and its five-dollar pitchers of Canadian beer (the owner, Pete, was an expatriate from Toronto). We sat at a corner booth, in a cramped, darkened nook with a thick, heavily scarred oaken table that reminded me of the Middle Ages—I could see us as travel-weary crusaders pausing for a drink at some roadside tavern tucked into the wooded mountains of Bulgaria. Howie ordered a "Tom and Jerry" served in a mug, steam rising from dark broth that smelled of spiced rum. Art got a pitcher of dark beer that I drank despite hating it. The pub was dimly lit by orange glass-covered wall sconces with those small, flickering bulbs that are supposed to resemble flames. *Medieval kitsch*, as Art called it. The patrons looked roughly hewn as well, shadows cut into their rugged features, faces carved from stone into cheekbone buttes and forehead escarpments. They talked in low tones, a steady rumble of conversation broken by the clink of glasses and the occasional outburst of laughter.

Three pitchers later we were talked out. We had covered school, career plans, and Dr. Cade's project. Howie told us he had just completed the final map—a portolano of 13th-century Byzantine trade routes—of the first three volumes. Art said he finished outlining the chapter on the Germanic invasion of Western Europe. Thanks to the beer I had a strong buzz going, tottering on that line where I still had some semblance of control, interspersed with moments of semiconsciousness. I'd suddenly become aware that I was just sitting there, staring at nothing, and like a driver falling asleep at the wheel I'd perk up with a jolt of adrenaline. The beer had also dulled my fears about the Ellen fault line. Everything seemed fine between Art and Howie. In fact, I'd never seen them so relaxed around each other.

Howie leaned on the table and rolled a quarter along the backs of the fingers on his left hand. He watched indifferently, eyes half-shut, fingers twitching like a sleeping cat's tail. Despite his drunkenness the quarter flipped from knuckle to knuckle without pause, slipping between pinky and ring finger onto the thumb, brought back to the index to start again. I stared, somewhat fascinated but mostly comatose. A plate of chicken bones sat in the middle of the table, colored red with leftover hot sauce.

"You watching the quarter?" Howie said. When I nodded, he dropped the quarter onto his thumb and rubbed it with his forefinger.

He held his hand out to me, fingers spread. He showed me both sides of his hand. The quarter was gone.

"Look in your glass," he said.

The quarter sat at the bottom.

"I didn't think you were going to finish it anyway," he said. I looked at the gash on his forehead and saw it had healed into a puckered, thin line.

How much have I had to drink? I thought. *Three glasses. A shot of something with Howie—scotch? Brandy? Whiskey?*

"Howie is a man of many talents." Art pulled out his pipe. It was the gargoyle, its round head polished to a dull glow. He set a pouch of tobacco on the table and pinched a wad from it. "Howie, why don't you play us a song," he said.

"You know I hate that piano. It's out of tune."

"Oh, come *on*. Eric's never seen you tear it up."

"And he's not going to now." Howie inspected his thumbnail. "I don't play on antiques."

I looked around and located the piano, a dusty brown upright, its lacquer peeling and chipped. It hid in the corner with an ashtray sitting atop it.

"Soundboard's all warped." Howie poured himself the rest of the pitcher, and continued as if Art had asked him a question. "It's a piece for show, not performance."

Art shrugged and lit a match. "You're probably right." He puffed twice, and then sat back, cradling the pipe in his hand. "Only Pete can play it because he knows its quirks." Art looked at me. "Sometimes Pete rattles off a couple of songs, nothing much. Old show tunes, stuff like that."

"And they sound like shit," Howie said, cracking his knuckles. He drained his glass in one gulp, then wiped his mouth with his sleeve. He looked back at the piano, then at his hands. They trembled slightly.

"It's pretty dry in here, though," he said. "The soundboard might not be as warped as it was last time. Maybe Pete shelled out some money for a tuning." He looked at the piano again.

He stood, unsteadily, holding onto the partition for support. Then he steeled himself and strode forward, like a gunslinger walking to a duel.

"Howie went to Juilliard for a semester, you know," Art said.

"Juilliard? In New York?"

He nodded and drew on his pipe. The gargoyle leered, smoke curling from the top of its head. "Full scholarship. He walked into the admissions office with his transcript and auditioned. Supposedly they admitted him right there, on the spot."

Howie had made it to the corner, where he sat on the piano stool, got up, wiped the seat, sat down again, and flipped open the fallboard. The bartender walked to the far side of the bar and said something to Howie. Howie nodded slowly and trilled the keys with his right hand.

"He flunked out, though," Art said. "His drinking became a problem."

The bartender returned with a highball and handed it to Howie, who set it atop the piano and played a quick scale.

"I'm surprised he got into Aberdeen," I said.

"He didn't." Art leaned back against the wall, one hand holding his pipe, the other tapping on the table. "Not in the traditional sense. He's taken a couple of classes part-time, as a nonmatriculated student. I think he was going to apply again but lost his ambition. Getting rejected once was enough, he said."

I had assumed we all went to Aberdeen. "So Howie just works for Dr. Cade?"

"Yep. If it wasn't for Dr. Cade, Howie would have to go back home and start working for his dad."

"I thought that's what he wanted to do," I said. "He told me he couldn't wait to get out of college and into the 'real world.'"

Art frowned. "Are you kidding me? That's the *last* thing Howie wants. His dad thinks he's in school. He keeps sending tuition checks; Howie keeps spending them. He saves a lot of it, though. He's got a big account at Fairwich Trust." Art stifled a yawn. "My folks do okay for themselves, but Howie comes from a whole different world. Money like you wouldn't *believe*. Filthy with the stuff."

I swallowed the last of my drink and set the glass down harder than I intended. I was drunk and unafraid. I said:

"I wish you hadn't said those things about Dan."

Art paused with his drink in midair. "Is that still bothering you?"

I said nothing.

"You know I was only joking around."

I shook my head, alcohol-emboldened. "I don't think it was right. I like Dan."

"I like him too," said Art.

"He doesn't have a crush on me," I said. "And I don't think he's gay."

"Fair enough," Art said. "Maybe you're right."

"Just because someone likes you doesn't mean they have a crush on you," I said.

"Agreed," said Art. "You like Ellen, right? But neither of us would say you have a *crush* on her."

Art smiled at me. Adrenaline shot up my stomach and I sat back and guzzled the rest of my beer, Howie's magic quarter clacking against my front teeth.

Howie was showing his stuff, both hands skimming along the keys, feet working the pedals, head bobbing with the music. It was a jazzy, New Orleans–type number, and a small crowd had formed around him. To my amazement, Howie started singing:

Oh please
Don't talk about me
When I'm gone
Although our friendship
Ceases from now on.

If you can't say anything real nice
Then you best not talk at all
That's my advice.

Someone opened the pub's front door, letting in a whoosh of frigid air. Art and I sat in awkward silence for a few moments. I continued to drink, frantically probing my glass for any remaining drops.

Art finally broke the silence. "How's your research coming along?"

I looked up from my glass.

"I'm falling behind at school," I said warily. "Dr. Cade's project has taken over my life."

"But isn't this the life you wanted?"

"I don't know," I said. My vision blurred, briefly. "I don't know what life I wanted."

Art ordered another beer. "You could always go back to the dorms," he said. "No one's keeping you at the house."

"But I like the house."

"Of course you do. I could rearrange the schedule, give more of your work to Dan."

"That's not fair to Dan," I said.

"Fair?" Art laughed. "Fairness is the enemy of ambition. If I was concerned with fairness, we'd be even farther behind on Dr. Cade's project. I spent all last semester putting together a proposal for a chapter on medieval science, and Dr. Cade said no. He didn't even read the whole thing because he said he didn't have the time. Now, that's certainly not fair, but it *is* necessary, and I've learned the difference between the two."

Howie finished his routine to a round of applause and immediately launched into another.

"I saw a book in the study," I said. *"Collectanea Chemica.* Was that for your science chapter?"

Art was clapping lightly and he stopped and looked at me. "Did you read the book?"

"Just the first page," I said.

"What did you think?"

"I've read stories about the Philosopher's Stone before," I said. "It's interesting. But it reminds me of the *Summa Theologica*, when Aquinas tries to mix the supernatural and the empirical—"

"Mixing faith and empiricism is always a risky venture."

"It's impossible," I said.

I was enjoying my stupor, caught floating in a fuzzy web. My toes tingled with warmth. Art and I sat in silence for a few minutes, while I pretended to watch Howie play.

"Not impossible," Art said, suddenly. "Look at what St. Anselm adopted as his life's motto: *fides quaerens intelligentiam*. Faith seeking understanding. He showed how reason can be used to illuminate the content of belief. The two can work together, faith on one end of the scale, reason on the other. The point where both sides even out." He held up his hands in imitation of a scale: palms down, both hands rising and falling in smaller and smaller increments until they stopped on the same plane. "That's where I think truth lies."

"Truth," I repeated.

Art looked at me, warily. "You feeling okay?"

"I'm sorry," I said. I truly felt so. I was sorry I'd drank so much. "I'm really wasted," I said.

"Indeed you are," Art said, and he grinned. "Our little Eric is becoming an alcoholic, right before our very eyes."

We left soon after, practically carrying Howie away from the piano, stopping in the parking lot while he threw up into a snowbank, and stuffing his limp body into the car's backseat where he immediately passed out, slouched against the door, his cheek pressed against the glass. The snow was starting to stick, piling up along the shoulder, covering the countryside in a thin white blanket that looked spotty and wan under the dim moonlight. I nearly fell asleep as well, lulled by the rhythm of the windshield wipers and the muted whoosh of the Jag's tires over slushy roads, and the alcohol that was hitting me like a shot of morphine.

The engine cut off and I woke up. I opened my eyes and saw Dan—I'm sure it was him by the shape of his profile—walking up the brick path to the front door, dressed in full winter gear and cradling a large earthen pot under his arm. His back was briefly lit by the headlights, and then Art switched them off. The clock on the dash read 1:00 A.M.

"Hey, *Howie.*" Art turned and jabbed Howie in the shoulder. "Get up. *Get up.*"

Howie opened one eye and quickly shut it. "I'm sleeping here," he said, his voice gravelly. He readjusted himself and folded his arms across his chest.

"You'll freeze."

"Then I'll freeze. Fuck it."

"Okay, then. Fuck it." Art got out of the car and slammed the door. I waited for a moment, unsure of what to do. I looked back at Howie. His face was relaxed, hair pressed down against his forehead, broad shoulders slack. The car smelled of booze.

The engine ticked. Snow bounced off the windows. "If you're not inside in fifteen minutes, I'm coming back," I said, and left.

The house was stifling hot. Dan's boots sat on the grooved, rubber mat in the foyer, melting snow puddling around them. The lights were off except for the kitchen, a thin ribbon of yellow shining from under the door. I walked, unsteadily, toward the kitchen, past the dining room table that smelled of a fresh polishing.

Dan was standing near the counter, his clay pot upright in the sink. It was a plain brown jug, covered in flecks of old grass and caked with dirt. The mouth was stopped with a large cork, which in turn was wrapped in clear plastic. An open book sat on the countertop, some colored illustration printed on the page. Dan turned to me and coughed, and then he quickly motioned to the jug.

"Herbs," he said. He had on his funny red hunting cap. Its flaps were pulled down, covering his ears.

Art thumped down the kitchen stairs, talking to Dan without seeing me. "You were supposed to dig it up earlier," he said, sounding irritated. "It's this kind of oversight that really—"

He stopped when he saw me. Something flashed across his face— guilt, apprehension, surprise, I couldn't tell—and then he smiled and walked to the sink. "Pretty nice artifact, isn't it?" He slowly brushed some of the dirt off with his hand.

"What's in it?" I said.

Art looked at Dan. "Herbs," Dan repeated.

Art laughed, unexpectedly. "Is that what you told him?"

Dan nodded. He looked at Art.

Art laughed again. "I guess you could call it that."

The kitchen door swung open and Howie stumbled in. A small clump of dissolving snow rested atop his head, half-hidden in his jumble of hair. His cheeks were a high, bright shade of red, as if windburnt. *"Fucking freezing out there,"* he said, teeth clenched, and then he looked at all of us, one at a time, stopping finally at the jug, where his unsteady gaze rested.

"There's horseshit in that," he said. "Get it away from me before I puke."

I looked at Art.

"Well,"Art said, and he crossed his arms and shook his head. *"In vino veritas."*

Chapter 8

For the next two hours I sat in Art's room and listened to him calmly and rationally explain why he believed three seemingly ridiculous notions:

1. Alchemy was not a psuedoscience, but rather a legitimate pursuit with some admittedly flawed theories.
2. Alchemists knew the formula for immortality, calling it by many names (*quinta essentia, aurum potabile,* and the more popular *Philosopher's Stone*) but the exact formula had been lost over the centuries.
3. That exact formula can be rediscovered.

We lay on Art's bed, a collection of papers spread before us on the comforter, while Art told me about Dr. Jacqueline Felicia, a French physician who defended herself against charges of medical malpractice brought by the University of Paris in 1322, the result of her invention and dispensation of *aqua clarissima,* a clear liquid medication that achieved miraculous results for hundreds of patients. He showed me the writings of Jabir ibn-Hayyan, who, in the 10th century, translated from the Greek a formula for creating the ultimate panacea, which he used on himself and his wife for more than two hundred years, before finally succumbing to an assassination by the sheik's guards in 1108. The volume of anecdotal evidence was astounding—tales of transmutation performed in royal courts, of massive clumps of lead turning into pillars of gleaming gold. Lepers and victims of the Black Death cured by mysterious elixirs. Rumors of the secret formula for the Philosopher's Stone spanning from Europe to Asia, always jealously guarded and steeped in allegory so that even if such formulae were stolen, the uninitiated would find themselves lost within poetic verse instead of laboratory instructions. *The green lion is the mineral substance used by alchemists to create a red lion, or eagle, by sublimation with mercury, which then must be united with the winged toad in order to achieve purification of the two-fold swan . . .*

Art had constructed timelines (1471—George Ripley's *Compound of Alchemy;* 1476—*Medulla alchemiae;* 1541—*In hoc volumine alchemia;* 1561—Peter Perna's compilation of fifty-three alchemical treatises; 1666—Baron Helvetius's *On Transmutation,* claims to have witnessed transmutation in The Hague) and traced routes over photocopies of old maps, every map a confusing network of crisscrosses and arrows with place names and dates scribbled in black pen and sometimes crossed out and sometimes underlined, occasionally with exclamation points or question marks or simply a red circle drawn around the word. It gave the impression of a long, frantic search for an elusive quarry. A monastery in the Romanian village of Churisov had been destroyed by fire in the mid-1950s, and it was rumored a wealthy prince sent an emissary to purchase an incunable from among the stacks of waterlogged books and codices, paying in excess of one million U.S. dollars for a book whose content, under terms of the sale, was not revealed. Ten years earlier, reports had spread from the Muztag mountains of China about a village elder who finally died at the age of 315, and who it was said drank the same substance throughout his entire life, a golden liquid resembling the *aurum potabile* of European medieval fame. According to Art, there had been glimpses of the Philosopher's Stone since the 8th century, passing beneath the table of history from black-gloved hand to black-gloved hand, shown only under the dim flicker of candlelight and in the darkened corners of Greek temples and Byzantine cathedrals and medieval taverns and mountaintop inns.

At the conclusion of Art's epic exegesis I stood up, looked around his room, and sat on the Oriental rug in the middle of the floor.

Art took off his glasses. His eyes looked watery and tired.

"I don't understand," I said. I was still too drunk to think clearly. "What was in that jug?"

"Sulphur, mercury, horse dung. It's a formula for Paracelsus's nutritive medicament. We combined the ingredients and buried the jug for fifty days."

"And then?"

"Well," Art shrugged, "then we test it. I admit the nutritive medicament is a shot in the dark. Neither Dan nor I expect it to work. But some of the other things we've been working on . . . now *that's* some mind-blowing stuff. We've been doing this for more than a year, officially. That's when we started, Dan and I, and even Howie sometimes, little experiments here and there. We had some bad luck about six months ago." He paused and looked down. "I had an accident. I miscalculated and took what I thought was a safe dosage of *Amanita pantherina*. Panther mushroom—don't ask me what I was thinking. I'd been thrown off track by the Crecentius manuscript, all that talk about 'noble poisons.' But I'm much more cautious now."

It was silent outside; the storm had stopped. The radiators started to tick.

"So you do all the testing on yourself?" I said.

Art shook his head, grimly. "Sometimes I use cats," he said. "I wish there was another way but there isn't . . ."

They wanted me. They wanted me down there. They were clawing at my ankles.

I'd seen Art that one night, carrying a sack to the pond. That's where he dumps the cats, I realized. *How many?* I thought. *Hundreds of bones scattered at the bottom of the pond.*

"Cats," I said, with a shudder. "Art, that's *terrible.*"

Art looked unfazed. "Scientists test on animals all the time," he said. "I use cats because they're more complex organisms than mice and there's no shortage of them, especially out here, in the country, where none of these old farmers neuter their pets. I would use dogs—

seeing as how their genetic sequence is pretty close to ours—but I have an ethical problem with that. I had a dog, as a child, and can't bring myself—"

I remembered the conversation with Howie, that night on the boat:

Don't worry about it. They'll tell you, if they want.

Tell me what?

I really can't say. It's not up to me.

"Howie almost told me," I said. "That night when he rammed your canoe. He almost told me something about the attic but stopped himself. Is that where you do your experiments?"

Art shook his head. "Howie can't ever keep his mouth shut," he said, disgusted. "I used to think it was the alcohol. He'd run his mouth off at parties, telling people how he's working on the secret to immortality. He's not into it for the same reasons Dan and I are. Really, his behavior runs contrary to the whole spirit of alchemy. He's like the charlatans who gave alchemy a bad reputation, duping kings into funding their con games. Howie has this insane notion that he'll become independently wealthy and cut off relations completely with his father."

"He thinks alchemy is going to make him rich?" I said.

"Sure. Transmutation. Converting worthless base metals into gold." Art yawned. "It's a natural by-product of the Philosopher's Stone."

"This is all theory, though, right?"

"Maybe," Art said. "It's all theory until we succeed. But it takes time. It isn't like you pour in the ingredients, flick a switch, and stand back. Transmutation is a very difficult process, and the yield is often so small that it isn't worth the trouble. Besides, transmutation is supposed to be the means to an end, not the end itself."

"Let me see the attic," I said.

Art shook his head. "The attic is off-limits."

"Why?"

"Contamination. You don't know your way around a lab. Most importantly, this isn't your project. You need to focus on Dr. Cade's work."

"Does Dr. Cade know about this?" I said.

Art stood up and gathered the papers from the bed. "Professor Cade respects what I do during my own free time, so long as I'm up to date on the project. Frankly, I could be running a brothel out of my room and Dr. Cade wouldn't know. He's so concerned with his books that he's blind to everything else."

"Is anyone else helping you?"

"Cornelius," Art said.

Of course, I thought. Cornelius and his pigeons. Art and his cats.

"Our methodology is different, though," said Art. "He does help me with the occasional translation, but most of the time he's just a babbling old man. I don't pay him much attention."

I suppose I should've been freaked out but I was too excited. Everything was coming together, those shadows behind the curtain— from the footsteps in the attic to the pigeon grave and Cornelius's weird story about Claude-Henri de Rouvroy, and even the three books Cornelius had wanted me to give to Art. They were rare-book guides. Art acquired rare books while searching for alchemical manuscripts under the guise of research for Dr. Cade.

"What about those mushrooms," I said. "That day I found you on the couch, passed out."

Art nodded. "The original alchemists—pre–Christian era, before Jesus allegories entered alchemic formulae and fucked everything up—felt the spiritual component of alchemy was just as important as the physical. They felt you had to be receptive to mystical knowledge before you could understand the scientific side. So they used hallucinogens, a shortcut to communing with the higher levels of consciousness. I've tried peyote, mescaline, and even a distillation of *Claviceps purpurea,* the same alkaloid that caused ergotism in the Middle Ages. Those mushrooms you saw that afternoon. *Stropharia cubensis.* Remember the night I rescued you from Peter?"

Of course I remembered.

"I came to that party to buy acid from Leon," Art said. "The bald-headed kid with the German glasses who was hitting on your girlfriend Nicole."

"Nicole's not my girlfriend," I said.

Art went on. "Leon sold me some supposedly new form of acid called ALD-52, derived from LSD-25. Touted it as very potent and totally 'mind-blowing.' It was all bullshit. I saw some colors for a few hours and then I got a wicked headache and fell asleep."

"Why?" I said.

"Probably low quality," Art said. "The good stuff isn't supposed to—"

"No," I said. "Why are you doing *this?*"

Art looked at me as if I'd asked the obvious.

"I'm searching for truth," he said. "Finding the balance between faith and reason. This is the root of alchemy. Can't you see the symbolism? Lead to gold, transmutation . . . it's all allegory. From the imperfect to the perfect. From death to life. *Immortality.* Can you imagine a more beautiful goal, a more noble pursuit?"

I said nothing. Art looked exasperated.

"Aren't you afraid of death?" he said.

I've deluded myself into thinking that if I'd answered differently and joined Art's quest, then maybe I could have guided it in a different direction. Who's to say—physicists claim a butterfly stirring the air in Beijing can influence weather patterns in New York. Maybe if I'd been more curious, or said something to Dr. Cade, or altered any of my behaviors in even the slightest manner, maybe the dark days ahead could have been avoided. But it's more likely, however, that such beliefs are just vestigial ideals left over from the days when I thought I had such power.

No, I told him. I'm not afraid of death at all, and even though I lied, at the time I believed it to be true.

◆ ◆ ◆

The next morning I awoke early and worked at my desk, pushing through the red haze of a hangover, while out my window I could see Howie and Nilus playing in the backyard under a brilliant sun that eventually melted most of the snow.

Charlemagne emerged into darkness, into a 7th-century Western Europe devoid of learning that had suffered under the rule of the Merovingian dynasty. His vision looked toward the future and kept its roots planted firmly in the past: Roman civilization was to be restored, infused with a new breed of Christianity, and his kingdom, Charlemagne's kingdom, was to be pleasing not only to the Church, but ultimately, and more importantly, to God.

Francia lacked the scholars necessary for Charlemagne's vision, and so he recruited from the surrounding lands. Paul the deacon, historian of the Lombards; Peter of Pisa, the grammarian; Angilbert, the abbot of St. Riquier; Theodulf the Visigoth came from Spain. Alcuin, the greatest scholar of his time, left his home of York and joined Charlemagne with even greater ambitions. Their kingdom was to be a reincarnation of antiquity, Hebrew, Greek, and Roman, risen from the ashes of a darkened Europe and restored to its former shining brilliance. Alcuin deemed himself "Horace," Angilbert was "Homer." Charlemagne the anointed king was now "David," and his eldest son, Pepin, was "Julius." Charlemagne's first edict was that all monks and clergy were to be literate, and the Rule of St. Benedict was to be the standard for all monks. It was not enough that Charlemagne provided protection for his people; he saw his duty as nothing less than the creation of God's rule on Earth, and this was, in Charlemagne's view, to be achieved by loving knowledge for its own sake.

Art had mentioned something weeks earlier, I remembered, while walking with Nilus and me through Dr. Cade's land. Dan and Howie were on another double date (which, I later discovered, failed miserably) and Art and I were fantasizing about our ideal futures in a way that only the college years seem to understand: no marriage, no kids, no real jobs. A bedrock of things never changing and loyalties always honored. Art made a vow that afternoon, that one day we'd emerge onto campus as professors ourselves, and usher in a revival of the Classical tradition, when knowledge was both sacred and profane, doled out to the deserving few and honed to a high art. Knowledge as an entity, rather than merely a commodity.

"And those who don't obey we conquer," Art had said. "Like Charlemagne did to the Saxons. Give them a choice: conversion or death."

Writing the piece on Charlemagne for Dr. Cade, I finally understood Arthur's comparison; perhaps he did see (or wanted to see) our home as Aachen revived. But it was doomed from the start, putting so much faith into knowledge, not realizing that knowledge by itself can be dangerous. We believed too strongly in our minds back then, and when I discovered the irony in Charlemagne's life it should have then become clear—intent isn't enough.

Charlemagne slept with pen and paper under his pillow, every night. It was said he suffered from insomnia, and practiced writing when he couldn't sleep. There are accounts of the warrior-king lying in his bed, candles burned to their stumps, all else quiet in Aachen except for the scribblings of his pen, and sometimes, other noises: a cry of frustration, papers tearing and objects hurled. The sounds of Charlemagne's torment—despite all his efforts he died an illiterate king, having learned only to sign his own name.

◆ ◆ ◆

Later that day I went to the library and found Cornelius asleep at the front desk. He looked as if he had spent the night there. A thermos and empty cup sat near him on the desk, and he had a blanket draped over his shoulders. I opened the curtains, careful not to let any light fall on him, and spent the next half hour straightening the rugs and shelving stray books. A ponderous old tome lay in his lap, bound in dry, cracked leather, the last remnants of gilt on the fore-edge now just flakes of gold. A magnifying glass sat atop the open page. I moved closer until I could read the print on the white parchment. It was a page from Deuteronomy, written in vulgate Latin.

Cornelius put his hand on the page, and I straightened up, startled. But he had no grumpy remark this time, just a tired expression and his creaking voice, dusty and stiff. *"Aliquando bonus dormitat Homerus,"* he said, and then shut his eyes again. Even good Homer nods.

"*Mutato nomine de te fabula narratur,*" I said. With the name changed the story applies to you.

"I know about the pigeons," I said, quietly.

I wasn't sure if Cornelius heard me. He put one hand on his knee and moved to stand. His cane trembled under his hand but somehow, like an old, rusted machine, he hauled himself upward by unseen gears and pulleys.

"Art told me about the Philosopher's Stone," I continued, gaining courage. "He said he does experiments on animals, and I met someone who used to work for you and he said you made him catch pigeons in the Quad."

Cornelius cleared his throat and held up a shaking hand. "A moment, a moment." He coughed and spat into the handkerchief.

"What is it you want to know?" he said. He stared at me.

It wasn't the response I'd expected. I had this whole scenario figured out, where Cornelius denies and I press on, and I'd even made a list before coming to work, of the facts of the case and how they were all connected. But Cornelius didn't look like he'd been caught doing anything wrong. In fact, it was I who suddenly felt cornered. Maybe everyone knew about the pigeons. Maybe it was all a part of his eccentricity, a harmless symptom (harmless, that is, to everyone except pigeons) that the school administration accepted in exchange for keeping Cornelius content. *Besides,* I thought, *why do you care if none of it is real, anyway?*

Cornelius tapped his finger on his cane. "Do you want to know if the Philosopher's Stone exists?" he said.

I didn't know what to say. I didn't know what I believed.

He sighed and touched my arm. "Come with me."

He led me to his office, through a door set against the far wall. I had never seen so much clutter in my life—mountains of files and books, leaning precariously as if they could collapse at any moment. Mounds of papers covered the small desk, their yellowed edges curling out from among the piles. Drizzled over the mounds of papers were broken clasps, assorted book hinges, locks, keys, overturned inkwells, nibs, pens, cracked magnifying glasses, razor blades, dried tins of glue, and a pocket watch with a shattered face. The wastebasket was overflowing and the walls were filled with tacked-on sheets of paper, along with unframed maps, crookedly hung prints, and opened envelopes with the return addresses circled in red marker. *This is what Cornelius's brain would look like if you opened him up,* I thought, and within the jumble I saw his diploma sitting behind a spidered piece of old glass, framed by dented and chipped wood. It looked like a religious icon for some extinct order and that now lay unused and forgotten.

Over his desk was a black-and-white print of a labyrinth with a citadel at its center. *Amphitheatrum aeternae sapientiae alchemicae,* the title read. In thin script, below it, the illustrator's name, in small type: *Heinrich Khunrath.* The picture was typically medieval in both proportion and style—men dressed in tunics and triangular hats wandered within the walls of the maze, some were on horseback, others traveled on foot. Some had stopped to talk with one another, or were looking at the sky as if trying to get their bearings. A few explorers had scaled the wall but could only peer over the top at the citadel that stood in a body of water filled with writhing sea serpents. There was one way to the tower—a wooden bridge with a dragon at the end, the dragon's coiled body resting atop an arch and looking down at an old man in a robe who had stopped at the entrance. The man held a beaker with lines emanating from it as if light was shining forth.

Cornelius stood at my side and pointed with his cane to the drawing on the wall. "Twenty false paths, all connected, so that an initiate may wander for years, thinking he has found the true way." He traced the labyrinth with the end of his cane, moving the rubber tip in a circle around the citadel. "There is no exit from the maze once entered, save for the twenty-first path." He stopped on the dragon. "The guardian of the tower of knowledge. Look here." He traced a line to the bridge. "The twenty-first path is a rite of passage. The dragon is the snake, you see. The archetypal tempter. Its head points north, its tail points south. Two choices, *caput draconis* or *cauda draconis*. Which path, which direction? As above, so below."

He stared a moment longer, then moved his cane to a man who

was lying on his stomach within one of the walls. "This one has fallen and lies dead. And this one here—" He pointed to a man standing over the dead man, his hand in the dead man's pocket. "What do you see?"

"He's stealing from him," I said.

"Stealing what? Money? Food?"

I looked again. "I don't know," I said.

"He steals *knowledge,*" Cornelius said. "That is why these impostors will forever remain lost. They think knowledge is something you can take. Look, here . . ." The point of Cornelius's cane stopped at the top of the illustration, at a man caught within the labyrinth whose pockets were overflowing with gold.

"He has found nothing extraordinary," Cornelius grunted with disapproval. "Transmutation, silver to gold, mercury to gold, amateur accomplishments . . . and yet he believes he is close—see the anticipation on his face? But look in the next room."

The next room showed two men locked in combat—one was choking the other, his face contorted in rage, the other held a knife overhead and was about to strike. Around them were tables covered in books and alchemist's tools: flasks, cylinders, bowls, scales. Black smoke billowed from an open furnace, almost enveloping the two combatants.

"This is what happens to the impure," Cornelius said. "The answers will only reveal themselves to the virtuous, and all others will destroy themselves in the heat of their own blind covetousness."

Cornelius smiled, his mouth black and cavernous. "Is this what Art has shown you?" he said.

"He showed me his research," I said. "He said you help him, sometimes. With translations."

Cornelius lost his smile. "And what do you think?"

Art had given me some alchemy books to read, and made me promise I wouldn't show them to anyone, not even Dr. Cade. I'd done my part and gotten through them as best as I could, but I was under deadline, again, and had an economics paper due. I wasn't able to finish some of the more obscure sections on the Rosicrucians and Masons.

"I don't know," I said. Was it fascinating because I believed some of it, or because, like all lonely boys, I sought solace in the unknown?

Cornelius nodded and sifted through some papers on his desk, licking his fingers methodically, pushing the papers into little piles and humming to himself.

"Do you know how long Gerald Hughes will be on sabbatical for?" he asked me.

I shook my head. Gerald Hughes was a philosophy professor, and I didn't know what Gerald Hughes had to do with alchemy and dragons and immortality, but at that point nothing would have surprised me.

"Such a shame," Cornelius said. "There are too few good philosophy professors at Aberdeen. Gerald was our best, but Russell Gibbs may one day approach greatness . . . He teaches the Aristotle course— what was that called? Either his rhetoric or logic class, I can't remember . . ."

He continued sorting his papers. "Have you finished for the afternoon?" he said, not looking at me.

"I just got here," I said.

Cornelius sighed and closed his eyes. "Then go home," he said. "There's very little for you to do today."

I could tell by his tone that he was tired, and by tired he often meant bored, and so I left, feeling embarrassed but unsure why.

I exited the library into a gorgeous day, crisp and bright, clear sun painting the patchy snow. The storm had stripped the trees in the Quad naked, their dead leaves scattered and bunched up around their trunks in sloping piles that I kicked through, on my way to Campus Bean.

Rationally, I had difficulty accepting any of what Art and Cornelius had shown me. But if I went deeper, past my everyday mind, my skepticism began to wane. After all, I figured, past notions of how the universe operated were once held as scripture, only to be blown away like straw in a storm with every new discovery. And paradigmatic shifts weren't even needed—I knew change occurred incrementally.

Accept gravity and you accept universal law. Accept universal law and you accept earth's place in the universe as being part of a system. Accept *that,* and you then seek to know how the system works, and your view goes skyward, past what you can see and toward what you can only hypothesize. This is where hermeticism and science converge, the epigram of mystics and occultists *ut supra, infra.* As above, below.

But I didn't believe in a universe of infinite possibilities. I knew there were rules that reality adhered to. As knowledge expands so do limits, always ahead, so that new phenomena are kept just behind its constraints. Alchemy seemed a reversal of this—here was a quantum leap in the truest sense, past the barrier of reality as I knew it and toward darker regions, places without rules. I knew what Art would say: *It's foolish to think you're capable of seeing the pattern for what it is. In its enormity it becomes impossible for the average mind to comprehend . . .*

Campus Bean was busy, and after a quick scan to see if I knew anyone there, I spotted Dr. Cade at the front of the coffee line, speaking with a young kid behind the counter. I hesitated a moment, torn between leaving immediately or walking up to him. But he made the decision for me—he saw and summoned.

We sat together at a table in a darkened corner, a cup of hot chocolate in front of me and a coffee for him.

"I have been impressed with your work," he said, brushing unseen crumbs off the lapel of his suit jacket. "So much, in fact, that I'm concerned you may be neglecting your studies in favor of my project."

"I'm pulling all A's," I said. This was true, although I wasn't sure how my grades would fare after my latest round of papers.

Dr. Cade nodded. "I've spoken recently with Dr. Lang," he said. "How are things going with him?"

"Fine," I said.

"And the time commitment isn't too strenuous?"

"It gets a bit tight," I said, fidgeting in my seat. "But once I'm finished with Professor Henson's econ course, I think—"

"Would you like me to speak with Professor Henson, perhaps? Ask him to lighten the load, in lieu of your other responsibilities?"

I stared at Dr. Cade.

"That's okay," I said.

"Very well." Dr. Cade stirred his coffee. "You should know that Professor Lang informed me you're in the running for the Chester Ellis Award."

The Chester Ellis Award was a two-thousand-dollar grant given to freshmen with a perfect GPA. Later that day I tried to write a postcard to Nana to tell her about the award, but after the first few lines I stopped and tossed the postcard in the garbage.

"Winning would be an impressive accomplishment," Dr. Cade said. He looked pleased, and my stomach leapt. "But if it's the money you're most concerned with, I have been known, on occasion, to provide grants for students with special financial needs. Your pursuit of a perfect GPA should not interfere with your work on our project, agreed?"

I nodded.

"And if you do find my work interfering with your classes, please let me know and I will make sure you're given special arrangements. My colleagues, for the most part, understand how important this project is, and I can't imagine them interfering with our schedule, seeing how quickly the deadline approaches. The administration appreciates the importance of the Pendleton Prize, not just to me, but to Aberdeen as a whole."

He faded off, looking away for a moment, and then returned.

"Have you thought about what you are doing for winter break?"

"I was going to stay at the house, I guess."

Dr. Cade *hmm*ed and sipped his coffee. "I should have told you this earlier." He set down his cup with a delicate *clink*. "I'm going to Cuba for four weeks and a friend of mine—an associate professor from Oxford—is staying in Fairwich for three weeks during vacation. I offered him the use of my house." He put the next sentence as delicately as he could. "*Sole* use of my house. I thought I told you when you first arrived. My apologies—I merely assumed you would be going away, like everyone else." He shook his head and slowly steepled his hands. "This is terribly awkward," he said.

"Don't worry about it," I said. I tried to suppress the blush that crept up my face. My options were limited—I had saved enough money, maybe, to stay in a hotel for a few weeks. There was international student housing that remained open during the winter, but I didn't know what Aberdeen did, if anything, for domestic students who had no place to go.

"You have no family you can stay with?"

I shook my head. "I have some friends in Chicago. A couple of my old high school friends go to Northwestern." An absolutely random lie. I knew no one in Chicago, or anywhere else besides Stulton and Aberdeen.

"And you don't foresee it being a problem? Staying with them for an entire month on such short notice?" He sipped from the white cup. When I didn't answer right away he continued. "It's simply unfair of me to expect you to make these last-minute plans. Don't worry—I'll explain everything to Thomas. If you—"

"Please don't," I said. It was the first time I had ever interrupted Dr. Cade, but my discomfort was becoming unbearable. "I'll be fine. Wherever I stay."

He paused and stared at me. "You're certain?"

"Without a doubt."

Dr. Cade nodded, as if the matter wasn't closed, as if I could change my mind if necessary, but there was a look of relief on his face, however subtle.

Art came into my room later that evening, well past midnight, a dark form sitting on the edge of my bed while the radiators clinked and moonlight spilled in under my drawn window shade. His late-night visits no longer startled me, as I'd been awakened by him in the same manner several times since moving in. Sometimes he'd have a medical question (*What are the symptoms of appendicitis? How do I know if I have an aneurysm or just a migraine?*) but mostly he just wanted to talk—he was a fellow insomniac, and suffered from it far worse than I—and I'd lie back and listen to him ramble about the most obscure of topics. Chemical warfare in ancient Greece. The Parnassian movement of late-19th-century France. The works of Chretien de Troyes. He was capable of speaking for hours, in hushed, excited tones that often invaded my dreams and I'd be sleeping even as he kept on, only I'd be dreaming of Lysander's assault upon Haliartus, or of the quest for the Holy Grail, riding horseback through some mountainous forest, my armor clanging under shafts of brilliant sun.

I sat up and asked him what he wanted.

"I need your help bringing Dan in. He's in the back, in the garden."

"Why do you need my help?"

"Because he's passed out."

I clicked on my light and Art threw his hand in front of his eyes. He looked awful. His skin was pale and sweat-slicked.

"Have you been drinking or something?" I asked him.

Art stood, unsteadily, and smoothed his shirt. "Or something. Are you going to help me or not?"

We carried Dan inside, from his spot on the stone bench in the garden off the study. Art had to stop at one point and throw up, concealing it in the shadows of the emptied fountain. He was sweating profusely, and looked as though he might faint at any moment, but he trudged on, helping me bring Dan upstairs and into his bedroom, where we lay him on his bed and left him there, mouth open, body slack as a corpse.

"Please don't say anything to Dr. Cade about this," Art said afterward. He slugged a glass of water and rinsed his face in the kitchen sink. "We were so amateur about the whole thing. We found some fly agaric mushrooms in the woods, little red caps speckled with white, just like in the fairy tales. Jabir ibn-Hayyan believed the secret ingredient in Paracelsus's Philosopher's Stone formula lay in the Vedic *soma*, and it's my understanding that this *soma* has since been discovered to be fly agaric. So of course we tried it, and of course we got nothing more than hallucinations, and dizziness, and severe nausea, and Dan took too much and you saw what happened to *him.*"

Art filled the glass with more water and gulped it down.

"But let's forget about Jabir's obvious mistranslation of the source material," he said. "Which I can't blame him for. Maybe the Vedic *soma* isn't fly agaric, but some other, as-yet-undiscovered plant, mineral, whatever. And maybe if Jabir had enough time, he would have discovered this. What I'm most interested in, however, is this important question, first posed by Edward Schultes in reference to the hallucinogenic drink *yaga:* how did all those primitive societies, with practically no knowledge of modern chemistry, ever figure out how to activate an alkaloid by using a monoamine oxidase inhibitor?"

I sat and stared.

Art set down his glass. "I'm going to bed."

I decided to remain in the kitchen, seated at the breakfast nook. I knew there would be no more sleep for me that night.

On a blustery Friday night (fire crackling, Nilus sleeping in a curled-up ball near the couch), Dan and I sat in the living room, playing backgammon, while Howie was in the study, talking on the phone to his father, his loud, braying voice easily penetrating the closed French doors. Dan was a timid backgammon player, always running, never leaving blots back if he could help it, disregarding pip counts and simply moving his pieces toward home as fast as possible. He also had terrible luck—rarely getting the numbers he needed, falling behind because of ill-timed doubles or a low roll, getting hit in even the most improbable circumstances.

We were drinking club soda—I noticed when Dan and I were alone we spurned alcohol; only in the presence of Art or Howie did we succumb to their subtle, but overwhelming peer pressure—and eating stew Art had made, something with turnips and carrots and bok choy. Howie's conversation echoed through the house, pieces of it spewing forth like snippets from some after-school special on dysfunctional families:

"I know *that,* if you'd just listen for a—"

"But what difference—"

"All right, then, why don't you just direct my life and—"

"Uh-huh. No, I didn't say that."

"Aw, *fuck you too.*"

Silence. Dan and I waited for Howie to burst through the doors, cursing and ranting. He had these arguments with his dad often, and they were usually followed by a thirty-minute discourse on how lucky I was to be an orphan, and how fortunate Art was that his parents took such a laissez-faire approach, and how Dan's mom was a model of how parents should be—sympathetic, unobtrusive, and financially supportive with no conditions attached. Howie's arguments, as I soon discovered, were always about money. His dad had been pushing him to buy a home somewhere in Fairwich, something Howie could live in until graduation and then sell at a profit, or, if he wished, keep as a rental once he left Connecticut and moved back to Chicago. As far as parental requests go, it was a fairly innocuous one—I wish I had the resources to buy my own mini-estate, maybe a pillared, three-story mansion, and a garden with temples and statues like the Greek Revivals of the early 20th century. But Howie refused, telling his dad he didn't want to manage a house by himself, that he was happy living with his friends, and that administration had "messed things up" and now he didn't know when he'd be graduating. Dan said Howie had been playing that cat-and-mouse game with his dad for years, putting off having to confess he was no longer in school.

Naturally, Howie would begin each ill-fated conversation with his dad with a bottle of Famous Grouse close at hand. By the end, a third of the scotch would be gone, and Howie would be disgustingly drunk. From what Dan told me—he'd met Mr. Beauford Spacks last spring, and watched him consume *eight* double martinis in an afternoon—they were probably both drunk every time they talked, which partially explained the inevitable collapse of any decorum, and the inevitable escalation into screaming and swearing.

"That's the last goddamn time," Howie said, stalking into the living room. "Next time he calls tell him I'm not home."

Dan glanced at me and threw his dice. They tumbled onto the board with a muffled clatter. He needed any combo of seven. Five-to-one odds. He rolled a three-two. Of course.

"Fuck it," Howie said, not talking to anyone in particular. "If he calls back tell him I moved out and went to St. Croix. Tell him I'm living on the beach, with nothing but a hammock and a tan. Skipping stones and drinking cocktails and eating coconuts off the trees."

He paced back and forth, running both hands through his hair.

There was a dark splotch of sweat across the back of his blue button-down. He stopped and turned to me.

"Do they have coconuts in St. Croix?"

I looked at Dan. We both smiled quickly. "I don't know," I said.

Howie waved me away impatiently. "He wants to know when I'm graduating," he said, with a shaking calmness that belied his panic more than hysteria would. "Said he's been thinking about *retiring*. Retiring," he said it slowly, as if trying to make sure he understood himself. "Can you fucking believe *that*? At his age? He's in his mid-fifties and healthy as a draft horse."

He fell into a chair and propped his feet up on the ottoman. "The jig is up. He'll want me to take over the business, fresh out of school with my *degree* . . ." He faded off. "Say," he stamped his feet on the floor and leaned forward. "Do you guys know anything about Fairwich Community College?"

"Oh, no. The situation can't be that desperate," said Dan.

"I'm afraid it is."

"An *associate's* degree? How will you explain—"

"I'll tell him it was the most time-efficient way. Do you think he cares? As long as I have a goddamn piece of paper with my name printed across in black calligraphy. The old man didn't go to college." He lowered his voice in what I presumed was an imitation of his father: *"I want my son to understand the value of education. I want him to have all the opportunities I didn't."*

"Meanwhile, he's making tons of money," I said. "Pretty ironic, isn't it?"

Howie stopped and stared at me. "Why would you say that?"

There was an awkward pause. Dan rolled his dice and fixed his attention on the board.

"I just mean that he's obviously doing fine, without the degree and all."

Howie still looked stunned, as if I'd slapped him across the face. *"Tons* of money? It's not like we're the fucking Rockefellers." He sank back into the chair, still staring at me. Sweat was collecting at his hairline.

"Poor bastard like you," he said, with a wicked smile and low voice, "never seen money, wouldn't know the difference between a hard-working businessman and the Sultan of fucking Brunei."

Dan stopped in mid-move, holding a blot between his thumb and forefinger. Howie's gaze was unwavering, focusing on me with a drunken glare. A log in the fire popped.

"Poor bastard," he said again, this time to himself, with a bitter snort that shook his body. He blinked slowly, stood up, steadied himself, and walked out, thumping up the stairs. Moments later I heard his door slam shut.

Dan and I didn't say anything for a few minutes, playing our game in silence. It had come to a race, naturally, and Dan was behind. I tried to focus but couldn't, my face sweating from the flush of embarrassment.

"He's just drunk," Dan said, picking up his dice. "You know how crazy he gets when his father calls . . ."

"Don't worry about it," I said. "I'm fine."

"Really, Eric . . . Howie's quite fond of you."

His attempts at comfort were more humiliating than Howie's insults. I kept quiet and played the game to its finish, beating Dan easily with a double-four roll.

◆ ◆ ◆

November passed quickly, snow fell often, and winter invaded in the hypnotic way it usually does. I discovered a motel on the edge of town that would let me stay the entire four weeks of vacation for a small fee, in a room located in the basement, but the television didn't really work, there was no phone, the heat was spotty, and the water pressure varied from trickle to drip. The room was kept available for transients, a kind gesture on the part of the owner, Henry Hobbes, himself a former "bum," as he claimed, who had worked his way up and now felt it was his karmic duty to return some of the good fortune he enjoyed. But the room was seldom used, since transients were rare in Fairwich, even on the outskirts of town, especially once the cold weather came. Nights were brutal, arctic air driving all but the hardiest of New Englanders indoors. My plan to stay in that motel room was, looking back, a foolish one, since I had more money than I knew what to do with (from my student loans and Dr. Lang's paychecks), and I could have easily afforded a decent room in one of Fairwich's nicer hotels. But I had been poor for so long, and thus my appreciation for the utility of money was severely underdeveloped. Cheap meant better, as far as I knew.

I spent the last week before vacation wandering around town, going to the movies with Dan at the single-theater movie house, and afterward the two of us would have dinner at Edna's, the only two college students in a room of paper-mill workers. Dan and I had become fast friends ever since I'd told him that Art spilled the beans about their alchemy experiments and the cats (which Dan insisted he took no part in).

Dan told me he was relieved, that he'd hated lying to me but he knew how serious and secretive Art was about the project, and Dan also said that he was going along with it more out of intellectual curiosity than anything else.

"So you don't think there's a formula?" I'd asked him.

"I didn't say that," he said. "Art believes in it, and I believe in Art, so there you go."

"But you put your life in danger," I said. "I helped Art carry you in that one night . . . the night you took those mushrooms and passed out in the garden."

"We made a mistake," Dan said. "It won't happen again."

I had a holiday dinner with Professor Cade, Howie, Art, and Dan, a Cornish hen for each of us with wild-mushroom stuffing, and a pumpkin pie that I brought home from Edna's. *This is my new family,* I decided. *This is my new past.*

My housemates all had things to do over winter break. Art was leaving for London to stay with friends before meeting up with Ellen for a one-week stay in Prague. Dan was going home to Boston, and Howie was off to New Orleans, staying with one of his many cousins in some "amazing loft" above Basin Street's biggest jazz club. I evaded, as best I could, their questions about what I was doing for the month. Dan and Howie both offered to take me along (*I can promise you this much*, Howie had said, slapping me on the back, *you will get laid every day of vacation if you go with me*), and Dan said I could stay in the guest bedroom of his mom's house. One night I got so drunk I nearly accepted Dan's offer, enticed by his description of civilized Boston with its mythical Brahmins lining every street corner.

"We'll go to the Harvard library," I said, spilling some of my drink in excitement. Gin and tonic soaked into my shirt cuff. "Shoot spitballs at the grad students and moon the faculty."

"Only Harvard students are allowed access," Art said. He was ironing his shirt over a towel laid across the dining room table. He had a date with Ellen; some Russian dance troupe was performing at the Mortensen Theater. Later that night she came to pick him up and she literally took my breath away: She wore a small, black dress, legs scissoring under wispy fabric, black folds rustling around her thighs.

"We could get in the library," Dan said. "My dad willed half his collection to their rare-books room."

"Or just have Dr. Cade call," Art held up his shirt for inspection. "It worked for me."

Howie left first, on a Friday night, throwing two suitcases into the trunk of his Jag and a bottle of white zinfandel on the front seat. He wore a T-shirt and shorts and sandals, and said he was driving nonstop, thirty hours straight through.

"You'll have a fucking blast, I'm telling you," he said, ducking under his car's hood. He checked the oil while I held the flashlight for him. The temperature was well below freezing, too cold for snowfall, but Howie seemed immune to it, standing in his summer wear. He wiped the dipstick clean. "It's hedonistic paradise down there. Have you ever been to New Orleans?"

He had asked me this before. I shook my head and tried to hold the flashlight steady. I was shivering. *Why not go?* The impulse was seductive, and as with most impulses, the seduction was the best part. I didn't want to spend the month alone with Howie. I knew if I spent it with him, I'd be drinking every day. I was sick of alcohol and a little sick of Dr. Cade's house, and all I wanted was a month to myself, with my books and maybe a few nights with Nicole before she left.

Howie and I said our goodbyes and I watched the sleepy red tail-lights of his Jag disappear down the driveway.

Dan left the next morning. When I made it downstairs there was a note from him to all of us, a piece of paper with his mom's phone number. I took Nilus for a walk—it was a bright, wintry day, sunlight glaring off the snow-covered surface of the pond—and when I returned Dr. Cade had just arrived home, carrying a set of new luggage.

"When do you leave for Chicago?" he said, as I helped him with the suitcases.

I was shocked he'd asked me that. I'd forgotten the lie I'd told him that day at Campus Bean. I was also shocked he hadn't heard the truth from anyone else in the house.

"I leave Monday," I said. *Confess now,* I thought. *He knows. Of course he knows.*

There was a moment of silence, perhaps left by Dr. Cade for me to use for confession, but I remained quiet. He took off his hat and smoothed his silvery hair back.

"Excellent timing. My flight departs tomorrow morning, and Thomas won't be arriving until Monday. I'm not certain when Arthur is leaving for London."

I realized he didn't know the truth. No one, it seemed, told Dr. Cade anything.

Dr. Cade left the next day. He wished me a "safe and wonderful New Year," and presented me with a Christmas gift, a beautiful deep blue cashmere scarf. Then he got into his taxi and drove away. Nilus remained at my side, tongue lolling and tail wagging, but his presence made me even lonelier, and I lost all ambition to go on the long hike I'd planned earlier in the day. Instead I went to my room and read at my desk while Nilus slept by my bed, the windblown crests of snow on Dr. Cade's lawn darkening from twilight to deep-sea blue, and then finally fading to black under a moonless sky. The radiators started to heat up, metal expanding in staccato ticks and baritone clanks.

Art, as far as I knew, was already in London. I had peeked into his room, earlier, and saw his bed made and all his papers gone. He'd left a travel checklist on his drafting table, words with boxes near them and checkmarks in each box *(Passport, Phone numbers, Traveler's checks, Pocket money)*. Another piece of paper lay nearby, with something typewritten in splotchy, uneven ink, as if the typewriter were very old:

> *. . . L'eternité.*
> *C'est la mer mêlée*
> *Au soleil.*

Eternity. It is the sea mingled with the sun.

Most likely one of Art's poems, I thought, and not a bad one at that, and then I left his room.

I called Nicole, but got her answering machine. She was probably walking around SoHo with her aunt, I figured, eating at trendy little cafés, flirting with the waiters.

I went to the attic and stood in front of the door. Behind it I imagined all those cages of cats, and ancient books spread over tables, and maybe even the heads of Bluebeard's wives, all lined up on fondue skewers, waiting with open mouths and staring eyes to greet me. I pressed my ear to the door, listened for a few moments, then opened it and stepped inside.

It wasn't at all what I'd expected. No long desks covered in flasks and beakers, no mortars containing brightly colored, pungent-smelling powders. No hanging bunches of drying herbs or pots of bubbling liquid, or blood-spattered walls and crates of feline body parts. It was a typical attic, a bit larger than most, if anything—and colder than the rest of the house, with a floor gray and fuzzy with age, an arched ceiling with cobwebs swaying between the exposed beams, a loose stack of aborted oil paintings (landscapes, still lifes, indiscernible portraits), rolled Oriental carpets stacked against the far wall like giant cloth logs, old furniture missing legs or drawers, and an armoire wide open with a bunch of clothes hanging inside. I searched through the clothes and found one jacket that fit—an old Harris tweed, herringbone print, with what looked like genuine gold buttons.

I rifled through old dressers and peered into the dark corners where mouse droppings were scattered around in dusty blots, and eventually I gave up and walked back downstairs. The house stood silent with me in its belly. The solitude I had once craved was now a slow fire in which I burned.

My friends were all gone. There was nothing for me there, so I left.

Chapter 9

When I arrived at the Paradise Motel, Henry Hobbes gave me a grand tour of my small room, which would have been comical were it not for the good-natured smile he kept up the entire time, as if he were setting an example for me of a man who, through sheer determination, had worked his way from financial disaster into private business ownership. He was short and fat, and his round, balding head made him look like a medieval friar. His clothes were outdated, like he'd owned them for years despite several changes in waist size.

"It's quiet, that's another good thing about down here," he said. "A person can get a whole lot done. Thoreau liked to keep to himself, you know, felt that it helped him to organize his thoughts." Henry pointed to the far wall opposite the bed. "Anyway, the boiler is on the other side, along with hot-water tanks. So if you hear any clunks or thunks, don't worry about it. It's just the sound of everything running smoothly." He winked.

My room was small, with a brown and yellow tiled floor, a single bed, and a beat-up chest of drawers leaning to one side because of a short leg. The bathroom had a toilet, a corroded, gray-paint-flecked industrial wash basin with two faucets, and an old-fashioned single-person shower with one of those circular curtains. Everything looked clean, but beneath the smell of pine products lingered the odor of mildew. There was little light—no windows, a lonely brown lamp atop the chest of drawers, and a lightbulb above, hanging like a gallows rope, casting chaotic shadows over the dull gray walls.

"There's no heating system proper, but because you're so close to the tanks and the boiler, heat should seep in through the walls and warm you just fine." Henry ceremoniously handed me two keys. "Big one is for the basement, little one is for your room. Just make sure you lock the basement door after you leave. I got a lot of cleaning equipment down here, and it has a tendency to walk." He lowered his voice as if the thieves could be listening. "I'm just as trusting as the next guy," he said, giving me a conspiratorial wink, "but I also know human nature. You know those Mexicans who work for me?"

I didn't, but I nodded.

"They'd just as soon rob me blind than earn an honest wage."

He straightened up. "*Any*way," he said, back to his old positive self, "you can use the front-desk phone anytime you want. I'm either up there or my son Luke is. Just make sure you keep incoming calls to a minimum, and honestly, I'd prefer it if you didn't take any incoming calls, period. It ties up the line."

I thanked him and put my bag on the bed. Henry smiled, a big, curvy grin arching up his round face. "Keep positive, son," he said, patting me on the back. "You can't let a woman get you down. Especially not at your age. You're a good-looking kid; there's plenty more fish in that sea."

I had lied to him earlier, telling him that I broke up with my girlfriend and she kicked me out of the apartment. I don't know why I lied—there wasn't any reason, and I started to feel guilty, which prompted me to get under the clammy sheets and figure out how I was going to keep myself from becoming insane.

There's nothing quite like being constantly cold. I woke up every morning stiff and sore, achy as if from the flu, my head pounding like it could split and burst at seams that ran along my temples and over the crown of my skull. Henry was wrong—the boiler's heat stopped at the wall rather than continuing through, so I was left with a warm spot over a patch of peeling paint, and little else. Every morning I swaddled myself in blankets, made tea on a hot plate, and sat back against the warm spot on the wall, drinking my tea until I summoned the courage to get undressed and shower. I began to dread mornings so much that I became anxious the night before, but by the afternoon I was free, either sitting in Edna's Coffee Shop or the Fairwich Public Library, leafing through plastic-covered magazines. I usually stayed in the library until close, and by that time I'd covered dozens of hobbies and recreational pursuits—car repair, home gardening, book binding, photography, watchmaking, cooking, antiquing, and the entire women's magazine collection, spanning topics from bridal gowns to the special needs of winter hair and skin care.

One night, while sitting against the wall and reading some trashy novel I'd checked out of the library, I discovered what I thought was the reason for my room's arctic chill. An icy draft sliced at my fore-head and I found a hole in the ceiling corner, water stains blooming out from its rotted edges. It went straight through to the outdoors at ground level, and I could even see the tip of an ice-crystallized leaf, sticking out of the thin layer of snow like some fossil from a time when it had been warm.

I told Luke, who was sitting behind the front desk, a newspaper in his lap and a half-eaten powdered doughnut in one hand. He looked at me, white sugar in the corners of his mouth, and said he'd inform his dad and that was all he could do. When I asked for some duct tape to at least patch up the hole, Luke said he didn't know where any was, and then he stuffed the remainder of the doughnut into his mouth, picked up his newspaper, and noisily spread it open, covering his face and shutting me out.

I bought duct tape myself but it didn't help much. While no more snow congregated in the corner of the tiled floor beneath the hole, as the nights lengthened and winter settled in, my living conditions bordered on deadly. I slept in fits and shiver-wracked spurts.

One evening I opened my Aberdeen daily planner and was dismayed to see that only two and a half weeks had passed. *Almost fourteen days left,* I told myself. I fantasized about going back to Dr. Cade's home, and living like a mouse, scurrying from my room in the middle of the night, stealing food from the refrigerator, waiting until Thomas left and then sitting in the living room in front of the fireplace, catching a quick nap while heat from the fire softly washed over me.

Sunday night I ate soup and watched the local news. At night the reception was better than during the day, and the picture was clear enough that I was able to masturbate to Cynthia Andrews, Channel 7's six o'clock anchorwoman. She was attractive in that nondescript anchorwoman kind of way, and every Sunday I'd fall asleep to the images of my fantasy, unaware of my own violent shivering, my knees pulled up to my chest and the incoherent mumble of the television in the background.

Monday morning someone knocked on my door. I pulled the pillow over my head, but there was another knock, this one louder than the first. I thought it was Luke or Henry, finally coming to fix the hole. I slipped out of my cocoon of blankets, already dressed, and answered the door.

At first I thought I was dreaming. Art stood in the doorway, dressed impeccably in a fitted black turtleneck sweater, tan corduroys, and a burgundy pea coat. His hair was cut short and he had new glasses. He smelled faintly of cologne and fresh snow, the icy scent of the outdoors still clinging to him.

He took off his glasses. "Me first," he said, holding up his gloved hand. He looked over my shoulder. "What the hell are you doing *here?*" He looked over my shoulder again and stared at me, incredulous.

"It's not as bad as it looks," I said. Art brushed past and strode into my room. He stood in the center of it, hands on his hips, and swept his gaze from wall to wall. He filled the space, his head only a few inches below the ceiling.

"It's worse," Art said, putting his glasses back on. "Mildew." He wrinkled his nose. "And it's *freezing*. How long have you been living like this?"

"Two weeks."

"And you were going to stay the entire vacation?"

I nodded.

"Why?"

I shrugged. "I didn't have anywhere else to go. Dr. Cade's friend is staying at the house," I said. "And Paderborne closes for winter vacation."

Art laughed. "Why on earth didn't you go stay with Dan? Or with Howie?"

"I didn't feel like it," I said. I couldn't think of a more honest answer.

Art sat on my bed. He had new shoes—ankle-high black leather boots, shiny like wet seal skin. "This is really amazing," he said. "You're like St. Daniel. Rejecting all earthly comforts."

Art glanced up at the hanging light bulb. "Nice touch. Very film noir."

"I thought you were in London," I said.

He leaned back against the wall and swung his legs onto the bed. "I *was* in London. Great time, as always. My friend—George Pinkus, did I mention him before? We rowed together freshman year. He transferred to Cambridge. Sharp fellow. Anyway, he got appendicitis two days ago. He's laid up in the hospital and I'm biding my time in coffeehouses, and you know, there's only so much dark roast one man can drink. Can you imagine I was stuck in London with nothing to do?"

"I could think of worse places," I said.

"I bet you could."

"What about Ellen?"

"What about her?"

"Weren't you going to meet her in Prague?"

"Oh, yeah." His expression soured. "She came to London. Showed up at my friend's flat completely unannounced. She said the train ride to Prague would be romantic, just the two of us." He looked at his thumbnail and started to pick at it. "Never mind the fact that I was looking forward to some quality time with George. I haven't seen him in over three years. Instead he gets appendicitis and Ellen thinks we should leave early for Prague. You know what I think," he looked up at me. "I think she didn't trust me. I think she figured I was fooling around."

"How insulting," I said, not really meaning it.

"It is, isn't it?" He nodded and sat up. His boots trailed dirt onto the bed. "What way is that to approach a relationship? It's difficult, you know. Trying to maintain this mature, adult relationship while she acts as if I'm her child. As if I need to be watched. It's not like I'm constantly looking over *her* shoulder." He brushed something off the tip of his boot. Art could be amusingly fastidious at times.

"So you came home," I said.

"She pissed me off, if you want to know the truth. Nothing good could've come from it. I was mad at her, she got mad because I was mad, we had this Prague trip hanging over our heads . . . so I decided to come back. Ellen ran off to her cousin's apartment in Paris. She's probably shopping right now, as we speak. Stuffing her face with chocolates."

Art picked up a pillow and smelled it. "More mildew. There's probably mold down here, too. Stuff can get in your lungs. Oomycota. Nasty critters." He tossed it aside.

"Anyway," he continued, "I got back into town last night and asked Thomas if he'd heard from you, which he hadn't. He didn't know what I was talking about, actually sounded concerned, as if you were missing. I told him I must have been confused, that I'm sure you're fine, and all that. And then I went into town and grabbed a bite at Edna's, and I know that's your favorite haunt so I asked the waitress if she'd seen you. She knew who you were, and as it turns out, her sister is married to the owner of this shithole."

"Henry Hobbes," I said, feeling a little like Watson, watching his good friend deduce a particularly complex problem.

"Have you lost weight? You look sick," Art said. "Your skin is the color of nonfat milk. How do you feel?"

I pushed the lightbulb and watched it swing on its thin cord. "Cold," I said.

Art winced and rubbed his neck. He stared at the lightbulb, squinting. "Does that look really bright to you? What's the wattage?"

I spun it around on its cord. "Forty-five."

He put his hand around his throat, up under his chin, and prodded with his thumb and forefinger. "You know anything about swollen glands?" When I answered *no* he sat up, on the edge of the bed, and started to roll his head from side to side.

"Meningitis," he said gravely. "The patient sharing George's room was recovering from it. The nurse assured me he was long past the infectious stage, but you know how those things linger in hospitals."

"You don't think you have it, do you?"

He stopped and stared at me. "I can't be certain. My neck does hurt, and I think I may have swollen salivary glands . . . and this light seems awfully glaring. You know that's one of the symptoms—hypersensitivity to light."

"Like rabies," I said. I don't know why I said that.

He frowned. "I suppose." He looked around—at my books piled atop the chest of drawers, at the small TV with tinfoil antenna sticking out like a poorly designed prop for some science fiction movie.

"Come to Prague," he said, as casually as if he were asking me to join him for coffee at Campus Bean.

"*What?*"

"I'll pay for your ticket. You have a passport?"

"Actually, I do," I said. "Before my mom died . . . we were planning a trip to England."

I stared at him in the dim light. Slender jawline, dirty-blond hair cropped close, small, rectangular glasses. The confident half smile. It was then I realized that no one matched Art's persuasiveness. It crossed age and gender lines. The seduction was complete.

Chapter 10

We left the next morning. I hadn't flown since my mom's death, when I'd taken a jet from West Falls to Stulton with a social worker by my side, who talked to me the entire time, assuring me how safe flying was, while I remained completely oblivious and drew dragons with a box of crayons the stewardess had given me. I didn't know what to expect this time, and Art tried nobly to distract me with his talk of Prague. Not thirty minutes into the trip, however, after some turbulence that prompted a flashing seat-belt sign, I had to sprint for the bathroom and throw up in the small metallic toilet, electric-blue water glowing like nuclear waste, fluorescent light buzzing overhead. Down went my raisin bagel and orange juice, and I stood up and splashed water on my face, looking into the mirror at my zombielike appearance—dark circles, pale skin, white lips.

I walked back to my seat, light-headed and sweating. Art had a small plastic cup of ginger ale waiting for me on the pullout tray, while he sat with his head propped against a pillow, reading a book. The plane lurched again, engines whining.

The pilot announced we were flying above a small storm system, and that we should expect "a few bumps, nothing to worry about." All I could imagine was something out of a disaster film: cabin lights flashing, oxygen masks dangling, flight attendants crashing into their meal carts.

"How are you feeling?" Art asked me.

"Like hell," I said.

Art closed the book with his finger inserted to mark his place. He had one of the books Cornelius had given me for him, the ones I'd kept hostage on my desk. Abram Oslo's *Index Expurgatorius*.

"Remember what I told you about Gurdjieff?"

The endless toil. The cunning man.

"I think I have food poisoning," I said.

"Food poisoning? You're airsick," Art said. He reached down into his bag and handed me a small book. *Labor et Paracelsus*.

"Try distracting yourself in work. Read this," he said. "Paracelsus was a 16th-century physician. Claimed to have a substance called azoth, a reddish powder that assisted him in miraculous cures. He supposedly carried a quantity of it in his sword pommel."

The plane pitched and dropped suddenly.

"There's some charlatanism in there." Art seemed completely unaffected by the turbulence. "But his success as a physician was remarkable. He cured the Margrave of Baden's dysentery by grinding semiprecious stones and adding a dash of this azoth, and then preparing it into a potion."

I tried reading the first few pages but I couldn't concentrate. There was another series of bumps as if we were riding full speed over a potholed road, and then I closed the book and sank into my seat.

"I can't do this," I said. "I'm sorry." Lightning flashed and I dropped the book onto the floor.

Art sighed. "You want some Valium?"

At that point I would have taken a horse tranquilizer. "Whatever," I said. "As long as it works."

"Oh, it'll work. Have you ever had Valium before?" Art whispered, reaching into his pocket. I shook my head. "Take only half," he said, dropping a small chartreuse tablet into my palm. I bit it in half, found it too crumbly for a clean break, then licked the bitter remainder off my lips and downed the entire pill with a swig of lukewarm ginger ale.

Forty minutes later I was on my own personal flight, skimming just over the clouds and relaxing under the soothing gaze of a cheerful sun.

• • •

My first lesson in Europe: In spite of fascism's demise, the trains, as Mussolini had promised, run on time.

Our flight landed in Paris, and from there we were going by train to Prague. We had a few hours, and so Art took me to Michel's, a small café along the Seine, owned by an American expatriate whom Art had met his first time in Paris five years earlier. I was overwhelmed by everything: the swooning aftereffects of the Valium, the speed with which Parisians talked, the icy glaze of the Seine and the colors of the buildings, slate and concrete, French Romanesque stone vaulted buildings with alabaster domes, and intricate Rayonnant Gothic churches, sunlight splashing onto their traceried glass and dripping down the tips of their delicate spires. Everyone was thin and everyone was smoking, and Art moved through the city streets like he had lived there his whole life while I was distracted at every corner by the narrow sidewalks and billboards and the small cars with their tinny horns and the singsong banter of spoken French from the mouths of modern-day Gauls and Franks.

Along the way he bought a bottle of wine and a pouch of Turkish tobacco. I was going to get a postcard to send to Nicole, but I forgot, and as we sat at a small wrought-iron table at Café Michel, Art guzzling his espresso and talking with Michael, the owner, I closed my eyes and just listened while the sunlight streamed in through the window and warmed my face.

There were two women seated across from us; both looked in their twenties. One was dressed in a fitted black suit with a short skirt and black boots reaching to her calves. The other wore a turtleneck sweater, red as blood to match her lips, and tight jeans, her bobbed black hair curving into her jawline. Michael smiled at them, and the one in the suit returned his smile with her eyes, her mouth hidden behind an espresso cup.

Art was looking at a pocket map. "The train to Prague should take us about twelve hours, barring any problems. We will be crossing the border into Germany at"—he traced a line with his finger—"Saarbrücken. Then we head east to Frankfurt—if we have time we'll head into the city for a couple of steins—and then onto Nürnberg, cross the border into the Czech Republic at the city of Cheb, and then Prague."

"You should've flown," Michael said. He tapped a cigarette on the back of his hand. His accent was still American, with flat *a*'s like a Midwesterner. "Paris to Prague. Easy trip by puddlejumper. Seventy dollars from a guy I know." His fingernails were short and ragged and his black hair was slicked close to his skull. He wore a tight black crewneck sweater. He vaguely reminded me of Peter, the molesting yogi.

"Eric's never been here before," Art said, folding the map. "I want him to see the countryside."

"Then he should also explore Paris. I got a killer rate on a hotel in the Left Bank. Ten minute walk from Luxembourg Gardens."

The woman in the red sweater was eyeing me, and she leaned over to her friend and they both laughed. I asked Michael how far the Church of St.-Germain des Prés was. He lit his cigarette, spat out a cloud of smoke, and answered while still looking at the two women.

"C'est à environ vingt minutes à pied, cinq minutes par le taxi."

"Don't be a dick," Art said, staring at Michael. He took out a pack of rolling papers and opened his pouch of tobacco. "Stick with English."

Michael looked at me. "How old did you say you were?"

"Sixteen."

He tapped ash onto the floor. "So is Art like your big brother?"

"Non," I said. *"Mais il est mon meilleur ami."*

Art laughed and nodded in my direction. "How do you like that?"

"Ça ne m'a fait pas bonne impression," Michael said, and he stood up and walked away, leaving his cigarette burning on his plate.

"Well," Art grinned. "If you still want to see St.-Germain des Prés, the train doesn't leave until two-thirty. We have approximately . . ."

He looked at his watch and frowned.

"Shit."

Exactly thirty minutes later we were sprinting through the Gare de l'Est, bags bouncing off our backs, pushing our way past tourists and businessmen and beggars. We turned a corner and saw our train beginning its slow acceleration away from the station. An attendant on the back rail was talking to one of the engineers on the platform.

I bolted, my one heavy bag tugging on my shoulder, and when I looked to see if Art was close, I saw him trip over a child who had darted in front of him. Art twisted and sidestepped like a running back evading a tackler, but his bags shifted and knocked into the child, who fell forward with a loud *thwack* and started to scream. I paused, unsure of what to do. The mother rushed over and knelt before her child, uttering a soothing stream of motherly pleasantries while touching his face as if looking for wounds.

"He's fine, he's fine," Art said, looking back at me. I jogged over and tried to apologize but the mom yelled at Art and clutched her son fiercely, grinding his face into her chest.

"Let's *go*," Art shouted, oblivious to the mom's rage. He continued to run, slowing down only to shout at me again.

I looked at Art, who was sprinting now, bags bouncing on the ends of their straps like marionettes. The mother had seemingly lost interest in us and was completely absorbed in her child, and so I fled.

We made it, the attendant taking our bags from his perch on the back railing while Art and I grabbed on to the metal bar and heaved ourselves up. We remained on the back platform as we left the station.

"I think that little boy was hurt," I said. "He hit the ground pretty hard, you know."

Art merely shrugged, and recited a short passage from one of Caesar's speeches about the rigors of war hardening youth to life's future tribulations.

◆ ◆ ◆

We passed through the town of Épernay, where Art told me Armand de Gontaut was killed in 1592 defending French Catholics from sieging Huguenots, and then we continued along the river Marne, and through the French countryside, past countless villages with small stone homes and vineyards scattered along hillocks, barren vines cascading over sunken fences. Fescue and pale-green sedge covered most of the land, with ridges and pockets of snow dotting the landscape like bales of cotton. The sun cast a dull, gold haze across the Marne, a river of light, twisting and winding in a slow rivulet alongside the rhythmic clank of our train cars, moving closer and then pulling away, as if playing a game of tag.

Art had put down his bed and lay on the bottom bunk while I leaned against the window and stared at the white and green landscape rushing by. We talked about Paris, and Art told me the story of his first arrival there five years earlier, during his junior year of high school. He had, naturally, fallen for a girl, a twenty-year-old medical student from Brussels, studying at the Sorbonne. She was tall and thin, with thick, long brown hair and frosty blue eyes that Art said reminded him of swirling water. Art told me he lied to her and said he was a musician touring through Europe, and then they had sex in the Luxembourg Gardens under an aster-colored moon. One week later he returned home and decided he was going to marry her, and he arranged everything—selling his car, contacting a housing agency in Paris, even inquiring about guitar lessons. He got into several arguments with his parents, who said he was acting too impulsively, but Art said he had never been more certain of anything in his life. One month later the letters slowed, however, and eight weeks after his return home, she stopped writing. Art said she was the kind of girl who, if he saw her again, he'd still ask her to marry him. Tomorrow or twenty years from now.

By dinnertime we had turned north, over the river Meuse and into the city of Verdun, which Art said began as a Roman outpost and then became the commercial center for the Carolingian empire. From Verdun to Metz, and the conductor announced over the cabin speakers that the dining car would be closing in an hour.

The food was delicious—chicken breast with cream sauce, served with fresh bread and a glass of heady Bordeaux. I ate voraciously, and by the time I finished it was dusk, the sun now just a sliver of fiery orange behind a faraway forest edge. I could see my reflection in the train window: wrinkled shirt, baggy pants, unwashed hair. I felt like a slob.

Art smiled contentedly and slumped back, patting his stomach. "This is probably the last good dinner we're going to have for a few days. Unless you like pork—that's all they eat in Prague. Big mounds of the stuff. Sliced, stuffed, braised, boiled . . ." He closed his eyes and breathed deeply. We said nothing for a few minutes.

"You ever read anything about Prague?" he said, his voice startling me. I thought he had fallen asleep.

I shifted in my seat and stared out the dark window. The car bobbed up and down rhythmically, in time with the steady *cla-clank* of the train. "A little," I said. I knew about the Hapsburg family, from a paper I wrote my high school junior year. I remembered photos of the city—dark jumbles of towering spires, the ubiquitous Vltava River slicing the city in half. Something else, a legend I had read in one of my favorite books, the ponderously titled *Unexplained Creatures, Beasts, and Phenomena of the Ancient and Modern World.* I must have read that book in my high school library at least a dozen times, keeping it hidden by putting it back high on the shelf, behind a thick text on geothermal dynamics. It was one of those fantastical tomes they don't seem to make anymore, with a black-and-white cover taken from a medieval woodcutting of a werewolf attacking some farmer. The articles had grainy photos (or, more often than not, gruesome illustrations) of so-called "monsters," and quotes by academics of questionable repute (mostly by a "Dr. H. L. Foster, professor of antiquities from St. Carmichael University"; for the record, to this day I have not located a university by that name). Each section usually ended with an unintentionally campy cliffhanger: *Will science ever penetrate the murky depths of the Loch? Will we one day discover the answers behind the mystery of this elusive sea beast? All we can do is wait, and hope old Nessie does not discover us first . . .*

From that book I knew of the legend of the golem, a hulking clay creature made in the image of man, inscribed in its forehead the secret name of God, and used by its creator for protection from evil. It was supposedly Rabbi Judah Loew, who, in Prague, first gave life to the golem, using clay from the banks of the Vltava. *Perhaps the golem still lies in an unknown tomb beneath the bustling streets of Prague, awaiting the signal from his master to walk amongst the living again . . .*

"This worked out well, actually," Art said, his eyes still closed. "You coming with me instead of Ellen."

We were the last ones remaining in the car. Behind us the waiter wiped down tables.

Art opened his eyes. "I've been looking for a book, for about six months," he said. "I finally found it, in Prague, which was such an obvious place that I didn't think to look there."

He waved the waiter over and asked for a soda water. "Did I ever tell you about Jaroslav Capek?" he asked me, once the waiter had left.

"A little," I said. I remembered seeing his name in one of the books Art had given me to read. "He was some Czech alchemist, right?"

Art reached down into the bag he'd brought to dinner, and pulled out Oslo's *Index Expurgatorius.*

"Page 123, second entry," he said, laying the book on the table. I opened it:

MALEZEL, JOHANN. Title: *Ad Majorem Dei Gloriam. MCCCLIX.*
Quarto, a.e.g. 163 pages with title page. No illustration.
Number of printings unknown. Declared heretical by Bishop
prelate nullius Terás of Lavigerie in 1363 for alchemic references,
diabolism.

"Jaroslav Capek based his work on the writings of Brother Johann Malezel," Art said. "Johann Malezel, also known as the Sacred Healer of St. Czerny, was the abbot of the St. Athanasius monastery in the Wallachian town of Brotöv, circa early 14th century. In 1350 Father Pisano of Milan, on order of the Roman Church, travelled to Brotöv to observe Brother Malezel's so-called miracles. Father Pisano didn't think he'd witnessed any miracles—in fact, what he saw he considered heretical. Johann Malezel could restore vision to the blind and make the crippled walk again, and he allegedly did it all with the aid of a white powder, which he would mix in holy water and give to the sick."

The waiter set Art's soda water down and walked away. Art plucked the lime wedge off the rim and squeezed it into the glass. The dining car was empty except for us, the light above our booth the only one still on.

"For his heresy, Johann Malezel was promptly excommunicated and imprisoned in Braşov, a small town in the foothills of the Transylvanian Alps. His punishment had little effect on his reputation—in fact, his fame grew, and scores of the sick and dying made the pilgrimage to his prison, where they left offerings and took anything they believed Brother Malezel had touched, from the waste-bucket slop to bits of stone chiselled from the prison walls.

"Finally, after years of this, rumors started to spread. The town priest claimed he saw an unearthly light shining from Johann Malezel's prison cell, and there was word that the devil himself visited Johann every night. A mysterious man was seen in the woods, riding the back of a huge goat, wearing a dark cloak painted with mysterious symbols. The statue of Jesus in St. Helvetius's church cried tears of chrism, surely a sign their lord was unhappy about *something*. And then a group of plague-ridden travellers came to Braşov to receive a cure, and the plague spread to the town, and that seemed to be when the villagers decided they'd had enough of Brother Malezel and his miracles.

"The villagers stormed the prison, planning to drag Johann Malezel from his cell and hang him in the town square. Only when they got there, he was gone. They found an empty cell, containing a blanket, a tattered monk's robe, and a book. *Ad Majorem Dei Gloriam*. 'To the Greater Glory of God'. The book describes all of Brother Malezel's alchemical experiments, with detailed instructions for each process, written by Brother Malezel in three languages: pre-Vulgate Latin, Hebrew, and, strangely, enough, Coptic. No one knows how he wrote it, because prisoners were strictly forbidden to possess pen and paper, especially someone of Malezel's reputation. So, naturally, it was decided *Ad Majorem Dei Gloriam* was the work of the devil, and the book was taken into custody by the church, until Jaroslav Capek somehow came into possession of it."

"Where's the book now?"

"St. Thölden Monastery," Art said. "Some old Benedictine order has it in their archives. But we'll see," he said. "It might be a forgery.

You never know with these old books. Sometimes the forgeries look better than the real thing . . ."

He stood up and stretched his arms. I looked around the dining car, ran my hand along the smooth, varnished edge of our table, felt the velvet curtains on our window and swished the melted ice around in my glass. *Where was I last year, at this time?* I thought. *Sitting on the brown carpet in my Stulton tenement? Suffering through Ms. Goiner's math class?*

"I'm going to stay here, for a bit," I said.

Art smiled. He got it, I think; he knew I didn't want to sleep because I was having too much fun. He said goodnight and he left, a rush of cold air and metallic clatter blowing in before the door between the cars slid shut.

The waiter suddenly reappeared, corporalizing from within the dim glow over our table. He asked me if I wanted anything else. His eyes were tired but friendly. I noticed how young he was, almost my age.

"A deck of cards, if you have them," I said.

He returned moments later with a sealed pack. For the next two hours I played my favorite solitaire game, Forty Thieves, supposedly Napoleon's preferred pastime while exiled on St. Helena.

◆ ◆ ◆

That night as I lay in my bunk, the gentle movement of the train rocking me into relaxation while we hurtled through the dark countryside, I obsessively replayed Art's story in my mind. It was, admittedly, fantastic. To my sixteen-year-old sensibilities it was entirely possible, but even then there was an element of the mythological. The monk in search of immortality. The fall from grace. The nervous townspeople and their local priest invoking the requisite voice of religious hysteria. The mysterious disappearance and the enigmatic clues (a book, a grail) left behind.

But unlike most legends I knew of, fantasy was seeping into reality. It was like an archaeologist had unearthed Paul Bunyan's axe blade, found lying near the massive fossilized femur of his blue ox. Perhaps it would turn out to be a hoax, a story more suited to *Unexplained Crea-*

tures, Beasts, and Phenomena of the Ancient and Modern World. I put my mind to rest by deciding there was no way of knowing until we saw the book, and with that I fell into a peaceful sleep.

I awoke to the clanking of the train and the whoosh of brown and gray country sliding by. Art was awake on the bottom bunk and holding his glasses to the window, cleaning the lenses with the edge of his T-shirt. He looked like he'd been up for some time. He was clean-shaven, his bed was made, and his bags sat patiently by the door.

There were mountains in the distance, a jagged black edge on the horizon. Evergreens surrounded us but as we drew closer the trees thinned out, eventually becoming a bare, cold, rugged landscape of small, craggy buttes and scrubland. It was flat, like the American Midwest, but colored in shades of lead and tin. A river sat in the distance, slow-moving and black, winding without purpose toward the mountains, crawling by a small town that sat in a blurry lump on the horizon. Distinct shapes began to appear—smokestacks, some dormant, some secreting black smoke, jutting into the gray sky like the fingers of a buried hand. *The remnants of communist industry,* Art said. We passed by a town, and looking at the square buildings and squatty flat homes, all the color of institutional cement, I believed I'd never seen a landscape so forlorn. The American Midwest had been vital; however broad and dusty, there was a soul to the land. When you cut the earth it bled. We were traveling over land that looked scarred and beaten, like an old bone with its marrow sucked dry.

Our train rolled uphill, over a narrow pass that cut a swath through thickening forest, behind us the barren plains receding like a tide. We soon passed into highlands, pine and dormant oak shooting up from snow-covered ground. A flock of black birds swooped by my window, and the train slowed as we went farther up the mountain. Snow dusted the treetops and the dense thicket on either side, silent pines towering above like the legs of a dinosaur.

It started to snow, and the sky was now like cracked slate. The landscape shifted subtly; snow-covered brush outside my window sloping into foothills, frosted evergreens and bare ash, and then the land gave way to farms with small cottages, sitting in the middle of plow-furrowed frozen ground.

"There she is," Art said, pointing out the window. Out of the snow-blurred horizon emerged the towering Gothic spires of the Hradcany Castle and the amorphous geometry of the cityscape below. Then there appeared the narrow swath of the Vltava River, perpendicular to us, running direct through the city's midline and continuing north, toward mountain ranges covered in a dark gray haze.

"That's her," he said. His eyes were dancing. "That's Prague."

Chapter 11

Prague is a city of juxtaposition, the jumbled mess remaining after the mystic collided with the pragmatist and the pagan warred against the Christian. It has been home to the Knights Templar, Casanova, Mozart, Tycho Brahe and Johannes Kepler. Its blazon is an arm holding a sword, emerging from a castle doorway, its wielder hidden. It warns those who do not understand: *There is danger in what you cannot see.* Throughout its history the paradox has emerged; the 16th-century Czech philosopher David Gans attempted to reconcile Copernican theory with Judaic beliefs, while across the river the Rudolfine rabbi Judah Loew dabbled in cabalistic rituals to raise golems from the clay of the banks of the Vltava. Again the same patterns—hermeticist versus scientist, dark versus light, sacred versus profane. Celetna Street's statue of the Black Virgin Mary, manifestation of the Egyptian goddess Isis, the Phrygian Cybele, the Greek Demeter. While Soviet tanks rumbled through the streets in 1968, old native Czechs, the ones who still remembered, prayed to the pagan prophetess Libuse, who sleeps with her army of knights in the catacombs beneath Vysehrad. Some people believe Prague is where the translucent fabric between the world we know and the underbelly of the unknown has ripped open. Art was a believer. It's what led him back to the city.

From the train station we walked to the Charles Bridge, stopping at the mouth of an arched stone underpass, the snow-covered bridge spread before us. It was crowded with nondescript tourists, some leaning against the side and looking down at the slow-moving dark river, others flowing in a human wave. A statue of Jesus had been erected on our right, his body mounted to a cross next to a gas lamp. Beneath him street vendors stood by their tables, selling hats and small flags and postcards and unframed sketches. In the distance, like a brooding king surveying his domain, the Hradcany Castle threw its towering spires into the sky, dark and ancient, flanked on both sides by the more delicate fleches of St. Vitus's Cathedral.

Art and I stood at the mouth of the bridge, cold wind ruffling our hair as we heaved our bags and began our trek across the bridge. Fat clouds, so dark gray they were almost black, rolled into position over our heads.

Where Paris had been a mix of cosmopolitan modernity and European history with leanings toward the former, the Prague I saw that wintry morning was a city of temporal stasis, with the occasional trace of Americana. Tourists in jeans and puffy ski jackets walked past us, seemingly oblivious to everything but the vendors positioned along the walkway. Random sculptures perched on the bridge's walls; a caged Turk, Mary cradling Jesus, and a massive gargoyle with slitted eyes and wagging tongue. In every direction were Gothic, Baroque, and Romanesque towers standing beside simple stone cottages. Nove Mesto (New Town) behind us was filled with cathedrals and churches, domed and spired, and ahead of us, Mala Strana looked the same except for the imposing bulk of the Hradcany.

At the end of the bridge we passed under another archway, this one spanning between two Romanesque towers of unequal height. To my left and right, on the banks of the Vltava River, stood homes colored in pale yellows with maroon and red tiled roofs, dark windows closed off to the cold and chimneys trailing smoke into the morning sky. A man wearing mirrored sunglasses and a leather jacket walked up to me and shoved a nightclub flyer at my chest. A woman walking in front of us lost her hat in the wind and had to chase it across the street, her heels clacking on the cobbled stone. A small cab sputtered past, with a red tram close behind clanging its warning bell. Tourists passively stared out the windows like they were watching television. I heard the wind, Art's long coat whipping and flapping, and the flat din of voices all around—English, Czech, French, German. My own footsteps clopping on the cobblestones, children running and laughing at the foot of a tower, one throwing clumps of snow at the other, who then screeched and ran past, red-faced and laughing.

Our path continued alongside tram tracks. The sky remained dark, but almost directly overhead there was a break in the clouds, through which a feeble shaft of sunlight shone. I had a powerful sense of déjà vu—surrounded by bastions and ramparts, closed in by the medieval vertical landscape, this was Europe as I had imagined it.

We walked uphill to the Mala Strana Square, past tightly spaced homes that towered on either side of the narrow street, and paused at St. Nicholas Church. People streamed from its open doors, Americans in blue jeans taking pictures, pointing to its green dome and cross-tipped minarets. We continued up and around a bend, where a small sign tacked to a black and patina-green gaslight read Nerudova.

"Mozart lived on this street," Art said, buttoning his coat to the collar.

The snow resumed, quickly changing from light, airy wisps to heavier clumps of wet sleet, and then, amazingly, a flash of light arced overhead, lighting the bloated belly of the storm clouds. A crack of thunder followed, and I looked behind us, down on the Charles Bridge and the Vltava River, imagining the Hapsburg artillery raining cannon shot on the city. I leaned into the wind, following Art by watching his shoes.

We turned down another short, narrow street, and emerged from its shadows into another main thoroughfare, cars buzzing past. Ahead of us sat a huge, modern building, built in hideous imitation of the Romanesque and Gothic buildings surrounding it, with new brick and a freshly paved and painted parking lot below. Twin towers stood atop either side of its three-gabled roof, the façade a glittering sheet of windows, some lit, others a shimmering black. Attendants, dressed in gray waist-length jackets, moved about busily, rolling luggage into the hotel and out of it, their steps efficient and brisk, like well-trained soldiers.

"The Mustovich Hotel," Art said. "Five years ago it wasn't here. There was an old church, with a collapsed southern wall, all mossy and ruinous. Wild dogs had made their home under the arcade, and if you came around at night you could hear them howling. Over there, at the parking ramp entrance," he pointed, "was the chancel. Tree trunks had busted through its wall. It looked like the Slavic gods came back to reclaim what Cyril and Methodius took from them."

We checked into the hotel and Art collapsed on the bed while I stood at the picture window. Our room was huge—a master suite with two separate sleeping quarters, a kitchen, a cherrywood bar, a living room with work space, and a gleaming marble and brass bathroom. We had an amazing view of the city, stuck into the side of a hillock, the Hradcany Castle above and behind us. I could see the spires of St. Nicholas Church, and snow falling onto the black waters of the Vltava. Every rooftop was covered in white. Below, faint outlines of people walked about, heads held low against the wind. I opened the window a crack and heard car horns and tram bells drifting up through the snow-lined alleyways and streets.

Another arc of lightning streaked across the sky. I moved away from the window.

"Get me a drink, would you?" Art pushed his shoes off and propped himself up against the headboard. "Preferably something with vodka in it."

I found a can of orange juice in the mini-refrigerator and poured it into a glass with a healthy splash of vodka from one of those mini-bottles. "I figure we'll take a stroll into town, grab a bite to eat, maybe do a little tourism," Art said. He sipped his drink. "We're meeting Brother Albo in about four hours. If we have the chance we'll hit some of the bars later tonight. There's this great jazz club, Reduta." He closed his eyes and rested the glass on his chest, both hands wrapped around it. "Czech women go crazy for American men, you know. They think we're all movie stars."

Our plans didn't work out—instead Art fell asleep after finishing his drink. We left the hotel just as the storm passed; the streets were now ankle-deep with snow. The winds had stopped completely and the city was remarkably still. There was some sun, a harsh yellow halo glaring through the snow clouds.

We ate at a corner café, ordering *eccle* rolls and cubed lamb with two pints of strong beer. After dinner we walked in the opposite direction of our hotel, down a twisting, narrow street lined with houses with tiny doors. We were going to the St. Thölden Monastery, Art explained. He said it was home to the oldest Benedictine order in Eastern Europe, and in addition to having the Malezel book, St. Thölden Monastery was reknowned for its large collection of medieval incunabula.

"When I told Dr. Cade that, he offered to pay for my flight," Art said.

"And did you accept?"

Art nodded, shoulders hunched against the cold.

"His perpetually stocked bar pays for Howie's nasty habit," he said. "That's Howie's bonus. This is mine."

We made our way down the narrow street and Art stopped at a low stone wall. Atop the wall was a black iron fence with rusted spikes, brown branches dangling over the fence like unkempt hair. Art and I peered through the fence.

"This is supposed to be it," Art said. "Corner of Ostra and Berec. Do you see anything?"

All I saw was a flat tract of snow with yellow bulldozers and backhoes dusted white, parked near mounds of dirt and stacks of lumber. Tall, gray buildings surrounded the empty lot. A dog loped into view, and it stopped and started sniffing around one of the bulldozers. Art whistled and the dog lifted its head, saw us, and went back to sniffing the bulldozer.

"Maybe you have the wrong address," I said.

"I just spoke with my contact at the university, last month," Art said. He turned around and leaned back against the wall. He didn't look too upset but I could tell it wouldn't take much to get him there. "Unless he gave me the wrong address but I don't see how that's possible," he said. "How many St. Thölden monasteries could there be?"

A young man was walking by and he stopped and turned to us.

"You American?" he said.

I nodded. Art didn't seem to notice him; instead he stared down at the street, deep in thought.

The young man smiled. He was wearing a bright orange ski

jacket, and he had on headphones. He pulled the headphones off. I could hear a tinny blast of music, and then the young man reached into his jacket and switched it off.

"Cool," he said. He sounded Czech. "You from New York?"

"Just outside of New York," I said.

The young man nodded. His forehead was dotted with pimples that were as red as his wind-flushed cheeks. "I'm going to New York this spring," he said. "Visit my sister. She's at college. You two at college?"

"Aberdeen," I said.

"You party at Aberdeen? Lots of women?"

"Lots of women," Art said, slowly. He looked up at the kid. "Do you know where St. Thölden Monastery is?"

The young man shook his head. "I'm not Christian," he said. "My parents go to church but not me."

He smiled again and looked past us. "There was something there," he said, pointing. "A church, I think. It burned last month. *Whoosh.*" He lifted his arms. "Big goddamn fire. My friends and I sat on my porch and smoked grass and watched the fire."

A gust of wind ruffled his hair. "You like grass?" he said.

Art looked at me. I shrugged.

"How much?" Art said.

The young man turned, looked down the street, and whistled with two fingers. Moments later I heard the buzz of a small engine, and I saw a guy on a moped driving toward us, wearing a helmet with a tinted face shield and a big motorcycle jacket like he was riding a Harley.

The moped rider stopped and took off his helmet. He had short, black hair like his friend, and he looked a bit older. The two of them talked, and the moped guy glanced at us cautiously.

"How much do you guys want?" he said. His Czech accent wasn't as thick as his friend's.

"A few buds," Art said. "If it's good, then maybe more."

The moped guy nodded. "It's good," he said. He unzipped his jacket, pulled a pipe out from one of the inside pockets, and surreptitiously handed the pipe to Art. Art nodded toward a small alley tucked between two tiny homes and we ducked into it, brick walls on either side, the sound of a television blaring down from one of the shuttered windows. The guy wearing the orange ski jacket stayed on the street, presumably to keep watch.

Art took a few hits and passed me the pipe. I took one long draw and it felt like someone dropped an ember down my throat. I doubled over and tried to stop myself from coughing but it was useless— the smoke exploded out of me and Art and the moped guy started laughing.

Not bad, I heard Art say.

Better than not bad, the moped guy said. *Fucking great. You want the whole bag?*

I coughed again and looked up. The weed was strong; I could already feel it stroking the front of my brain. I rubbed my face and looked toward the wintry, dusky sky and took a few deep breaths. *Nice.*

"You know anything about the church that burned across the street?" Art said. He handed the moped guy a few folded bills.

The moped guy quickly counted the money, then slipped it into his pocket and gave Art a rolled-up baggie, something dark and green inside.

"It wasn't a church. It was a monastery," he said. He sniffled and zipped up his jacket. The wind was getting colder. "The place burned to the fucking ground, man. They're building a McDonald's, I think. Big Macs and fries," he said, and he smiled and rubbed his stomach. "You hungry?"

Art shook his head. "Where did the monks go?"

The moped guy thought for a moment, then he snapped his fingers. "Hotel Paris," he said. "In Stare Mestro. You know where Máchova Street is?"

Art nodded. He looked at the baggie, unrolled it, and lowered his nose to it.

"This isn't what we smoked," he said.

The moped guy frowned. "Yes it is."

Art took out one of the buds and crushed it between his fingers. "No, it's not," he said. "It doesn't smell the same, and see how short and dense these are?" He held up a bud. "Looks like an indica strain. We just smoked sativa. I'm sure of it. I can tell from the high."

The moped guy looked nonplussed.

"It doesn't matter," Art said to me, pointedly ignoring the moped guy. "Really, the weed here is so cheap it doesn't matter." He flashed a smile and dropped the bag in the snow. The moped guy laughed, incredulous, but Art walked back onto the street. He looked eager to get going.

"Go with God," the moped guy said, and he put his helmet back on and fired up his moped. The kid in the orange ski jacket was holding the baggie Art had dropped, staring at it and talking rapidly in Czech to his friend.

Art thrust his hands into his pockets and we continued down the narrow street. It's always the small moments that define someone, and watching Art trudge through the snow, head down, oblivious to the wonders all around us—the spires, the cobbled streets, the ancient churches stuck like stone fists into the hillside—I finally understood the extent of his obsession, and rather than frighten me, it made me respect him even more.

We crossed the Charles Bridge and headed into Stare Mesto, the old town square. Even though I'd taken one hit I was very stoned, and I think Art was too because we wandered for an hour before finding Máchova Street. It had started snowing again, a light downy shake that floated languorously from a soft black sky, swallowed by the slow-moving dark waters of the Vltava or curling in the wind around streetlights like fluttering moths.

Groups of people spilled out of bars and onto the street, laughing and holding onto each other, some with bottles in hand triumphantly raised to the night sky like pagan kings howling at the moon. I saw a man bend over and throw up into a snowbank and there was a woman rubbing his back while she talked to her friend, and I marvelled at how many good people there were in the world, and how I couldn't imagine being anywhere else at that moment, gliding through the snowy streets of Stare Mesto on a winter night in Prague, Art walking by my side, his black greatcoat trailing in the wind, bag slung over his shoulder, while I listened to his stories about the Přemysl family, Bohemia's first dynasty, and their rise to power in the 10th century.

And then suddenly we were there: standing in front of a gabled, low-lying, boarded-up brick building that ran the length of the sidewalk to the street corner, *Hotel Paris* painted on an old, faded sign in peeling black paint, with a silhouette of a dancing girl under the name.

Art and I stood there for a moment, gazing up at the sign. Every window had a board nailed over it, and the front door was spray-painted with graffiti.

"That moped guy was full of shit," Art said. He closed his eyes and rubbed his forehead.

"Are you still high?" I said.

Art kept rubbing his forehead. "I think so," he said. He exhaled sharply and opened his eyes. "Actually," he said, "I'm really stoned."

He stared at me and we burst out laughing. We laughed so hard we collapsed onto the soft snow, and then we sat on the curb and gazed out over the river at the twinkling lights of Mala Strana.

"Let's stay here," Art said.

"We'll freeze to death," I said.

"I mean in Prague," Art said, and he drew his knees into his chest and wrapped the front of his coat over them. "I have enough money. We could rent a place near the university, get our degrees there. We wouldn't ever have to go back."

"What about Dr. Cade's project?" I said.

Art remained quiet for a moment.

"He'd find someone else," he said. "There's always someone else."

It was a strangely seductive proposition. I had nothing. I was beholden to no one. Would I be missed? Would anyone even notice I'd left? I'd be another story for Dr. Lang, another boy from the city who'd dropped out, and maybe one day I'd run into some student at Aberdeen, and I too would warn them about Cornelius, crazy old Cornelius who kills pigeons in his search for immortality, and Art would continue looking for the Philosopher's Stone while I lived out my life among the dim bookshelves of Charles University, lost in antiquity.

If our existence has weight, then I believe that weight has to remain in place long enough to sink into the earth and make its mark. My problem was I felt I hadn't stayed anywhere long enough to sink in, that I was a footprint in the dusty earth of my West Falls farm and a footprint in the grimy stairwells of my Stulton tenement, and if I left Aberdeen I'd be a footprint there, too, a faint smudge on its burnished wooden floors and marble stairs. The existential vertigo would be too much. I believed it was entirely possible that if I left, one day I would wake up in our Prague apartment and find myself invisible, weightless. An afterthought.

I took a deep breath and tried to clear my head.

"We should go back to the Mustovich," I said, turning to Art. "Tomorrow we can ask around and see if—"

Art stood up and walked to the front door of the Hotel Paris and knocked. He waited, ear pressed to the door, and knocked again, and to my utter amazement, it opened.

A boy appeared, wearing a dark brown robe, his young face staring at Art from the doorway. He blinked once, twice, and then pulled his cowl back. His hair was short and simple, cropped close to his scalp. He had gentle, soft features, and a lilting, almost feminine voice that floated onto the night air like a wisp of smoke.

"*Dobrý večer,*" the boy said. "*Máte přáni?*"

"*Dovolte mi, abych se představil,*" Art said. "*Jmenuji se Arthur Fitch.*" Art gestured to me. "*Toto je pan Eric Dunne.*"

The boy nodded and smiled.

"*Mluvite anglicky?*" Art said. I knew that phrase. *Do you speak English?*

The boy lifted his hand, palm down, and turned it over, then back, several times.

"Albo Luschini," Art said, and at the mention of that name the boy smiled and opened the door wide.

. . .

The boy led us down a short hallway with wooden panelled walls that smelled like old cigarettes. I watched the snow melting from the back of Art's coat, dripping onto the scarred wooden floor.

At the end of the hall the boy opened the door into a large room with a low ceiling. Little round tables were scattered about, some with older monks seated at them, talking and eating, and other tables had boxes stacked atop. The floor was carpeted in red and the walls were papered in yellow, with alternating strips of gold and fading red fleur-de-lis running from floor to ceiling. A staircase sat to the left of a raised stage at the far wall, curving slightly to the right, a tattered red runner going up the stairs. There was a brass pole in the middle of the stage, and Christmas lights were wrapped around the pole.

The young monk hurried ahead and bent down to talk to one of the monks sitting alone at a table with open books scattered around him and a calculator at his hand. After a brief moment the monk stood, slowly, beckoning to Art and me.

"Come," he said, speaking across the room in a strong, clear voice. His English was lightly accented. "Come join us. We have more food if you wish."

Art and I sat at the table. The old monk smiled at me and I nervously smiled back. He was short and lean, with big, thick white eyebrows, like bushes rooted to a cliff edge. He wasn't wearing a robe like the others; instead he had on brown sweatpants and a faded T-shirt that read *Cats! The Musical!*

The old monk filled two cups from a half-empty bottle of red wine, and pushed them across the table to us.

"God be praised," he said, and he raised his glass and gulped noisily. *"And wine that maketh glad the heart of man . . ."* He set the cup down and smacked his lips, and then he sat back and folded his hands together and smiled, wrinkles spreading from the corners of his mouth. I looked at the other monks, who were simply staring at us, obviously enjoying the entertainment.

"I am Brother Albo," the old monk said. "Peter says you've come to see me."

Art put his bag on the floor and introduced us. "Mr. Corso from

Charles University gave me your name," Art said. "I've come to see your collection of manuscripts."

Albo nodded. "Most were saved," he said. "God be praised. The library was the last to burn, and what we lost was mostly to smoke and water."

"I'm so sorry to hear about your monastery," Art said. He looked around and flashed his winning smile. "But this looks like a good place to start over."

"It's adequate," Albo said. "Do you know about the Hotel Paris? It was . . . what is the word . . ." He looked down in thought. "A *burlesque* hall," he said, grinning. "Lady dancers, on that stage," he pointed to the stage, "and the rooms upstairs? Sometimes for tourists, mostly for the patrons and whatever lady dancer caught their eye."

Monks living in an abandoned strip club. If I wasn't high I would've started asking a thousand questions, but as marijuana tends to raise the ridiculous up to the sublime, all I could do was sit there with my mouth shut and my eyes wide, sipping the sour wine Albo had poured for me, trying to stay focused on their conversation.

Albo told us about the Paris Hotel, how it had been previously owned by Nikolai Donegar, one of Prague's most famous magicians, who'd originally opened the hotel as a night club. Nikolai was hit by a streetcar and killed, and his son Nikola turned the Paris Hotel into a den of drugs and prostitution. Nikola was arrested sometime later, and the Paris Hotel was slated for demolition, but for ten years nothing happened. It just sat there, rotting and abandoned, until Albo approached the city council and told them of his need for a new abbey. *It was God's will that this blessed building be given to us,* Albo said.

"Now," he said, "we continue God's will by raising money and restoring what was once a beautiful building. We plan to take down the stage, remove the bar"—he gestured to the opposite wall, where a bar ran the length of the room, boxes and cookware on the back wall where liquor bottles used to be—"maybe even start an orphanage in the spare rooms. But it is all a question of money." He rubbed his thumb and forefinger together.

"Do you miss your old monastery?" I said.

Albo looked at me, a queer smile spreading across his wrinkled face.

"Yes," he said, slowly. "I suppose I do. But if God had intended us to remain there, we would still be there. *The glory of the Lord shall endure for ever; the Lord shall rejoice in his works.* This is the new path he has intended for us."

Just like my old farm, I thought. And everywhere else I'd been. I found comfort in the old monk's words. *If God had intended me to remain there, I would still be there.*

Art reached into his bag and took out his Oslo book and Gilbert's *Universal Compendia.* He opened the Gilbert and slid it to Albo. While Albo read, a cat appeared, slinking along the floor, black with white paws and a white nose. It brushed by the table leg, tail curling high, and then wound its way around Albo's feet, arching its back and rubbing its face against his calf.

"Mr. Corso said you have the Malezel book," Art said.

Albo scratched his head. "We have many books," he said. "I don't know them all. Who did you say you spoke to?"

"Mr. Corso," Art said. "From the university. He works in the library archives . . ."

Albo slapped the table, rattling our wine cups. "Of course, of course," he said. "He helped us catalogue our holdings a few years ago. He would know better than I. Did you say you were college students?"

We nodded.

"And you came to Prague for a *book?*"

"It's part of a research project," Art said, quickly.

"Must be an important research project," said Albo.

"Very," Art said.

Albo raised his eyebrows and nodded slightly. He took a sip of his wine and remained there, staring at the two of us as if we were eminently fascinating. Which, perhaps, to a Czech monk, we were.

"You," he said, pointing at me. "Are you part of this research project?"

Before I could think of a good answer I'd already spoken. "No," I said. "I'm on vacation."

"This is how you spend your vacation?" he said. "Following your friend to monasteries in search of an old book?"

"It's either this," I said, "or cable TV."

Brother Albo laughed, as did some of the monks who'd been listening. "That's good," Albo said, slapping the table again. He looked a little drunk. "Very good," he said. "*Cable TV.* Very, very good."

Albo finished his wine in one gulp and stood up, patting his belly and looking around like he'd forgotten something.

"Okay," he said. "I'll take you to the books. We'll see if Mr. Corso was right."

◆ ◆ ◆

From Gilbert's *Universal Compendia:*

1359, JOHANN MALEZEL MANUSCRIPT, *"Ad Majorem Dei Gloriam"*
     Binding: Full, alum-tawed pigskin over wooden, partially bevelled boards, blind-stamped, -tooled, and -embossed. Rows of acorns fill the center panels, whose borders incorporate the names of the theological virtues of Faith, Hope, and Charity, plus the cardinal virtue of Justice. The owner's initials (L.D.) are also blind-stamped on the front cover, and the volume retains the bottom clasp and a remnant of the top one.
     Reported Condition (as of May 1910): Binding as above, spine and covers moderately stained and abraded with loss of leather at the corners, a small hole in the front cover, few small wormholes in the spine. Pages variously age-toned and foxed, with occasional wax and water-drop stains (also, possibly chrism); obscuring of letters in one place (p. 38–40) where a drop of wax has burned a small hole through the page.

Albo led us out of the dance room, down a narrow corridor, and through a set of double doors. We walked down a stone staircase, silent as thieves, and when we got to the bottom Albo pulled on a lightbulb and there, in towers and stacked piles and heaps and mounds, was the largest collection of books and miscellany I'd ever seen.

The books were confined to the center of the room, in chest-high stacks, and piles of them lined the walls and sat in huge wooden crates. The rest of the basement was filled with junk: lamps and broken chairs and tables; bundles of curled, yellowed newspapers and magazines; old carpets rolled and piled atop each other like logs. An entire wall was filled with mirrors, some smoked, others speckled, most cracked, casting the room's reflection in a dark jumble of shapes. A big statue of a mermaid hung on the far wall, with long, turquoise ceramic hair and large breasts painted the color of a manila envelope. The room had a musty odor of old leather and mildew and stale smoke.

Albo plucked a spray can from atop a book and scanned the floor. He muttered something in Czech and aimed a plume of white mist at an insect scuttling from one stack of books to the next.

"Cockroaches," Albo said. He sprayed again. "They eat the book bindings."

Art stepped forward and looked at one of the books stacked atop a waist-high pile.

"Finellan's *Le Triple Vocabularie Infernal*," Art said, touching the cover delicately. He gazed around the room. "Are these books organized in any particular order?" he said.

Albo shook his head and stroked one of the books closest to him, as a father would his child. "We are still unpacking. Mr. Corso's catalogue was among my belongings that were lost in the fire. It may take us years to once again document what we have. We do not even know what we lost."

"So where would I find the Malezel book?"

Albo shrugged and smiled gently. "Pray God will lead you to it," he said.

Art turned and surveyed the room. He put his hands on his hips and sighed.

"Is this stuff all yours?" I said. I spotted a dusty jukebox with cracked glass, an electric guitar lying across what looked like the top part of a piano.

Albo laughed softly. "No. Nikolai Donegar was a collector, as you can see. This was all here when we arrived . . ."

He looked out over the room, lips pursed, a hint of a disapproving frown sneaking its way onto his face.

"I will have Brother Falldin bring tea, if you'd like," Albo said, his smile returning. "I would help you but the damp chills my old bones . . ."

"We'll be fine," Art said. He was already searching the piles, picking his way delicately among the stacks and towers.

I helped Art for a while but eventually made my way into the junk, imagining I'd find some lost cache of gold coins. Instead I found a box of pornographic pens, the kind where the women's clothes come off when you tip the pen upside-down, and I also found hundreds of envelopes stuffed with flyers advertising a Czech rock group. Another box held official-looking forms—taxes or something like that—and the box near it had a bunch of moldy albums I'd never heard of. There was a door on the far wall but it was locked.

Art was sitting on the floor, sifting through a bunch of papers. He looked tired—shoulders slumped, eyes heavy.

I tried the door again. I thought for a moment, and decided that since the door probably hadn't been opened in years (a trickle of rust sifted down from the knob when I'd first turned it) I wasn't entering someplace I shouldn't. At least, I figured, nothing the monks owned would be in there.

"Can you pick locks?" I asked Art.

With anyone else it would have been a crazy question, but Art had all sorts of quirky, random skills, like card tricks and origami (I once saw him make a woman with a parasol, out of a restaurant receipt), and he could do complicated math problems in his head, square roots and cube roots and long division, and he could even fix his car—over the course of the semester I'd watched him replace the brakes, perform a tune-up, and give the engine a partial overhaul.

"The door might be locked for a reason," Art said.

"It hasn't been opened in years," I said.

Art dropped the papers and looked at me, wearily, and then he stood and made his way across the room. He stopped, looked around the floor, and picked up a bicycle wheel. He began to work on one of the spokes.

"There's a chance the Malezel book was lost in the fire," he said.

I didn't say anything. What was there to say?

"If that's the case," Art grunted and ripped a spoke free from the wheel, "we might have to go to Sofia." He started bending the spoke. "I'll pay for your ticket, don't worry about that. But I haven't even started the next section for Dr. Cade, and I'd planned on getting back in time to at least finish the first third of the Crusades, and if we have to travel to Sofia I don't see how I'll be able to translate Malezel before the semester starts."

I wasn't sure I'd heard him correctly. *"Sofia?"* I said. "In Bulgaria?"

Art nodded. "The Petrusal Library has a decent selection of hand-copied works, courtesy of all those poor monks who destroyed their eyes sitting in the scriptoria. I don't like to use copied works, but we may not have much of a choice. Of course, that's assuming there'd even be a copy of Malezel, given its heretical status, but I figure anything with *Dei* may have been preserved on principle alone . . ."

Art was right to be wary. The scriptoria were dreadful places, consisting of a senior monk sitting in the front of a dimly lit room, reading from a text for hours on end, while his fellow monks (especially those who had to perform penance, for scriptorium duty was often given as punishment) remained hunched over at their cramped desks, transcribing his words. Monks would often nod off, waking up and continuing their transcription as if they hadn't missed a beat, and sometimes, when the tedium became unbearable, monks would doodle nasty little notes in the margins: *A curse upon the author of this wretched text. My back is broken, my neck is stiff, my eyes dim and still there are six months before the end.* As a result, many transcribed manuscripts (including, as many Christians are loathe to admit, the Bible) are filled with gross errors in continuity and syntax.

Art held up the bicycle spoke, its end bent at ninety degrees.

"Now, help me find a paper clip," he said. "Anything thin and strong will do."

I searched around for a bit, then had a minor revelation and pulled a metal clip off one of the porno pens' caps. Art was already at the door when I gave it to him.

He inspected the clip for a moment and slipped it into the lock, along with the bent end of the bicycle spoke. After a few tense minutes Art's face relaxed and he turned the bicycle spoke. I heard a distinct *click*.

"Incredible," I said.

Art dropped the tools on the floor and wiped his palms on his pants. "Repetition," he said plainly, and he walked back to his books.

I entered a small room, dark outlines in front of me lit dimly by the single bulb in the basement, and once my eyes adjusted I saw the far corner of the room was littered with jars and glass boxes, and the walls were covered in posters, old posters from the turn of the century, advertising magicians *(The Wondrous Bandini! The Mysterious Necromancy of Corvinus the Hungarian!)* and elixirs that claimed to cure everything from dropsy to consumption. One such poster showed a muscle-bound man with a mustache and iron wristbands, swigging a bottle of "McGillicuty's Samson Oil." In the next panel, with feet firmly planted and arms extended, the newly empowered muscleman resists the pull of three horses, gripping their thick reins in his hands, while people in the audience stand and cheer.

I walked past a desk, a large day calendar centered on top. Notes were scribbled on a few of the days. Someone had sketched a naked lady, and written a phone number beneath. A deck of cards lay near the calendar, and a stiff rubber clown nose that cracked in half when I squeezed it. One of the drawers held an open jar of wax or Vaseline or something like it, with the ancient corpse of a fly on its back, stuck in the goo. Another drawer had silk handkerchiefs tied in various knots. Another had a baggie filled with an ominous white powder, twist-tied shut, lying next to some plastic spoons and a packet of sugar and a jumble of coffee stirrers. There was a familiar smell in the room, vinegary and sweet under the must and damp, and I soon realized what it was: formaldehyde. It reminded me of high school bio lab.

The jars and glass boxes were covered in a thick coat of dust, and when I wiped off the front of one of the larger jars, I discovered where the smell was coming from. Floating, motionless inside the jar, was a hand. It was swollen and its peeling skin looked like beeswax.

I turned the jar and looked at the hand from all sides. *Whose hand?* I thought. Nikolai Donegar? Nikola Donegar? A thief cut from the gallows? I knew about the Hand of Glory: the hand of a gibbeted criminal, lopped off and used as protection against burglary. *Lot of good it did you,* I thought, and I wiped clean another jar.

Inside was a foot with two missing toes. I cleaned off the glass boxes. Various organs, all labelled in English. A spleen, a gall bladder, a liver. The biggest box contained a large grayish lump with the label *The Heart of Nicephorus, the Adriatic Giant* glued to the outside of the glass.

A black towel had been draped over the largest jar. I took a deep breath, and pulled the towel off.

There was a head in a glass globe, a monstrous staring thing with swirling black hair and puffy, misshapen lips, bared teeth the color of skim milk, sunken eyes that still bulged and looked as though they might blink at any moment. Below it, engraved in English on the globe's wooden base:

DR. HORATIO J. GRIMEK
CLAIRVOYANT, SPIRITUALIST, TRUTH SEER
ASK, AND YE SHALL RECEIVE

I stared, both fascinated and repulsed. I knocked on the globe with my knuckle. Horatio stared back. His hair hung in mid-swirl, black lines crisscrossing his forehead.

"Does the Philosopher's Stone exist?" I said.

One of his ears looked like it was falling off.

"Will Art find his book?"

"How old is Cornelius?"

I leaned in and whispered:

Does Ellen love me?

Horatio J. Grimek continued his thousand-mile stare. A poster of

Carmine the Magnificent loomed above, Carmine holding a black wand in one hand and a ball of fire in the other, his eyes colored bright blue like the summer sky.

I replaced the black towel. *Silly,* I thought, and I turned and walked away and that's when I heard a hollow thump, the kind of noise something sloshing against the inside of a bucket of water would make. Since then I've convinced myself that hollow thump was a mouse, roused from its hiding place, scurrying among the jars and glass boxes, but at the time, when I still believed anything was possible, when I'd already found myself in the basement of a strip-club-turned-Benedictine-monastery searching for an ancient manuscript that held the secret of immortality between its alum-tawed pigskin covers, I believed that maybe, *maybe* the head of Dr. Horatio J. Grimek still had some leftover mojo from his days as soothsayer, and I bolted, banging my hip against the desk, kicking over a box of plastic magic wands, careening out of the room and slamming the door behind me.

Art looked up from the stacks, slowly, with a sort of detached interest.

"Anything good?" he said.

I was breathing heavily, my heart a trip-hammer.

"A human head in a jar," I said, and to my amazement, Art simply nodded and went back to work.

Albo was kind enough to put me up in one of the spare rooms, with a cot and a thin wool blanket and one of those old space heaters with exposed, red-hot coils. Art told Albo that, with his permission of course, he'd continue his search through the night, and if he did find the manuscript, he'd present his offer to Albo in the morning.

"Offer?" Albo said.

"To purchase the book," Art said. "I have some idea of its worth, but you can certainly name your—"

"Our books are not for sale," Albo said, with a kind smile. "Certainly we could use the money, but I could not bear to part with my books. They have become our only link to the past."

Art was going to say something, I think, but Albo smiled reassuringly. "You may, of course, copy whatever it is you need. If you'd like, I could ask Brother Luschausen to assist you."

"That won't be necessary," Art said. "My assistant here will take care of it."

Art looked at me and raised his eyebrows.

"Hoc opus, hic labor est," I said. This is the hard work, this is the toil.

Albo laughed, wrinkles spreading from the corners of his eyes like the branches of a dried-up riverbed.

I was awakened sometime in the night. Art was standing over me, gently shaking my shoulder. For a second I thought I was back home, in Dr. Cade's house.

"Eric," Art whispered.

The space heater glowed red. The wool blanket was down near my waist and I was shivering. Art's face was a half-moon, one side lit orange from the heater, the other cloaked in darkness.

He has cancer this time, I thought. *Or maybe some rare blood disease. Or maybe Art just wants to talk about the usual; the Byzantine literary salons of Thessalonica; the astronomy laboratories in Trebizond; the rise and fall of the Saxon empire.*

I pulled up the blanket.

"I found it," Art said, excitedly. *"I found the book."*

I wanted to be thrilled but jet lag had taken its toll, and I couldn't imagine getting out of my bed and walking across the frigid stone floor.

"I'm exhausted," I said.

"Keep your voice down," Art hissed. *"I need you to look at something."*

"What time is it?" I said.

"Three, maybe four," he said. He ran his hands through his hair and looked around the small room. *"Get your stuff together and follow me,"* he said. *"And for Christ's sake, keep quiet."*

We sat on the stage in the main room, near the pole, letting the white Christmas lights illuminate the book. The rest of the room was dark;

small round tables, the Christmas lights reflecting like distant stars in the smoked mirror behind the bar. Art was wearing a pair of latex gloves, and he had a jeweler's loupe in his hand.

A row of acorns filled the center of the book's cover, just like the Gilbert book had described, and in the four corners, in Cyrillic script, were the words *Fides, Lux Lucis, Caritas,* and *Aequitas.* Faith, Hope, Charity, Justice.

Lux lucis, I thought. *What an odd choice of words.*

The hope of *lux lucis* is entirely different from *spes,* the theological virtue of Hope. *Spes* is the desire for a future good, which the medieval Church believed was only possible to attain with the help of God. (However, I now know that *spes* also implies the hope for an eternal life, which glorifies God because, according to the Church, only through God is eternal life possible. Knowing that, Johann Malezel's decision to replace *spes* with *lux lucis* made even more sense.)

Lux lucis is an elucidation, a seeing eye, the light of day that shines upon something unknown. Such double entendres aren't rare in heretical works; the very nature of heretical works implies hidden meanings clear only to the initiated. But it seemed as if Brother Malezel hadn't been as clever as he'd believed, or maybe he just didn't care if the Church took notice.

Art, however, wasn't interested in any of this. When I asked him what he thought of Malezel's *lux lucis,* he merely shushed me and read aloud, in a harsh whisper, from the top of the first page:

"'I emit the hypothesis that arsenic acts as a catalyzer and the sulphur as a ferment in this transmutation.'"

Art turned to page 38. As the Gilbert book had noted, a small hole had been burned in the page, passing through to the next. Art put the jeweler's loupe in his eye and delicately brushed the hole with a gloved finger.

"You can still see traces of the wax, I think." He popped out the loupe and handed it to me. "Tell me what you see."

I didn't need the loupe. "It looks like a hole," I said.

"Yeah, but what kind of hole."

"I don't know," I said. "A small hole."

"I wish I knew the number and location of wormholes in the spine," Art said. "A wax burn you can fake, but bookworm trails are trickier. If the holes have smooth curves it can indicate a punch or drill of some kind. Of course, if you burr the edges it could pass off as legit but that takes some talent . . ."

At this point he was talking to himself. He wasn't even looking at me, just staring at the page, rambling on about forgeries and fakes and the Church planting false information in copies of heretical texts.

Art gently turned the page, then another, then he closed the book and patted the cover. He wrapped the book in long strips of white cloth, and when he finished he slipped it into his bag and pulled off his latex gloves.

"What are you doing?" I said.

"Borrowing what I need," he said.

"You mean stealing what you need."

Art shook his head emphatically. "I intend to return it when I'm done."

"Then why don't you just ask Brother Albo?"

Art buckled his bag shut. "They don't even read their books. They just store them away. This book isn't meant to be forgotten on some shelf in the dark corner of a monastery basement."

He quietly slipped off the stage and slung the bag over his shoulder. "You ready?"

I looked around the room. Albo wouldn't know his book had been taken. He wouldn't ever know—even years later, when their inventory is done, he would just assume it was lost in the fire. I recalled Albo's kind smile, and the bad wine he'd given me, and his delight at my lame little attempt at a Latin joke (*hoc opus, hic labor est*). I don't believe in a god—at least not a moral one who's concerned with our affairs—but I'm sure that stealing from monks is marked down somewhere in the cosmic registry.

Art, however, didn't look concerned at all. In fact, he looked the happiest I'd seen him since he'd walked into my basement apartment at the Paradise Motel. I looked at his bag, made a silent apology to whatever god may be listening, and followed him across the room, buttoning my coat and trying to push the image of Dr. Horatio J. Grimek's head out of my mind. *I know what you've done,* Horatio was saying. *Ask, and ye shall receive.*

We wandered back to the hotel, treading heavily through the rising stratum of snow, our path lit by streetlamps and the moon floating behind a scrim of clouds.

"We shouldn't have taken the book," I said.

Art adjusted the bag at his side. "I'll send an anonymous check," he said, irritated. "Stop worrying about it."

I kicked at a soot-blackened icy chunk that looked like it had fallen off the underside of a car. Art took out his pipe and began to pack the bowl.

"Don't you feel *any* remorse?" I said.

I thought maybe Art was going to start yelling at me, and I didn't care, but instead he stopped and struck a match, pulling on his pipe in long, soft drags. He exhaled, head back, gazing at the night sky. "I believe in necessity," he said. "If anything, I pity Albo Luschini. He had the key to unlocking the mysteries of the universe, and he never even knew it."

Aeneas, I thought. *Pitying Dido.*

The wind had returned and it whipped around us, shrieking across snow-covered cobblestones and careening off brick buildings, echoing over the valley and fading away into the mountains, breaking atop craggy peaks and icy pine, scattering about like dust.

Chapter 12

I worked through the night, seated at the desk with my schoolbooks laid out in a row. Working for Dr. Lang allowed me access to the faculty files, which meant I saw class syllabi before anyone else, and thus I had bought my books early and completed the semester assignments for two of my upcoming classes. I finished just as the first rays of sunlight crawled over the Gothic skyline of Nove Mesto, running over the pale, snow-frosted buildings and across the river in a cascade of fierce yellow light.

Art slept soundly, fully clothed, sprawled atop the blankets with a pillow over his face. He had started to translate the Malezel book, and he also drank a good deal, emptying five more mini-bottles, three of vodka and two of whiskey, their little plastic shapes scattered around the bed like miniature bowling pins.

I gazed out the window. Bathed in the light of dawn the cityscape appeared two-dimensional, a movie set cut from plywood and painted hues of gray, black, and ashen. I had been in Europe for almost two days, and yet I felt the same. I don't know what I had expected—a revelation, some instant change in my worldview, a dramatic shift in maturity. I turned on the TV and watched some French film with Czech subtitles. It was awful—a man running around town with a briefcase, getting shot at by men in suits, followed by car chases and secret documents and close-ups of ringing phones. I switched it off halfway through because the one attractive woman in the movie, a French prostitute, had just been stabbed and was dying in the protagonist's arms.

Perhaps I should have a drink, I thought. I scanned the bottles on the silver tray, found them all unappealing, and finally I settled on a weak mixture of gin and tonic, not enough gin to affect me, just enough to sour my mouth. After two sips I poured it down the drain.

I drew myself a bath and imagined I was some Roman emperor, watching the peach-colored walls sweat steam, running my hands along the smooth swirling marble pillars that surrounded the large oval tub, submerging myself up to my chin and pretending I was at Hierapolis. Maybe I'd catch a coliseum event later, something gruesome—Christian vs. lion, Anatolian vs. Jew. Battle of the criminals for the emperor's pardon; the marketplace pickpocket vs. the unethical businessman who fixes his scales. Tridents and netting and blood-soaked dirt scattered and thrashed under dusty sandals.

"Luscius," I said to the wall. "Fetch me the slave girls."

The faucet dripped in response. *Perhaps I should get a call girl,* I thought. We were in Eastern Europe, how much could it cost? Maybe I could get two women, give one to Art, or give him both in an even swap for Ellen. I laughed out loud. The funny thing is that Art was the kind of guy who just might have gone for such a deal.

Art has remained my first love—does that sound strange? I fell in love with him before Ellen, and the subsequent women in my life all had to live up to the specter of Arthur Fitch. As far as specters go he remains oblivious: long white coat, five o'clock shadow permanently tattooed across his face, mixing formulas and grinding herbs, hurrying from one flask to the other with ancient cookbook in hand.

My love for Art still remains inexplicable, because it ran deeper than friendship, the type of feelings I'd expect in a marriage of thirty or forty years, all compressed into that one year at Aberdeen. C. S. Lewis wrote that to tell the difference between love of a friendship kind and love of a romantic kind, one must decide whether one would rather spend exclusive time with the beloved, or time within the company of other friends. Friendship love, he said, desires a larger group. Romantic love, however, is jealous, and wants only the lover and the beloved, at the exclusion of everyone else. If this is the case—and I hold anything a Christian writer says as highly suspect—then I must have loved Art, in the Classical tradition of battlefield heroes and lusty emperors. And this is the paradox I've struggled with, which is exactly how Art would have wanted it.

In late November an old high school friend of Art's had come to visit—Charlie Cosman, a lanky, long-haired engineering graduate student at M.I.T.—and in celebration Art organized a *bal des ardents* in the deep forests surrounding Dr. Cade's land. We held it at midnight, attended by Ellen and some of her friends, along with Charlie, Howie, Dan, and myself, and we came dressed in costumes of straw and grass and shredded newspaper as per Art's instructions, masquerading as wild men and women, with twisted horns made of papier-mâché and long, flowing beards of burlap and string. Art had cleared a circle in the woods and lit the area with flaming tiki torches, which were supposed to provide an irresistible element of danger to the affair; in medieval times, torch sparks sometimes lit upon the costumed revelers, engulfing them in flames. When we all arrived at the torch circle and saw flames leaping and licking at the night air we all promptly left, all save Charlie and Art, who danced and hooted under a gibbous moon. *This stupid behavior,* Ellen had said to me on the way back, *from a man who won't touch doorknobs in restaurants because he's afraid he'll contract some terrible disease.*

He also was prone to sudden moods of a darker nature, however, remaining in his room for days on end, absent from Dr. Tindley's class, not joining us for dinner, not responding to Ellen's phone calls or Howie's drunken implorations. I had no experience with depression up to that point, so I simply saw Art's behavior as brooding and pensive, maybe even a little sophisticated. It's the way I envisioned Poe or Milton acting, the role of the genius-madman, cutting himself off from the world, the lone wolf. Christ in the desert. St. Daniel on his pillar. Art in his bedroom.

Art was rooted in both pragmatism and mysticism. A firm believer in the existence of ghosts and malevolent spirits, he scorned psychics and astrologers. Conspiracy theorists of any kind angered him, and he lumped them into the same category as religious conservatives, environmentalists, vegetarians, and peaceniks. He was the sworn enemy of Aberdeen's political activism club, confronting them at any opportunity—at their semipermanent booth set up inside Garringer Hall (across from the Campus Republicans table), and at their rallies in the Quad protesting America's trade embargo of certain Middle East nations (Howie often joined him, shouting *Long live Charles Martel!* during such events).

It quickly became clear to me that Art's zealous, almost fanatical quest for glimpses of the unknown were due in large part to Professor Cade's influence, coupled with Art's personal frustrations at his own limitations. He had claimed to follow Gurdjieff's teachings, but there was more to it. Art was a sliver short of brilliance—his temperament prevented the necessary emotional maturity inherent in all world-class minds—and I believe he knew this, and I believe it infuriated him, and in some ways, drove him to limits beyond what he was normally capable of achieving. We both possessed a strong, unyielding work ethic, but Art's sanguine ferocity allowed for little rest. Where I could close my books and be done with them, clearing my mind by taking a walk along the pond or playing fetch with Nilus in the backyard, Art was incapable of shutting down. Any problem required twenty-four-hour surveillance, throwing Art into the worst mood, followed by elation once the problem was solved. But this Roman candle–like burst of joy would quickly fade as soon as another problem presented itself. That's why I think alchemy suited Art perfectly. It was forever elusive, teasingly fruitful, flitting around on the edges of his vision and impossible to fully grasp.

I remember one dinner in particular, around the beginning of December, with only Art, Dr. Cade, and myself present. We had lost power from a blown transformer at the Fairwich central station, and we'd lit candles around the dining room. Dr. Cade, blue eyes shining in the candlelight, sipping a red Burgundy, spoke on his favorite topic: the limitations of intellect.

"I don't dispute how far we've come because of science and rational thought," he said, "but I caution those who hold up science as the only paragon of truth, in the same way I caution those religious zealots who blindly adhere to the beliefs of their various churches. Religion and science are, after all, slaves to man, and can only see as far as their tethers stretch."

Art was leaning back in his chair, hands resting in his lap, his gaze fixed upon Dr. Cade.

Dr. Cade sipped his wine again. "Agrippa spoke of the occult virtue," he said. "The inexplicable, inherently powerful elements affecting human existence. What did they reside in? Trees, stones, fire, and comets. The call of an animal and the rustle of wind through a thicket. Agrippa knew that human intellect and reason alone could not discern these potent qualities, that only experience and intuition could. His was a rejection of the notion of absolute truth. He believed that man could have complete and total understanding of the universe through faith and toil.

"But there were others, of course, who believed the path to ultimate truth led to direct knowledge of God, and in doing so, enabled one to achieve immortality. Do you remember Buridan and Oresme's argument, Arthur?"

"Temporal sufficient truth versus tentative useful truth," said Art. "Both mere vergings toward absolute truth."

Dr. Cade nodded. "The alchemists thought it possible to peer behind the universe's veil and glimpse knowledge of the eternal. What did the Philosopher's Stone represent but the highest wisdom, the final achievement of emotional and intellectual perfection. It was seen as a direct path to God. Transmutation of base metals into gold mirrored transformation of the alchemist."

"It was a shortcut," Art said. "Alchemy was the perfect marriage between the sacred and the profane."

"That's one interpretation." Dr. Cade twirled his glass by its stem. "Discover the Philosopher's Stone, and all the mysteries of the universe fall at your feet. Of course, in studying the Middle Ages one may be tempted to believe the many absurdities of that era, for they are presented with such sureness by the most celebrated minds of that age. Our modern empiricism can have a similar effect, making us cleave toward the unknown, like children begging their parents to tell them a ghost story. We crave mystery and secreted knowledge. It makes us feel special, and powerful."

"So you don't believe the Philosopher's Stone existed?" Art asked.

Dr. Cade smiled sympathetically. "I have chosen to view the

world rationally," he said. "And to my delight the world has presented itself as such. Everything else is faith, for which I have no use."

I submit this as a pardon for Art's later actions: He was a man of faith. For all his failings, he kept a hold on his faith longer than anyone I've ever known.

I got out of the bath, wrapped myself in the hotel bathrobe and walked softly into the living room. Daylight had streamed in, washing over the blue carpeting. Art was at the desk, steaming mug of coffee close at hand, the Malezel book laid out before him. A blanket was draped over his shoulders, and he was still in his clothes from the day before, minus one sock.

"We're taking the four o'clock flight," Art said, his back to me. "I extended our checkout until three."

"I thought we were going to do some sightseeing," I said.

"No time," he said. "The semester starts in a week. I have to get this translated by Wednesday at the latest."

He sipped his coffee. I noticed an empty mini-bottle of crème de menthe near the coffee cup.

I got dressed and Art remained absorbed in his work the entire time, even as I slipped on my coat and hat. He didn't look up until he heard me self-consciously rattle the room key.

"Going somewhere?" He turned, puzzled. Dark circles loomed beneath his eyes.

"I want to see the Hradcany," I said.

"But we have so much work." He looked down, at the book, and then at the key in my hand. "I need some translation help," he said. "I figured you could take over at some point, let me rest my brain . . ."

"You've been here before," I said. "I haven't, and I want—"

"Fine, fine. No speeches, please." He turned away. "If you see the concierge on your way out, have him send up breakfast. Three eggs, lightly scrambled, rye toast, large OJ. And tell him to water down the juice. My stomach doesn't feel so good, and I don't think the acidity will help."

. . .

I walked aimlessly for hours, buying a map from a vendor and heading toward the castle until I lost interest, and then I headed back down, toward the river. It was a brilliant day, painfully bright and cold, the sun magnifying off the sparkling snow that had settled overnight into a fine powder that blew off the rooftops in icy sprays. I kept my distance from the throngs of tourists and instead walked along the Vltava. Someone at school—Josh Briggs, maybe—had mentioned he was going to southern France for winter break. He had described it to me on a hot fall day, a day when I had dressed too warmly and found myself sweaty and uncomfortable in the back of French class, and the last thing I wanted to hear about were the beaches of Cannes: white sand, black bikinis, the ocean spread out in a warm, aquamarine haze, scraping softly against a footstep-pocked shoreline.

And now I had the Vltava, a black swath of water, crawling almost imperceptibly along, its surface like a sheet of obsidian. I kept hearing someone behind me—*Albo Luschini,* I thought, *with a gang of angry monks*—but every time I looked there was no one. A crow landed nearby, flapping and cawing, and I threw up my hands at its shadow. I thought about Ellen, and whether I'd ever see her again if she and Art were finished. What was the proper etiquette? Would she forever be off-limits, someone tainted by having dated my best friend?

I came upon a street fair, the buttery smell of fresh bread drawing me in, a pig rotating on a long spit over an iron trough filled with glowing embers. I was in a small town square, surrounded by steeply pitched alleys cutting between houses jostling for space like tall trees in a forest canopy. I looked into the faces of those who shouted at me to buy their wares or taste their food; I gazed directly into their eyes and continued past, trying to make myself invisible, just another anonymous tourist. They too were all anonymous, vendors with one-dollar goods strewn over folding tables, cooks working with fingerless gloves, swaddled in grease-laden steam rising from the sizzling pans. I finally stopped at a stand and bought sausage made from some sort of gray meat. It was salty and surprisingly good, tasting of fennel and mint, and then I bought a cup of hot chocolate and sat on the stoop of a church, eating in silence.

The food woke me up some, and I continued my walk, stopping at the edge of the street fair at a table covered with a tasseled, Arabesque rug draped over four poles like a tent. A cone of incense burned inside a dirty shot glass blackened with soot and smoke. An old woman sat alone on the other side of the table, facing the street, dressed in a tattered Boston Celtics jacket, with a brown and magenta skirt. A red paisley babushka covered her head, and before her, on the table, were a row of tarot cards. I smiled at her and she nodded in return, her expression unreadable. It could have been many things: fatigue, disinterest, or even a dreamy languor that only looked sad under the weight of decades marking her wrinkled face.

The tarot cards bore the mark of a popular American toy company, printed across their backs, and I noticed there was a Ouija board at her feet, bearing the same American toy company marks. She beckoned for me to sit, but I walked on. Having my future read with mass-produced divinatory tools was not something I wanted to pay for.

Fatigue seemed to be pulling me into the earth, coaxing me to sit for a moment and close my eyes. I thought if I rested I might freeze to death—maybe an irrational fear but maybe not. Who would wake me, suspecting I was just another American college student suffering from a night of excess, sleeping off his hangover in the threshold of some building?

I rarely drank coffee but decided it would give me the strength to return to the hotel, and so I ducked into the first café I saw, a small shop on the corner of Plaska and Ujezd. I sat at a table and ordered some Turkish blend. The coffee was stronger than I expected, smoky and sweet. I unzipped my coat and sank back into the chair, drinking in silence, watching customers pass in and out of the shop.

Thirty minutes later, bored and jittery from the caffeine, I asked the waitress if she knew where a pay phone was. She pointed toward the restroom and I followed, stopping in a narrow hallway with an old pay phone stuck against the wall. Someone had written on the wall in black marker, in English: *Nick and Tina were here.*

If I knew Ellen's number I would have dialed it. The memory of her voice wreaked havoc on my stomach. *Look at these hands,* she'd said, holding my hands on the tips of her fingers, palms up, as if reading my fortune. I remembered seeing the faintest of blond hairs lining the curve of her earlobe. *That was the night we made brownies,* I thought. *And the night of Howie's accident.*

I dialed the operator, reversed the charges to my number at school, and got through to the Aberdeen campus. Nicole's room. Her phone rang twice and then amazingly, someone answered.

"Nicole?"

"Yeah." She was chewing gum or something. "Who is this? *Eric?*"

She sounded closer than I imagined she would. There was a faint hum on the line, and music playing in the background.

"It's me," I said. "I'm in Prague."

"Hold on a sec," she put the phone down and I heard the music stop. "You're where? In *Prague?*"

"Yes." I leaned against the wall. Her voice was comforting. "I'm on a pay phone in some coffee shop."

"Shit, that is so cool," she laughed. "What are you doing there?"

"I'm on vacation with Art. We're"—I looked toward the picture window facing the street—"sightseeing. There's a castle near our hotel."

"Wow," she said. "Is it cold there? We got nailed with a huge storm—roads closed down and everything. They had to call in the fucking National Guard."

"What are you doing back so early?" I said.

She let out an exasperated huff. "I'm helping run orientation for spring semester transfers. We're doing all these stupid icebreaker events . . . it's pretty lame. I'm the only one here, me and the international students. They've served noodles almost *every* day for dinner. *Hey.*" She snapped her gum. "I saw your friend, what's-his-name, the big redhead."

"Howie?"

"Yeah. He was absolutely *smashed.* I saw him at the Cellar about three weeks ago."

Howie was at the Cellar often, and as a result, was known by most of Aberdeen's students. He was like one of those frat brothers, as Art described it, who keep partying at the frat house long after they've left school.

"He got into a fight with one of the bouncers," she said. "The cops came and everything. Your friend was shouting all this stuff, like how he was going to come back and buy the bar and give everyone free drinks all the time. You should've seen him—it was hysterical. The cops had to drag him out. We were all cracking up, really. He said he couldn't be hurt, that he's immortal, and he's all drunk and practically passing out even as he's screaming this garbage. Oh my God it was *so* funny." She giggled.

It couldn't have been Howie, I thought. And then I realized it was entirely possible he'd taken a detour during his New Orleans trip, and stopped at the Cellar for one last drink.

"So when are you coming back? Not that I ever see you anyway. After that one week when we saw each other every night . . ." She lapsed into silence. We both were thinking the same thing, I knew it. Sex on her carpet. Both of us stoned. It seemed like so long ago.

"Yeah, well, I'll come over when I get back," I said. I dropped my eyes as if she were standing in front of me.

"Don't worry about it," she said, suddenly flippant. *Good old Nicole.*

We said our goodbyes and I hung up and walked into the bathroom. I thought of Howie, the raging bull, the stink of alcohol on his breath, his red hair falling in a belligerent bang over his forehead. What had he possibly gotten into a fight over? An insult? A wrong look? Was he in jail? Had he hurt anyone? What would Dr. Cade think?

I paid for my coffee and left, raising my collar against the stiffening wind, and headed back to the hotel, back to the pit of obsession.

I got to the suite around 10 A.M., to find Art still seated at the desk, glasses way down on his nose, eyes heavy-lidded and red. He wore a robe, now, and white slippers with *Hotel Mustovich* embroidered across the top. The room was stiflingly hot.

"How was the castle," he said. His voice was raw with exhaustion.

"I didn't go," I said. I noticed a thermometer lying on the night-stand. "Are you sick?"

"I'm fine . . . tired, that's all. Jet lag probably catching up with me." Art smiled weakly. He looked bad. "I've made some progress," he said, nodding toward the book on his desk. "Not as much as I hoped. The going is slow."

He stood up, shuffled over to the bar, and cracked open a beer. "The Malezel book is remarkable. Like nothing I've ever read." He took a few gulps and rested on a stool. A slipper dangled off the edge of his foot. He looked at me unsteadily. "By the way, did you see the castle?"

"I already told you no," I said. I drew closer. His eyes were glassy. "Are you *sure* you're feeling okay?"

"I'm fine. Can't stop now, just a pause to collect my strength." He inhaled deeply and let his shoulders drop.

"I called Nicole," I said. "Remember her, the girl in my dorm?"

He feigned interest.

"She said Howie got into a fight at the Cellar," I said.

Art refocused on me. "Really."

I nodded. "The police were involved—"

Art shook his head.

"—and Nicole told me Howie was yelling something about being immortal."

Art drank the remainder of the beer. *Well,* is all he said. Then he got off the stool and walked back to the desk. Something fell out of his pocket, a little rolled plastic bag. I picked it up off the blue carpet.

"What is this?"

He looked back. "Belladonna leaves." His face was red, and I noticed his pupils were dilated. "They help me see things," he said slowly. "Gregory of Nyssa used it, even though the risk of poisoning is high. He understood the payoff is proportional to the risk. *Listen.*" He held up his hand. "Do you hear that?"

I thought it was someone playing music below our room, loud bass thumping through the floor. And then I discovered it was coming from Art. *Tha-dump, tha-dump.*

"My God," I said. "Is that your *heart?*"

He smiled blithely. "A symptom of belladonna poisoning."

I went to move away but he grabbed my arm. "Don't tell anyone," he said sharply. "I'll be fine. I know the dosage. It'll wear off in a few hours. Why don't you have a drink downstairs and come back up around three."

I looked at his hand wrapped around my arm. I pulled my arm away but Art held firm.

"Promise you won't say anything," he said. His black eyes were fixed upon me. And his heart, beating like marching doom.

"Promise."

"Okay, Art. I promise."

He dropped his hand and rubbed his eyes. "Look behind you," he said.

I turned quickly. The bar, the television cabinet, an empty beer can sitting on the marble countertop.

"Do you see anything?" he said.

"Like what?"

Art stared at the floor for a moment, and then turned back to the desk, Malezel's book lying open in front of him.

"I think you better get going," he said. "And please hang the *Do Not Disturb* sign outside the door."

◆ ◆ ◆

Two Bloody Marys later, sleep smothered me and I passed out in the lobby on a plush chair, my feet dangling off the side. I drifted in and out of consciousness, lulled by the quiet shuffle of people, the smoothly rolling wheels of their luggage, the din of their conversation. I heard some American businessman complaining about the size of his room, a youngish couple asking one of the bellhops if he knew of any sports bars that would show tonight's Knicks game, and the breathy voice of an Italian woman speaking with quiet vehemence to the concierge (I forced open my eyes, and only saw the rush of her raven-black hair, the swoop of her black greatcoat, and the daggerlike points of her heels clacking away briskly, toward the elevators).

I knew I looked terrible—hair messy, clothes wrinkled—but I was so tired I didn't care. Art, for all I knew, was in our room invoking the spirits of alchemy or whatever the hell they were. I simply wanted to go home. It was crazy that I'd come with him in the first place. He could have gotten to Prague by himself, stolen the Malezel book on his own, and had a nice leisurely stay for a few extra days without me to worry about. But that would have meant him being alone, and Art hated being alone.

Someone tapped on my shoulder. I expected it to be the concierge, asking me to please go back to my room. I ignored the tapping and fell slack.

"I know you're awake."

It was Art. I opened my eyes. He was fully dressed and shaven, and he had our bags waiting nearby in a luggage cart. He looked incredibly well rested, considering the condition I had seen him in earlier.

"It's time to go." He looked at his watch. "Our flight leaves in an hour."

I sat up and scratched my head. Men and women all around in suits and skirts. To my left, across the room, bar denizens talked to one another, lined up on stools, drinks in hand, the bartender rubbing the copper-top bar with a white shammy. To my right the entrance, rotating doors in constant motion, melting snow in white trails along the carpet, bellhops in their red jackets streaming in and out like bees from a hive.

"How come no one woke me up?" I said, tucking in my shirt and smoothing back my hair. I caught a glimpse of myself in the mirrors lining the far wall to my left. A young kid sitting in a big chair. That's it—no stubble shadowing my face, no puffiness under my eyes. No crinkled brown paper bag at my feet. I expected to see someone haggard, like a private investigator after an all-night bender at the local tavern, or a cardsharp after a night of high-stakes poker. It was a look I secretly envied—worn, dark, mysterious, aloof.

"Why would anyone wake you up?" Art said, smiling. "You look like someone's kid."

"But the bartender served me . . . I drank two Bloody Marys."

Art raised his eyebrows. "This is Europe, and we're paying five hundred a night for this place. You think they're going to say no?"

We took a cab to the airport. I was half-drunk and staring blankly out the window at the snowbanks, crowded streets, and clanking trams. The sun was a white smear behind a veil of scraggly clouds.

"What happened up there," I said. "After I left the room."

Art didn't respond for a few moments. Then, quietly: "I can't say. I saw . . . I don't know. Some of it, most of it, I'm sure, was the belladonna. Dark flickering on the edge of my vision, footsteps in the bathroom. Something knocked my beer can off the counter. And there was a smell."

I turned to look at him.

"Musty, like old wool. Like a wet dog. The way Nilus smells in the summer after a swim in the pond." He wouldn't look at me, staring forward instead. "There was something in our room. With me."

"A cleaning person," I said.

Art shook his head. "I read about this a while back but thought it was nonsense. Spirits and garbage like that. Do you know when Paracelsus discovered the secret to transmutation, it came to him in a vision? A beast carrying a golden vial in its mouth. He gave the beast a name—Berith. Said it was a large black dog. Jung called it an archetype for forbidden knowledge. The vial represents knowledge, held in the jaws of a dangerous beast."

"You don't really believe there was a giant black dog in our hotel suite," I said. The cab slowed as we approached the airport. "You said yourself that belladonna causes hallucinations."

Art shrugged and pulled out his pipe. He struck a match and pulled slowly, letting the smoke waft from his mouth and crawl up his face.

PART II

—

Aberdeen, Revisited

All things truly wicked start from an innocence.
—ERNEST HEMINGWAY

Chapter 1

I had been in Europe two days. During that time, we learned, the entire Eastern Seaboard had been hit with two ice storms as well as a blizzard that dumped more than three feet of snow in metro New York City. Now Connecticut was under siege by subzero winds, downed power lines, and bursting water pipes. The National Guard had been called into New Haven to clear two feet of snow and ice from the roads, and from Canaan to Middletown all travel was banned until further notice. Our bus ride from New York to Fairwich was slow and careful, taking us five hours, and the entire time I slept.

In Prague my eyes had been given a feast, and yet as the bus turned down Ash Street and into the village of Fairwich, rolling past Edna's Coffee Shop and the Sans Facon Tobacconist, past the Cellar and the Governor Lane intersection, I kept looking up, expecting to see graceful spires and towering steeples. But they weren't there, of course. Just the quaint simplicity of 19th-century red-brick storefronts, shoveled sidewalks, and small homes with clapboard shutters and tiny chimneys jutting from their roofs. The streets were quiet, dotted with snowed-in cars and knots of students back from break, their faces tanned and relaxed. I looked at myself in the reflection of the window. My eyes were sunken and wan and my hair was a matted tangle, pressed flat like a bad toupee.

Art and I waited for our taxi on the same bench I had sat upon my first day at Aberdeen. The sky was a brooding dark gray smothering the hills to the west, and snow skittered and shifted across the street, swept by the wind.

"It's nice to be back," Art said, narrowing his eyes against the cold. "I missed it here."

It was almost funny to hear him say that, especially with bitter wind whipping all around, but I felt the same way.

"I'll meet you back at the house," I said, just as the taxi pulled up to the curb. Art stood up and looked at me quizzically.

"I'm going to campus . . . I want to check my mail, maybe see if Nicole's around," I said. The truth was I needed some time away from Art. I think he felt the same because he simply nodded and got into the cab, and they drove away as I began my trek to school.

I'm not sure why I thought I could walk there—Aberdeen was a solid three miles from the Fairwich bus terminal, and the only way to school was via a long stretch of country road with a thin strip of shoulder on the right side and a snow-filled ditch on the other. I put my head down and counted my steps, tips of my shoes soaked with roadside slush, gravel pellets grinding beneath my soles. A jet roared faintly overhead, and I looked up to see the remnants of white exhaust trails in dissipating crisscrosses. I looked at the hills in the distance. *We had driven into those hills,* I thought, *Dan and I, months ago.*

I made it to campus just as the sky darkened into a sooty gray and snowflakes began to waft down like white ash. I headed toward Paderborne, where a few students stood on its steps, smoking and talking. One of them I recognized as Jacob Blum, a gangly New Yorker known for supplying very good weed. He had also supposedly slept with Nicole. Jacob nodded at me, flicked his cigarette away, and then launched into one of his diatribes about how amazing New York was during the holidays (he was one of those people who constantly remind you they're from New York, though I'd heard he actually lived on Long Island, in a quiet little suburb). I brushed by him and marched through the lobby.

The usual litter of flyers and brochures was missing from the corkboards. I went up the stairs (empty Styrofoam coffee cup sitting forlornly on the edge of a step, flattened cigarette butts, a few pennies) and stopped at Nicole's door. Complete silence. I knocked twice, waited, then knocked again. A radiator creaked and moaned. Fluorescent lights buzzed overhead, flickering at the end of the hall. I waited for another minute, and then walked down the hall to my room.

It was shockingly cold—I had left the window open a crack, and the white drapes fluttered weakly. Everything was frozen in stasis as if I'd never left: my unmade bed, an open notebook atop the dresser, an uncapped pen on the floor lying next to a balled-up sock. It reminded me of a story in the *Unexplained Creatures, Beasts, and Phenomena* book: the tale of the ghost ship *Mary Celeste* found sailing aimlessly in the Atlantic, with no one aboard, meals prepared and left uneaten on tables. The crew had disappeared without a trace, leaving everything behind.

I went to Campus Bean and found it busier than expected, as students talked about their holidays and their vacations and what their upcoming class schedules were like. I wanted to tell someone about my trip but realized there was too much to say, and none of it was believable. What had *I* done? I'd taken a train ride from Paris to Prague, found a room full of preserved body parts, helped Art steal an ancient manuscript from Benedictine monks, and then I drank and passed out in the lobby of a five-star hotel while Art took belladonna and hallucinated about a giant black dog roaming around our suite.

Great stuff. *Wish you were here.*

I sat in the corner and drank hot chocolate and read the *Quill*, a literary magazine published by the English honors students. I thumbed through it, became bored, and sat back and wondered what I was going to do for the next few hours. I still didn't feel like going to the house. *Maybe I should take a cab back into town and do some window-shopping,* I thought. Fiddle around in an antique store, or go to Edna's and see if anyone still recognized me.

And then I looked up and saw her: Ellen. She was stepping away from the cash register. The boy who just took her money watched her walk away, transfixed (*yes, I know,* I thought), and with a panicky mixture of terror and painful longing I realized she was smiling and coming toward me. I wanted to leave, maybe even bolt out the back door.

"What are *you* doing here?" she said, stopping at my table. I felt as if I hadn't seen her in years. She looked exquisite—a shorter haircut, colored a darker shade of honey, with a sky-blue turtleneck that curled up and under her chin. She wore slim black pants and a long navy wool coat, with a small red handbag clutched in a black-gloved hand. I was at once reminded of why I loved her: the reservedness of her beauty. It demanded your attention, but showed itself in glimmers and flashes. Ellen revealed one delicate piece at a time, and let you put them together yourself.

She had a cup of coffee in her other hand, red stirrer jutting out. "I thought you were in Prague, with Art," she said, peeling the top of the cup off. Steam plumed. "Did you end up going?"

I motioned for her to sit. I was still stunned by her appearance. "Yeah . . ." I said, without much conviction. "He came to get me and then we flew the next day."

"I suppose he told you about our argument." She sat down and didn't sound at all upset, maybe a little embarrassed but not angry like I expected. "We don't travel well together. After our argument in London he told me he was going home to get you. I told him I thought it was a terrific idea." She forced a smile. "But enough about that. Tell me what you thought of Europe."

I gave her the usual—birthplace of history, the wine, the food, the architecture.

"And how was Prague?" she asked. "Did you see the Hradcany?"

"No," I said. "I almost got my fortune read. Tarot cards." It was the most glamorous thing I could think to tell her.

She sipped her coffee. "*Ooh.* Sounds exciting. What else did you do?"

I shrugged. "That's it." I didn't know if Art had told her about the Malezel book.

She pulled back. "That's it? No tours? Did you at least go to *Reduta?*"

"We stayed at the hotel, mostly," I said. "We were really only there for a day."

She narrowed her eyes. "How strange. Art usually likes to explore." She looked down at the table. Her lips were parted slightly. "Did Art conduct any business while you two were in Prague?"

I paused. A brief mental skirmish between loyalties, and then: "No."

"He didn't mention anything about a book?"

"No."

"Am I making you uncomfortable?" Ellen asked gently. She pushed her hair behind her ears.

"I'm okay," I said.

"Sure. Sure you are," she smiled, not unkindly, and sipped her coffee again. "And you're Art's friend. I understand."

She glanced at her sweater, picking something off it. "I know he was going to buy a book," she said flatly. Her eyes met mine. "It has something to do with his alchemy project. He wouldn't give me any specifics but I know he's spending a lot of money on it. I don't care, really. I just wish he wasn't so secretive about the whole thing."

She sighed. "He called *me*, you know, from London. He told me how sick George was, and how he's bored and tired of walking around the city by himself, and could I please come early. And so I did. I love London. Art took me to Mantra, that new Chef Burke place." She stopped, aware that such references were entirely lost on me. "Anyway, over dinner he started talking about the Philosopher's Stone, and immortality, and the usual. You know how he gets when he's obsessing about something."

I did. Very well.

"And then he tells me he's going to test the formula on himself one of these days, because that's the only way he'll know for sure. Now, cats I can understand, but humans are an entirely different story."

Ellen half-covered her mouth. "You don't know, do you?"

"He already told me about the cats," I said.

"And you're okay with it? It doesn't freak you out?"

"It did," I said. "But then I figured Dr. Cade must know, and if it's okay with him . . ."

"Professor Cade?" She shook her head. "If he knew he'd send Art to a psychiatrist."

Ellen stirred her coffee. "So are you involved in it now?"

"No," I said. I was too embarrassed to admit otherwise. "I don't believe any of it."

Ellen didn't seem to have heard me. "I should've known," she said. "I told him over dinner that I thought this entire alchemy thing was a waste of time. And I'm not the only person who thinks so—Howie's come to his senses and wants nothing to do with it. The only reason he got involved in the first place was because he needed something to keep his mind occupied. You know how much Howie drinks, but you probably don't know why."

"Alcoholism comes to mind," I said.

Ellen smiled. "Sure there's that . . . But he also drinks because there's nothing else for him to do. Look at the poor guy—he's a city mouse stuck in the country. And as for Dan . . . he just follows whatever Art says." She said this with a hint of reproach. "I think there's more than just a friendly attraction there. You want to know the truth?"

"I don't know," I said.

She laughed, throat pulsing, her eyes glistening. Razor-edged beauty drawing blood with a quick slice. *I honestly would not mind,* I thought darkly, *if Art died in a car crash.*

"This stays between us." She leaned in and lowered her voice. "Not that I care in the least what a person's sexuality is, but I think Dan might be . . . confused. You know?"

I nodded.

"Art's a flirt," Ellen said. "Men, women, he doesn't discriminate, as long as the attention remains focused on *him*. If Dan had any propensities in that direction to begin with, I'm sure some of the strange things . . ."

She faded off. "Some of it's silly," she said, sipping her coffee. "Hanging out in the woods behind Dr. Cade's house, the three of them carrying candles and chanting. Alchemy is mixed up with the occult—why do you think the Church eventually banned it? Magic circles and spirit-summoning and, sometimes, even human sacrifice." When she saw my look of horror she immediately put her hand on mine. "Art's not crazy. *Please.* He's more into the academic approach.

Do you know he and Dan took cuneiform last semester so they could perform some sort of Babylonian rite on Halloween?"

"I remember that," I said. "They told me they were all going to a costume party."

"Consider yourself lucky you didn't go," said Ellen. "Most thaumaturgic rites are sexual in nature. I wrote a paper my freshman year," she smiled, "about the homosexual undertones of orgiastic religious observance. Semen as the main ingredient in any kind of spiritual passage and so on . . ."

"I had no idea," I said. "I didn't think Art or Howie was into—"

"Oh, they're not *gay*," she said sternly. "Not at all. In fact, Howie's a genuine homophobe. And Art's a typical medievalist, terrified of women. When I say 'sexual,' I mean nothing more than a circle jerk into a cup. But I'm sure Dan didn't mind."

The images were all very sordid, and very unsettling. My housemates had previously aligned themselves into simple categories: the smart one, the drunk one, the young one. *What next*, I thought. *Dr. Cade keeps a harem of chained virgins in the basement?*

The crowd at Campus Bean had thinned out and a few students remained, scattered about the room, sitting at the small round tables, hunched over their books.

"And then there's you," Ellen said playfully, crossing her legs. "Art's always thought you were a bit of a puzzle. The orphan-genius. Quiet and brooding, sitting in his bedroom all day and night like a little monk. That's how he described you, you know. We all thought you were putting us on. *The poor kid from the projects*. Howie suspected you were a pathological liar."

"Why would I make up a past I'm embarrassed of?" I said. "If anything I would've concocted some story about, I don't know . . . my dad winning the Nobel Prize in physics."

"That's just it—you think your past is so terrible." Ellen narrowed her eyes. "Do you know how *envious* Howie and Art are of you? It's true. They like to think of themselves as survivors, the ascetic ideal and everything. Art still clings to this bizarre notion that the proletariat are somehow more noble than the rest of us. It's very Christian of him. Though he'd go crazy if I ever said that to his face. And

Howie—he portrays his dad as some turn-of-the-century robber baron. *Right.* His dad fell into the family money. Their money is as old as it comes. We're the nouveaux riches, my family and I. But you don't have a history, really. You're making it up as you go along."

Ellen glanced into her coffee cup and pushed it away. My mind raced as I tried to organize everything she'd just told me. Everything she'd revealed had been followed by a quiet voice of recognition in my mind: *Ah, yes.* I guess I should have been disturbed by what she'd said, but I still saw it all—the alchemy, the experiments—as nothing more than a formidable intellectual puzzle Art wanted desperately to solve. And he wanted to solve it not because he believed it—how could he?—but *because* it was so daunting, *because* its answers had eluded so many for so long. Sure it was all very strange but how was any of it more surreal (or unreal) than my life had been thus far?

"I forgot how we got on this topic," Ellen said, reaching into her handbag. She pulled out a tube of lipstick and dabbed her lips.

"Your argument with Art," I said.

"I wouldn't call it an *argument.*" She clicked her purse shut. "I just finally told him I thought this alchemy business had gone too far, and he got angry, and I stayed in London and he came back and got you."

"Art's a very intense person," she continued, smiling. "He goes through these phases sometimes. It gives him an outlet for all the stuff running around in his brain. He's really quite brilliant, you know. He always needs something to work on."

Ellen looked at her watch and then started to button her coat.

"Would you like to come over for some dinner?" she said, her tone indicating she didn't care one way or the other. "I can't promise a full-course meal like Dr. Cade, but there's this terrific Chinese place a block down from my apartment."

"I'd like that," I said, and then I tried to convince myself that I was really only interested in dinner.

I rode in Ellen's car for the first time, an old Saab, British racing green with a faded tan interior. Masculine looks but somehow fitting, smelling of lotion and perfume, very clean and mature, a grown-up car. A spiral notebook lay on the backseat, a balled-up piece of paper stuck out from the ashtray. Ellen apologized for the mess.

Her apartment was the top floor of a three-story Victorian home on Posey Street, a small, one-way lane on the eastern tip of Fairwich. East Fairwich was strictly residential, and wealthy, from what I understood; it was where the college president lived, along with several professors and the mayor of Fairwich. Ellen's landlord was a retired Aberdeen art professor, some famous painter who had supposedly donated his salary every year to the Connecticut Fine Arts Museum and made a fortune selling oil paintings. He let her live there for reduced rent on the condition that she was to help tend his garden. For two years she'd been there, and had never once seen his garden (the backyard was a heavily treed plot), and had only seen him four or five times.

I expected a modern décor—sparse, expensive furniture, some artwork, maybe a rug with funky geometric designs. I was right about everything except the rug. Her hardwood floor gleamed under small track lights ("I just got it polished last month," she said), and true to form, she had a few modern pieces hanging on the walls: Lichtenstein and Gauguin, a small Dali. She had a portrait of herself above the fireplace, an abstract painting with severe lines and slashes, but the artist had pared down her features perfectly—two strokes for her jaw, an elongated comma for her nose. Translucent hair cascading down her neck like a silken waterfall. A wet shade of green filled her almond-shaped eyes, the brightest and richest color in the entire painting.

"That's very good," I said, staring up at it. Ellen threw her coat over the back of her couch.

"Howie did it," she said. "Last year."

I looked at her. "Howie did this?"

She nodded. "That's what I said."

"That's cool," I said.

Ellen eyed me warily.

"Is there something you'd like to ask me?" she said.

"Not at all," I said. Actually, I wanted to ask her why Howie had painted her portrait. And whether Art knew. But of course I said nothing, and I looked around the rest of her apartment. The living room led into a small galley kitchen, with a hallway beyond that.

Ellen walked into the kitchen. "Would you care for something to drink?" she said. "I have some Chardonnay . . ." She opened the refrigerator. "Orange juice, cranberry juice, soda water . . ."

I told her some tap water would be fine, and instead she opened a bottle of spring water and poured me a glass, her shoes clicking across the floor as she handed it to me. *Just a minute,* she said, and she disappeared into the hallway while I sat on the couch, all the way to one side, sipping my water and gazing around the room. My watch read 4:30. I tapped out some random song on my knee. I set my glass down on the coffee table and inspected an old scab on my wrist. A magazine sat on the table, some French fashion publication, with a pouty model on the cover wearing thin strips of clothing around her waist and breasts.

Ellen walked into the living room, barefoot, wearing jeans and a loose cable-knit sweater, and holding a glass of wine. She sat across from me, in a sand-colored leather chair. Her bare feet gleamed white and soft, thin ankles, bluish veins snaking over bone.

"I had to get out of my work clothes . . . I only worked a half shift today," she said, tousling her hair with one hand. "You know, I've never seen you at Campus Bean before."

"I don't spend much time there," I said.

"Yeah, the coffee isn't so good." She sounded as if that was the reason I didn't go. "But it's a nice change of place—every other coffeehouse in town usually has someone I work with, and outside the office I want *nothing* to do with bankers. They're worse than academics, if you can believe it. Lecherous, uptight middle-aged men. You wouldn't believe how they ogle me." She shuddered.

Oh yes I would, I thought.

"Tell me more about where you grew up," Ellen said, drawing in her legs and tucking them under her body. She sipped her wine, cradling the glass in her hands, stroking the stem, staring at me. "Not that nasty city place, but your childhood. Where was it? Somewhere out West?"

"West Falls, Minnesota," I said, and launched into my little tale.

◆ ◆ ◆

We ended up ordering from Han's Kitchen and sitting across from each other on the floor, my back against the couch, hers against the chair, eating pork fried rice and moo goo gai pan straight from their little white boxes. We finished the bottle of Chardonnay and Ellen made martinis, but I found the taste unbearable and mine remained twice-sipped, sitting on the coffee table while Ellen poured herself a second.

She was fantastic company, a wonderful conversationalist, an impressive scholar in her own right, telling me about French literature, modern art, and her favorite topic: old movies, specifically from the '30s and '40s, the type of films I've always associated with beautiful women with sleepy eyes, men in fedoras, and the bad guys holding their guns at waist level. Ellen loved photography and sculptures, and after a few requests she got her portfolio from her room and showed me the photos. They were stunning black and whites, pictures of snowy trees at dusk, a lone dog skulking around the corner of a concrete building, an old woman resting on a bench. There was even a picture of Howie, lying in his bed, asleep, mouth half-open, pillow on his chest. Ellen quickly turned the page, like she'd forgotten that photo was in there.

She told me about her cousin Lucinda, a famous photographer who had apprenticed under Helen Levitt and whose work was seen regularly in *Le Monde*. Lucinda killed herself, Ellen told me, an overdose of Percodan, and she had taken a final photo of herself, lying on the hardwood floor of her Greenwich Village apartment, mouth open, eyes fading, arm looming toward the lens as its hand prepared for that final *click*. Ellen said she had the photo in a shoebox in her closet, but she hadn't looked at it in years because it gave her nightmares.

"This is Lawrence, my father," said Ellen, pointing to a picture of a tall, handsome man standing shirtless on a beach, the distant outlines of waterfront homes all along the shore. "Five years ago at our house in San Francisco." Her father looked like the successful hand surgeon he was: self-confident, relaxed, a light tan, and a thick head of black hair. Her mother, Rebecca, was in the next photo, and for a brief moment I thought it was Ellen, until I noticed the wrinkles and the darker hair. Her mom was a beauty, regal in the way she smiled at the camera, completely at ease with having her photo taken. Ellen had her mother's mouth and eyes, but her mother had a high forehead, giving her the look of some European model.

"Your mom is beautiful," I said.

Ellen laughed. "She is beautiful, and she lets you know it. *Miss Tennessee.*" Ellen said it with a heavy Southern accent, and laughed again. "She still has the ribbon hanging in her closet."

We were kneeling side by side, portfolio opened in front of us, Chinese-food boxes scattered about. Ellen had her head cocked to one side in the most astounding way—for a second she was a sculpture in profile, frozen, every line and curve of her face deepened and enhanced. The upward tilt of her lips, the dip and swell of her chin. And her hair, as before, as it always was, fine silk, smooth strands, brushing against her ears, curling behind, tumbling down her neck. I felt powerful and daring, a confident sleepiness to my actions and thoughts. I swallowed hard and took a long, deep breath.

And I kissed her. I balanced her chin on the tips of my fingers and I turned her lips to mine and I kissed them.

She pulled away gently and stared at me. Her mouth had been unresponsive. My hand trailed down to her black sweater, thick cotton soft against my skin.

"What was that?" she said. Her breath smelled of sweet wine.

I drew in again but she pulled away.

"Do you know what you're doing?" she said.

I was speechless. I cannot describe adequately the scope of my longing for her, only that it was so overwhelming I felt as if it could snap my mind in two.

"I love you," I confessed.

"No, you don't," said Ellen. She smiled sympathetically.

It was not the response I had expected. Maybe a laugh, or a flattered smile, or even, in my most disconnected fantasies, a passionate embrace. But not refusal. It broke my trance, and I stood up.

"I think I should go," I said.

Ellen laughed. Her laughter was many things at that moment, some real, others imagined: cruel, amused, pitying. "My goodness, relax," she said, leaning back against the chair. "You haven't even finished your fried rice." She peered into the box and fished around in it with her chopsticks.

I spotted my coat, on the rack, and rushed over to it. "It's late," I said. "And I'm totally humiliated."

"It's not a big deal, Eric. Come on . . . Look, if you're not going to stay, let me at least give you a ride home." She made to get up but I turned to her and fumbled my house keys, dropping them on the hardwood floor.

"Just don't do *anything*," I said, harsher than I would have liked. I thrust my keys into my pants pocket and yanked open the front door, and I looked back, in some desperate attempt to convince myself that she'd been right, that I didn't love her, that in fact, maybe I'd hated her for what she'd done to Art, and for what she'd done to me.

She was standing there, in the living room, barefoot, arms crossed, her head cocked to one side. A lock of hair had fallen across her forehead. Her green eyes studied me. Her jeans were set low on her hips and her sweater was bunched up at the bottom, revealing a glimpse of white skin and the half circle of her navel.

"I'm sorry," I said, and then I hurried out and slammed the door.

Chapter 2

I took a cab back to the house, and I almost flew into a panic as the taxi pulled into Dr. Cade's driveway. I was suddenly convinced Art would be able to smell Ellen on my hands, and that he'd beat me senseless or, worse, maybe reveal my betrayal to Professor Cade, who would then banish me from the house, and send me back to my dorm room. My emotions ranged from self-loathing to ecstasy, pitching and rolling like a ship in a storm. I had lost self-control; that was harder to accept than anything.

It was a calm evening, no wind, little sound, everything muted in a blanket of snow and ice and cold. The living room light was on, and I saw Dan walking in from the dining room. I stopped at the front door, steeled myself, and walked in.

The house was as if I'd never left—same comforting smell of polished wood and the charred, piney scent of the fireplace. Everything was spotless, the dining room table was buffed to a glow. A colossal bouquet of flowers was centered upon it (courtesy of Thomas, as I later found out), and an unopened crate of wine sat against the dining room wall (also courtesy of Thomas). Nilus loped over and snuffled my hand and bumped up against my leg. *He smells her*, I thought. *Art's got him trained, like those airport dogs.*

Dan turned to me, smiled, and held his arms out in a grand gesture.

"Hey, hey," he said, giving me a quick hug. His brown hair was a bit longer, but still parted on the left. He withdrew into the same old Dan—hands in pockets, head down thoughtfully. "Art told me he found you living like a Franciscan in the basement of the Paradise, wrapped in blankets and speaking in tongues," he said.

Dan told me about Boston, about the snow they had, long, lazy days of boredom, shopping with his cousins on Newbury Street, hiking through the Arboretum, hanging out at the Harvard library and browsing through old atlases. He had spoken with Howie once—a drunken call at two in the morning on a Wednesday, Howie slurring on the other end, loud blues blaring in the background, something about a girl who wanted Dan to fly down and go to bed with her.

Art walked into the foyer, yawning, wearing plaid flannel pajamas. He scratched Nilus behind the ears. "Nicole called," he said. His glasses sat low on his nose. "She said she'll be home after nine. Where did you head off to?"

I thought of a dozen lies.

"Dr. Lang's," I said, finally. "I had to pick up a paycheck and work out my schedule for the semester."

Art was already not paying attention, looking down at his hands, turning them over. *Ellen called,* I thought. *She thought the whole episode funny and wanted to share the experience with Art.*

"You going to bed?" Art asked me. The memory of Ellen shrieked away.

"It's only eight," I said.

"Oh." He scratched his head and smiled sheepishly. "Feels much later. Jet lag, you know." He sighed and grabbed the stair railing, and then walked upstairs, his pace plodding and slow as if he were shackled.

Dan and I lit a fire and played backgammon. At around ten it started to snow hard. Dan told me Dr. Cade had left Art a mountain of work: translations and expanded chapter outlines, along with the more Byzantine assignment of gathering information on Dr. Linwood Thayers's project. Art had posed as some academic journal reporter and called Dr. Thayers's Stanford office. His secretary (*Which journal is this for? The Plume? That must be new . . . Who did you say you were again?*) knew nothing, and suggested Art call Dr. Thayers's publicist.

We talked about Prague, and Art's experiments. The belladonna, and his visions of the black dog and the knocked-over beer can.

"Don't you think it's dangerous?" I said, rolling my dice. "The belladonna could've easily killed him."

Dan shook his head. "Art knows what he's doing."

"What about that one night, when you passed out in the garden," I said.

Dan frowned. "Didn't we already talk about that?"

"Yeah, but—"

"It was a mistake," Dan said. "It's all a part of the process."

"So you're not into this alchemy thing for the fun of it," I said.

Dan looked at me with mild disgust. "Not at all."

"And you believe it. Immortality and everything. You believe that if you died you could come back."

"I don't *dis*believe it."

The fire crackled and a flaming log split in half, a rush of sparks spurting out.

"So why haven't we seen any proof yet?" I said. "If this knowledge has been floating around for centuries, where are all these immortals?"

"How about Cornelius?" Dan said. "Art told me he's two hundred years old."

"Cornelius is senile," I said, though I didn't fully believe that.

Dan didn't look convinced either. "It is a fantastic notion," he said. "I'll grant you that much. But it's not entirely outside the realm of possibility. Why are you so reluctant to at least admit the possibility?"

"Because it's common *sense*," I said. I was accustomed to Art's fantasies, I was even taken in by them occasionally, but hearing the same lines from Dan didn't sound right. He was too logical, too even-keeled. And yet . . . I thought of the rituals that Ellen had told me about, and envisioned Dan in a black robe, hood drawn over his head, masturbating into a golden chalice.

"Would you want to live forever?" I asked Dan.

He thought for a while, watching the fire, turning his glass in his hand.

"Not forever," he said. Shadows played across his face. "I'd get tired of seeing everyone I care for die."

"You could give them the potion, too," I said. "Buy a big house somewhere and watch the centuries roll by."

"Or I could be a college student for the next hundred years," he said. "Get degrees in every field."

"Molecular biology."

"Engine repair."

We sat around for another few hours, talking about how we'd spend our lives if we had a thousand years to live: amassing wealth and power, buying clifftop mansions and two-hundred-foot yachts, summer expeditions hacking through the rain forests of Madagascar and winters spent climbing the Karakorum mountains. To fill the centuries we'd learn every existing language, like Sumatran Lubu and the Aztec Nahuatl. Given enough time, Dan said, we could master every musical instrument, or write the great American novel ten times over. Or we could do nothing and fritter away the centuries like divine flaneurs. With a millennium of time the accumulation of knowledge would be staggering. We would be gods, Dan said, and we laughed.

Two gin and tonics later the snow had stopped, and through the picture window of Dr. Cade's living room his front yard looked like a black-and-white photo. A rising and falling line of trees, the low field-stone wall cutting us off from the road. Nothing moved—no wind, no swaying branches, no sifting, shifting snow.

◆ ◆ ◆

I awoke early the next morning to take Nilus for a walk, but the air was so cold it froze my nostrils shut, and Nilus was able to last only ten minutes before ice built up between his toes and I had to bring him back inside. I then sat in the kitchen and ate breakfast while Nilus slopped and slavered over his bowl that I'd filled.

Howie was supposed to be coming home either that Thursday night or Friday, followed by Dr. Cade that weekend. School started Monday, and I dreaded the upcoming semester. My class load was heavy—six courses, including an additional hour-long symposium for my History of Slavic Peoples class—and Dr. Lang wanted me to pick up an additional shift, since his grad assistant had taken a leave of absence for the remainder of the year. Before vacation, Cornelius hadn't said much to me about returning to the library, so I planned to simply not show up for work, hoping he'd forget or just not care. As it was, the work-study agreement had been for one semester only, with a reassessment at the end, and I was certain that Professor Lang could arrange something on my behalf, perhaps shift my obligations to his office.

I went back to my room and started my translations, monastic writings from the 11th and 12th centuries, some prescribing reform while others spoke of darker things, militaristic musings of monks as soldiers of Christ waging war against the Devil and his minions. There were miracles, too, extraordinary phenomena attesting to the power of various saints.

A MIRACLE OF ST. RIPALTA

(S. Ripalta. Vita Prima. Lib. IX [ex. exordio magno Cisterc], cap, VII)

We happened upon the village of Amien and thereupon our arrival saw many ill and suffering, and the abbot did approach us seeking assistance in removing the bodies from the chapel of St. Georgius. They were all his monks [and had served him loyally and without complaint] and he had prayed for their salvation but death still came. "Surely this is the work of the Devil" said the abbot, and we agreed, being men of God we had seen the Devil's work before, [wrapped within] the cloak of disease. "Show me where the people are baptized" I said and the abbot led us to a small river above which stood the monastery, thereupon which I sat upon its bank and wept to the Lord. His guidance did come to me in the form of St. Ripalta, and I instructed for the bodies to be brought to the river and placed under its waters, and upon doing so there was a gathering of clouds and the river ran red, and we all fell to our knees and praised the Lord, for the dead monks were now living, clothed in white raiment and giving thanks for what we had done.

I skipped dinner and worked straight through until 8 P.M., and then came downstairs to a suprisingly empty house. Art's car was gone, a rectangular outline in the snow where it had been. His boots were gone from the front hall, along with Dan's.

I wandered into the kitchen, opened the door leading to the back, and looked out over the pond. Frigid air rushed in and stung my face. A quarter moon reflected off the water, its white horns wavering gently upon the surface, skeletal trees looming all along the shore. The night sky spread above in milky darkness, swirling with stars, vertiginous and infinite. It's a sky I've dreamt of many times, since then.

◆ ◆ ◆

At around three in the morning I was awakened by Art sitting on my bed. I imagined any variety of reasons—another suspicious birthmark or freckle that he wanted me to inspect, perhaps a splotchy rash on his arm indicating scarlet fever—but when I felt his hand grab my shoulder and shake firmly, I thought of the only reason it could be: Ellen had told.

He said my name, but I kept my eyes closed. Another shake, this one so hard I couldn't possibly pretend I was still asleep. I steeled myself and opened my eyes. I had prepared for this, somewhat.

I rolled onto my back. The room was dark, Art a jet-black figure sitting on the edge of my bed.

"Something's happened," Art said. His breathing was heavy and quick. "You have to come downstairs."

The radiator in my room clanked and hissed. "It's late," I said. "We can do this tomorrow morning."

"This can't wait until tomorrow."

"Come on, Art. It's almost three—"

"We tried the formula."

It took me a moment to understand what he was talking about.

Art stood and clicked on my lamp. One look at his expression and I scurried out of bed, pulled on my sweatpants, and followed him downstairs.

I'm reluctant to recount the first few minutes after I followed Art downstairs and saw Dan's body lying on the foyer floor. I no longer believe that traumatic experiences are indelibly burned into our minds, and what I do remember of that night may contain unconscious mental elaboration, but I am certain of at least one image: Dan lying on his back, head rolled to the side, arms and legs splayed out like a child making angels in the snow. Drying spittle on his face and white froth at the corners of his mouth. Dead eyes, pupils like two pools of spilt ink. A fleck of dirt perched on the tip of an eyelash. The point of his tongue sticking straight out.

I remember grabbing his wrist and searching for a pulse, and then thrusting two fingers under his jaw and not feeling anything there, either. And then I did something I'd seen on TV—on those frantic medical dramas where handsome young doctors are forever running alongside blood-soaked gurneys. I got a flashlight from the kitchen drawer and shone it directly into Dan's eyes—his pupils didn't change. I slapped his face and shook him by the shoulders and said his name. *Dan . . . Dan . . .*

Cold foyer, Art in a red cable-knit sweater, stubble darkening into the beginnings of a beard. Knees drawn to my chest, sleep crumbling from my eyes. Nilus underneath the dining room table, watching.

What happened, I said, and I said it again and again, and I don't even know when I stopped saying it, or if I've just been asking different people the same question since that night.

I soon found myself seated at the breakfast nook, in the dark, the kitchen lit only by the moon and the night-light over the sink. Art sat across from me, talking, explaining. He talked about dosages gone awry, a miscalculation of Malezel's procedures, errors in translation, impure ingredients, and Dan drinking the formula despite Art's warnings. They had waited in the living room, sitting across from each other on the couches, tense and silent, and after an hour Dan stood up and said he felt nothing. Nothing at all, he insisted, and then he mumbled incoherently and dropped to his knees. Convulsions and foaming at the mouth followed. He collapsed onto his back, unconscious, and his heartbeat faded even as Art listened, head pressed tightly to Dan's chest, counting the beats, hearing them slow from stuttering uneven flutters, then to weak slaps, and finally to nothing.

Art stopped and got himself a bottle of scotch from one of the cabinets. He collapsed onto the bench, uncapped the bottle, and guzzled, dark liquid trickling down his chin.

"We have to do something," he said.

There was nothing I wanted to do. I was numb, but I knew panic was coming. I could see its dark shape far away, on a shadowy ridge, and it began its journey while I watched. A beast bounding through bog and field, Grendel coming to eat Hrothgar's men.

I stood up and turned to the swinging door.

"What are you doing?"

"Maybe he's alive," I said. "We can't say for certain—did we check to see if he's breathing? He might be in a coma. I saw a show once, this guy accidentally ate a poisonous fish and everyone thought he died but—"

"There's no pulse," Art said. He took another swig of the scotch. "I kept my head to his chest for a long time."

Something scratched at the swinging door.

I jerked back and banged into the corner of the breakfast table. Art clutched the bottle of scotch to his chest. Our eyes met for a brief, terrible moment. Some passage—a translation of a battlefield account, the war at Cortenuova, I remembered, insanely—sprung to mind. *They arose, still, though bloody and battered, arose with arms outstretched and cursed us while we stood silently and watched.*

Another scratch, and the door swung in feebly and swung back.

A snout lodged itself between door and jamb. I pulled gently and Nilus scrambled in, tail wagging, ears pinned back. A horrible glimpse of Dan's body lying in the foyer—pale face, open eyes, rumpled clothes.

"I can't go back in there," I said. "We have to call someone."

"Who?"

"I don't know. The police. The paramedics . . ."

"Wait, wait. Just *hold on* a sec." Art exhaled and ran both his hands through his hair. "Nilus, *sit.* I can't concentrate with that goddamn dog running around."

Nilus skulked away to the back stairwell and curled himself up against the bottom step.

"Okay." Art pushed away the bottle of scotch. "We call the cops. Then what."

"You tell them what happened."

"I tell them he drank poison, convulsed, and collapsed, and— they'll love this—I waited an *hour* before calling for help. Wait, make that," Art glanced at the stove clock, "an hour and a half."

"No . . . that can't be right. You woke me up at 2:47. It's only a quarter after three," I said.

"I sat here for an hour," Art said quietly. "I couldn't decide what to do. What could I have done? Jesus, if you'd seen him. It was *horrible* . . . the *sounds* he made . . ."

I closed my eyes. *I don't want to know. Shut up.*

"It hasn't been that long," I said. "They won't know the difference."

Art laughed, a bitter little snort that reminded me of Howie. "They'll find out. Forensics can determine the time of death. It's their fucking job."

I sat down on the kitchen tile, eyes closed, my back leaning against the door.

Ten minutes later I opened my eyes. Art was slumped back into the bench, hands resting on the edge of the breakfast table. He was staring at the wall, expressionless.

"We have to call someone," I said.

Nilus barked in his sleep, legs jerking and twitching. Something howled from the forest, a high, mournful wail. *Coyote,* I thought, and then I remembered what Art had said, months ago, when we'd first had coffee in Campus Bean and I'd told him about the pigeon grave in the woods behind Kellner. *Maybe you saw a coyote den. Like the scorched bones marking the entrance to the dragon in* Beowulf.

I kept my eyes down, afraid to look at the window above the sink. I was sure Grendel would be there, bristle-haired face pressed to the glass, feral eyes glinting in the dark.

At four-thirty Art stood up, re-capped the now half-empty bottle of scotch, and unlocked the back door.

"We'll put him in the pond," he said, and he clasped his hands together and looked out over the backyard. "We'll take out the boat and push him over near the mouth of Birchkill . . . it should carry him right to the Quinnipiac . . ."

"You're not serious—"

"Of course, there's always the risk he'd get caught up in the reeds, or get snagged on a fallen tree, but the Birchkill is deep enough, and the weeds all die off in the winter."

No, I said. *This is crazy.*

Art stalked toward me. "Do you have a better solution?"

"We call for help."

"We've already been through this." Art pushed the swinging door open. "Look at him, Eric."

"Please close that door," I said, trying not to beg but it nevertheless came out that way. "Please, Art. I don't want to see him again."

"Dan's gone. Do you understand me? There's nothing to help. You want to call the morgue, arrange a proper burial? Call his mom, perhaps, ask her what we should do?"

"We should do the right thing," I said.

Art let the door swing shut, and he paced, work boots thudding heavy on the tile. "The right thing. Whatever that is. Nice cozy country estate, a few students living with a famous professor, and now an accidental death by poison. Or should I be more specific, and say our friend died from ingesting a three-hundred-year-old alchemical formula. That'll go over *real* well. Fucking puritans would go *nuts*. All of Connecticut would shout for our heads." He stared at the floor, still pacing. "We'd be on the front pages. Strung up and stoned. Maybe Dr. Cade, too. And Howie, for good measure. I've got money; I'd get a good attorney. What about you? You trust some public defender with the rest of your life?"

His face glowed in the moonlight. His words terrified me.

"The farther the body is from this house the better," he said. "The Quinnipiac might carry him all the way to the Long Island Sound if we're lucky."

"We're not doing it," I said.

Art didn't hear me. "I can carry him myself, but I'll need your help in the boat."

"You should've left me in bed." I closed my eyes. "You should've never woken me up."

I opened my eyes and he was staring at me.

"Jesus Christ, Art, I *can't do this.*"

"Okay," he said, buttoning the top of his shirt.

He headed for the dining room and I burrowed my face into my arms and remained on the floor.

I heard terrible things. Art's labored breathing as he dragged Dan through the kitchen. The swish of fabric across tile, the thud-thud of shoes slipping over the threshold. The twist and creak of a doorknob and shrill, icy wind. Crunching of snow, rattle-bang as the back door swung shut.

I raised my head to see Nilus padding softly across the kitchen. It was 4:45. I walked to the window and there they were. Art and Dan, one hunched over and lurching backward, dragging the other across the ground. One on his back, arms overhead, shoes cutting two trails in the snow. Charlemagne and Pepin. David and Julius. My friends.

To the Long Island Sound if we're lucky, I told myself. As I walked toward the back door my stomach lurched and I threw up.

• • •

I woke up that day at 4:45 P.M. My window curtain was a dark square framed by pale light. I rolled over and pulled a pillow over my head and fell back into a dead sleep, not wanting to remember anything, hoping the Valium Art had given me was tainted with something that would prevent me from ever opening my eyes again.

I awoke again, this time to darkness. I sat up against the head-board and looked around my room. Dan was there, standing casually by my chest of drawers, wearing his Sherlock outfit, his hair and clothes dripping black water that had pooled around his shoes.

"Hornwort," he said, smiling and tipping his head to one side. He lifted his leg, and I saw it was wrapped in green plant tendrils, twined around his ankle and shin like snakes. "Didn't I tell you they were a problem? Art and I filled the boat *four* times last summer with these suckers . . . and then Art got sunburned so badly on the back of his neck that he peeled for weeks."

You already told me this story, I said.

"Oh, that's right." He let his leg down, and water sploshed out of his brown oxford. I heard Nilus scratching on the other side of my door, whining to be let in.

I'm so sorry, I said. *I'm so sorry . . . We should've called an ambulance. I don't know how this happened . . .*

Dan smiled wistfully. "It's okay," he said. "Art can be very persua-sive. But eventually I'll need a proper burial." He stepped closer. Leafy vines trailed behind him, leaving wet smears along the floor.

But you are buried, I said. *You were carried away by the sea.*

Dan stopped at the side of my bed. I could smell him—wet, cold, like mud from a pond. A rotting birch leaf was tangled in his hair. He shook his head sadly.

"Have you already forgotten your Aeneid passage? *'Until my bones rest in the grave, or till I flutter and roam this side a hundred years.'* I know time isn't supposed to matter over here." He looked away, to my window, and then back to me, his expression suddenly angry. "But I'll tell you, Eric. A hundred years is still *a long fucking time.*"

I woke up with a start, breathing heavily, my back slicked with sweat. Darkness all around, the green glow of my clock read 6 P.M. Heartbeat pulsing in my ears. I fumbled around my nightstand and found the other pill Art had given me, and I popped it in my mouth and let the bitter powder dissolve on my tongue. I closed my eyes and tried to remember summers spent at my house in West Falls—the crisp scent of impending rain, the rumble of faraway thunderheads, and the rich orange tint of the soil falling from my hand in a silty waterfall.

Chapter 3

I'd like to think I spent the next week in panicky seclusion, holed up in my room, paranoid, unable to walk downstairs past the point where Art had dragged Dan's stiff body from foyer to kitchen. And the nights should have been equally intolerable, with nightmare after nightmare playing endlessly, Dan's grinning corpse rising up to me from out of the dark water, hands outstretched, his voice bubbly and clotted the way I imagine a drowned man would sound. But while I've come to know the incapacitating pain of guilt I've also come to know how invigorating it can be. Guilt drove me out of my room and into a blur of physical activity—shoveling the driveway every morning, splitting firewood in the garage, hiking for miles through Dr. Cade's land with Nilus at my side. I had no desire to sit at my desk and read, and I couldn't have anyway; it was my room, oddly enough, that most reminded me of what I'd done. Its silence was damning and its blank walls provided a screen upon which evil memories played: a crust of jagged black ice along the pond's shore, the dark outline of a body on the snow. Art and me pushing the canoe out, the clunk of our oars. Art heaving Dan over the side of the boat and me—trying not to cry—watching Dan's hair floating for a moment like black moss, before his body disappeared into the inky water. These images only came back in my room, and so I stayed away.

Art and I worked around each other, eating dinner separately, arriving home at different times, leaving the house in the morning before the other came downstairs. We got into a sad rhythm of avoidance, like an estranged married couple. I think we both needed the time alone to somehow come to terms with what we'd done. It had been five days and nothing had happened—the police hadn't shown up banging on the front door, there were no moments of panic that we'd been found out. Nothing seemed different. I saw my own death vicariously through Dan's, and because of that I can now recall exactly when my mind made the momentous shift from believing everything revolved around me to understanding that nothing did at all. It was both comforting and scary to know reality didn't hinge upon my perception of it. The circumstances could have been easily reversed, Dan still alive and me at the bottom of the Birchkill or the Quinnipiac or wherever he was, skimming along the riverbed, brushing against creek stones, hair swirling around my face like strands of silk.

By Saturday afternoon the sky was covered in a vortex of gray clouds that threatened to snow but never got around to it. Art had offered me a ride to school that morning, since I had to pick up my work schedule from Dr. Lang, but the car stalled several times sitting in Dr. Cade's driveway, and while waiting for the engine to warm the tension between us dissolved. Sitting in silence, in the front seat, was more than either one of us could bear.

"I saw Ellen yesterday," said Art, looking ahead. His glasses had a thin layer of moisture beading up on their lenses. "She said you guys had dinner last week."

I stared out my window. "We ate Chinese." I didn't even care if she'd told him about what happened.

"Yeah—Han's Kitchen," Art laughed. "For a New York girl, Ellen sure doesn't know good Chinese."

"She's from San Francisco," I said.

Art turned to me, curiosity skittering across his face. He smiled.

"Anyway, I'm glad you two got to spend some time together, away from the house."

I looked at him. "Really?"

"Oh, yeah. Ellen's a great girl. I see myself marrying her one day. It's nice to have her get along so well with my friends."

I don't know what I felt—some gruesome hybrid of guilt and jealousy. "I didn't know you thought about marriage," I said, attempting to sound as disinterested as possible.

Art looked over his shoulder as he backed down the driveway. "There comes a time when you have to make a decision. Ellen's a traditional girl, you know, likes to have her eggs lined up. She gets a lot of pressure from her folks, always asking her when she's going to settle down, so I figure, why not me? I can't imagine her finding anyone else who knows her as well as I do."

"For example," I said.

"Well, I know Ellen is a bit . . . how can I put this . . . she's a bit of a free spirit. Gets bored easily. So the more I pull away, the more she tries to get close. If I show any kind of commitment she feels trapped. I see it as the perfect situation—it allows me to enjoy the company of other women, knowing I'm only helping my current relationship by doing so."

"Sounds like a rationalization."

"It would," Art smiled. "But you don't know Ellen. Not like I do."

Howie might know her too, I thought.

We stopped at a traffic light. The town sign was straight ahead, atop two stout poles, a small, brown rectangular block of wood with FAIRWICH branded across in straight lettering, and below, almost as an afterthought:

Our Home
Est. 1760

As we rolled down Main Street, Nicole drove by in her little silver sports car, honking to us and waving out her window. There was a girl next to her in the passenger seat, a high-haired blonde who stared at her nails while we waved back, and the moment Nicole's car turned off Main Street I sank back into my seat and covered my face with my hands. I didn't know what I was going to feel once my mental shield of denials and justifications was exposed to the public, and yet there was Nicole, someone who knew Dan only in passing, and already I felt as if she somehow suspected what had happened, as if it were obvious in my every action and expression.

We drove past Aberdeen's patinaed front gates and onto the smooth black surface of its long entranceway, rolling by Paderborne, until Garringer Hall came into view, jutting out against the swirling gray sky in robes of granite.

Art stopped the car. A couple of students stared at us from their small smoker's group huddled near the building's entrance.

"I've been dreaming about him," I said. I leaned my head against the door window. "He visits me every night. Sometimes we play backgammon, or just talk about silly stuff, like the weather or what I had for dinner."

"Who are you talking about?" Art asked, staring ahead.

"Dan," I said, surprised. *Who else?*

"Oh, I see . . ." Art took his pipe out of his jacket pocket and peered into the bowl. "You think he's haunting you, is that it?"

"I don't know," I said, disturbed by Art's measured movements: the unraveling of the foil pouch, the pinching of clove and the packing of it into the bowl, and then the flick of the match and a wispy curl of smoke dissolving into the air.

Art puffed once, twice. "You could try tracing a thaumaturgic triangle around your bed. Or sleeping with a solace stone under your pillow. Antonio Ebreo recommended heated azurite." Art opened his mouth slightly and let the white smoke seep out.

"You can't be serious," I said.

He shrugged. "It's just a suggestion. At the very least it can't hurt. I don't know what else to tell you, Eric."

"I think I'm being punished," I said. "Remember Palinurus, doomed to wander for a hundred years? Or Cato, unable to cross the threshold between Hell and Purgatory? Until Dan's body is found I don't think I'll ever have a decent—"

"Nonsense." Art puffed again. "You simply have to let go of your guilt. I suspect the only ghost haunting you is up here," he tapped his temple. "Besides, if there is an afterlife, I'm sure Dan has more important things to do than haunt your dreams."

"And how would you know that?"

He ignored, or didn't detect, my sarcasm. "Even if we assume the pagans all exist in Hell, there are still enough interesting Christians in heaven to keep one occupied. Think of Justinian and Constantine . . . Aquinas, Anselm, and St. Jerome . . . With millennia of people to choose from, don't you think it's egotistical to assume Dan would rather spend his time with you?"

• • •

Howie came home that afternoon, tan and relaxed, wearing a short-sleeved yellow button-down and faded tan shorts, his hair longer than I'd ever seen it. He'd put on some weight, a heaviness to his face that hadn't been there before vacation, and when he greeted me with a crushing bear hug and a thundering slap on the shoulder, I realized I'd forgotten how big a man he was. Art was diminishing in size, it seemed, head now always lowered in thought, face pinched, obsession and compulsion molding him into a two-dimensional object that took up less space than it should have. But Howie was bound by nothing, and his presence shoved aside the somber silence that had pervaded the house the past week. He talked about New Orleans's beautiful women and seedy bars, bragging that he knew all the places the average tourist doesn't find. He told us about a dangerous affair he had with a Creole woman he'd met in a jazz club his first night in town—two nights of crazy sex that was ended abruptly by her boyfriend bursting into the house and threatening to cut off their heads with a machete.

"Was he armed?" I said.

"Oh, yeah. He was wielding the goddamn thing like a samurai." Howie sipped from his glass—filled, incredibly enough, with plain orange juice. We sat in the kitchen at the breakfast nook. "I mean, I can understand why he was so pissed. We were in his *bed*, for Christ's sake. But still, if you're going to threaten me, you better make good on it." Howie looked away for a moment and then continued:

"So I stood up real slow—mind you, I'm naked as the day I'm born—and I said, 'Look, there's been a misunderstanding here, I didn't know this was your woman,' but he's getting madder, screaming at me in Creole, screaming at his woman, she's screaming back, and I'm caught in the middle with my dick hanging out and a two-foot-long razor-sharp instrument not more than a few paces away. He notices me walking toward him and then he raises his arm like he's going to slice me in half, and so I ran into him full speed, just like a tackling dummy, *wham*—"

Howie punched his fist into his open palm.

"—and this guy goes *flying*. His arms shoot up, his legs stick out, and he crashes back into the wall and collapses onto the floor. Out cold."

Howie took another sip of his orange juice.

"So," he said. "How the fuck was your break?"

I told him about Prague, about the train trip and the hotel. I said nothing of Albo or the Malezel book, and instead I filled in the time with descriptions of the city and my experience with the gypsy in the street fair.

"I didn't know you got your fortune read," Art said.

"I didn't," I said. "I told you I just walked by."

"Voodoo's big in New Orleans," Howie said.

Art ignored him. "You shouldn't mess around with things like that," Art said to me.

"Didn't you hear what I said? I didn't do anything." I tried to push my anger away. "And maybe I should've. At least I'd have something fun to do, with you back at the hotel doing whatever—"

"All right sweethearts, *enough.*" Howie stood up and heaved a thick cardboard box from the floor, plopping it down on the kitchen table. "Look here." He produced a penknife, sliced open the box, and took out two tightly packed bags of ice, and then a Styrofoam cooler filled halfway with oysters.

"They're still alive," Howie said. "I picked them from their bed two days ago."

Art took a few oysters from the cooler and handed them to me. He smiled. Everything was fine. Everything was normal.

"We'll eat them raw," Howie said, "'on the half shell,' as they say. Dash of hot sauce and you're good to go. And they didn't cost me one red cent."

I dropped the oysters on the table. "I heard in Maine, if you're caught stealing lobster from traps, the lobstermen are allowed to shoot you."

"Same in New Orleans," said Howie. "I risked my life for these critters so you better enjoy them. Say," he looked around, as if he'd forgotten something, "where's Danny-boy at? I bought him something."

I looked at Art. He was perfectly composed and casual, leaning against the counter, arms crossed. "Don't know. He left this afternoon. Said he had some errands to do."

This is it, I thought. *This is where it all starts.*

But Howie just sat down on the bench, took another swig of his orange juice, and pried open one of the oysters, sucking the glistening gray flesh into his mouth with a satisfied smile.

Later that night, Art, Howie, and I sat in the living room, engaged in our own little pursuits—Art read from some small book written in French, Howie leafed through old holiday catalogues that had stacked up on the coffee table, and I tried to focus on my notes for Monday's classes.

"Did Dan say he was going on a date?" Howie said, looking at his watch. The fire crackled in response and Nilus barked in his sleep.

"Not that I know of," said Art. He glanced at me.

I turned to Howie. "I don't know," I said. "I didn't even know he'd left."

"I bet you he ended up going over to Katie Mott's room."

"Who's that?" I said.

"Some girl he liked last semester. They hooked up right before break. Frankly, I didn't think Dan had the guts to follow through. Usually he never does. The big-city Boston girls probably taught him a lesson this past month. Good for him."

Howie went back to his holiday catalogues—gifts for him and for her under twenty dollars—while for the next hour I stared at my notes without reading a single word.

The next morning Art left to pick up Dr. Cade at the airport and I stayed at my desk, daydreaming and gazing out the window. I could just see the edge of the pond from my room, a crescent of snow covering the water at the shoreline, which had already frozen over, and a lone crow walking across the side yard. Around 10 A.M. Nilus started barking and I heard the front door open, the crash-bang of luggage, and then Howie's booming baritone welcoming Professor Cade home. I crept to the hallway and listened from the top of the stairs.

A few minutes of small talk—*vacation was fun but we're looking forward to getting back to work,* stuff like that—then Dr. Cade spoke: *I hadn't been to Havana in nearly thirty years. It's more impoverished than I remember.* He'd had dinner with Castro and signed a copy of his book *This Too Must Pass* for one of Castro's sons. Fishing trips in Guantanamo Bay and talking to some old sailor who'd cleaned Hemingway's boat, long evenings spent in *palapas* telling the locals about America, and hearing horror stories about mothers who'd lost their children while sending them to supposed freedom on timber-lashed rafts headed for Key West.

Howie offered to make dinner for him that night, a seafood gumbo using the oysters and some fish he and Art were going to pick up that afternoon. Dr. Cade thanked them and said he was going upstairs to lie down, and if Dean Richardson called, would they mind just taking a message?

Before I stole back to my room I heard Art ask Howie if he'd heard from Dan. Howie laughed and said Dan was probably having the time of his life with Katie Mott, and that at any time he expected him to show up at the front door, bedraggled and exhausted, suffering from dehydration and in need of a B-12 shot.

I worked until dusk descended in a bluish veil and I could smell sautéing onions and garlic wafting up from the kitchen. In the kitchen I found Howie slicing haddock at the counter while a kettle simmered on the stove and a tired-looking Art stood over a skillet, stirring a whitish mixture with a wooden spoon. A pile of shucked oysters sat in a gray wet heap atop a plate.

There was an open bottle of club soda on the kitchen table and what looked like a matching glass of the stuff sitting on the counter near Howie. A pale green disc of lime floated among the bubbles and ice cubes.

"Art's burnt the roux twice already," Howie said, with a grin. He pulled a strip of haddock apart with his fingers.

I glanced at Art. He looked sick, dressed in an old Aberdeen sweatshirt and plaid flannel pajama bottoms. His hair stuck out at crazy angles like he'd just gotten up from a nap.

"During the ride home Dr. Cade said we're way behind schedule," Art said, in a low monotone. "Don't be surprised if he doubles our workload. He plans to submit the first draft of Volume One by the end of this semester."

Howie dropped the haddock onto the cutting board. "Is he serious? I've barely begun inking."

"I still have another thirty pages of translations," I said. "And he wants me to write something on Emperor Barbarossa. Twenty pages *minimum.*"

Dinner was amazing. Howie was a much better cook sober than drunk, and thanks to the Chardonnay that Thomas left us, I felt as relaxed as I had the entire week. We sat at the dining room table, Dr. Cade at the head, Howie and myself seated across from each other, and Art at the opposite end. Dan's chair was conspicuously empty.

"I'm surprised we haven't heard from Dan," said Art, spooning the last of the gumbo into his bowl. He'd drunk a great deal of wine, about three glasses, while Howie continued to sip club soda.

Dr. Cade showed concern. "Has he not yet returned from Boston?" he said.

"He came back last week," Art said. His speech was slightly

slurred. "He left here to do some errands . . . yesterday afternoon, was it?" He looked at me.

"Yes," I said quickly.

"I see," Dr. Cade said. "And no one has heard from him since?"

We all shook our heads.

"I had some time in Cuba to look over what we've accomplished so far." Dr. Cade steepled his hands. "While our progress has quickened, we are still behind schedule. Sections on the papacy are quite rough, and what you've given me on the Saxon empire . . ." He shook his head. "Let's just say it lacks depth. Howie, you were supposed to have had those portolanos completed and on my desk. *Eric*"—he raised his voice to stop Howie from interrupting—"Eric, how are the translations coming along?"

I had a sudden memory of shivering under a dark sky, kneeling in the canoe, struggling to lift Dan while the rush of the Birchkill bubbled and gurgled close by. *Make sure nothing comes off of him yet—not his sneakers or his belt or anything else,* Art had said, his voice shaking from the cold, and when we checked—everything in order? nothing left in the boat?—we pushed him over the side, the canoe rocking gently as he slipped below the black surface of the pond. I'd cut my hand without even knowing, and I remember later watching the long slit run from red to clear under the bathroom faucet, blood winding in thin tendrils over the glassy white porcelain. Blood had pattered on the floor, on my pants, and smeared across my cheeks where I had rubbed them after coming inside.

My God, I thought. *What have we done?*

"Eric?"

I blinked. "The translations," I said. "I finished St. Ripalta's Miracle."

"Ah," Dr. Cade nodded. "Yes, one of my favorites. A retelling of the Lazarus tale. And the others?"

"Almost done," I said. "Tonight . . . maybe tomorrow."

My eyes began to tear up. I excused myself and hurried to my room. I didn't care what Howie and Dr. Cade thought, and I knew it didn't matter, because everyone would pretend everything was okay. No one would ever ask me what was wrong, and I hated myself because I was becoming one of them, sweeping emotions under the rug, drinking until the world took on a dull haze. I fell back on my bed and closed my eyes and saw the head of Horatio J. Grimek, sitting in his jar in that musty basement in Prague. *Memento mori,* he said. *Remember that you too must die.*

◆ ◆ ◆

Monday morning brought painful cold. I floated through the first day of classes, listening to endless throngs of students talk excitedly about what they'd done over the past month. Nearly every story was like something out of *Condé Nast Traveler:* sunning on the beaches of the Balearic Islands, backpacking through New Zealand, staying at the family estate in San Filipe.

My last class of the day was Professor Wallace's The 18th-Century Gothic Novel, with Allison Feinstein in all her dark cosmopolitan elegance sitting beside me, dressed in a black pantsuit and wearing a pair of slender tortoiseshell eyeglasses that sat low upon her thin, aquiline nose. Allison Feinstein was the daughter of a senator from Rhode Island, and the closest thing to a student celebrity at Aberdeen. She was beautiful, of course, with Semitic features and preternatural confidence, often followed by a swirling trail of cigarette smoke and surrounded by an entourage of fawning men and envious women. I'd seen her a few times before, walking across the Quad, eating a bagel at Campus Bean, sunning herself in a black bikini on a lawn chair behind Thorren Hall. Some semesters ago she had supposedly received a D from Professor Cade in his Ottoman Empire course, and as a result the school received a phone call from her irate father, who threatened to pull his funding if Allison wasn't given an incomplete and allowed to retake the class the following semester. But Dr. Cade stood firm (rumor has it he matched Senator Feinstein's yearly donation as a swipe at the administration), which only solidified his already sanctified reputation as Aberdeen's arbiter of uncompromising values.

She was dressed in all browns and blacks, not a hint of bright color about her, from her raven-colored hair to her chestnut eyes to her nails painted deep red. I noticed she used a Mont Blanc, not the fat ones that Dr. Lang preferred but a thin, rapierlike silver pen. Her beauty was the complete opposite to Ellen's—dusky and amorphous, blurred around the edges.

"Please stop," she whispered harshly.

I turned to look at her. She was staring at me, wide mouth turned down in disapproval.

"Excuse me?" I said.

"You're tapping." She motioned to my feet with a nod of her head. "I can't concentrate."

Any other day I would've mumbled an apology and looked away. But recent events had imbued me with a sense of power—that invigorating guilt was now a pair of gray lenses through which I viewed the world, making me feel invisible. *Nothing can hurt me,* I thought.

"'The great man is he who in the midst of the crowd," I said, quoting Emerson, *"keeps with perfect sweetness the independence of solitude.'"*

Allison looked at her nails. "Whatever . . . just stop tapping," she said, and turned to the front again.

Professor Wallace talked about the elements of the gothic novel, its common themes of ruined castles and monasteries, deep, dark forests crawling with serpentine vegetation, the melancholic ghost and the distraught heroine. Walpole and Radcliffe and Shelley—all of them, I felt, could have had a field day with any of my memories from the night Art and I dumped Dan into the pond. There had been the hooting of an owl, the tattered veil of clouds passing over a full moon, the black water swirling beneath our oars, and Dan's body sinking into Stygian nothingness.

"Has anyone ever traveled to Prague?" Dr. Wallace said, leaning forward against the podium, looking out over the class. He was a tall, thin man, as New England as they come with his gaunt face and rocky features, hands long and knobby-knuckled.

I was certain several of my classmates owned at least one home in the Czech Republic. When no one responded I held up my hand.

"I was there over winter break," I said. Allison looked at me.

"And your impressions?" said Professor Wallace.

I could see where he was heading so I talked about the solemnity of the architecture, the cold waters of the Vltava, and the decrepit remnants of the church that had once stood where our hotel was. I wanted to impress everyone but think I ended up sounding pretentious, and Professor Wallace merely thanked me and went on to tell about his years spent in Prague where he wrote his thesis on similarities between Mary Shelley's Frankenstein and Rabbi Loew's golem.

After class Allison Feinstein approached me as I gathered up my books. She introduced herself with a curt little handshake.

"You know, I haven't been to Prague, yet," she said, taking off her glasses and slipping them into a slim leather case. A few of the male students lingered at their desks, eyeing me enviously. "I wanted to study there last summer at Charles University, but my dad insisted I go to Israel instead. Of course, it ended up being way too hot, and the men were all these psycho army guys." She smiled quickly. "If you don't mind me asking, where was it you stayed again in Prague?"

"The Mustovich," I said.

"I knew it sounded familiar," she said, nodding. "My dad stays there when he visits."

I smiled. We had absolutely nothing more in common save a working knowledge of Prague's finest hotel.

"I know this may be short notice," Allison said, opening her pocketbook, "but I'm having a party tomorrow night, at my place on Linwood Terrace." She handed me a silver-embossed calling card. I thought of Dan's card, that day in the Quad with Nicole when she called out to him and he walked toward us in his big suit with the pants bunched up around his ankles. I still have his card, I think, somewhere, in one of those shoeboxes that reside in our closets like ossuaries, holding the bones of our past.

"Bring a friend, if you'd like," she said, with a trace of a smile. *What had that meant?* I thought. *Attraction? Curiosity? Sympathy?*

I thought of possible dates—Nicole, Art, or Howie—but none of them seemed particularly appealing. Allison gave me a quick, formal handshake, closed her pocketbook with an authoritative *click,* and whisked away, dark hair streaming over her shoulders like a falling shadow.

Chapter 4

Instead of going back to Dr. Cade's I took a cab into town and shopped at the Haberdashery, Fairwich's finest men's clothing store. I bought shoes, pants, and two shirts, along with a pair of fourteen-karat gold cufflinks. I then stayed in my dorm room for the rest of the day, worked on my translations, and drank tea that I made on a borrowed hot plate with some old orange pekoe Josh gave to me. There wasn't much going on in my dorm—jazz rang softly through the halls, the radiators whined and clanked, someone knocked on my door around dinnertime but I didn't bother to answer. I finished my work and tried solitaire for an hour or so, grew bored, then headed downstairs to grab something to eat before the dining hall closed.

The usual scraps remained—a browning banana, a bruised apple, a prepackaged single serving of cereal. When I asked the guy behind the hot-food counter if anything was left from that evening's dinner, he only grunted some kind of response and walked away, scratching the back of his head through his hairnet. I took a muffin from the community bins and sat by myself in the corner of the hall, listening to the sounds of a few students talking on the other side of the room. It was comforting, actually, staring at the brown, scarred wooden walls, reading the countless initials that had been scrawled and etched into the panels over the decades. Most were two letters followed by a year: *AM '78, JT '85*. A few had left their first name, in aged, faded letters that looked as old as the names themselves: *Horace, Marvin, Esther.*

I glanced quickly around the room and then took my key and began to scrape out my initials, shielding my left hand with my right arm.

"Eric?"

I looked up and there stood Nicole, flanked on either side by artsy-looking young girls. She wore all black—tightly fitting pants and a trim sweater that appeared hopelessly overstretched by her breasts. My initials were half-finished on the wall, a scraggly *E* and the back line of *D.*

"I had no idea," she said, with her hands on her hips, "that you were such a *vandal.*"

"Hi, Nicole," I said.

She pouted and rushed forward, embracing me in a rush of vanilla scent.

"I saw you with your friend the other day, the tall, handsome guy who never smiles, what's-his-name . . ."

"Arthur."

"Yeah, him. In his car—"

"I know, we waved to you."

She nodded and smiled, obviously already bored with the topic. "Say, we're going to see the Bluelight Specials play at the Cellar. You want to come? I can get you in for free."

"No, thank you," I said, pushing my half-eaten corn muffin around on my tray. "I'm not feeling so well."

"You do look kind of sick," Nicole said, and she put her hand to my forehead. "Maybe you picked up something in Prague. The Czech flu or something like that."

The girls' eyes widened. Nicole, sensing this, I think, draped her arm over my shoulder. "He was in Prague over winter break," Nicole said proudly. "Can you imagine? He called me from a pay phone in some street café. Remember, Eric?"

"Yes."

"I couldn't believe it. Of all the people to call and you picked *me."* She tousled my hair. "I stayed in lousy old New York. SoHo actually, if you want to be picky about it."

"How was it?" one of the wide-eyed girls asked me. She was pretty and blonde, with wet blue eyes and a fresh face. I felt like I could fall in love with her.

"It was dark," I said, referring to Prague. "Dark and cold."

"We really should get going," Nicole said suddenly. I knew I'd attracted the attention of the blonde girl, but I didn't know why (now I know—it's always the brooding malcontents who attract young women). I wanted to take that girl back to my room and lie in bed with her and talk about her life and listen to her stories. She represented everywhere and everything I wanted to be at that moment.

But it wasn't to be. Instead, Nicole kissed me on the cheek and told me to call. I watched them flit away, talking excitedly about nothing.

◆　◆　◆

The next day I went to Allison Feinstein's party. She lived in a two-story cape on Linwood Terrace, a one-way street with only seven homes. Her parents had bought the house for her, Allison later explained, figuring they could always sell it after her graduation, or, if she liked Fairwich, keep it as a vacation home. Either way, Allison said it was a much-needed alternative to dorm life and apartment living—she'd heard too many stories about rapists who frequent student housing, and thieves partial to dormitories.

Allison greeted me at the door, dressed in a black cocktail dress, her slender arms bare and finely muscled, her hair pulled back into a high ponytail with a shimmering silvery bow. All the sounds I had ever associated with "adult" parties streamed out from behind her—clink of glasses, low chatter of conversation broken by the occasional polite laugh, music playing softly in the background. Allison took my hand and led me inside. She smelled of alcohol—something medicinal like vodka or gin—and her cheeks were lightly flushed. "Drinks are in the kitchen," she said, "and the bartender is here until ten, so you still have a couple hours. Not that *I* need any more . . ." She laughed and patted my arm, and then pointed (with limp wrist and glittering diamond bracelet) to a large table in what looked like the dining room. "Food is over there, but I'm afraid you didn't arrive in time for the shrimp." She laughed again, kissed me on the cheek, and wafted away.

An hour later I found myself standing in the kitchen doorway next to a cute freshman who'd been in my literature class last semester. We watched a girl sit cross-legged on the living room floor and snort lines of coke off a compact mirror. Someone turned up the stereo and played Art Tatum. The cute freshman gave me a little blue pill and I swallowed it without hesitating, and I wondered if she'd be game for going back to my dorm room, but I was too sad and tired to flirt, and instead I stood there like a zombie and listened to her go on and on about some tragedy involving her friend's parents both dying in a car accident over winter break.

"I'm an orphan," I said.

"You are not," she had said, poking my ribs. She was short and blonde, with thin wrists, a thin neck, and nonexistent breasts. She had a hint of a Southern accent that became more pronounced with each swig of booze.

"I am," I said. "I lived with a foster family in New Jersey."

She crinkled her little upturned nose. "I don't believe you," she said. *You* came out like *yee-ew*.

When I didn't say anything, she gave me a sideways glance and ran her finger around the rim of her glass.

"Are you serious?" she said.

I looked around to make sure no one else was listening. *"Yes,"* I said dramatically.

She gasped. "What happened to your parents?"

"My dad just left one day—"

She put her hand to her mouth.

"—and my mom died of cancer."

The mystery pill had begun to take effect, tilting the floor at a slight angle. I was suddenly tired of the freshman girl. She said something else to me but I just shushed her and kissed her on the forehead and walked away, floated actually, to the living room, hovered just above the hardwood floor, and collapsed onto a leather couch.

A kid in a jacket and loosened tie dropped down next to me and leaned forward, taking a small baggie of white powder out of his jacket pocket. He untied it and sprinkled some out onto the glass coffee table.

"Do you have a credit card on you?" he asked me.

"Excuse me?"

"Never mind," he said impatiently, and he pushed the coke into a wavy line with the edge of his index finger. He then leaned down, pressed his face against the glass top, sniffed the entire trail, and shot up, wide-eyed and mouth agape.

"Finish it off if you want," he croaked, tossing the bag into my lap. "I'm fucking *blasted.*"

"Eric?"

I looked up. Ellen stood in front of me.

"Hi," I said, casually, as if I'd been waiting for her all evening. I looked down at the baggie. "This isn't mine."

"I figured." She plucked it off my lap and dropped it on the table. "What are you doing here?"

The kid came back for the bag and left. Ellen took his place on the couch. She smelled amazing. "Rachel and I stopped in to say hello to Allison," she said. "Do you know her?"

"Sort of," I said, looking away. "She invited me."

"That's nice."

"Yes, it is."

We said nothing for a few moments. I looked straight ahead, at the small group of students dancing in the middle of the living room. The party had thinned out, and now only the serious guests remained, the ones who'd drank the most and eaten the most and done the most drugs. Allison moved among them, flitting around in her silver hair bow and black dress, as vaporous as a ghost. I don't know if her friends noticed her. I don't think they even noticed each other.

Ellen touched my arm. "Eric," she said cautiously, "are you angry with me?"

I turned to her. She looked the way she always did. Honeyed hair, emerald eyes, soft white neck. Beautiful. That's all she ever was, really. Just that one word was enough.

"I'm stoned," I said. "And drunk." Someone else entered my field of vision—a tall, leggy redhead, wearing a poofy baby-blue sweater and tight jeans. She towered over me, standing to my left, her arms crossed and her mouth set into a hard, straight line.

"This crowd is too young," she said to Ellen. "Let's go to Murray's. Roger said he'd be there."

"I think I'm going to stay," said Ellen, sinking back and crossing her legs. "I haven't seen Eric in a while."

"Oh . . ." The tall woman looked down at me. *She's like an Amazon,* I thought. "So you're Eric—Art's housemate, right?" she said.

I nodded.

She jabbed her long finger at me, the nail curved like a talon. "You tell Art he fucked up. Tell him Rachel said that. Got it?" I nodded again, and she turned on her heels, strutted across the room, and left out the front door. I ran my hand over my face and thought about the last time I'd seen Ellen. I remembered her laughing in her apartment as I'd fumbled for my keys, and the excruciating cab ride back to Dr. Cade's, feeling as if I were heading to my executioner. Every night I'd waited for Art to burst through my door and pounce upon me, and even though it had taken a dimmer place in my mind—in light of recent events—having Ellen sitting beside me brought everything back with a stunning clarity.

"Art said he's marrying you." I stared down at my hands.

"When did he tell you this?"

I shrugged. I couldn't remember—had it been before Dan's death or after? His *death* . . . The word hissed like a hot brand plunged into cold water.

"Well, that's news to me," said Ellen. "We haven't spoken in quite some time. He said we were getting *married?*" She laughed humorlessly. A kid fell onto the living room floor, just missing the coffee table. He giggled and rolled around, his pinstripe shirt unbuttoned enough to show one of his nipples. The edges of his nostrils were dusted white. Fellow partiers danced around him in a semicircle, women in stockinged feet and men in dark socks spilling their drinks held aloft, Allison among them, black hair, diamond bracelet gleaming wicked around her bony wrist.

I shrank into the couch, into the corner between the back cushion and the armrest. I wanted to leave but couldn't see how I'd be able to escape past the Dionysian throng of revelers without being pulled into their midst. I felt a hand on my arm and I jerked away.

It was Ellen, staring at me clinically, the way a doctor or a nurse would. "How much have you had to drink?" she said.

"Enough," I said. "And I took a pill, something small and blue."

She leaned in closer. "How do you feel? Drowsy or fidgety?"

"Neither."

Ellen nodded. "Would you like me to take you home?"

"No," I said, and I must have sounded thoroughly repulsed because she pulled away in surprise. "I don't want to go back there." I tried not to plead. "Take me back to Paderborne."

As soon as I said it, I envisioned my dark dorm room, cold and dusty, with my old sheets still on the bed. And that smell of emptiness that I hated so much.

"No, take me to the Paradise," I said, sitting up. The room swayed dramatically, like a rolling ship. "I know Henry Hobbes, the owner."

Ellen extended her hand to me and I took it and followed her past the swirling mass of revelers and out the front door. The air was thin and icy, and every snow-crunching footstep was the felling of a tree, and the moon was pinned to the black sky in a perfect half circle, and never before had I felt so wonderful and so terrible at the same time.

I remember a short car ride and a long flight of stairs, and then the sound of answering machine messages being played back. I was on a couch, and I remained there for I don't know how long—it could have been thirty minutes or five hours. Someone was humming in the background, the floor creaking beneath their feet. I heard the soft whisper of a refrigerator door and then the gurgle of a faucet. I opened my eyes. Ellen's apartment in dim lighting, Ellen seated across from me on the floor, barefoot, legs crossed Indian-style. She wore a Yale sweatshirt and gray sweatpants. She was reading a magazine.

I looked at my watch. It was almost midnight. My head felt much better. A glass of water awaited me on the coffee table. I took a sip and Ellen looked up.

"How are you feeling?"

Fine, I said.

"Art called." She closed her magazine. "He told me about Dan."

A bolt of adrenaline rocketed up and burned into my stomach wall.

"It is strange," she said, picking a strand of hair off her forehead. "Dan's such a homebody. Except for vacations, I don't think he's ever been away from that house for more than a day or two. Do you have any idea where he might be?"

"I know nothing," I said.

"Well," she raised her eyebrows, "that's just the kind of thing someone who *did* know something would say. You know what I think . . . I think Howie may have said something that offended him. Dan and he have had their troubles in the past."

We sat in silence for a few minutes. I counted the ticks of her kitchen clock.

"Eric," she said slowly, carrying that pained expression particular to uncomfortable topics, "I think we should talk about the other night." She closed the magazine and sat back, arms locked behind her, propping her up. "I don't think I handled it well. I want to apologize."

If I'd had the mental resources I would've rushed out, just as before. Instead I crossed my arms and looked down. "I was just acting foolish," I said.

"Oh, come on, you've already confessed your innermost desires," she smiled. "No reason to hold back now."

Why the hell not.

"I do love you," I said. I looked directly into her eyes.

She opened her mouth to laugh or perhaps say something witty, but my gaze gave her pause. I was so sick of lying. I wanted to confess everything: that I fantasized about her nearly every night, that I both wished for Art's death and felt horribly guilty about it, that all I wanted was a single evening of physical pleasure to store away in memory and recall whenever needed. Memories of her touch whispering sweetly in my mind would be enough; even if memory passed into illusion as old memories often do, I would choose those illusions over a thousand real women.

"I doubt you know what love is," she said, not unkindly.

"You're probably right," I said.

She smiled, and, keeping mercifully silent, walked over and bent down to kiss my forehead. The touch of her lips cooled on my skin.

"You can sleep here if you'd like." She yawned. "The couch pulls out into only a twin but the mattress is comfortable. Dan stayed here last year and he swore by it."

I could smell him, suddenly, a clean, woolly scent, reminding me of his old jackets and funny little hats and his scratchy green pants. A flood of emotion, so powerful that initially I didn't know what I was feeling, and then the dam shivered and exploded and I let out tremendous whooping sobs, my body wracked with convulsions, sorrow and guilt and shame filling my mouth like acid, choking me. I cried uncontrollably, hearing lashings snap and twang as the moorings that had held my mind in check ripped free from their supports and the entire structure reeled and crashed.

Ellen hurried over and tried to comfort me, obviously thinking I was having some reaction to the drugs, and it was fortunate that she didn't ask me what was wrong because I would have confessed everything. I cried until I fell asleep, and even then I think I still cried, because I dreamt it so.

◆　◆　◆

The heater's broken, the cabby said, as he tossed me a blanket and turned onto Main Street. It was sometime after 5 A.M., and the only reason I'd left Ellen's apartment was because I knew I needed to go back home to Dr. Cade's.

Instead I told the cabby to drop me off at Paderborne, my courage failing as I imagined a night alone in my room and all manner of ghosts and spirits swirling about. Everywhere was snow and gloom, a morass of shadows and jagged icicles jutting from underneath Paderborne's eaves. I passed under those icicles warily, convinced they would descend in swift silence and impale me where I stood, spattering my blood across the cigarette butt–strewn threshold of Paderborne. The Paderborne lobby was empty and cold, modular furniture heaped into corners, an abandoned can of soda sitting forlorn atop a garbage bin. The air smelled of cold cement and stale smoke.

I carried my mail upstairs. I hadn't checked my box in months—there was an invitation to some symposium on cuneiform (courtesy of the history department), a postcard addressed to my box number but to the wrong student, and an envelope from Mr. Daniel Higgins, dated three weeks earlier, around the time I was shivering uncontrollably in the basement of the Paradise Motel.

I entered my room, clicked on my desk lamp, and sat down on my bed, tearing the envelope open. There was a folded page of spiral notebook paper, its top edge crenellated with ripped half circles, and Dan's smooth handwriting running across the page in fine black ink. Dan always used notebooks that opened vertically, I remembered, because he was left-handed and couldn't write with the metal spirals digging into the side of his hand.

Dear Eric,

I'll probably return home before you get this letter, because I don't know how often you check your box at school, and I can't remember where you said you were staying over break. But hopefully you'll receive this on time and accept my invitation to join mother and me for Christmas dinner here in good old Boston. Mother said she'd pay for your ticket, so if you're reading this at any time before Christmas day, you have no excuse.

What else. Boston is gray and rainy, and I've had a cold since arriving. Mother keeps asking about Dr. Cade and when he'll be coming to visit. If I haven't told you before (and I don't think I did), mother idolizes Dr. Cade. But don't we all?

*When I get back to school I have to tell Art I'm no longer
interested in his search for the stone, which is a funny thing for
me to say because I'm the one who came up with the idea. But
it was just a lark, really, something clever to fill the time, and
somewhere along the way it got too serious. I'm not saying it's
all nonsense—I still think there might be something to it, but
getting to that point is too dangerous. Or maybe there's nothing
to it and we're all just bored.*

*Either way, please don't say "I told you so" when you see
me, or I'll throw out Howie's stash of single malt and blame it
on you.*

Waiting in Boston,
Dan

I sat at my bed, staring at the letter. I stayed that way until the blue
light of dawn crept across my room, and then I shoved the letter
under my mattress and took a long shower.

The phone rang when I got out. I knew who it was. I'd been
thinking about him.

"Eric?" It was Art. "Hey, listen, you haven't heard from Dan,
have you?"

"No," I said. I watched water drip from my hair and fall onto the
wooden floor. It started snowing again. I closed my eyes and thought
about the letter.

Somewhere along the way it got too serious.

It was Wednesday morning. Dan was still missing.

I heard conversations in the background on Art's end of the line,
Dr. Cade and Howie and a new voice, deep and official-sounding.
Art spoke again. "Well, you might want to come over. Campus security is here—I'm sorry, what's that?" he pulled away from the phone
and had a brief discussion with the deep-voiced man. *Sure, I'll tell
him,* I heard him say, and then he returned.

"Security will send someone to your room if you'd like, or you
can stop by their office."

"What is this about?" I said.

Art paused, gauging, I'm sure, what to say within earshot of the others in the room. "They just have some questions about Dan," he said, and then after, in a subtle tone that only I could understand the significance of: "Not much else is going on."

I took two deep breaths and after he hung up I lay there, listening to the stuttering blare of the disconnected line.

The snow was relentless, pouring out of burnt-silver clouds. Snow clung to Garringer's spires, blew against Thorren's clock, and covered the last of the Mores's red roof in an unbroken blanket that stretched out like a glacier sheared off at the top.

Campus security was located in the first floor of Thorren, toward the rear of the building, in a small, cramped office with yellowish lighting and '70s-style décor: wood-panelled walls, an orange, thin carpet, and frosted-glass windows. I gave the receptionist my name and sat on a mud-brown Naugahyde couch and waited, picking at an old crack that had split along the bottom of the cushion. After a few minutes a tall, heavy man plodded from the back hall into the waiting room, carrying a clipboard, his uniform spotless and pressed, a lineup of fat pens sticking up from his shirt pocket. He looked at me with a kind smile.

"Mr. Dunne?"

I stood up.

"Officer James Lumble," he said. He motioned toward the hall. "I just have a few questions for you," he said. "Officer Pitts should be on his way back from Professor Cade's house, and I'm sure he can fill you in about the situation better than I can. My office is the next door on the right. Pardon the mess . . . I took an extended stay in Miami with the kids and I'm still getting organized."

He accompanied me into his office, rushing ahead to move a small cardboard box from a chair. His desk was littered with papers and manila file folders and Styrofoam cups. A jumble of small photos sat in gold and silver frames all along the edge of his desk, with pictures of laughing children.

Officer Lumble fell back into his chair, swiveling toward his desk. I sat in the small chair across from him. "Now then," he said, scanning his clipboard. "This is regarding your friend . . . Daniel Higgins, is it?" He took one of his pens from his shirt pocket.

I nodded and he scribbled something on the clipboard. "And you live with Daniel Higgins at Professor Cade's home, correct?"

"Yes, sir."

"The names of your other housemates are . . ."

I answered and he smiled, continuing to write.

"When was the last time you saw Daniel?"

"Last week. Saturday afternoon, I think. He said he was going out to do errands."

"Did he drive?"

I shook my head. "Dan doesn't own a car. He usually takes cabs everywhere."

"I see. And did he take a cab that afternoon?"

"I don't know."

Officer Lumble smiled again, put the clipboard down, and capped the pen.

"Now son, every year we get one or two of these . . ." He picked at a hangnail. "And it always turns out to be one of two things: either the student went away without telling anyone, in which case they usually end up calling their folks from some motel in Mexico, or this is some kind of frat trick, and the student's friends eventually confess once we threaten to bring in the police."

I nodded.

He looked up. "So which one is it?"

"I'm sorry?"

Officer Lumble sighed. "Is this a stunt of some sort, or has your friend Daniel decided to take a little extra time off this semester?"

"I don't know," I said.

"You don't?" He narrowed his eyes and leaned forward, the chair creaking helplessly. Behind him, through the window, snow swirled and swooped, a whirlpool of white pressing against the thin glass.

"No, sir," I said. "I don't know where he is."

"Okay . . ." He pursed his lips and stared at me. A pause, then:

"I guess I have some more questions for you." He sat back, crossed his legs, and rested the clipboard on one knee.

I told him that Dan didn't have any girlfriends I knew of. He asked about Dan's other friends, and I said that I thought he only socialized with us, his housemates. No, I didn't know anything about Dan's parents, but I believed he only had his mom and that his dad had died. There hadn't been anything unusual about Dan's behavior, and he never drank or used drugs, at least not that I knew of. Yes, I said, I did consider him a good friend, and I did believe if he was going somewhere he'd tell me. And no, he wasn't the adventurous type. He was, in fact, very studious and a bit of an introvert.

"Daniel's an excellent student," Officer Lumble said, riffling through a handful of papers. "So this *is* a bit weird—not the usual party animal that things like this happen to—but if there's one thing I've learned here at Aberdeen, it's to never judge anyone by their appearance. Especially the smart ones. You have to keep a close eye on them—one day they're fine and then *boom,* they can't take the pressure and they're off somewhere with their parent's credit card and an exotic dancer from one of them clubs in Bookertown." He laughed. "You'd never believe the shit these students put us through." He spoke to me with an air of confidentiality, as if I weren't a student but a fellow public safety officer from a neighboring college. "Mostly drug stuff—ODs, bad trips, coke cut with baby laxative and weed dipped in formaldehyde. I caught a kid dealing pot right in the Quad, clear as day, last spring. Hauled him in, called the Fairwich police, and before they could do anything the kid's dad sent a lawyer from New York and that was the end of *that.* This kid was from a very famous family—if I told you the name you'd know it. That's why we'd rather keep things under Aberdeen jurisdiction; no sense in rousing the locals, and they can't seem to stand the rich kids making a mess of their town. They're an okay bunch, though, these kids here." He smiled affectionately. "Spoiled, that's all. And who can blame them. Throw enough at a kid and something's bound to stick. What about you? Your dad some big shot?"

"No," I said. "He's a traveling salesman."

"Probably taught you the value of hard work."

"Yes he did."

"Good for you, then. You got yourself a leg up on your fellow students."

The office door swung open and a short man clomped in, his ski hat and matching coat covered in snow, boots trailing water and slush. He wiped his thick black mustache with the back of his gloved hand. "*Je*-sus it is blustery out there," he said, speaking to Officer Lumble.

"This is Eric Dunne," Lumble said, tipping his head toward me. "Eric, Officer Pitts."

"Anything new?" Officer Pitts said to Lumble, who shook his head and went back to writing.

Pitts walked over to the desk and dropped a folded bunch of papers onto it. "No one has seen this kid since Saturday. Thank God nobody's called his parents yet. No reason to get them into a frenzy. Things like this happen every so often." Officer Pitts turned to me. "You see, usually it's one of two things—"

"He knows," Lumble said. "I already told him."

Pitts cleared his throat and looked around the room, as if searching for something important to do. "Anyway, all I'm getting at is that these matters usually resolve themselves. We just have to be patient. You staying in the dorm or at Professor Cade's?"

I thought for a moment. "Professor Cade's," I said.

"Good. If anything changes give us a call. Otherwise, we'll be in touch. You know," Pitts smiled and leaned against the desk with his arms crossed, "that Howie is a real cutup. Can you believe he offered me a drink? A Harvey Wallbanger, for Christ's sake. I haven't had one of those since the Dark Ages."

They both laughed while I thanked them and left, hoping they didn't notice how sweat-soaked the back of my shirt was.

◆ ◆ ◆

That's how it all started, like that child's game where a metal ball rolls down a trough and into a cup, which sinks and trips a lever that drops another ball onto a seesaw, and so on until the entire contraption has been altered by one simple motion in the very beginning.

When I arrived home from my meeting with Officer Lumble, Howie was fiddling around on the piano while Art played Go with Professor Cade at the dining room table. Dr. Cade said he'd just gotten off the phone with one of Dan's professors, Dr. Junta, who claimed he'd seen Dan in class that day, sitting in one of the back rows. I had a brief stab of panic—Did Dan rise from the dead? Did the elixir actually work?—before remembering that Dr. Junta's course, The Medicis: Fact and Fiction, was famed for both its enormous class size and Dr. Junta's senility and poor eyesight, which made cheating mandatory in a course so confusing that any other approach meant certain doom.

Katie Motts had returned Art's call, and said she hadn't heard from Dan since before vacation, so now Dr. Cade's curiosity shifted from where to why. Was Dan avoiding them? Had someone gotten into an argument with him? Was he dissatisfied with school? Work? His personal life, perhaps?

"I should like to think," Professor Cade said, as he surrounded the last of Art's black stones, "that Dan would approach me if he was having difficulties in the house. I'm expected to produce a workable manuscript by the end of this semester, and not having Dan's assistance puts serious demands upon the rest of you."

Dr. Cade had been repeating himself lately, always about his book, and how he didn't want it to interfere with our studies.

"He was unusually quiet when we last saw him," Art said, scanning the Go board for any possible escape routes. "He didn't even say goodbye. He just left."

"Yes, for errands, you said. I remember." Dr. Cade sat back, knowing—as did I—that Art had lost the game. "I can't imagine why he failed to come back. I really must look for him on campus, as should all of you. Perhaps one of you said something that angered him . . ." He glanced in Howie's direction. "Whatever it was, let's put it behind us. I don't care who was at fault, I only care that a member of our team is missing."

It was strange to hear him talk like that, calling us a *team*. Dr. Cade never played the role of mediator or advice giver; in fact, he'd been remarkably neutral when it came to our personal lives. I'd always had the impression that he didn't really care what we did outside the house, and I think my impression was accurate. For a man who had no children of his own, we served as his children, but I realized he was more like an impersonal deity than a parent, something like Aristotle's unmoved mover or Copernicus's grand clock maker.

"We did have an argument," Art said quietly. I looked at him but he kept his gaze on Professor Cade. "A few days before I saw him last. It was over something silly, like who's turn it was to do dishes. He seemed short-tempered. Not like himself."

Dr. Cade nodded curtly, stood up, and glanced at his watch. Hearing about our daily lives always displeased him. "I'll be at my department office for the remainder of the day," he said. "Should anyone come in contact with Dan, please call me immediately."

There was silence as Dr. Cade stared at Howie, who was trilling the piano keys. After a few moments Howie stopped playing and looked up.

"What?" he said, bouncing his gaze from person to person.

I knocked on Art's door that night, making sure that Howie was downstairs and that Dr. Cade hadn't yet returned home from campus. Art opened his door just wide enough to show his face. He didn't have his glasses on, and his eyes were red and dazed, as if he'd been reading for a long time.

"We need to talk," I said.

"Bad dreams again?"

"Just let me in."

"First tell me what's wrong," Art said.

I leaned in closer. "Dan sent me a letter over Christmas break," I whispered harshly. "It was in my mailbox at school."

Art shrugged. "So."

"He told me he was quitting," I said. "He said he didn't want to help you anymore with your alchemy project."

"And?"

"Well," I said, "did Dan say anything to you?"

Art thought for a moment. "Dan wanted to quit but I convinced him otherwise."

Art stared at me. "You have another theory?" he said.

I stood there, staring back at him.

"You need to get your mind off it," Art said, rubbing his eyes. "Go see a movie, read a book. Finish those translations. Write that section on Barbarossa or whoever the fuck it was. The walk could use some shoveling, actually . . ."

"Why did you tell Dr. Cade you got into an argument with Dan?"

Art raised an eyebrow. "Figure it out. Here, take this—"

His face disappeared and reappeared, and his hand emerged from the narrow slit between door and doorpost. In his palm was a tiny green pill.

"To help you sleep," he said.

I looked at the pill for a moment. "Is it?"

His expression darkened and he withdrew his hand.

"Sweet dreams, then," he said, and he closed the door.

The rest of the week brought more snow, another six inches that fell redundantly upon the swelling white dunes heaped across Dr. Cade's land. I could barely make out the pond, now just a shallow crater surrounded by trees fuzzy with snow, and winter birds sometimes landed briefly on the snow-covered ice, crows and sparrows and chickadees, huddled together like bolts of gray and black cloth. Even Nilus trotted onto the pond's surface, cautiously, at first, as if remembering a time when it had been water. I wondered if he could smell Dan out there, under the black ice, if that's where Dan was, or maybe he could smell a shoe of Dan's that had fallen off before Dan was swept into the Quinnipiac, the shoe now lying nestled among the rotting birch leaves and dormant hornwort at the pond's bottom. But if Nilus smelled Dan, he never gave any sign, and he would only lope back to me with the fluorescent tennis ball, ready to retrieve again.

When Dan didn't show up for Friday evening's dinner, Dr. Cade decided he was going to call Dan's mom.

"Perhaps she could give us some insight as to his whereabouts, or why he left in the first place. I do know they're quite close, Dan and his mother. If he was having difficulties I'm certain she'd be the first to know."

"I could call," Art said, seated at his usual place, on the other end of the table. He speared a carrot chip from his plate. We'd eaten the last of the vegetable lasagna Dr. Cade had prepared, and as always, whenever Dr. Cade cooked (a rare occurrence), the food was outstanding.

"Two years ago I spent Christmas at their Back Bay condo," Art continued. "We played bridge the entire time. She sent me a holiday card this year."

I don't believe anything you say, I thought. *Everything you say is a lie.*

"Very well, whatever you'd like," Dr. Cade said as he folded his napkin. "But please call her tonight. I need this problem resolved. The deadline for Dan's sections is fast approaching, and the work he's done thus far has been nearly perfect. I can't imagine any of you taking over at this point . . . there isn't enough time."

Howie snorted into his napkin. He'd come down with a bad cold a few days earlier, and was suffering publicly since then, wandering around the house in bathrobe and slippers, glass of warmed rum in one hand and box of tissues in the other. His alcohol abstinence was short-lived; why it began or ended he didn't say. But I think he was more affected by Dan's absence than he let on, because although Howie enjoyed teasing Dan, Dan was also, out of all of us, the most tolerant of Howie's teasing. I think Howie blamed himself for Dan supposedly leaving the house. Some argument before vacation, maybe, or one too many slights and insults, had ended in Dan finally deciding he'd had enough.

A day earlier Howie had pulled me aside and asked if I was keeping anything secret.

"You can tell old Howie," he said, winking. His breath smelled of

Irish coffee. "I won't say a word. It's because of me, isn't it? Because of what I said."

I put my hand on his shoulder. He looked desperate. "If I knew anything, I'd tell you."

Howie closed one eye and pulled away from me. "About a month ago Dan and I got into a little . . . debate, I guess you'd call it. Nothing much, you know, nothing much at all. It was about that Philosopher's Stone bullshit." He looked around the living room to see if anyone had sneaked in during our conversation. "Before vacation. I told Art I wasn't interested in it anymore. He had this whole thing planned, some big ceremony in the woods—" Howie stopped.

"Aw, what the hell," he said. "He probably told you anyway."

"Actually," I said, "Art hasn't told me anything."

"Doesn't matter now. What's done is done. Art told us when he returned from Prague he'd have the real formula for the elixir. I told him I didn't give a shit because I'm *done*. I told him this alchemy business stopped being fun a while ago. You know how it is, sometimes those types of things are interesting, like ouija boards and seances . . . not that I ever believed any of it anyway. But you know Art. Once he gets something in his head he won't quit. So I told him I wasn't interested, and Dan said I was being stubborn, and that got me going . . ." He trailed off, a sad look in his wide, green eyes. "Maybe I said some things I shouldn't have said."

"Like what?"

Howie sniffled. "Well, I sort of stated the obvious."

I held out my hands to indicate I didn't get it.

"Oh, come on, Eric. You may be young but you aren't blind. You know Dan is . . . you know." He rolled his eyes.

"Gay," I said.

"Yeah." Howie sighed, as if relieved I'd said it first. "Or at least he's leaning in that direction. Frankly, I just think he's confused—he doesn't act like a queer, and usually with those types you can tell the second you meet them. And God knows I've tried to help. I can't tell you how many dates I've set him up on. Something about fags draws women like stink to shit. But I think Dan could go either way, and I don't think some of the things he does with Art are right."

"Ellen told me about the forest ceremonies," I said. "About the circle jerks and everything."

Howie fell silent, his red hair in swirls and whorls, a couple of days' worth of facial hair covering his chin.

"She wasn't there," he said, quietly. "She took it out of context."

I could see we were heading into dangerous territory and I quickly asked him again about Dan. Howie sniffled.

"I told him I thought he was only into this whole alchemy thing for the sex."

"Oh, *man*," I said.

Howie ran his hands through his hair and exhaled sharply. If I hadn't known the truth about Dan's disappearance, I would have believed Howie's comment was the reason.

So it was only fitting that Howie was the catalyst that Friday evening, since he'd burdened himself with unnecessary guilt, and although I'm sure, in his drunken stupor, he thought what he'd found wasn't anything important, a part of me still wonders if Howie suspected something subconsciously, and with alcohol as solvent the grains of doubt swirled and collected at the bottom of his mind, waiting to be plucked between his outstretched fingers and held to the light and inspected with a revelatory *Ah-ha!* He looked up from his plate, speech slurred, eyes unsteady. "There was a poem on Dan's bed when I got back from vacation," he said. "I went into his room to drop off the book I got for him, and I found a poem. In French. Does Dan speak French?"

I looked to Art, who looked to Dr. Cade, who looked to Howie. "Where is this poem now?" Dr. Cade said.

"In my room," Howie said. The radiator groaned. "On my dresser. I translated it, and totally forgot about it."

Professor Cade set down his napkin and left the table. For five minutes we waited in silence, listening to footsteps creak across the upstairs floor. Howie refilled his glass with wine, and Art refused to look at me, instead rooting through the remainder of his lasagna wedge, giving it a few desultory jabs with the tip of his knife. Nilus padded softly across the living room and moved to his favorite spot in front of the fireplace. A yellowing leaf toppled from the stalk of Dr. Cade's ficus tree framing the archway and fell to the floor.

Dr. Cade returned, holding out a folded sheet of paper between thumb and forefinger, his forehead wrinkled with worry, his mouth turned down at the corners. He looked concerned, and a little afraid, but most of all he looked *curious,* as if he were watching a great tragedy unfold and found it fascinating.

Soon after I realized why—Professor Cade was holding what he believed was Dan's suicide note.

Chapter 5

There was the phone call, Dr. Cade's solemn voice coming from the kitchen, telling the Fairwich police he has reason to believe one of his students may have harmed himself. There was the suicide note itself, laid out for us on the dining room table, between the vegetable lasagna dish and the radicchio and olive salad, a piece of white, unlined paper, containing a single stanza typewritten in the center of the page:

> *. . . L'eternité.*
> *C'est la mer mêlée*
> *Au soleil.*

There was the long wait in silence and the flashing red lights of a police cruiser, and then Nilus barking and knocks on the door and Dr. Cade welcoming in two policemen, who looked at our strange scene with what must have been astonishment. The three of us, Art, Howie, and myself, sitting equidistant from one another at the dining room table, the cryptic note as the centerpiece lying there as if we were waiting for it to morph into human form and sing its sad tale.

Questions and questions, so many of the same, voiced as gently as possible, but always sharp and double-edged, more probing than campus security's had been, and I remember one of the officers asking Dr. Cade why, if his student hadn't been seen for a week, didn't anyone do anything sooner. Dr. Cade said that Professor Junta thought he'd seen Dan in Wednesday's class.

"So he saw him a few days ago, correct?" one of the officers said.

"I believe so, yes. But Dr. Junta is one of our older—let's just say he's not what I would deem a reliable witness."

"But when you spoke to him, he clearly stated he had seen Daniel Higgins in class, on Wednesday."

"Correct."

The officers exchanged glances. The shorter, stockier of the two, Officer Bellis, asked the questions—*And there is no history of depression, as far as you know?*—while his taller, leaner partner, Officer Inman, stayed in the background, jotting down notes, wandering casually about the first floor. No to everything, we'd all said, Howie and Art and myself, while Dr. Cade made phone calls and talked with Officer Bellis about what I can't remember, though I recall some conversation about runaways and high IQs. No, there wasn't any drug use in Dan's life. No, he was an excellent student and felt little anxiety about schoolwork. No, his relationships all seemed healthy and prospering. Howie had switched to coffee, and he was sweating with the effort of trying to maintain a sober façade while a grim-faced policeman asked a seemingly endless stream of morbid questions. There was no mystery—I could have taken them to the exact spot in the pond, like Poe's madman in "Tell-Tale Heart," and dropped a stone into the water and screamed *Dissemble no more! I admit the deed! Here! Here lies his body!*

Officer Bellis looked at the note again and shook his head. *This doesn't look like much of a suicide note to me,* he said to Dr. Cade. *How can you be sure?*

Dr. Cade translated the note for them, and sighed. "It is a message that does not bode well," Dr. Cade said, with tired patience, as if weary of dealing with what he no doubt viewed as two well-intentioned ignoramuses. They, in turn, merely nodded solemnly, though I could see in their expressions they thought the whole matter was being blown out of proportion.

They asked us if we'd searched the surrounding woods, and Art said we'd walked nearly a mile back, all the way to the end of Dr.

Cade's property line where a big ravine cut him off from Troyer Nursery. And of course we hadn't yet spoken with *all* of Dan's friends, although we didn't think he had that many, and certainly none he'd be staying with without letting us know. We were his closest friends, I told them.

"So all of you live here, is that it?" Officer Inman spoke up from the background.

"They are in my employment," said Dr. Cade proudly. "In exchange for which I provide room and board."

"Nice setup," Officer Inman said, and he flashed a strictly professional smile and went back to his clipboard.

We stayed up until two in the morning, the fire again a small mound of sparks and embers, stoked recently by Art, the police having left with Dan's note and his wallet, on their way to Aberdeen to meet with campus security. Officer Inman, in a routine sweep of Dan's room, had found the wallet under Dan's bed, and when he brought it downstairs everything changed. Officer Bellis turned to a new page in his notebook and silently scribbled something; Officer Inman asked if he could use the phone. Howie paced across the room until Art asked him to stop, and Dr. Cade asked if anyone wanted some tea. An announcement would be made tomorrow morning, the police assured us—all students and professors would know "to keep an eye out" for Dan. Dan's relative would be called, Dan's file would be pulled, and the whole situation would work itself out. But it was obvious, judging by the now serious looks on the policemen's faces, that having found Dan's wallet was a bad sign.

Dr. Cade called Mrs. Higgins and left a message on her machine, something about a problem with her son and could she please call immediately. And when the police left and Dr. Cade went upstairs to bed, Art, Howie, and I remained in the living room, each of us wallowing in guilt, whether deserved or not. And the only image I can think of, no matter how outlandish, is from something out of the *Inferno:* Art and I on Geryon's back, clutching its reeking fur, spiraling down to the circle of the deceivers, while Howie looked out over the desert sands under the fury of raining fire, searching for his lost friend.

◆ ◆ ◆

It was all a grim mess, and I think I might have done something dras-tic had I not ripped free from my bedroom the next morning and made my way to campus. I was insanely tired but that was a good thing, because it allowed me to amble without much thought, heavy-lidded and dazed. Art had kept me up the previous night, stealing into my room around four in the morning to talk about Origen's three-fold interpretation of literature. Snippets floated up from my subconscious . . . *Somatic, psychic, pneumatic* . . . Saint Augustine's four-fold interpretation . . . *Littera gesta docet quid credas allegoria; moralis quid agas, quo tendas anagogia.*

Word had gotten out about Dan's disappearance and spread among the halls and eateries and faculty lounges like fire across a dry plain. I heard Dan's name mentioned in every conversation, from the steps of Thorren to the first-floor men's room in Garringer to the cof-fee line at Campus Bean. *Missing* was the mantra, whispered in melo-dramatic breaths. Prayer groups formed and dissolved, impromptu search parties set out into the woods surrounding campus, shouting excitedly, their voices ringing off the snowy hills. Photocopies of a picture of Dan had been stapled to every corkboard in every hallway, but the print had been too dark and the quality was poor, making Dan look like an aborigine in shirt and tie.

It was a very clear day, crisp and windy, the sky a cradle of blue, the distant ridges of Stanton Valley like a row of storm clouds set on the horizon. I wandered from building to building, unseen, clutching a cup of hot chocolate. I saw Howie walking briskly across the Quad, underdressed for the weather as usual, hands stuffed in his pockets, head down. For a moment I wanted to call out, but then I realized there was nothing to say.

Around mid-afternoon I found myself in the H. F. Mores for the first time in weeks, reading some book on Mesopotamia. I'd been scanning the same sentence over and over, finding comfort in the rep-etition. *Flat was the land between the Euphrates and Tigris Rivers, but here and there mysterious mounds rose out of the plain.*

The door swung open and Art walked in, black greatcoat flapping behind him like the wings of a giant crow, curly hair slicked back and the smoking bowl of his pipe jutting from his mouth. His face was red from the cold and he was dressed in what looked like a new suit, dark navy blue with a maroon tie. He didn't seem to notice me at first, his gaze sweeping from side to side and then peering ahead into the recesses of the dusty bookshelves. I closed my book and sat back, while Art stopped at the edge of the massive Oriental rug and looked at me. He loomed tall and silent in the dim light of the room.

He remained at bay, on the edge of the rug, taking the pipe out of his mouth. "Have you seen Cornelius?" he said.

Not for a while, I told him. I hadn't been going to work, and I didn't care if I got in trouble.

"He's sick," Art said. "He's been getting chemotherapy at St. Michael's. Stomach cancer, I think. I thought maybe he'd been released . . ." Art puffed his pipe, despite the library's no-smoking policy.

Cornelius had stomach cancer. He wasn't immortal. It was all crazy, just like I'd suspected. The maps with dragons and his dumb old books and his pigeons . . . all of it, completely crazy.

"How bad is it?" I said.

"The cancer?" Art shrugged. "I visited him last week. He didn't look too good."

"He's never looked good," I said. I wanted to shout *It's a dead end! Cornelius is dying! There is no Philosopher's Stone!*

"I saw Howie earlier," I said. "What's he doing on campus?"

"Organizing a search party," Art said. "Couldn't have picked a colder day."

We fell silent for a few moments.

"Dan's mom is flying in tonight," Art said. "She's staying at the Riverside." The Riverside was Fairwich's only four-star hotel, a renovated Victorian resting on the banks of the Quinnipiac.

"And I saw your friend Nicole at Campus Bean. She asked about you, how you were holding up. I told her you were doing as well as could be expected."

"I'm worried about Dr. Cade," I said, wanting to say much more, but there were a few students scattered about, wandering the aisles or

284 — MICAH NATHAN

seated at study carrels with bowed heads and bent backs. The truth is I wasn't worried about Dr. Cade at all—I'm sure he was concerned, but he was handling Dan's disappearance in classic fashion, neither too upset nor too calm, comfortably straddling the medium without settling on any particular emotion. I imagined he was philosophical about the whole thing, fearing Dan had killed himself, yet believing there were far worse fates, and I just couldn't see Dr. Cade joining in the mass hysteria. Even if Dr. Cade himself were to discover Dan's body, I couldn't envision it in anything other than Apollonian terms: a brief surprise, a moment of sadness, and then solemn reflection upon the excesses of youth's emotion and the quiet tragedy of a fine life lost.

Art puffed twice. "I wouldn't be too concerned with Dr. Cade. I think in some ways he's rather enjoying this . . . assuming the outcome is as positive as we all hope. There's a certain epic quality to it all, you know? Like those sweeping tragedies . . . something out of *Wuthering Heights.*"

I agreed, actually, in a cynical way, as much as my guilt would allow.

"You don't know the half of it," Art said, pausing with the pipe in his mouth. "Dan attempted suicide about three years ago." One of the students in the study carrels stiffened noticeably, and turned his head. "When he was about fourteen," Art continued. "After his father died. He took a bunch of his mother's Valium. Dan told us about it a while ago, and it wasn't that big of a deal, we all understood." Art shook his head. He was either a superb actor or being honest, because he looked truly dismayed.

"So you think it's happened again," I said, trying to contain my sarcasm. "Another suicide attempt, is that it?"

"Who's to say. We won't know until we find him." Art puffed again. "Which reminds me—tomorrow morning Howie and I are taking a drive to Wiktor's Orchard. I think you should join us. We can cover more area with another person helping out."

He released a cloud of smoke, and then turned on his heels and left, the tail of his coat licking the edge of the door as it shut, snapping in the wind like a tongue of black flame. *He's working on something,* I thought. *This is all going according to his plans.*

I stayed in the library until dark, and as I walked down its front steps it started snowing, flakes materializing from the night sky reflected off the lamppost lights lining the main path through the Quad. Over the previous four hours I'd made many resolutions and broken them all; I decided to tell the police the truth, I decided to show Dr. Cade the letter under my dorm-room mattress, I decided to confront Art about the suicide note and ask why he'd had the same poem on his desk, weeks earlier.

Instead I walked to Paderborne, hurrying through the lobby with my head down, hoping to pass unnoticed into my room, where I could crawl into bed until the next phone call or startling revelation. Maybe Howie had gone missing, or Dr. Cade, or even Art. It was all beginning to feel preposterous, as if I'd walked onto the set of a play and slipped into a role as one of the extras. I was fairly certain I'd been a central character, at one point, but somewhere in the production my name had fallen off the marquee, and its block letters were now trampled underfoot by the hordes of people crowding into the theater to get a look at the next scene. *Maybe I'm invisible,* I thought, *or maybe I'm giving off some sort of macabre scent that keeps everyone away, the rank odor of anguish that ghouls are said to emit while skulking around graveyards and charnel houses.*

I passed by a couple of freshmen in the stairwell, and caught a fragment of their conversation. Dean Richardson was giving a speech tomorrow, in the former chancel of Garringer, some sort of public service announcement offering counseling services for any students who feel overwhelming academic pressure. This, I'm sure, was a back-handed way of stating a reason for Dan's disappearance. Crisis management at its finest, corking the hole after the leak.

I saw Nicole leaving her room, dressed in her favorite tight black pants and mint-green turtleneck sweater. She immediately rushed up and gave me a full-frontal hug and then assaulted me with sympathetic questions and fawning looks.

"So is everyone in the house going crazy or what?"

"It's very hard for all of us," I said. *There's that phrase again. Like some line in a soap opera, with the pretty heroine in a coma and her family and friends surrounding her hospital bed.*

"This is *so* weird," Nicole said. "I remember talking to him like it was yesterday, that day in the Quad, remember? He was such a cutie. Do you think he's okay? Someone told me there was a suicide note, but I told them they were fucking nuts because I served on the peer helpers board last semester, and Dan exhibited *none* of the suicidal behaviors we learned about. I didn't know him that well, of course, but you can tell the minute you meet someone . . ."

She looked down at her nails, eyes narrowed in ruthless inspection, and picked at a cuticle. "By the way, I've got some very good smoke," she said. "Do you want some? To help you relax?"

"Do you think it'd help?" I said.

Nicole nodded emphatically and grabbed my arm. "Oh, most definitely. When my mom was being a total bitch after the divorce, I smoked just about every day for a month. It's so much better than drinking, which depresses the shit out of you, and on top of *that,* did you know pot isn't even addictive? It's true—you can smoke it for thirty days straight and quit whenever you want. Try that with coke; you'd be running around like a chicken with its head chopped off."

I finally returned to Professor Cade's late that night, my head muddy from the aftereffects of an evening spent at Nicole's. She'd been a good sport, making apple-cinnamon tea on her hot plate and feeding me little powdered doughnuts. People came and went, faces I'd seen during the previous months, kind, inquisitive faces that talked in hushed, respectful tones while Nicole watched over me and ensured no one asked about Dan or mentioned anything "inappropriate." I remained on her bed the entire time, bong on the nightstand, book of matches nearby, open box of doughnuts close at hand and a mug of steaming tea sitting on a black lacquer Oriental tray at the end of the bed. I felt like some Persian king, with Nicole as my courtesan, receiving guests who spoke in strange tongues that I didn't care to understand. When I decided it was time to leave, I had her call me a cab and I floated back out into the cold winter night, clinging tightly to the cocoon I'd spent the last four hours weaving around myself.

A single light shone from the living room window of Dr. Cade's house. I saw a tall shadow flash across the living room followed by another shadow, this one smaller and feminine. *It's Ellen,* I thought.

The inside of the house smelled like spring. There were fresh flowers everywhere, bundles of jonquils and daffodils and tulips and long-stemmed red roses with stems thick as my fingers. A ceramic white bowl held pennyroyal and spikenard in a thick tuft of purple and white. A spray of mums sat atop the dining room table, russet orange and almond brown and soft bronze. Someone had sent a massive bushel of lilac and damask rose that remained in its clear plastic delivery box by the bottom of the stairs.

Dr. Cade walked into the dining room from the kitchen, holding a bottle of dark wine and wearing one of his signature cable-knit sweaters. *"Eric,"* he said, approaching me with a kind smile. "How are you?"

I told him I was okay, a little tired, that's all. He nodded and beckoned me into the living room. *There's someone I want you to meet,* he said.

It was Dan's mother of course, Mrs. Elizabeth Higgins, looking exactly as I'd imagined, with jet-black hair pulled painfully tight into a bun that stuck out from the back of her head like it had been glued on. She was a tiny woman, shorter than Ellen and about fifteen pounds lighter, all sun-freckled skin and tendon and bone. Her eyes were beautiful—deep-set, teardrop-shaped, and creamy brown like chocolate, offset by a glittering diamond chain wound tightly around her willowy neck. She looked as though a strong wind could sweep her away, or even a mean glance, and her ivory-colored silk blouse clung gently to her delicate frame, above a pair of slender chestnut-brown pants. When Professor Cade introduced me she allowed herself a brief smile, flashing a row of miniature, straight white teeth, before closing that diminutive mouth in a tight clamp of worry surrounded by wrinkles and creases that suggested worry was as familiar as an old scar that had marked its territory upon her face.

I sat across from her, on the couch facing the study, Nilus at my feet and a scatter of papers lying on the coffee table. A wallet-sized photo of Dan was paper-clipped to one of the sheets, showing his head and upper torso in a gray suit with a light blue background; it looked like a high school senior portait.

"We missed you at Christmas," Mrs. Higgins said, staring at the fire for a moment before turning to me. Her voice was clear and measured.

"I'm sorry?" I said, then I remembered Dan's letter. *But, hopefully, you'll receive this on time and accept my invitation to join mother and me for Christmas dinner in good old Boston.*

I'm so sorry, I thought. *Dan, I'm so sorry.*

Mrs. Higgins uncrossed her legs and set them side by side, hands resting in her lap. "You look exactly as Daniel described. Very young. Like him—two peas in a pod, I suppose you are. Daniel is quite fond of you."

"Thank you," I said, and for a moment I thought I would cry.

She smiled politely. A massive diamond ring shone brilliant in the firelight, encircling her third finger. She rubbed it with her thumb.

Dr. Cade sat on the other end of her couch. "Liz is an accomplished philologist," he said, looking in her direction. "She's taught seminars at nearly every prestigious institution in the country, except for Aberdeen, of course."

She *hmm*ed and reached for her wine glass. "This college isn't quite big enough for the two of us," she said. "I'm afraid your ego would smother me."

Dr. Cade laughed, the first time I'd ever seen him do so. "When everything is resolved, perhaps I should have you conduct a seminar here. I don't know why we've waited so long. I saw you speak last at Princeton, correct? That series on Juvenal."

She said nothing, only stared at the fire, hands interlocked again and knees touching one another, her form a slender, dark straw. I could see Dan in her face, in the shape and delicateness, but there was a hardness that Dan didn't share, a graceful stiffness to her expressions that seemed much older than her current worries. She blinked and turned to us, her eyes watering.

"Goodness," she said, unclicking her purse and pulling out a small square of tissue. "The heat is irritating my eyes . . . what are you burning in there, William?"

Dr. Cade rose quickly and walked to the fireplace. I watched a moment longer as Mrs. Higgins dabbed her cheeks, and then I awkwardly excused myself and left, hearing Dr. Cade's voice: *Please don't worry . . . Another day and he'll be found . . . Dan is a responsible boy.*

I waited at the bottom of the stairs for Nilus to follow, and then I went to my room, warily keeping my hand upon Nilus's head the entire time. The Romans believed dogs can sense the dead, and warn of them by barking.

Sunday—cold, clear, and windy—I remained in my room, ignoring the phone, sleeping on and off, and I emerged, after dark, once Art and Howie returned home. They were both red-faced and exhausted from hours first spent searching Wiktor's Orchard and then the deep forests surrounding Aberdeen, joining a search party made up of undergraduate ski bums *(They used it as an excuse to cross-country ski,* Howie told me, unwrapping his black scarf from around his neck; *I called them a bunch of shameless pricks).* Then, when conditions turned from sunny and clear to dark and blustery, they switched to a smaller group of more serious volunteers—hunters and fishermen from Stanton Valley who'd heard about the disappearance on the local news, grizzled old veterans of local tragedies like the great flood of '64, when the Quinnipiac absorbed five feet of melting snow and washed away eight homes, killing a family of six. Some of the older members brought along their dogs, hounds, and retrievers trotting through knee-deep snow. Howie said it reminded him of old horror movies where grim-faced villagers set out to trap the werewolf or vampire or what have you, treading through misty forests with hunting dogs in tow.

"I'm surprised we didn't see you out there," Howie said to me. He unlaced his boots and rubbed his feet. "What did you do all day?"

I coughed into my fist. "I stayed in. I think I'm getting sick."

Art shot me a reproachful look.

"Well, it's probably for the best," said Howie. "It was a waste of time. A little drama to cure the boredom, you know? First time I've seen townies on campus, though. That alone was almost worth the price of admission."

Art hung up his coat and collapsed onto the living room couch. "These kind of things bring small towns together," he said, covering his eyes with his forearm. "Edna's Coffee Shop donated ten gallons of hot chocolate and a huge crate of doughnuts. Father Reynold led prayer groups in Garringer all afternoon."

"Which I was totally against," Howie said. He sat on the couch opposite Art and yawned. "Any excuse to ply their wares and the Church'll rise to the occasion. *Opportunistic,* that's what I say, always riding on the tails of crisis. And you know what else? Wait, hold that thought . . ."

Howie walked out and returned moments later with a bottle of brandy in one hand and a snifter in the other. "Here's what I think." He uncorked and poured. "I think Dan decided he needed to get away for whatever reason, checked himself into a hotel under a fake name, and then went for a stroll a few days ago and got lost. Remember last year when he went on that hike near Horsehead Falls? We searched *three* hours for him, wandering around the forest, shouting his name, and it started raining . . . And then we finally took a break and went to that little diner, what's-it-called—"

"*The Whistle Stop,*" Art said, his eyes still covered.

Howie nodded. "Yeah, so we stroll in and sure enough, there's Dan sitting on a stool, dry as a bone, reading the paper and drinking coffee."

"You let him have it," Art said. "You guys had it out right in front of everyone."

Howie paused in mid-drink and looked away. A troubled look passed across his face, and then he shrugged and drained the snifter in one gulp. "Yeah, well, he deserved it," he said, and he refilled the glass and sank back into the couch.

We decided to watch the six o'clock news, so Howie retrieved the small black-and-white stored in the basement. We set it on the floor in front of the fireplace and huddled around, our faces lit by the fire and the flash of commercials for laundry detergent and beer and Jim

Blakely's Used Cars (*You've never seen lower prices for cars this amazing, and after this week, you never will again!*). The Channel 7 news came back on with my old girlfriend, Cynthia Andrews, staring out at us, her face framed in a new, shorter haircut.

"The search continued today," she said solemnly, "for a local Aberdeen student—"

"How's that for a lousy photo," said Howie. "Dan looks eleven years old."

"Shush," Art said.

"—in this new development, which police say may shed some light onto the whereabouts of Boston native Daniel Higgins. With more on that, we turn to Harris Gavin, who's reporting live from Aberdeen College."

Cut to Harris Gavin, wearing a ski jacket and black earmuffs, standing on the steps of Garringer, a small throng of students behind him pointing and chuckling at the camera. He had a piece of paper in his hand, and his hair flipped up in the wind.

"I'm standing on the steps of Garringer Hall, in the heart of Aberdeen College, where the search for Daniel Higgins has completed its second day—"

"Oh man, is this moronic," said Howie, to which Art responded *Will you shut up and let me hear this?*

"—and, in this breaking story exclusive to Channel 7 news, an anonymous source has informed us Daniel Higgins was spotted early this morning, at approximately 6 A.M., driving a white sedan on Route 128 in the town of Brant, with, and I quote, 'a large man of African-American descent.' Local officials have refused to speculate, but have released this composite sketch of Daniel Higgins's passenger—"

(At that point the camera cut to a charcoal etching.)

"—and ask that anyone with information on this case should please contact the Fairwich Police Department at area code . . ."

"Whoah," said Howie, and he gulped from his snifter.

Art sat back. I looked at him and our eyes met, for a moment, a rush of confusion passing between us.

Harris Gavin was interviewing a student, a kid dressed in an Aberdeen sweatshirt, splotchy blemishes shining angrily under the flat camera lights. *Yeah, I knew Dan. He was in my freshman comp class last year . . .*

Howie stood up, towering over me, snifter in hand, one of his white socks with a hole in it and his big toe poking through.

"A *black* guy?" Howie said. He guzzled his brandy. "I don't think Dan's ever even *talked* to a black guy."

Art shot up from the floor and ran both his hands through his hair.

"What is it?" I said.

"He's still alive," Art said, staring at me but not seeing.

I was speechless. Art walked out of the living room, slowly, and went upstairs. His door slammed shut and Nilus sat up and barked.

"Of course he's alive," Howie said to no one in particular, emptying his glass in one swallow. "He's eloped with a fucking black man."

Howie and I stayed up for another hour, sharing the bottle of brandy until it ran out, while I listened to Howie ruminate about how confused Dan must be, how his decision to "run off with some black guy" was really a direct refutation of the Waspy lifestyle he obviously wanted no part of. I didn't know what to think—so much had happened that anything seemed possible. Dan being alive, however remote a possibility, was certainly more reasonable than him having joined an African-American man on some cross-state road trip. Rasputin had been poisoned and shot and finally drowned; perhaps Dan had proved just as resilient. Or had the witness been mistaken? There were a lot of everyday people who resembled Dan, so nondescript was he that I often find myself forgetting how he looked.

It was much easier to pretend I was just as confounded as everyone else, that I went to bed wondering where Dan was (which, in a sense, I did), and woke up hoping he'd come home safely (which, in another sense, I also did). Self-preservation had muted the pangs of guilt, and I'd developed an emotional callous that protected me from the numerous breakdowns I'd suffered through the past week. Now I was content to close my conscience and view every event like fiction, like a book or a movie, disassociating myself as much as possible so that I no longer felt everyday emotions but rather a dead calm. *The life of a junkie must feel like this,* I thought, *wandering from one fix to the next. Feeling nothing, tasting nothing, hearing nothing, wanting nothing save that rush of nullity so often mistaken for bliss, when in fact it's only blissful because the pain stops.* I craved the absence of existence. Nothing more.

His speech on Dan's rebellion now completed, Howie told me about the day's events—police buzzing around campus like hornets at a picnic, darting into buildings, accosting students and professors alike who had come to either help in the search or gawk at the unfolding drama. The administration, Howie said, was very nervous, viewing the police as a necessary annoyance and little else; they were still convinced Dan was part of some elaborate prank that had gone too far. If this was a prank, Dean Richardson assured everyone, in as poor a display of timing as anyone could remember, suspensions and perhaps even expulsions would be meted out. Professor Cade was seen gliding across campus, Mrs. Higgins at his side, the two of them like phantoms dressed in gray and black. Howie had seen them several times throughout the day—standing at the edge of the woods behind Kellner Hall, apart from a knot of noisy students; in the Thorren lobby, reading the various announcements tacked to the corkboard; even at Campus Bean, sitting in the corner sipping from Styrofoam cups, which, Howie had said, Mrs. Higgins held primly between her gloved hands as if she'd never touched Styrofoam before.

We talked until we both passed out from exhaustion and alcohol. I fell asleep on the couch, Nilus nearby, and Howie slept across from me on the other couch. I think I heard him mumble something to himself before fading into drunken oblivion.

Art awakened me in the middle of the night. I started to say something but he put his finger to his lips and dissolved back into the darkness.

I sat up and looked around, momentarily disoriented. The living room was bathed in pale blue moonlight, running across the floor, washing over Howie's face. He'd fallen asleep with his head back and his mouth open, one foot dangling over the end of the couch and the other resting on the floor. On the coffee table was an empty bottle of brandy. I was still drunk, as I recall, because my mouth had a strong medicinal taste and I had difficulty remembering how I'd ended up on the couch.

My watch read 12:30. The fireplace held a few crumbled, glowing embers. Art straightened up slowly and walked away, and I followed him, up the stairs, unsure if I was awake or dreaming.

Once in his room—he kept the lights off—Art moved to his window, swift and silent, a silhouette gliding across the room, and beckoned me with an outstretched hand.

"There," he whispered, pointing toward the backyard. Black trees cast long shadows across the snow like the legs of a giant. *"Do you see him?"*

I looked, but saw nothing.

Art breathed heavily. *"He's down there . . ."* he said. *"I saw someone run from the woods, across the lawn."*

"Who?" I whispered back.

Art craned his head and stared toward the pond. *"Dan,"* he said.

Something moved at the edge of the forest, a dark shape, barely noticeable. It was too far away for me to get any kind of perspective, but whatever it was dashed back into the woods.

"Oh my God," I said.

Art remained at the window a moment longer, then pulled down the shade and turned on his desk lamp. I squinted from the harsh light.

Art was shockingly well-dressed for such a late hour. His blue shirt was pressed and clean, and he wore a simple dark blue tie held tight by a silver bar.

I had too many questions. I started with the most pressing:

"How do you know that was Dan?"

Art sat at his desk and faced me, leaning forward, forearms resting on his knees. He had on his leather boots, the pair he'd bought in London. "I can't be certain," he said, looking down. "But I'm pretty sure whoever it was followed me home from Ellen's."

That explained his clothes. A pang of jealousy struck.

"I thought I was going to lose my mind tonight," Art said. "After that piece on the news. I told myself there was no way he could be alive. I mean, you were there . . . you saw."

I didn't need to be reminded. Dan's head lolling on a limp neck as we hefted him from the bottom of the canoe, one eyelid fluttering open, flashing a sickening white . . . I'd already seen too much.

"But tonight, after I dropped Ellen off . . . we ate at Orezi's, you know, that new Neapolitan place." He raised his finger and cocked his head to one side. "Did you hear that?"

"No," I said.

"Hmm. Anyway, I dropped Ellen off and was about to turn onto Main when I saw a white sedan pull out from a parking lot. I wouldn't have paid attention, normally, but after that news piece . . . I drove up Route 80 and back down to school, just to see if this sedan was really following me. I'd think I lost it and then at a traffic light I'd look behind me and there it would be, headlights in the distance. It was like something out of a horror film."

"You should've gone to the police," I said, but Art shook his head.

"You know they brought me and Howie down to the station this afternoon. Asked us a bunch of questions."

I was shocked.

"Don't worry," Art said, getting up off his chair and loosening his tie. "They didn't mention your name." Despite the current situation, Art was remarkably relaxed—it was a change I'd soon become accustomed to; Art distant and nervous in crowds, and then back to his old self when with me, despite the memories we now shared. I think it may have been the guilt, since guilt can make one feel torturously alone, except when there's someone else to share it with.

Art folded his tie and walked over to his dresser. "Like I said, I'm not one hundred percent certain it's him, but that white car followed me all the way home, and then drove past once I pulled in the driveway. So I came in, found you two passed out on the couch, and ran upstairs with a pair of binoculars. And I waited. Two hours went by and I finally saw something—some*one*—run across the backyard and into the woods."

There was too much to think about. The police questioning Art, the figure in the woods, and incredibly, in the back of my memory, like a splinter in my palm, was Ellen. *Had she told Art anything about my confession?* I wondered. Did Art care even if she had?

"What if it is Dan?" I asked. Art was now unlacing his boots. "What then?"

"We leave," Art said. "We get out of the country."

"Pardon me?"

He looked up. "If it's Dan, that means the formula works."

"But I thought that's what you wanted."

"It is. It's just . . ." Art kicked off his boots and sat on the edge of his bed, stretching his toes out. "I don't know," he said, and he fell back and slapped his palm over his eyes. "We got lazy. We skipped the purification rites."

"So?"

"*So,* they're the most important part. The body—actually, the soul, or the spirit, or whatever you want to call it—has to be ready for immortality." He rolled onto his side and stared at the headboard. "I have a hard time accepting all the ritual, even though I know it's the most important element."

"What are you getting at?"

Art looked at me. "Dan hadn't been cleansed. If he's still alive, then he may have . . . *changed.* I don't know how else to say it."

"What, like into a monster?" In spite of myself I laughed.

"Not in the corporeal sense," said Art. He was being surprisingly patient. "Jung said alchemy is the bridge between the subconscious and the conscious. The cleansing rites are meant to lengthen the bridge. To make sure nothing dangerous bubbles up. Some of the drugs Dan took were very psychoactive, and under certain conditions there is a danger of the subject losing his mind, quite literally. Reverting back to a primal state."

I glanced at the window shade.

"Transmutation goes both ways," Art said. "And not always for the better."

Something wasn't adding up. We were talking like madmen. I'd seen Dan disappear under the water, seen his face fade into inky nothingness. Even if there were a formula for increasing longevity, how could it possibly apply to someone already dead? And, assuming he was now alive (the most insane notion I've ever come close to believing), why would he be slinking around the woods at night? Why wouldn't he just come forward and proclaim the entire thing to be one giant misunderstanding? And why was Art afraid? It wasn't the police he seemed afraid of—in fact, Art approached them with almost dangerous confidence, as if believing his superior intelligence was the ultimate protection, an attitude which rubbed off a bit onto me—but there was something else. It was Dan, Dan who scared him. But why, I asked myself.

When I get back I have to tell Art I'm no longer interested in his search for the stone.

They were too far in, I thought. *They were too far in and Art couldn't let Dan go.*

I'm not saying it's all nonsense—I still think there might be something to it, but getting to that point is too dangerous.

More murder-mystery idiocy, I thought. *Don't be foolish. Occam's razor. Law of parsimony. Simplest explanation, nothing more. Art convinced Dan to stay on just a little longer, just like Art said. And Art isn't scared. He feels guilt. He's mistaking fear for guilt.*

"Tell me about Dan's suicide note," I said.

Art crossed his arms over his stomach, serene as a monk. *"L'eternité . . ."* he said. "It's by Rimbaud, Dan's favorite poet. I wrote it the night of the accident and left it on his bed. At first I thought Dr. Cade would find it, or maybe campus security once we called them, but having Howie discover the note worked out perfectly. The wallet under the bed was even better—I didn't know where it was, and thank God because I would've done something foolish, like throw it in the trash for Hector the garbageman to find."

Or maybe there's nothing to it and we're all just bored.

"Did Dan know what he was drinking?" I said, slowly.

Art looked at me. "Of course. Why do you ask?"

"Then why didn't he go through the purification rites?"

Art didn't answer.

"Art?"

He closed his eyes and lay there, still as a stone.

"Art," I said, cautiously, "I saw that poem before winter break. I saw it in your room."

"What were you doing in my room," he said. He kept his eyes shut.

"I don't know," I said. "And that's not the point."

I remembered the book on Cornelius's desk, my first day in the library. *Fiat experimentum in corpore vili.* Let experiment be made on a worthless body.

"Dan didn't know, did he?" I said. "You gave him something to drink and he didn't know what it was. You'd been planning it, and that's why—"

"I'm exhausted," Art said, turning on his side. He faced the wall, his back to me. "We can talk about this some other time."

"I think we should talk about this now."

Art kept quiet, then:

"We have another search party tomorrow," he said. "You should get some sleep. Really, Eric. It's been a draining week for both of us."

That was it. It seemed so easy for him. Shutting down. Closing off. I could have sat there, asking the same question for hours, and he wouldn't have said anything.

I took my pillow and blankets from my room and slept on Art's floor. I was too scared to sleep alone.

◆ ◆ ◆

I joined the search party early the next day, at 7 A.M. I'd planned to go with Art and Howie but by the time I came downstairs they'd already gone, and had left me a note on the dining room table. When I got to campus I found the tables set up as markers for where the search party was going to start, and I stood by myself, drinking hot chocolate out of a paper cup. When the party was finally ready to set out there were about twenty of us, some Aberdeen students, but most townie volunteers. We canvassed the forest east of campus, past the well-worn trails and toward the ravines and boulder-strewn hillocks of the deep woods. Sometimes the snow reached to mid-thigh, and we ended up only covering half the area we had intended because it was too cold. I returned to campus about an hour later, my toes and fingers numb.

I spotted Art and Howie in the Quad, among a small group of students and campus security officers.

"I'm surprised to see you out here," Art said to me, gazing toward the snowy forests. "I was beginning to think you'd miss another day."

Howie rolled his eyes and nodded his head in Art's direction. "How far back did you guys go?" Howie said.

"We reached the first ravine after the main trails," I said.

Art narrowed his eyes. "That's not far at all," he said. "Yesterday we covered at least twice that."

"Yeah, but that was the north forest—denser growth and not as much snow," Howie said. "And it was warmer. The windchill today must be close to single digits."

"Regardless . . ." Art looked at me. "I don't see how these searches are going to help unless a more serious attempt is made."

"Well, I'm not in charge," I said, annoyed.

Art didn't respond. A security officer walked over to us, red-faced and bundled in a ski outfit, with a badge pinned to his puffy orange coat. It was Officer Lumble.

"Afternoon, gentlemen," he said, smiling. "Hell of a day to be outdoors. Coldest day of the year, I bet." He took a cup of hot chocolate from the table.

We all mumbled a response.

"Have you heard anything new?" Art said, chopping at the ground with the toe of his boot.

"Nothing you haven't heard," said Officer Lumble. "There were a couple of troopers sent from Boston, though. They stopped by our office last night."

Art nodded—too emphatically, I thought. "Any reason why?"

Officer Lumble took off his hat and scratched his head. The sun shone off his peach-colored pate, mottled red with cold. "I guess Mrs. Higgins has some connection with the state police in Boston. Her late husband was friends with the senior detective . . . something like that. To be honest, we didn't do much of the talking."

Art asked why.

"They had a bunch of questions, stuff we'd already found out. Like those questions we asked you guys." He put his hat back on. "But they wanted to go over the whole thing again. You know," he dropped his voice and leaned in closer to Art, "it *was* kind of insulting. It's not like we're totally incompetent. I told—"

"But we are dealing with a missing person, here," Art said. He took out his pipe and inspected the bowl. "With all due respect, this is a bit more important than busting some senior for selling dope in the Garringer bathroom."

"Is that so?" Officer Lumble crossed his arms. His normally jovial smile faded quickly into something much darker.

"It's disappointing," Art said, not in a conciliatory way. "Everyone is acting as if Dan is fine. And while I appreciate the delicacy of this situation"—his expression indicated otherwise—"the lack of urgency is, ultimately, counterproductive to solving this problem. We must assume the worst and act accordingly."

Officer Lumble nodded. "Fascinating stuff," he said. "And what assumption would that be?"

"The one everyone fears but no one has said yet. That Dan is dead."

Officer Lumble was going to say something else but stopped himself, and once Art had lit his pipe and taken a few long draws, Officer Lumble walked away, tossing his cup of hot chocolate into a green garbage can.

I went to all my afternoon classes, ignoring the stares and hushed whispers, uncomfortable in my celebrity status as a friend of the missing. Even Allison Feinstein, who seldom showed any emotion other than bored indifference, paused and stared while I walked past her on the front steps of Thorren, her smoky perfume encircling me. But I trudged on, determined to put everything out of my mind, and instead I tried to focus on school. I wondered if it would make things easier if I disappeared, maybe go back to the Paradise and meet with my old friend Henry Hobbes. *Maybe by now he's fixed the heat,* I thought. Maybe the duct-taped hole still held.

Sometime during the afternoon even more snow had fallen, another two or three inches, plowed into sand-speckled mountains at all edges of the parking lots. The police, from what I heard, had questioned the witness who claimed to have seen Dan yesterday; now, under closer scrutiny, the man (Roy Elmore, a sixty-something alfalfa farmer who'd served a one-year tour in the Mekong Delta) was supposedly backing away from his earlier statements. He wasn't sure, he said, whether that kid in the white sedan looked like Dan. And maybe his passenger hadn't been black, maybe he'd been Puerto Rican or possibly even Cuban (not that a townie from Brant knew the difference, anyway). But rumors still swirled, and there was talk of a kidnapping, since the showing of the mug shot of a black man on Fairwich's local news had spawned several conspiracy theories. There'd been a fire in Bookertown about twenty miles over, which somehow became connected to Dan's disappearance, along with a furniture store burglary in Stanton Valley. The *Fairwich Sentinel* had decided to post the police sketch of the black man on its front page, along with the headline A POSSIBLE LEAD? despite the local authorities' insistence that Mr. Elmore was a completely unreliable witness. And in a strangely self-damning piece, the following day the *Sentinel* reported a "possibly racially motivated assault" at a Stanton Valley diner, something about an African-American man and two local highway workers getting into a scuffle in the parking lot.

I took a cab into town after my classes and got dropped off at St. Michael's Hospital. It was a small, low-lying brick building with tinted windows and pressed-concrete walkways leading up to a set of automatic sliding doors. There was a television at the reception desk, and on it I saw that the lead story on the five o'clock news was the disappearance of Dan Higgins. They even had a graphic, a black outline of what I presumed was Dan's head, with a giant red question mark superimposed over it. *The search now enters its third day and police still have little information as to the whereabouts of Daniel Higgins, who was last seen. . . .*

I asked to see Cornelius Graves, and the receptionist—a middle-aged, heavy woman with deep blue eye shadow that matched her rayon sweater—had me sign some sheet with a chained pen and then shooed me away, but not before asking me if I was a student at Aberdeen. I told her I was.

"You know anything about this missing kid?" She talked to me while staring at the news. Cynthia Andrews was standing in front of Garringer Hall and speaking solemnly into a microphone.

"No," I said.

"Something like this happened ten years ago," the receptionist said, somehow sounding both sympathetic and reproachful. "Some poor girl was hitchhiking up on Route 128, I think it was. They found her a week later in a field. She was obviously, you know—" She made some motion with her hands that indicated the girl was dead and it was best not to mention it. "They picked up the guy who did it, about a month later. He was living in New York, of course, and had killed a couple of other kids over the years. I think he even told them where he'd buried them all. Just goes to show you." She waggled a finger at me. "City kids like you think nothing bad can happen out here. But bad things do happen, you know. Small town or big city, it doesn't make a difference."

I know, I thought, and walked away.

Cornelius looked like he'd shrunken into a little old man under a pile of white blankets, with an IV dangling from one withered arm and oxygen tubes extending from his nose like the roots of a tiny, shriveled tree. His room was private and silent, the heavy curtains drawn, and it smelled like antiseptic and baby powder. It reminded me of my mother's room when she lay dying in the cancer ward. Glowing LEDs from medical equipment, the droning beep of monitors, and everything gray and white, cold and sterile.

I realized, standing at the foot of his bed, that I had no idea why I'd come or what I was going to do or say. I watched Cornelius's sunken chest rise and fall with each raspy breath. *He's dying,* I thought, *and I'm going to watch him die.*

"Eh? Who is that?"

I stepped back.

Cornelius moved his head and peered in my direction. I knew he couldn't see me clearly.

"Paul? Is that you?"

"It's Eric," I said, finding my voice. I cleared my throat. "Eric Dunne, from the library. I worked—"

"I know who you are." He coughed and raised his hand. "What do you want?"

"I don't know," I said.

"I'm happy to see that nothing has changed in my absence," Cornelius said. "Eric Dunne still doesn't know what he wants." He coughed again and struggled to sit up. "Why don't you step closer."

I moved to the side of his bed. I could feel the blue monitors and drab green scanners emanating heat like a car's engine.

"I've been watching the news," he said, staring at the small TV that hung suspended from the corner of the room like a giant metallic spider. Its black screen stared back at us like a baleful eye. "Some boy has gone missing at the school . . . His name sounded familiar."

"Daniel Higgins," I said. "He's a friend of mine. And Art's."

Cornelius sighed. "I still don't recognize that name. Say, you don't know who Dean Richardson has put in charge of the library, do you? Nobody good, I imagine." He grabbed my wrist suddenly. "Has anyone said anything to you? Is it a grad student? A member of the faculty?"

I nearly yelled in fright and had to resist yanking my arm back. "I don't know," I said, pulling away gently, but Cornelius held firm. "I think they just hired some extra help to keep it organized."

He released his grip. "Has anyone access to my office?"

I shrugged.

"You *must* tell the dean I will not allow it." Cornelius made as if to grab me again but I had backed away. "Do you understand? I cannot have children rooting around among my papers and stealing into my personal things. It is unacceptable. Are you listening to me?"

"Yes, sir," I said. His breathing quickened. "I'll tell Dean Richardson first thing tomorrow."

This seemed to pacify him. He closed his eyes and sank back into the bed, threatening to disappear altogether. Loose skin hung from his jaw in pale folds and his features had nearly lost all form or order—his cheeks were cracked and creased flat plains, above which lay twin burrows, no glimmer in those eyes anymore.

We said nothing for a few minutes, kept company by the beep of monitors and the rumble of a snowplow working on the parking lot outside Cornelius's window.

"I've done something terrible," I said.

Cornelius's eyes fluttered open. He looked at me. "If it's so terrible," he said, "then why burden me with a confession?"

"Art still believes in the Philosopher's Stone," I said. "He believes your stories. He follows your methods. He does experiments on cats, like you with your pigeons, but something awful happened, and now, even with Dan missing and Dr. Cade's deadline—"

"Deadline?" Cornelius said. "For his book series?"

"We're competing for the Pendleton," I said.

Cornelius looked unimpressed. "William has always believed the ephemeral will somehow lead to the immortal. The race of scholars died long ago, and yet William still thinks their crypts to be birthing rooms."

"You have to tell Art to stop," I said.

Cornelius shrugged. "Art will stop when he knows."

"When he knows what?"

"The truth," Cornelius said.

"But it's all lies," I said. "Look at you. You're *dying*. You're not immortal."

Cornelius smiled. "I never said I was. Would you hand me my water?"

I saw a small cup sitting on the nightstand. I didn't move. I was too angry.

"We all seek transformation," Cornelius said, wearily. He took the cup himself, oxygen tubes dangling and swaying. "We all want to become something we are not. Do you remember the map I showed you? The one in my office?"

I remembered it. The maze of the alchemist. The dragon guarding the tower of knowledge.

"When the initiate has lost his way," Cornelius said, "he may find it again by retracing his steps and coming to that one moment where he chose a path counter to his nature. No one can lead him out of the maze. The initiate must act of his own will—it is his failure to act of his own will that led to his wandering astray."

"So Art shouldn't have listened to you," I said. I focused all my anger on Cornelius. His fault. His lies.

"Dan's gone because of *you*," I said. I wiped away my furious tears. "You're the dragon. The archetypal tempter. You led Art down a false path."

Cornelius shook his head slowly. "My days of temptation are long past," he said. "But Arthur is not the one who's lost within the maze."

He stared at me.

"You are the initiate," he said. "And who do you now suppose is the dragon?"

Chapter 6

Much happened over the next twenty-four hours. The local media had been joined by stations from Hartford, New York, and Boston, and their reporters swarmed campus. The extras in my life were suddenly given major roles—I saw Josh Briggs and Kenny Hauseman being interviewed outside Paderborne, and Jacob Blum, in all his chain-smoking, gangly glory, chatting with some Asian woman reporter in a quiet corner at Campus Bean.

Mrs. Higgins offered a $100,000 reward for any information lead-ing to her son's whereabouts, making her announcement on the local news on Channel 7. She stared into the camera, while in the back-ground stood an entourage of men in dark suits—attorneys? detectives? I didn't know. Her hair was pulled into a bun, her diminutive body clothed in shades of black. She was flanked by Senator Feinstein and Dr. Lang, who, I discovered, had lost a son fifteen years ago; the son had gone on a cross-country road trip with his dog and was never heard from again.

Howie had contacted his family, and Beauford Spacks announced his own reward, an additional $10,000 dollars, courtesy of Spacks Shipping Inc. I heard that Mrs. Higgins's suite at the Riverside had been transformed into a war room, with a full-time private investiga-tor situated at the dining room table, Mrs. Higgins at his side, and regiments of professional search-and-rescue teams reporting back via two-way radio. There was a massive green and black grid map, Howie told me, crisscrossed with red marker, and the private investigator (a semifamous retired police chief named Teddy Wolford) pored over it, chewing his pen furiously because Mrs. Higgins didn't allow any smoking in her room.

Later that day, Dean Richardson called the first of what were eventually to be three press conferences. I attended the first conference, held in Garringer's chancel, and I stood in the back of the room while students chattered excitedly and the press propped their batteries of microphones upon the long table. Questions ranged from provocative *(Is it true that Daniel Higgins was missing for a full week before the school did anything about it?)* to scandalous *(Is there any evidence that drugs may have played a role in his disappearance?)*. I had never actually seen Dr. Richardson before, and he looked much different than what I'd imagined—he was short and slightly built, with salt-and-pepper hair and a sickly pallor that suggested either lack of sleep, frazzled nerves, or both. He was obviously unaccustomed to such mass attention, and he ended up sounding so defensive the press had a field day in the next day's papers: *Of course we took reports of Mr. Higgins's disappearance seriously; all such reports are given full and immediate attention . . . I highly doubt that Mr. Higgins's disappearance has anything to do with illegal substances whatsoever. Aberdeen College is a drug-free institution, and I resent such implications . . .*

I left after about ten minutes, and ran into Howie on my way across the Quad. I had tried to avoid him, but he spotted me and lumbered over, nearly tripping on a patch of ice.

"Eric, my boy . . ." He smiled sadly and slapped me on the back. His silver flask stuck out from his black jacket pocket. "I hope you're a bearer of good fortune for this poor soul," he said. His hair stood up at odd angles and he was in need of a shave.

"I haven't heard anything new," I said.

"So it goes, so it goes. Ah, hell." Howie leaned on my shoulder and looked up, toward the gray sky. "You don't suppose anything has happened to Dan, do you?"

"I don't know," I said, kicking at a chunk of ice. "I don't know why people keep asking me."

Howie tousled my hair. "You look like someone who would

know, that's all." He backed away and stood with his hands on his hips, like he was about to make an announcement. "Here's what I say: Dan's gone too far this time. I bet you he's just like Huck Finn, waiting for his own goddamn funeral so he can strut in and shock the hell out of everyone."

"It was Tom Sawyer," I said.

"Huh?" Howie frowned.

"Tom Sawyer," I said. "Tom Sawyer walked in on his own funeral."

"*Right* . . ." Howie scratched his face. "Well, I'm off. Got a date with a shower and a razor. You haven't seen Art around, have you?"

I shook my head.

"You don't suppose he's at Ellen's?"

"Why do you ask?" I said.

Howie shrugged. "No reason. Except it seems the whole fucking house is gone missing. Hope to God you at least stay put. *Vaya con Dios*," he said, and he walked away, unsteadily, hands in his pockets and jacket tail ruffling in the cold wind.

I did finally see Art, in the most unexpected of places—the St. Michael's parking lot, later that afternoon. I'd taken a cab to visit Cornelius, but the receptionist told me that Mr. Graves had been released that morning.

"But last time I was here—"

"Yeah, I know." She shook her head and laughed, a loud, honking sound. "He said he needed to go back to work. What could we do? We can't keep him here against his will. To tell you the truth, honey, he didn't look any worse leaving than when he came in."

I wandered into the parking lot, flipping up my coat collar against the bitter cold, and spotted Art exiting the hospital through a side door. At first I didn't recognize him—he wore sunglasses and a ski cap pulled low—but then I saw his station wagon and so called his name and ran over.

"What are you doing here?" he said immediately. He took off his sunglasses and looked around.

"Visiting Cornelius. They said he's been released."

"Is that so."

"Yeah. Are you okay?"

Art walked away, toward his car. "If you want a ride to campus I'm headed there now," he said. "Otherwise, I'm sorry, but I don't have the time to chat."

I followed him. "What's going on?" I said, but Art refused to answer until we got in his car. Once inside, he locked the doors and took off his hat. His face was red from the cold and he looked like he hadn't slept all night.

"I think he's following me," Art said, peering out the windows.

"What?"

"Dan," he said, and he started the car. "I think he's following me. I saw him again. Maybe it was him . . . this morning, walking past Edna's."

"Didn't you see the news?" I said. "The police said that alfalfa farmer is delusional."

Art pulled out of the parking lot slowly. "Yes, I did read that in the paper. It's good news for us. I was afraid if that theory didn't go away the feds might get involved. Kidnapping is a federal offense, you know."

"How much sleep have you been getting?" I said.

Art didn't respond. He wore a faded, tattered Aberdeen sweatshirt and jeans, and he smelled sour, like unwashed clothes. It was strange to see him like that.

He rubbed his eyes. "I had a CAT scan this morning. Killer headache all night, real bad, not like my usual migraines. It felt like someone was taking an ice pick to my temple. I thought maybe it was an aneurysm. That's how my grandfather died, and his brother, and . . . well, wait a second." He paused. "No . . . no, his brother died of a ruptured aorta."

We headed back toward campus, driving down freshly plowed Main Street. I watched people window-shop, the kids and their moms, students, old men shuffling along with their old wives. I wondered how many times I'd walked past a murderer on the street. Maybe I'd even talked to one; someone bagging my groceries or a bus driver admonishing me for not having exact change. Maybe they'd even had a couple of bodies back at their respective apartments, hacked up and dripping gore into the bathtub, lying in a jumbled pile, heads and hands and feet, red-slicked torsos, eyes wide and staring, specks of blood dotting their faces . . .

Enough.

"You might want to stay away from campus," I said. "The place is swarming with reporters."

On the horizon I saw snow rolling in from Stanton Valley in a gray sheet, dark clouds dangling leaden tendrils. Fairwich was silent—dreary, static, the torpid calm before the storm.

"I want to show you something," Art said, glancing in his rearview. "What's that you said about the reporters?"

"Campus is filled with them. They've set up some kind of bivouac just outside the gates—I heard that Dean Richardson threatened to charge them with trespassing if they didn't get off the grounds."

"Okay. Then we'll go around back. We can park near Kellner. Have I ever told you about the Aberdeen tunnels?"

Aberdeen's tunnels had supposedly been used as storm drains, secret passageways during Prohibition (rumor had it that Aberdeen's former priest, Father Mullen, was the proprietor of Fairwich's only speakeasy), and they also served as an emergency holding center during the infamous 1968 "Paderborne Riot," in which two freshmen were trampled to death during a scuffle between Fairwich police and undergrads protesting America's involvement in Vietnam. No one really knew why the tunnels existed and what they'd originally been built for (they extended to all major buildings on campus—Thorren, Paderborne, Garringer, Kellner, and the H. F. Mores), but, like the forests surrounding campus, they'd taken on a sinister mythology. The tunnels were allegedly home to secret societies and satanic rites, coupled with more frivolous legends, like the existence of the genetically miraculous "Brooklyn White" strain of marijuana, native to New York sewers and tunnels, spawned from decades of panicked drug dealers flushing their goods down the toilet.

Of course, no one I knew had ever actually been in the tunnels, and that's because there wasn't much to see. When I finally got my first look, walking with Art from Kellner to Thorren in what appeared to be an abandoned storm drain, I saw nothing more than cracked cement floors, cigarette butts, and rusted ladders leading to sealed manholes. No spray-painted pentagrams or crushed beer cans or even dimly lit corridors; instead, fluorescent tubes stretched from end to end, casting flickering light over the dirty white walls.

"They're service tunnels," Art explained, kicking a discarded metal clamp, watching it skip and clatter across the floor. "Sometimes during the night, if you find the right spot above ground, you can put your ear to the dirt and hear carts rumbling around, people talking . . . Each one of these tunnels leads to a basement. The chem students use them if they're at the Thorren labs after hours."

We turned at an intersection and found ourselves in a smaller tunnel, with candy bar wrappers and small potato chip bags lying in crumpled balls on the dusty floor. There was a wide, gray door at the end of the tunnel, about fifty feet ahead, with a metal handle like one from an old refrigerator. Someone had written on the door in black marker: *Snorin' Hall.*

Art stopped suddenly, and put his finger to his lips. His other hand grabbed my shoulder.

"Listen," he said, his eyes widening.

At first, nothing. Then, a hollow clapping, like footsteps, far away, coming from which direction I couldn't tell.

"That's him," Art said. "I told you, didn't I?"

I peered down the tunnel, toward the intersection. A moth fluttered up to the fluorescent lights. "It could be another student," I said.

The footsteps continued their pace, measured, coming closer. They were soft, scraping, like sneakers on a sandy floor.

"We should be safe in Thorren," Art said. "I don't think he'd come after us." He looked down the hallway again. "He wouldn't want to risk being seen."

. . .

Thorren's basement halls were dryer than the tunnel, constructed of cement blocks painted white, with caged lightbulbs at evenly spaced intervals and glowing red EXIT signs both above the tunnel door and at the opposite end. The air smelled like cold sulphur.

We passed by several doors, and then Art stopped and took out a key. "Fifty bucks a month," he said, looking down either end of the hall. "I pay the janitor to let me use this room."

He led me into a surprisingly large space: low ceiling, checkered tile floor, black countertops with silver gas spigots, lined up four rows deep. There was a sink at the end of each row, and empty metal shelving screwed to the walls. A chalkboard, cracked down the middle, was set against the far wall, remnants of writing (numbers and chemical diagrams, it looked like) still visible in ghostly lines upon its black surface. Only a single strip of lights worked, toward the back.

"What is this place?" I said, running my hands along the closest countertop. Dust piled up along the edge of my index finger.

Art unzipped his coat and stuffed it into one of the wall shelves. "The administration tried to improve their science and technology departments a while ago. Dr. Cade said they added something like ten new labs, and lured a couple of MIT professors, but nothing ever came of it."

"I wondered where you moved your operation," I said. "The attic was empty."

Art nodded. "It's for the best. Can you imagine if the police decided to search Dr. Cade's? How could I possibly explain what I'm doing? They'd think I was crazy."

"I thought maybe you'd given it up," I said. "After what happened."

Art looked at me with disappointment.

"I had a setback," he said.

"A major setback," I said.

"True . . ." Art ducked behind one of the counters. I heard him rummaging through a cabinet. "Although with things as they are, it looks like maybe I wasn't wrong, after all." He stood up, holding a jumble of tubes and trays.

"I don't see any cats around," I said, acidly. "At least you've made some progress."

Art shook his head. He continued to set things up, plugging in tubes, positioning beakers and flasks, setting out a row of baggies, each containing a different colored powder. "I don't use them any-more," he said. "Only in the beginning, when I was searching for any kind of small success." He pulled a book out from under the counter, some large, dusty tome with faded gilt lettering on the cover, and dropped it onto the countertop.

"I know you think I'm crazy," he said. "But have you ever seen someone crazy put so much time into one singular pursuit? Crazy people are all over the place." He threw his hands in the air. "Always bouncing from one thing to next. Not me. I'm like a fucking laser. I focus on that one . . . single . . . point."

He tapped the dusty tome with his index finger. "You know noth-ing of the work"—he jabbed the book with each word—"and the *time,* and the *dedication,* and the *sacrifice* required for all this." He stopped and looked down. His finger curled and his hand just lay on top of the book.

"Do you remember my lecture on Book Six of the Aeneid?" he said.

Of course I did. It made me sad to think about it. That was way back in Dr. Tindley's class, before any of the madness that had en-veloped us all.

"I'm prepared to sacrifice anything for the greater good," Art said, quietly. "Even if it means losing everything that's important to me."

He looked at me then, and at once my anger faded. Just as Art could shut down, showing the ultimate poker face, he could also open up, instantly, revealing all. And I felt I could suddenly see it: the fatigue, the fear, the uncertainty, the guilt. My anger turned to pity. *How could I have been so callous, I thought.* And now, I realize, how could I have been so incredibly stupid. He didn't deserve my pity. *I* didn't deserve my pity.

He went back to work, taking out his glasses from his jeans pocket and slipping them on. "I talked to the police this morning," he said. "Before my CAT scan. It was terrible. Stifling hot office, bad coffee, the cop assigned to me had the worst breath." He shuddered. "They asked me if Dan was involved in drugs of any kind. I laughed, can you believe that? I didn't mean to. It just seemed so silly, Dan being involved in drugs. It was hard enough getting him to take a drink."

"What else did they ask?" I said. I bit my thumbnail, became aware I was doing so, and stopped, but not before ripping off a thick strip that made my thumb bleed.

"It was strange. I was there of my own free will, of course, but I got the sense I couldn't leave. Not that they would've done anything, but it was as if I had to answer all their questions or else it *would* be suspicious. They asked about the last time we saw him. Remember what we told the cops that night?"

"Of course I do. *He left for some errands.*"

"They asked me to elaborate at least ten times. 'What kind of errands? What was he wearing? Did he say when he was coming back?' Thank God I remembered what he wore on the night of the . . . accident . . .'"

"Jeans," I said. "And a green wool sweater. And his favorite pair of shoes, those brown oxfords."

"Was that it?" Art wrinkled his brow. "Are you sure it wasn't a blue sweater?"

"Positive."

"Hmm." Art lit a Bunsen burner. "I didn't tell them the color of the sweater. Those are the details they get you on. The small stuff. Maybe I'm being paranoid, but it was like they *wanted* me to contradict myself. They kept asking me if I was absolutely certain about the time he'd left, and I told them no. Why would I have been? If it wasn't important at the time . . . Those are the questions you have to watch out for. Liars give too many details."

"Do you think they'll question me?" I couldn't imagine keeping my composure under such circumstances. Dealing with my own inner voices of accusation was enough.

Art shrugged. "It would make sense. I just don't know when they'd do it."

"Would you get me the flask marked H_2SO_4, please," he said, pointing to the metal shelving on the far wall. He adjusted the Bunsen burner flame and swiped his forearm across his forehead.

I'd be lying if I said some part of me wasn't expecting Dan to burst into the room before I reached the wall.

One part vitriol, two parts cinnabar, one part powder of Algaroth. Calcine until all that remains is a mass of gray. Apply to this with an open flame a quantity of heat sufficient to change the gray to crystalline white. This may then be scraped into a powder, dissolvable within any liquid, and through ingestion of a few grains all disease will be expurgated, both curable and incurable, known and unknown, and life may be prolonged indefinitely until the good Lord deems otherwise.

"The Malezel book has been a huge help," Art said, tapping a small amount of coppery powder into a crucible. "But you still have to sift through the Christian allegory, as well as the traps set up within the texts. Sometimes authors would give directions for a poison, instead of the antidote, or vice versa. Gregory of Nyssa, for example, thought he'd found the formula for the Greek anodyne nepenthe, but after giving it to his daughter for her labor pains, she died."

Art showed me much that afternoon, including the notes he and Dan had been working on, their progress over the past year, the mistakes and the minor successes they'd had. It was, if nothing else, an impressive show of perseverance. They'd covered nearly every region of the world, from Chinese formulas for the ill-fated *aurum potable* to Sendivogius's *lapis philosophorum*. One particular experiment—trying to isolate what chemicals had been used in theriac, a universal antidote first discovered in Bologna—involved more than five hundred different combinations, and yielded nothing in the end. "Just a foul-smelling stew," Art said.

It was a strange scene, watching him mix and separate and pour, burning off powder in acrid-smelling puffs of smoke and boiling milky fluid in the crucible and catching the condensation with a bell jar. And all the while he made small talk about our plans for the future and another possible trip he wanted to take in the summer, to Venice, perhaps, or Mykonos, with Ellen and Howie tagging along, and maybe even Nicole, as if there were nothing wrong and no tension between any of us. As if nothing bad had happened at all. For those few hours, at least, Dan was alive, back at the house, playing cards with Howie and waiting for us to arrive home for dinner with Professor Cade. It was in the midst of denial that I realized Dan's death was permanently tattooed across my psyche, an indelible emotion that would forever affect every decision and action I'd ever make from that point on, and it wasn't so much the guilt (which had become so ubiquitous as to be unnoticeable) but the scar, an injury that I knew would never heal. I could, and would, only get accustomed to it.

"Look at this," Art said, sliding a small, cloth-covered book over to me. There was no writing on the cover or spine. "The work of Antonio Exili, 17th-century poisoner. Do you know how rare this is?" He opened the cover. "The 15th to the end of the 17th century was considered the golden age of poisons. So many of the formulas are lost. Some exist, like Exili's work, but are very difficult to get. I bought this in Granada, last year. It's one of only four known 19th-century reprints."

"Similia similibus curentur," I said. Like cures like. Use of the poison is its antidote, one of the few medieval medical practices actually shown to have any validity.

Art took back the book.

"Part of your work?" I said.

He poured yellowish liquid from beaker to cylinder, and stirred it with glass piping. "I'm making *Aqua Toffana,* actually," he said. "Favorite of the Medicis. Composed mostly of arsenic and cantharides. Death is painless, occurring within a few hours."

I remembered the belladonna poisoning in our hotel room back in Prague, and Art's talk about the payoff being proportionate to the risk.

I asked Art what the poison was for.

"Dan," he said, calmly. "If he's after us, I intend to kill him first." He set the cylinder down and wiped the piping with a cloth.

Of course you do.

"I should go," I said.

Art motioned toward the door with a nod of his head, and then started to pour the yellow liquid into a crucible.

◆ ◆ ◆

I grabbed a coffee at Campus Bean and sat by myself in the corner, relieved that snow and darkness had banished the media from school. The search was entering its fifth day and the initial excitement had dissipated; it had become a more professional affair, as local rescue parties thinned out and eventually disbanded, giving way to Mrs. Higgins's personal investigation team. Even with all her connections the police were only willing to go so far—there had been no evidence of any criminal activity, according to the newspapers and television, and the Fairwich residents were starting to grumble about the attention paid to Daniel Higgins, claiming a local kid had gone missing a few years back and no one had given him half as much thought.

The media was leaning toward suicide as the reason for Dan's disappearance, and they latched onto the notion that Dan's mother was a callous, driven woman, whose ambition pushed her son too far. It was an unfair portrayal of Dan's mother, who, when I watched her impromptu press conference, wore a cast of shock and despondency that went beyond normal grief. She'd answered some questions, standing alone on the steps of the Fairwich police station under a midday sun, her entourage milling about in the background, and she looked perfectly dressed and coiffed—hardly the sort of image one would expect from a grieving mother. Reporters mistook the moribund silence for apathy, but for me her expression was familiar. It was the look of defeat worn on a well-dressed corpse. Tears often imply some trace of hope, the catharsis of a wounded spirit that at a subconscious level knows things will get better. But when grief transcends normality it spurs no action, no catharsis or fear. There is only emptiness. It was something I felt I knew better than most.

The weather predicted more snow until Sunday and then a thaw, with temperatures reaching the mid-50s, which threatened to flood the Quinnipiac. Waterfront residents were warned to clear their basements and keep an eye on river levels, as conditions could, as one weatherman put it, "be as severe as the great flood of '64." But that night the concept of a thaw was as far away as summer itself, and instead I put my head down and walked back to Thorren, the blinding snowfall filling my footsteps as fast as I left them behind.

I stopped by Dr. Lang's office to catch up on some work, and let myself in. The upper floors of Thorren were completely empty. There was usually at least one professor staying late in his or her office, warm light seeping out from under the door, but that evening I saw no one, and at every corner I half-expected to find Dan waiting for me, dressed in wrinkled clothes that smelled of pond water, leaning against the wall and smiling sadly.

I have often asked myself why I didn't put an end to all the drama when it would have been so easy—a phone call, a visit to the police station, a five-minute confession. The only answer I've ever come up with (and admittedly it's not much of an answer) has been this: I didn't do it because I felt I had no other alternative. I decided to see everything through to the end, no matter the outcome, no matter how surreal it got. When you believe you've escaped from Hell—and despite it all, Aberdeen was still paradise compared to that tenement in Stulton—nothing else seems that bad.

Chapter 7

Dr. Cade called an emergency meeting, leaving notes under our doors, written in his neat script on small sheets of thick cream-colored paper:

> *I will be conducting a mandatory meeting this Friday at 5:00 P.M., on the status of the project and other important matters. Dinner will be served afterwards.*
> *Sincerely,*
> *Dr. H. William Cade*

I hadn't seen Art since Thursday morning, but he banged open the front door at four-thirty and rushed upstairs without even taking off his coat, Nilus wagging his tail and following close behind. Howie stumbled in fifteen minutes later, glassy-eyed, his cheeks flushed and his movements slow and deliberate. His shirt was half-tucked, and there were red stains splattered across the front of it.

I waited in the living room and saw Dr. Cade walking up the driveway, briefcase in hand, with a troubled look on his face that I don't think I'd ever seen before.

By some miracle Art managed to pull himself together and reappeared freshly shaven, clothes clean and pressed, hair slicked back looking like he'd just had it cut (afterward I found the remains in the upstairs bathroom sink).

Even Howie had done his best—he'd downed a pot of coffee (I had to make it for him; black, no sugar) and showered and shaved, though a dollop of white cream still remained in his ear. From his fragmented story I pieced together an explanation for his semicomatose state: There had been some cocktail party at the Cellar, and Jacob Blum was selling various pills at five bucks a pop.

We sat at the dining room table, Dr. Cade at the head, panning his gaze from me to Howie to Art. "These are, unquestionably, trying times," Dr. Cade said gravely. "For all of us. But we must persist with our daily lives and obligations. It is the only way to assure we do not become paralyzed with grief. Especially now. Deadlines are fast approaching, and according to the schedule we are nearly two weeks behind. Therefore," he folded his hands, placid as a Buddhist monk, "I must double the work load due by the end of next month—"

Howie's face registered mild surprise, muted by the drugs. Art's expression remained the same.

"—and I am dividing Daniel's portion among the three of you. It is the only way we can be assured of making our deadlines."

Dr. Cade rested his chin atop his steepled hands. "Dan's well-being is of great concern, obviously, and no prize or contractual obligation should change our priorities in *any* way," he said.

"He is our dear friend, and until he has returned home safely I do not expect any of you to be at your best. Conversely, we should not be at our worst, either." He glanced at Howie. *"Labor omnia vincit.* Let us distract ourselves with work, so the days do not pass too slowly while we wait for news of our friend."

Dr. Cade pulled his jacket sleeve back and looked at his watch. "I have hired a chef for the evening," he said. "Clive Besk, head chef at the Riverside Hotel. He will be arriving shortly with a fully prepared meal. I'm sorry I will not be able to join you for dinner, but I promised Daniel's mother I would take her to the new Italian restaurant in the village."

"Orezi's?" Art asked.

Dr. Cade nodded.

"How is she doing?" Art said.

"Quite well, in light of the considerable stress she must find herself under. Can you imagine?" He adjusted his tie. "In a way, the four of you are the closest thing I have to children, and knowing that just *one* may be in danger . . . well," he stood and pushed in his chair, "it's something I prefer to not think about."

He bid us goodnight, wished us well, and then went upstairs through the kitchen.

Art drummed his fingers on the table.

"Orezi's," Howie said, staring off into space.

Despite Clive Besk's impressive culinary skills, it was not the most engaging of dinners.

◆ ◆ ◆

The next day I walked from Main Street all the way to East Fairwich, ending up at Posey Street, where Ellen lived. It was a beautiful day at last, clear and calm, everywhere puddles of melting snow and piles of gravelly slush and icicles dripping holes into pockmarked drifts. I rang the doorbell to Ellen's apartment and tossed a few snowballs against a telephone pole while waiting. A crow perched upon the edge of a dripping gutter. I rang the doorbell again, waited for another minute, and left.

I got back onto Main Street just as a dark car splashed past, turning down Posey and continuing to the end. Sunlight glinted off its windows in sharp streaks, and I looked back, thinking maybe it was Ellen's Saab; instead I saw it was a black Jaguar.

It turned into the driveway without slowing, skidding to a stop, lurching forward on its wheels. Howie got out—sunglasses, turtleneck, paper bag shaped like a wine bottle in hand—and Ellen exited the passenger side. Her red scarf trailed in the wind, and Howie said something and she laughed, black-gloved hand to her cheek. I started to raise my hand and shout out to them, and then Ellen stretched her legs over the puddle-spotted driveway, looking for a dry path, and Howie reached out and took her hand.

Their hands clasped, Howie's fingers encircling her wrist; there was her laughter, his careless smile. I thought of the photo of Howie in Ellen's portfolio, Howie just waking up, messy red hair, shirtless, pillow lines creasing his face. Medieval fortune-tellers sometimes looked for the future in the hidden faces within the folds and wrinkles of a pillow. *Maybe I should have done the same,* I thought.

I looked again, and saw her slender legs, clad in black tights, and her black shoes, and her gray skirt at mid-thigh. Black sweater wrapped tightly around her torso, narrow waist, a gentle swell of breasts. Howie's hand brushing her side. *Amor de lonh.* He drew her in and she poked him in the side with a quick jab of her finger, and then they walked up the front steps. A breeze rattled some branches nearby.

I walked away, not back the way I came but onward, toward the edge of town, passing by the clay-green Fairwich water tower and the soot-blackened St. Ignatius Church, blinded by the sun ricocheting off silvery puddles of melted snow. I stopped at some wood-and-brick tavern filled with old men and dark paneling and silence, and I took a seat in the back, on a cushioned bench with a thick wooden table, near an unplugged jukebox that sat forlorn and dusty. Chintzy heraldic crests adorned the walls, a white prancing stallion crossed with two gray swords, underlit by orange glass-covered wall sconces. A row of old men sat at the bar, their heads down, and the bartender moved to each one swiftly and silently, refilling their glasses, his sleeves rolled up to the elbows, long white cloth draped over one shoulder, bald head gleaming softly under the bar lights.

I sat back against the cushioned bench and stared at the ceiling, letting the shadows dissolve and form into whatever shapes they desired: swirling molecules, dark stripes, wavering geometric blocks swinging from the crisscrossing beams. My thoughts were discordant and disconnected: the black gleam of Howie's Jaguar, the dead cat I'd seen with Nicole in the forest, the stoner who'd waited on our table at the Whistle Stop, back when Dan was alive and we'd gone apple-picking. *Labor omnia vincit. Amor vincit omnia.* I laughed to myself.

Something moved on the edge of my vision—a woman, clad in an old green and white gingham apron and a sour mood, her graying hair corralled and pinned atop her head. She placed a small napkin on my table and glanced back in the direction of the bar before returning her wary gaze to me.

"You want a soda or something?" she said.

"With scotch, please."

She raised her eyebrows and put one hand on her hip.

"Is that so?" she said. Her voice was sharp and rusty, like an old razor blade.

I smiled. "Unless you're fresh out."

A pause. "Ain't that something," she said, not unkindly, and she sauntered away, shaking her head, one hand still on her hip.

A couple of minutes later she returned with a glass of soda, tinted caramel from a splash of scotch. I took a sip, fished in my pocket for some change, and then located the pay phone, near the restrooms.

I dialed Nicole's number and leaned against the wall, glass in hand. The sign on the door in front of me read GENTS. On the third ring Nicole picked up. I could hear the TV in the background, one of those vile game shows she liked to watch.

"Hey Nicole," I said, taking another gulp. "It's Eric. Listen, are you—"

"Holy shit, Eric, can you believe it? I mean, my God, you must be totally freaked out. If you need *anything*—"

"Hold on," I said. One of the old men turned to look at me, and I turned around, facing the darkness. "What are you talking about?" I said, lowering my voice.

Nicole squawked in disbelief. "You haven't heard? Oh my God, I don't want to be the first to tell you but if anything, I can relate to what you're going through . . . Jesus, Eric, they found his body this morning. I just saw it on the news. I'm so sorry, I know—"

I hung up and remained there a moment longer, staring at the GENTS sign, and then I left, tossing a five-dollar bill onto the bar. It wasn't until I was past Posey Street that I realized I was running, and that I still held my glass of scotch and soda. It had spilled all over my arm, soaking my sleeve and giving off an odor that reminded me of the first time I met Howie.

◆　◆　◆

I arrived by cab on campus and found students standing in groups in doorways and lobbies, some of them crying and hugging each other, some just talking and looking around warily, waiting to see what was going to happen next. I wandered from building to building, looking for someone to ask information of—Where did they find him? Who found him? What are they going to do now?—but everyone I saw looked just as lost as I, so instead I went to Dr. Lang's office.

The secretary was gone but I found Dr. Lang there, seated at his desk, talking on the phone. When he saw me his eyes lit, and he hastily said goodbye to the caller and beckoned me into his office. Deep lines spread across his forehead.

"I trust you've heard the reports," he said solemnly. He sighed, leaned back into his chair, and rested his chin on his chest, jowls serving as a cushion. "You must be very upset."

I nodded. I don't know what I felt, really. It was hard to pinpoint any particular emotion, as if so many had tried to push through at the same time and had gotten jammed in the entrance.

"I lost my son, you know. Many years ago." Dr. Lang smoothed his tie. "The police found his dog, wandering around Hyde Park, in Chicago. I couldn't bear to take the dog in. My wife told me I was crazy to let that poor animal go to the shelter . . ." He inhaled deeply. "At least with Daniel there's closure now. It's better that we know for certain. Not knowing is far worse, no matter how terrible the truth may be."

I looked into his eyes. "The truth can be terrible, sometimes," I said.

Dr. Lang nodded, and quoted Emerson. *"There is always a choice between truth and repose,"* he said. *"Take which you please; you can never have both."*

◆　◆　◆

The infirmary treated a few students throughout the day. Some had fainted, a fight broke out between two seniors standing in line at Campus Bean, three freshman girls showed up for class drunk, and Louise Hulse, our crazy RD at Paderborne, got into a screaming match with a student and security had to be called. Reporters descended like jackals, nipping and tearing at the flanks of school officials and students alike, dispersed by shouts of anger from administrative representatives, only to re-form and stalk other hapless prey, anyone and everyone who had even the most indirect connection to Dan. On my way to Paderborne a tiny blonde thirty-something woman with a bob haircut and deep red suit rushed up to me, bearded cameraman in tow, and thrust a black microphone at my face. *How has this tragedy affected you? Did you know Daniel Higgins personally? What do you think this says about your college? Have you felt overwhelmed by academic pressures recently?*

I put my hand up to my face like a movie star hounded by paparazzi, and rushed away, into Paderborne, to my cold room, where I closed the curtains and crawled into bed fully clothed. The silence, which before had been so damning, was now a welcome sanctuary. It was as if I'd never done anything wrong, and I convinced myself that perhaps that was the case. *After all,* I thought, lying on my bed and staring at the blank ceiling, *maybe it was a dream. What proof is there one way or the other?*

I met with the police early that evening, called into the station for what they said was a "formality." It was less than that; it was like a mall survey, complete with clipboard and rapid-fire questions, none as difficult as I imagined, nothing at all like the scenes I'd watched in movies and television crime dramas. There was no two-way mirror or pacing cop with cigarette jutting from mouth and hands thrust deep into pockets. I was put in a small room with a long table, given a powdered doughnut and a cup of hot chocolate, and asked a series of questions about Dan's behavior in the months leading up to what police were now calling "the accident." Officer Inman was there, standing in the background while Officer Bellis tapped his foot nervously and rattled off the questions. *Any unusual behavior that you can think of? Did he seem more withdrawn than usual? Did he give you anything of his, any unexpected gifts?*

"Now that I think of it," I said, staring at Officer Bellis calmly, "he had been uncharacteristically short-tempered. And he did give me his favorite pair of pants, about a month ago."

"His *pants?*"

"Yes . . . they were English hunting pants. He had them custom-made in London. Brown wool. He loved them."

Officer Bellis nodded and wrote on his clipboard. "Why do you think he gave them to you? Did you express interest in them?"

"No," I said. "I never asked Dan for anything."

Officer Bellis continued to write. "Where are they now, these pants?"

"I'm wearing them."

"I see." Officer Bellis rubbed his eyes under his glasses and scanned the clipboard sheet.

"Where was he found?" I said.

"In the Quinnipiac." Officer Inman hooked his thumbs into his front pockets. "Near Yale . . . Some student was walking his dog. Saddest thing, you know. No kid should have to see something like that." Officer Bellis shook his head and set down the clipboard. "I'm really very sorry, son," Officer Inman said. "No one wanted it to end like this."

"What did he look like?"

"Who?" said Officer Bellis. "The kid who found the body?"

"No. Dan. What did he look like?"

Officer Bellis looked quickly to Officer Inman.

"Son, have you ever seen a dead body before?" Officer Inman said.

"Yes. My mother's."

Uncomfortable silence. Officer Bellis coughed into his fist and stood up, and then pointed away as if he had somewhere important to go.

"I'll say this," Officer Inman intoned with a serious frown, "your friend Daniel looked at peace." He clapped his huge hand on my shoulder and squeezed, lightly. "God rest his soul."

I am impervious, I thought. *Nothing can penetrate my shell.* And I covered my face with my hands, thinking I was going to cry, but nothing came out.

I went from the police station directly to Edna's, taking a cab even though it was within walking distance (it was drizzling when I first got to the station, and by the end of my short interview the rain was almost falling sideways, driven by the wind). There I spent three hours drinking iced tea and eating turkey club sandwiches. I sat at the counter, on a stool, with my head lowered. A small television perched on a rickety shelf above the wash basin first showed reruns. (There was a show about a rich white guy who adopted two black children, and then a dark series about the New York homicide department. I hated the first show and was engrossed in the second; something about its violence and rapid resolution of problems gave me comfort.) Then a movie of the week started, with Richard Chamberlain as an archaeologist on the trail of a missing gold artifact. It was an awful film, made worse by the running commentary of a fat, bearded man seated a few stools down from me, who, during every action scene (which always seemed to involve Richard Chamberlain punching out natives), mumbled to himself how the natives were getting what they rightly deserved.

Finally the eleven o'clock news came on. Channel 4 news, with Ted Wright and Patricia Cullen. The lead story was, of course, the discovery of Dan's body.

"Hey Lucy," one of the patrons shouted from the other end of the counter. "Turn it up."

"I'm sick of this shit," said the fat man. "Try the other channels."

Lucy waved her hand dismissively, turned up the volume, and stood back, arms crossed across her chest, her tired expression saying *This better be good.*

"The week-long search is finally over, but the questions have just begun in the death of Aberdeen student Daniel Higgins"—Ted Wright looked into the camera with gleeful seriousness—"whose body was found today in the Quinnipiac River, just outside of New Haven. Police and school officials have refused to comment—"

"What else is new," one of the guys sitting in the back tables shouted out.

"—but an anonymous source close to Channel 4 news says that at this time, police have not ruled out any cause of death."

I put down my sandwich.

Ted Wright turned a page in the shuffle of papers laid out before him, and then looked up with a start, as if unaware the camera was still on. "Patricia Cullen was at the scene"—he shifted in his seat and quickly looked off to the side—"soon after the Yale student made his gruesome discovery." The shot lingered a moment longer, Ted Wright blinking uncomfortably, and cut to Patricia, a brunette, counterpart to Cynthia Andrews (Patricia had more of a girl-next-door look, with her small, pug nose and freckles and large, brown eyes). She wore a dark suit, skirt just above her knee, and she walked awkwardly through a muddy patch by the river as she talked into a microphone. Grim-faced police stood in the background, atop a snowy bank, looking down at the river, yellow POLICE tape flapping in the wind.

"I'm standing near the banks of the Quinnipiac River, in New Haven, where dozens of Yale students go to relax, reflect, or, as in the case of Gregory Forrest, take their dog for a walk. But for Gregory Forrest, this particular walk soon turned into something much different, and something nobody"—she clasped the microphone in both hands—"ever expected."

Another cut, this one to a curly-haired, upset-looking college student—Gregory Forrest, according to the caption below his face—talking into a microphone held by someone off-camera. He didn't look into the camera and instead stared off to the side, eyes narrowed against the wind.

"I let Theo run free all the time . . . He likes splashing around in the river, so I didn't even bother to see what he had until I called him and he wouldn't come . . . The first thing I saw was a mess of broken branches jammed against some rocks, then something big caught against the shore . . . like a bunch of old clothes, and his shoe, you know, covered in frost, and his hair . . . I thought it was a wig someone had thrown into the river."

My appetite was gone. I put down a twenty and left.

◆ ◆ ◆

On the way home the rain continued, taxi windshield wipers squeaking rhythmically, car headlights wavering past, distorted and wobbly. It rained all night and through to the next morning, streaking the windows of my room and muffling everything in the quiet shadows of a soft gray sky.

◆ ◆ ◆

I remember what it was like after my mother died, the drawing of curtains between my family and the rest of the world. I remember I couldn't believe how *normal* everything still seemed, how other people could go about their daily routines when my mother had just died and the world suddenly went flat. Oddly enough, I felt similar emotions not after Dan had died, but after his body was discovered. Self-preservation had held everything back and now the grief burst forth, unabated and almost joyous in the havoc it wrought, hacking away at the emotional struts and supports I'd so meticulously constructed, kicking over the walls and ripping apart the ropes and chains that held my monster at bay.

The most difficult days of my life were those weeks immediately following the discovery of Dan's body. I'd thought the hardest part was over, that if I'd gotten through all those previous guilt-soaked days then I'd be okay. But I was totally unprepared and I still don't know how I got through it, through the funeral and the gathering at Mrs. Higgins's home, and the return to school and the horrid days leading up to my eventual breakdown. It would be dishonest if I claimed my endurance came from a lucid understanding of what I'd done and what the consequences were—I understood very little, back then—but, for the exception of one particular moment that shone painfully clear and distinct, I was simply an observer, buffeted by the emotions of whomever I was near.

Everyone had a story to tell—professors, students, even the food service employees and the sleepy-eyed janitors. The most inconsequential of encounters with Dan—a "thank you" after paying for a pumpkin spice muffin, a brief comment in class, a passing nod and smile—had taken on monumental gravity, recounted in solemn tones in the days after his body was found. I watched Dean Richardson's press conference on the evening news, and he had said, with red eyes and gravelly voice, that Daniel Higgins was a *vibrant, active member of the Aberdeen community, and his loss is our loss . . . In his passing a part of us has passed as well."* This was true for us, members of Dr. Cade's house, but I doubted it translated to the rest of the college.

I don't know why I was so sickened by my peers' reactions to Dan's death, but it got so bad I contemplated taking a leave of absence and staying in my room at Dr. Cade's. I couldn't stand the prayer groups and the crisis hotlines that advertised in flyers pushed under my dorm door, and the posters tacked to every corkboard in every building. "So that this tragedy never happens again," read one flyer, "Campus Catholic Services (formerly Campus Christian Services) invites you to a special two-hour session at St. Paul's Church, Wednesday evening at 6 P.M. We encourage all participants to bring a guest." Aberdeen's religious groups had split into their separate factions, seeing the tragedy as proof of the increasing need for God. And God was in heavy supply, invoked by the ghost of Father Garringer, perhaps, transforming what had been a staunchly secular environment into a spiritual revival. Even Nicole got in on the act, wearing a sparkling crucifix around her neck encrusted with red and black gems like the centerpiece in some Spanish cathedral.

I saw Dan's mom briefly, at the house, during a small gathering Dr. Cade organized. It was a wake, I guess, although more like a quasi-cocktail party, subdued and awkward, despite Dr. Cade's gracious efforts. I hovered on the edges, out of place among the Aberdeen, Yale, and Harvard professors who'd come to pay their respects but actually spent the hours talking about their various projects. Howie was in his room, presumably finishing off the bottle of Glenfiddich I saw him with earlier, and Art was somewhere else, Ellen's or campus or wherever. I was sick of him and relieved I hadn't seen him since the discovery of Dan's body.

Mrs. Higgins, from what Howie told me, was inconsolable. Dr. Cade had been with her when the police called and said she needed to come down to the New Haven station and identify the body. There hadn't been any tears, Howie said, with a tinge of awe. Only silence and purpose. *She displayed remarkable poise,* Dr. Cade said to Howie. Her grief had turned to catatonia, however, by the time the wake began, and she stared blankly ahead the entire time, seated on the couch, impeccably dressed in a deep gray suit, raven-black hair pulled into a bun, drink in slender hand, receiving guests like some revered oracle. I wanted to talk to her but was too terrified; I'd heard, somewhere, that mothers have psychic connections with their children, and I was convinced she already suspected I had some equivocal role in her son's death.

The next day Art's friend, Charlie Cosman, drove in from MIT, new beagle puppy in tow, and he stayed in Art's room, sleeping on a makeshift bed while his puppy, Leo, played constantly with Nilus, growling, nipping, and stopping only to urinate on the floor. Howie's parents sent their condolences and were staying in Chicago until the funeral, which, Howie told me, was going to be held in Boston, with Dan set to be buried in Mount Auburn Cemetery. Dr. Cade spent more time in his office, taking a similar route as I, spending most of the day doing work; the three days following the discovery of Dan's body were the most productive I'd had the entire semester. Dan's mother had been whisked away immediately after the wake, and from what I heard she was back in Boston.

Art and Howie got into an argument the night before we left for Boston. Dr. Cade was at school, where he'd been staying every night until one or two in the morning, working furiously on Dan's unfinished sections. The house was finally empty and quiet. Gone were the well-wishers and sympathetic visitors, and Charlie had gone back to MIT after Professor Cade told us, as discreetly as possible, that

"Daniel's funeral will most likely be a closed affair." And in the regained solitude of our existence, whatever unspoken tensions that'd been growing between Art and Howie finally erupted.

It started with a shout—Art or Howie I couldn't tell—and then silence, and then a loud crash, like breaking glass. More arguing, followed by thumping and Nilus barking. I bolted from my room, headed downstairs, and stopped halfway. Art was leaning out the front door, his back to me, and Nilus was in the foyer, barking still, hackles raised and tail erect. I heard the roar of an engine and Howie's Jag zipped down the driveway before squealing onto the road. I looked to the right, into the living room, and saw the source of the crash: the French doors were rent and smashed out, one opened back into the darkness of the study, the other opened into the living room. Glass panels lay bare with jagged borders.

Art closed the door and turned, surprised, I think, to see me standing there. He wore a tie, off-center, and his face was flushed.

"What happened," I said.

"You heard."

"I don't know what I heard."

"Ellen has to make a choice, it's that simple," Art said, running his hand through his hair. He wasn't really talking to me—I think we both realized this. "I know I haven't been the most attentive of boyfriends . . . but she must understand that attraction is almost completely based upon proximity. There was a study conducted years ago, in a college dorm, based upon the number of relationships formed between men and women living on the same floor. They found the closer two people lived, the more likely they were to become involved. It's all proximity, nothing more. Howie ended up spending more time with her, and things progressed." He smiled bitterly. "Did you know Ellen's father is a drunk? It's true. A perfect case for an Electra complex if there ever was one."

"What are you talking about?"

"Oh, come on. That ingenue routine is getting old." Art's expression darkened. "Surely you know about Howie and Ellen."

I shook my head.

Art laughed—that laugh of his I hated. All-knowing. Piously self-assured. "No idea, huh?" He mimicked my gesture—shaking his head—and then he smiled wickedly. "It's so obvious. Almost as obvious as your attraction for her."

"That's not true."

"Don't lie on account of me," he said. "I've known all along."

I stared at him.

"She told me," he said. "She told me how you professed your love for her. And about the letter she found, in your pants. The night Howie tried to kill me." He laughed again. "Oh, I don't mind," Art said, reaching down to pet Nilus. "I know Ellen is a beautiful woman. Besides, you're no threat."

His words stung. I wanted to say something hurtful back to him.

"She hates you," I said.

Art stroked Nilus's back and left a dewy streak of red. I saw Art's hand was bleeding, sliced along the fingers. He sighed and straightened up, and looked at his injured hand. Blood pattered on the floor.

"Didn't you hear what I said?" My voice trembled. "Ellen hates you. She thinks I'm a better man than you. She told me so. And I saw her with Howie, last week. At her apartment. They were holding hands."

There was blood everywhere—on Nilus's back, on the floor, along the edge of Art's shirt cuff. Art cradled his injured hand in his other hand while Nilus began to lick the blood off the floor.

"We're leaving tomorrow morning," Art said. "The funeral service starts at nine. If we get out of here by five we should be in Boston by seven at the latest."

It was a scene I remember vividly. Blood all over Art's left hand, trickles and dribbles along Nilus's black back, bristly fur tipped with glistening red drops. Blood on the floor in spoked dots, licked into smears by Nilus's lapping pink tongue, blood across Art's forehead where he had pushed his hair back. I told Art again how much Ellen hated him, and how everyone knew she'd been cheating on him with Howie, and how much she respected me and how much I cared for her, and even as I said all that Art simply talked over me as if nothing had happened, ruminating about the possibility of traffic during tomorrow's drive to Boston, and now, when I think back to that evening, it reminds me of the sinking of the Titanic, and how the band kept playing even as the ship creaked and tottered, cello bows against a starry sky, heedless of the Atlantic's dark icy waters swirling at their feet.

Chapter 8

Boston. Everything dapple-gray and mottled brown, steady rain darkening the sidewalks and streets, steady procession of cars and bowfront row houses settled quietly under a leaden sky. In the back of Howie's Jag I leaned my head against the window and let the scenery roll past—businessmen and women hurrying under traffic lights, dirty strips of snow lying beneath black leafless trees. Wintry air with a saline tinge. Narrow streets and bricked sidewalks. And everything gray gray gray.

Art and Howie had made up, or at least called a truce, talking around each other during the car ride. Art was in one of his didactive moods, engaged in a ridiculous debate with Howie about the Donation of Constantine, an 8th-century document designed to increase the power of the Church, and whose authenticity was disproven in the 15th century by Nicholas of Cusa. Art claimed Nicholas had been wrong, on account of his support of the supremacy of church councils over the pope. Howie half-heartedly countered by reminding Art that Nicholas had later reversed his position and claimed the pope was supreme. I spent most of the two-hour trip drifting in and out of sleep.

We arrived at the Hingham Hotel, an austere brick and stone building crammed between two modernistic office structures. The lobby was small and dark, with ornately carved stairwells and a plaster medallion ceiling. The concierge was working the front desk, his delicate voice lowered in a whisper, and once Art informed him who we were, he greeted us with a kind, plaintive smile, as if he knew the circumstances of our visit.

"Breakfast is available until ten, or you may choose to have it delivered to your room for no extra fee, gentlemen—"

"And the wet bar?" Howie said, hefting his bag over his shoulder.

"Pardon me?"

Howie leaned in closer. "The wet bar. What kind of booze can I look forward to?"

Art pocketed his room key and pressed the elevator button, eager, it seemed, to get to his room before anyone else. We'd said little to each other since our argument the evening before, but because of the day's somber occasion neither of us had the energy for anything but avoidance, which was fine with me.

"I believe you'll find the liquor and wine selection most adequate," the concierge said, bowing his head slightly. "If you should need anything, perhaps a particular brand—"

"Famous Grouse and Glenfiddich," Howie said.

The concierge paused, eyes raised in thought.

"I'll have those sent up right away, sir."

"That's service for you," said Howie, and he slapped the concierge on the shoulder and winked at me.

Dr. Cade had reserved separate rooms for all of us, quaint rooms on the seventh floor with queen-size beds and small office areas, and a spectacular view of the city. We were meeting at St. Frederick Church at nine, according to the itinerary that Professor Cade had slipped under our doors the night before we left. Service was to be short—a half hour—followed by a car procession to Mount Auburn for the interment, and then a brunch at Mrs. Higgins's place. Art and Howie were pallbearers. I, thankfully, was not.

As I showered and shaved (I couldn't look at myself in the mirror, at least not at my eyes) I realized I'd never been in a church before and that I didn't know whether Dan's body would be laid out for viewing. My mother, true to her socially rebellious nature, had stipulated no church service and no viewing, instead opting for something similar to an Orthodox Jewish funeral. She died on a Monday and was in the ground by Tuesday afternoon. Her friends said their words at the grave site, my mom's cousins gave a small blessing, and that was it. She was buried in a plain box with a false bottom, despite the protests of her close friends, who'd always teased her about her "hippie" lifestyle, and I remember when I rushed to the side of the grave as her casket was lowered, ripping free from Nana's sweaty grasp, I caught a glimpse of my mom's pale arm when the bottom gave way and her body thudded into the earth. She had on her favorite dress, a gauzy yellow thing with sunflower patterns stitched into the bottom hem. Dirt had gotten on it, dark clods sticking to the fabric. I remember that, more vividly than anything else that day.

Dr. Cade was staying at the Ritz-Carlton, having flown in early that morning. His manuscript deadline was in three days and despite the circumstances we were all working feverishly to complete our sections, maybe finding solace, as I did, in the mind-numbing tasks of organizing and indexing our references. I was, essentially, writing one long string of footnotes, *ibidem* after *ibidem*, letters staying in my line of vision whenever I closed my eyes. I also had schoolwork, my one-thousand-word translation of the *Aeneid*'s Death of Turnus.

Howie called my room at 8:20 A.M., loud and drunk and telling me how we had to "get the fuck moving because we're gonna be late," and after I told him I'd meet him in the lobby, a wave of nausea washed over me and I ran to the bathroom and sat on the edge of the tub, my memory still clinging to the last passage I'd translated before the phone call, before the final realization I was on my way to Dan's funeral:

He sank his blade with great anger.
The body of Turnus fell limp in death's cold grasp,
And with a groan for such disgrace
His spirit wisped into the gloom below.

◆ ◆ ◆

The service was horrific. A few tears, mostly stone-faced grief carved deep into the high-cheekboned faces of Dan's immediate and extended family, all of them looking like Dan in some subtle way, all of them sharing his nondescript good looks. Dr. Cade—I'd never been so relieved to see him—was the only shining spot, subdued but still animated, drawing small crowds who asked about his upcoming books and if he would sign a few copies of *This Too Must Pass*. Dan's body hadn't been laid out; instead there was a small table with a photo (a larger copy of the portrait I'd seen at Dr. Cade's), and his various plaques and awards set close by. I passed by the table once but couldn't look at it.

Before the service I had tried to approach Mrs. Higgins but she stared through me, her gaze blank and fixed, sitting in the front row flanked on either side by wealthy-looking women in black dresses with long, black-stockinged legs and shoes that matched their handbags. Art and Howie mingled with some tall men on the other side of the room, all of them wearing suits that looked the same. I felt poor in the suit I'd bought at the Haberdashery the day earlier, despite being assured by the proprietor that it was "much classier than the new styles," and had come from the Winslow family, one of Fairwich's oldest and most prestigious pedigrees.

Dr. Cade found me, mercifully, catching my glance from across the room and excusing himself from an attentive crowd. He floated past the aisle and down the back row of pews, silver hair swept back, hands clasped in front, blue eyes shining.

"You are all alone, I see, as usual," he touched my arm kindly. "Today is not a day to be by one's self. Let me introduce you to some of Daniel's family. Have you met any of his aunts yet? There are three of them, triplets." He smiled. "All delightful women. They sent me over here to fetch you. I understand Daniel talked about you often to them."

"I can't," I said, afraid I was going to start crying. "I'm not feeling so well."

Dr. Cade nodded. "You and Arthur both. He's running a fever." I looked across the room, to Art. He stood, unsmiling, next to Howie in one of the front aisles, still engaged in that forest of tall men in dark suits. Howie was gesticulating and rocking on his heels. I wondered if any of them knew how drunk he was.

"This is a beautiful church," Dr. Cade said, gazing upward. "Very understated, very eloquent." We were standing in the nave, to our right the transept, the priest (white-haired, imperial, garbed in an ivory-colored robe with a green stole) talking with Mrs. Higgins while more people walked in, speaking quietly, hushes and whispers and the brief sound of street traffic before the church doors swung shut.

"This is my first time in a church," I said.

Dr. Cade raised his eyebrows. "Really?" he said, visibly pleased. He was a proudly unreligious man, viewing the Church with the respect and intense curiosity of a staunch intellectual pagan. "You aren't Jewish, are you?" He asked me this with a glitter in his eyes, as if were I to say yes, that he'd find himself in the company of a most fascinating and unusual specimen.

"No," I said. "I don't know what I am."

"Then you are wiser than most. Look here." He reached down and took a prayer book from behind the pew. "I suggest, should you have the time, that you look through this. You will find, in one passage whose exact location escapes me, an amusing typographical error; the original phrase, amended after the Council of Toledo, read *'I believe in the one holy Catholic and Apostolic Church.'* But you will find, in this version, the preposition *'in'* is omitted, and by accident the word *'holy'* does not appear. So instead you have *'I believe one Catholic and Apostolic Church.'* I have always been surprised such an error has never been corrected, though with the speed the Church recognizes and corrects its past mistakes"—Dr. Cade handed the book to me—"I should not expect otherwise."

I sat in the fourth row, at the end, nearest Howie, with Art on the other side and a row of four noisy children to his right dressed in little suits, slipping off the pews, poking and prodding each other, giggling and stomping their feet despite their frazzled mother's repeated attempts to shut them up. It wasn't until an older man turned around and hushed them with a thunderous stare that they finally stopped moving, and when they did it was as if they had turned to stone, petrified by the male Gorgon in their midst.

Dr. Cade sat in the front row with Dan's mom, her two sisters on her other side, their husbands directly behind them, staring straight ahead, chins held high. The priest spoke in low tones, glasses resting on the tip of his nose, hands grasping either side of the pulpit. *That thou givest them they gather: thou openest thine hand, they are filled with good. Thou hidest thy face, they are troubled—*

Howie was mumbling the words in unison with the priest. He stank of liquor and cologne, and had missed a spot shaving, on the underside of his jaw.

Thou sendest forth thy spirit, they are created: and thou renewest the face of the earth. The glory of the Lord shall endure for ever: the Lord shall rejoice in his works—

A wail rose from the back of the pews. I kept my face forward, concentrating on a spot on the wall in the back of the transept. The old man sitting in front of us coughed.

I will sing unto the Lord as long as I live.

St. Augustine had proposed striking the breast while reciting the *Confiteor*, as a form of penance. A partial version of the 8th-century confessional prayer was later finished in the 11th century and subsequently added to the Mass. It utilizes the sacredness of the number 3, as revealed in the thrice-asking for forgiveness. *Quia peccavi nimis cogitatione, verbo et opere: mea culpa, mea culpa, mea maxima culpa.*

Through my fault, through my fault, through my most grievous fault.

Dan's mom had asked Art to speak; I didn't know this until I saw him make his way to the pulpit. His face was flushed, like he had a fever. When he reached the pulpit he took a folded piece of paper out of his pocket and opened it slowly, crinkling it in the microphone. Howie shuddered and rubbed his eyes, hard, pressing his palms into his sockets, and when he dropped his hands his eyes were watery and red.

Art cleared his throat and looked out onto the congregation. His gaze swept past me without pause or recognition. He gripped the sides of the pulpit and spoke:

Once we were three, with but one heart among us.
Scarce are we two, now that the third is fled.
Fled is he, fled is he, but the grief remaineth;
Bitter the weeping, for so dear a head.

Art slowly refolded the piece of paper and slipped it back into his pocket, and then walked back to his seat, head held low, eyes staring down. No one said a word. *What a strange passage,* I remember thinking. It had been from an 8th-century poem Alcuin had written for a cuckoo bird.

◆ ◆ ◆

Mount Auburn was completely different from what I'd expected. During the funeral procession from St. Frederick to the cemetery (I rode in the front seat with Howie, who could barely drive straight, while Art rode in the chauffeured Bentley with Dr. Cade and one of Mrs. Higgins's nieces), I imagined a misty, Gothic graveyard, with crumbling tombstones and thorny, twisted trees, ravens croaking atop crypts and black wrought-iron fencing weaving a spiky circle around land churned and muddied like a battlefield. But it was the opposite—Mount Auburn was a graceful tree-filled place, full of knolls and hills, sedge green with white folds of snow and ice tucked beneath root-tangled crests and overhangs.

We drove up a hill, looping around a semicircle lined with naked chestnut and oak trees. I spotted the grave site, a mound of dirt rising up from the quiet earth like a miniature stupa, two men in blue overalls standing near the mound, leaning on their shovels, talking casually just like any other day at work. One of them was smoking, and when he saw the cars slow to a stop he took two final pulls, stripped the cigarette, and crushed it underfoot.

Howie had said nothing the entire ride. Finally, when he parked, he turned to me.

"I can't do this, Eric," he said, his mouth trembling. "Tell them I got sick and had to go back to the hotel." He exhaled sharply and swept his hair back.

"They need you," I said.

"No," he said. "I'll lose it. I swear to God I will."

"Everyone loses it at funerals," I said.

"But I've never been to one before." Howie wiped his eyes. "No one I know has died." He sniffled. "I mean, there was my grandfather last year, but to tell you the truth I didn't really know him. He and my dad hadn't talked in years."

I tried to change the subject. "Are your parents coming today?"

Howie shrugged. "They said they'd be here about five hours ago. Chicago got socked with a storm this morning . . . but they'll make it."

"What about Art's parents? Are they coming?"

"His dad is. His mom's down in Belize, on a dig."

Howie blinked and moved his head back, as if trying to refocus.

We said nothing for a few moments, sitting in Howie's Jag, watching the cars unload. Dr. Cade emerged from the silver Bentley, followed by Art and a beautiful woman with long, straight hair. She patted the sides of her head as if making sure her hair was still in place, and Dan's mom walked past, arm in arm with her sisters. They were triplets and all looked alike, dark hair, white skin, slender, and graceful. The sky was a light shade of gray, like fog at dawn. There was no wind.

Howie sighed and wiped his eyes again. "I suppose you've heard about me and Ellen," he said matter-of-factly.

"I've heard rumors."

"Whatever," Howie said. "She's just a woman. Not reason enough to destroy the friendships we have."

Someone knocked on Howie's window. One of the tall men. Howie opened the door.

"Let's go," the tall man said, glancing at me before turning his attention back to Howie. "We're ready."

He was referring to the casket, which Howie and I could see jutting from the back of the opened hearse. Art stood close to it, hands in his jacket pockets, looking away.

Howie turned to me, terror flashing across his dazed eyes, and he unbuckled his seat belt and stepped out, slowly and fearfully, like a man walking to his own execution.

Howie broke down during the recitation of the Lord's Prayer, burying his face in his large hands, standing alone at the end of the line, his suit jacket flapping gently in the wind that started the moment Dan's casket was laid on the bier. It looked like Art's fever was peaking—his skin was sallow and his eyes were red-rimmed and sunken, and after he'd carried the coffin he took off his jacket and sat on the ground, his back soaked with sweat, the ridge of his spine clearly outlined under the back of his shirt.

The low voice of the priest, white robe against dark earth. Bare tree limbs clicking in the breeze. Dan's mother's face shining pale, red lips set in a line like the edges of a wound. Soft moans and hitched sobs. Strength now, I wanted to say. I've been through this before. It'll all be over soon.

We lined up to toss dirt onto Dan's casket. The soil felt soft and cool in my hands, and it trickled from my fingers, falling soundlessly upon the coffin. I don't know if I was crying, then. I honestly can't remember.

Chapter 9

"Here's the thing—let's say I'm looking to buy something simple and cheap, like an office building in a less-than-desirable section of downtown. I'm not looking for junkies on the corner or hookers standing in the middle of the street." Beauford Spacks gulped from his highball and smacked his thick lips. "But the area has to be on the edge, on its way up but still pretty damn low. Now, you think I'm going to ask the broker what the city's like? No, *sir*. I'm not going to get an honest answer. I can look at housing values, sure, but those don't tell you the personality of a city. I'm interested in the city's *character*, and anybody who knows anything will tell you that character is destiny."

He handed his empty glass to a passing waiter without taking his eyes off the small crowd that was gathered around, standing in the living room of Mrs. Higgins's Back Bay condo.

"I look at the local paper," Beauford said, with a knowing smile. "Not the news sections—they're filtered through reporters—but the *classifieds*. They never lie."

The group of Boston Brahmins nodded approvingly, pressing in close to Beauford, who was obviously reveling in all the attention.

"Low car prices show the local economy is down. Cheap guns and openings for security guards tell me the city has a crime problem. You know those little classified ads for 'artist's models'?"

This didn't get a response from his listeners, but he continued.

"They're a scam. 'Artist models' means hookers. Same thing with a personals column packed with ads from single women." The waiter returned with another highball, whiskey and water. Beauford took it without any acknowledgment. "On the other hand, if I'm seeing personal ads from divorced women with children, looking for a husband, I know I'm dealing with a conservative community. No Hester Prynnes allowed."

Beauford gulped and smacked again, and patted his large stomach.

"So which is it," one of the listeners asked, a thirty-something man with light blond hair whom Howie had identified earlier as one of Dan's many cousins. "Do you buy property in a conservative city or one with . . . you know . . . a seedier underbelly?"

"Well, now, if I told you *that*," Beauford waved a thick finger, "I'd be giving up my trade secrets, wouldn't I?"

The crowd laughed politely and broke apart. I was seated against a maroon wall, to the right of a fireplace with an alabaster mantle carved in cherub faces and Celtic-style knots. Mrs. Higgins's place was big, even by non-Boston standards, a high, long living room with a coppery hardwood floor, a soft white kitchen with a central island and a stainless-steel refrigerator built into the wall like something from a Fritz Lang film. Food had been set out in the dining room, which had bowfront windows overlooking the Commonwealth Avenue mall. The dining room walls were colored purple, luxurious and rich, with a massive table positioned in the middle of the room, atop a gold and hyacinth Oriental rug.

Beauford Spacks and his wife, Charlene, had arrived at Mrs. Higgins's just as the rest of us did, Charlene greeting Dan's mom with a hug and a kiss, and Beauford doing the same, but continuing to hold Mrs. Higgins's hands in his own while he quietly gave his condolences. Howie's father was a towering, massive man, dressed in a black greatcoat of enormous size with a black suit, his red dotted tie sloping down his broad chest and over his large stomach. He had dark brown hair cut close to his round head, and a well-trimmed beard and mustache. Everything about him bristled with energy, his eyes most of all, two piercing pits of blue set deep above fleshy cheeks. He walked with a slight hitch like he had a bad back, and this only drew more attention; the uneven gait of a lumbering behemoth was presumably a rare sight in Mrs. Higgins's condo.

Charlene Spacks was, by contrast, as insubstantial as the wispy black dress she wore. No matter where she stood in the room, it seemed Beauford's shadow fell over her. She had a gorgeous mane of auburn hair, and she looked much younger than she was. She stood by Howie and talked with him quietly, while Beauford made his rounds, drinking and telling stories and doling out advice.

Dr. Cade appeared to be particularly fascinated with Beauford, and the two of them engaged in a lively debate near the dining room table.

"But surely you can't be *against* higher education, Mr. Spacks." Dr. Cade tipped his head to one side, as he often did when in a serious discussion. "Education can only make one a better person."

"Not the way I see it." Beauford munched on a spinach pastry. "Look here—I'm a perfect example. No college degree, jumped right into the business world. Doing just fine, thank you very much. Why? *Experience.* Your type confuses education with information. Books give me information but only experience can educate. You think college is the real world?"

"Well, I suppose that depends upon how one defines 'real world.'" Dr. Cade sipped from his wine. "In my profession, academia is the real world, as you call it."

"True, true." Beauford emptied his highball again. "But academics make up one, maybe two percent of the workforce. The rest is filled with people like me. Pragmatics. Salt-of-the-earth types. You know why I sent my son to college?" Another pastry disappeared into his mouth. "I want him to get it out of his system before reality comes up and slaps him in the face. And, I'll admit," he leaned in closer to Dr. Cade, towering over him like a tree on the verge of crashing down onto a small forest animal, "it is a vicarious thrill. Seeing my boy get the degree I never did."

Beauford snapped his fingers at a passing waiter, who promptly took his glass.

I left my seat and headed for the bathroom. It was located at the end of a short hallway past the kitchen, small, gilded-frame paintings hanging at eye level on the wall. The bathroom door was ajar and when I entered, I was startled to see Art sitting on the edge of the bathtub, with the toilet seat up and something dark and foul swirling in the water.

"I'm sorry," I said, backing away, but Art shook his head.

"Stay," he muttered. "Close the door."

I locked it.

"You don't look too good," I said.

His face was pale and drenched in sweat. His shirtsleeves were rolled up to his elbows, his tie was loosened, his collar was unbuttoned, and his hair fell over his forehead in thick, wet locks.

"I have to leave right after brunch," he said. "I rented a car and I'm driving back to school. The police want to interview me again."

My stomach roiled. "What for?"

He shrugged weakly. "More questions. This is my fourth or fifth interview with them. I've lost count."

I had a premonition of returning to Dr. Cade's and being greeted by Officers Bellis and Inman. *We need you to come down to the station for a couple of hours . . .*

"Hopefully this is the last one," Art said. "They're a lot smarter than I gave them credit for. I think we'd be in trouble if it wasn't for Mrs. Higgins. Once that kid discovered Dan's body and the initial report didn't indicate anything suspicious, Mrs. Higgins wanted the whole thing wrapped up. She's terrified of the media, and with Dan's previous suicide attempt . . ."

"How do you know all this?"

Art wiped his forehead with a balled-up napkin. "I met with Teddy Wolford, Mrs. Higgins's PI. We compared notes." He sighed. "I don't think you can appreciate how tough this past week has been."

He flushed the toilet and held his head in his hands. "I think this is it, though. I think the cops are ready to throw in the towel. A couple of days ago I told them Dan was gay. They asked if anything was going on between him and Dr. Cade, you know, anything intimate."

"Oh my God," I said. "If that gets out don't you think—"

"It won't. Mrs. Higgins caught wind of the rumor and went *nuts*.

Threatened to sue everyone: the school, the local police, campus security. She doesn't want this hanging around. What's done is done. He's dead. It's over."

"It is," I said. I wasn't just talking about Dan. The world I'd constructed for myself, that we'd all constructed—delusional or not—was now destroyed.

Art looked up at me, dark eyes bleary and sick. "Dr. Cade's been leaning on me pretty hard. Did you complete the Charlemagne section?" I didn't respond and he continued. "I had to sit in that goddamn Bentley and listen to Dan's cousin Alicia drone on and on about whatever . . . She's graduating this year and wants to go to Cornell. She wants to hike through Europe this summer. She's afraid a long-distance relationship with her boyfriend won't work. Blah blah blah."

"Art, listen," I said. This was as good a time as any. All pretenses were gone, dissolved like ice crystals under warm water. "About Ellen . . ."

He looked puzzled. "You're still worrying about that? It's ancient history. We're through. Let Howie have her." He clutched his stomach and winced. "She thinks I killed Dan."

"So do I," I said.

We stared at each other.

"Eric, you're being—"

"What about Dan's letter?" I said.

Art sighed in frustration. "What about it?"

"He told me he was quitting," I said, and I struggled to hold back the unexpected rage I felt creeping into my voice. "He told me it was getting too dangerous. Why would he change his mind?"

"Because of the Malezel book," Art said. "All the work I'd done over break . . . We were closer than we'd ever been. And then . . ."

Art paused, and anger swept over his face, twisting it into a knot.

"For fuck's sake," he said. "How many times do we have to go over this?"

"Dan didn't believe in it anymore," I said. "You did."

Someone knocked on the door. Art looked down and shook his head. There was another knock and a small child's voice, pleading for entry.

"Go away," mumbled Art—to me or the child, I didn't know—and he stood unsteadily and lurched to the sink.

"The aconite is making me sick," he said. His voice was ragged. The anger was drained from his face.

Funny thing was, I didn't even care about the truth anymore. None of it would have made a difference, anyway. Whether Art killed Dan or whether it was an accident, or whether Nicole killed Dan or a black man killed Dan or anchorwoman Cynthia Andrews killed Dan with a pitchfork and tossed his body in the Quinnipiac before continuing on a multistate murder spree. Where was the power in truth, I despaired. Truth's not a companion to reality. It's a slave.

"You might know aconite by its more common name, monkshood," Art continued, and he splashed water on his face. "Aconitine and aconine are causing the nausea and the sweating, along with my blurred vision. I miscalculated the amount, last time. Not enough monkshood, too much tansy."

I took a step toward him. I was suddenly furious, the futility and the sorrow and the guilt concentrating itself into a red geyser that I thought would burst through my chest.

Art looked at me and smiled weakly. "You look like you could kill me," he said.

I shoved him, as hard as I could. Art tripped over the bathtub and fell into it, cracking his head against the blue tiled wall.

Another knock, this one louder than the others. Art stared at me, dazed. He brought his hand to his head, rubbed his scalp, and a thin trickle of blood ran down over his temple.

"My God," he said, gazing at his bloodied hand. "Look what you've done."

"Is everything okay in there?"

I froze. Art's eyes widened and he stood up, slowly, grabbing the shower curtain for support. The curtain hooks popped off *ting ting ting* and Art caught himself before falling back into the tub. Someone pounded on the door.

"What's going on in there? Is everything all right?"

Art looked at me. I unlocked the door and opened it just as Art pressed a hand towel to his head.

One of Mrs. Higgins's sisters was standing there, holding her small black purse in both hands. She surveyed the scene—shower curtain on the floor, blood trickling down Art's forehead. I was breathing hard, like I'd just run up a flight of stairs.

"I'm sorry," she said, her tone indicating she wasn't. "I thought something may have been the matter."

"We're okay," I said.

Art sat down on the edge of the bathtub. "Yeah," he said. "Everything's peachy."

"I just wanted to tell you your father arrived," she said to Art, and she frowned at me, and walked away.

Art doubled over suddenly. He stumbled to the floor and vomited into the toilet. I stayed a moment longer, and then left him, slamming the door shut.

◆　◆　◆

Art's father was tall and slender, very quiet-spoken, with sandy blond hair, like his son. He wore small, black-rimmed glasses and everything about him seemed pinched: his nose, his mouth, his eyes, even the way he stood, with his hands in his pockets and his shoulders drawn in, like he was trying to hold himself.

His name was Elias, a direct descendant, from what I heard, of the original Mayflower pilgrims. When Art came into the living room, he greeted him with a handshake and a nod, and concern registered briefly across Elias's face—Art was pale and there was a smeared bloodstain on his collar—but no one said anything. I thought that if Art collapsed in the middle of the living room the brunch would continue as planned, guests merely stepping over Art's fallen body like he was a fold in one of the Oriental carpets.

"—and finishing some work for the State Department," I heard Elias say to one of the triplet aunts. "I took a leave from Princeton for the year until this contract is up, and then Diana and I are hoping to travel to Sicily . . ."

I looked for Dr. Cade and found him, in the corner, talking with another of the triplets. She had her hand on his arm and was smiling;

as always he was as enigmatic as a Zen garden. Serene in the most asymmetrical way. The longer I stared the less I knew.

I turned away and wandered into the crowd. I wasn't hungry and the thought of alcohol made me sick, and so I sipped a cranberry juice and club soda and talked with one of Dan's cousins, a guy named Emerson who was a senior at Dartmouth, majoring in business and on his way to London for an internship. We talked for about ten minutes until the conversation ran dry, and then we just sort of wandered away from each other.

Beauford had cornered Howie and was lecturing him on money management. In what was to be my only helpful act of the day, I walked over to them and asked Howie if he wanted me to get him anything to drink. I planned to get Howie alone and tell him about Art, about our fight in the bathroom and what he'd said about Ellen, and about my decision to move out of the house.

"No, goddamnit," Beauford said sharply, piercing me with his stare. "Who taught you service protocol? If I wanted a drink I'd—"

"*Pops.*" Howie shot me an apologetic glance. "This is Eric. Eric, my housemate. Remember?"

"Oh." Beauford smiled, a canyon stretching across his perspiration-beaded face. "Pardon me. Judging by your suit I thought you were the help. My back is acting up and I get a bit hot-headed, that's all." He wrapped a massive arm around my shoulders. "You're the little genius, I hear."

"I'm afraid rumors of my abilities are greatly exaggerated," I said.

"Is that so?" He laughed, his body quaking with the effort. "A humble teenager, how rare a sight. Howie tells me you're from the Midwest."

"West Falls, Minnesota," I said. I wanted to get Howie alone but I couldn't see how.

"West Falls, eh?" Beauford narrowed his eyes in thought. "Never heard of it. I used to own some property in St. Paul. That was years ago, though, before Howie got himself off into the big bad world. Before he knew *every*thing, isn't that right, Howie?"

Beauford smiled and pulled me in. "You seem like a good kid. Hope some of your humility rubs off on my boy here."

I realized how drunk they both were; surrounded by a miasma of reeking liquor that I'd always associated with Howie, nothing seemed out of the ordinary, until Beauford swayed and nearly pulled me off-balance, and I noticed that Howie was leaning against the wall for support.

"If anyone could use a lesson in humility it's you," Howie said, staring at his father.

Beauford released me and started arguing with Howie. I left them and walked toward the front door. I was overcome by a feeling of deep dread, claustrophobia making the walls swell. I rushed out, fumbling for a few panicky seconds at the front door when I thought I was locked in, until I realized I was pushing instead of pulling, and I finally escaped and ran out onto the sidewalk. Across the street, in the mall, two dogs greeted one another, tails held high, sniffing, jumping. A squirrel chittered and dashed up a tree, pausing on the trunk and staring out as if remembering something it had forgotten. Sweat ran down my sides. I could feel my heart pounding inside my head.

I wanted to go home.

◆ ◆ ◆

At the hotel I fell asleep, still dressed in my suit. The next morning I rode home with Howie. Art had left the day before and our trip was without incident—Howie just stared ahead and drove like an automaton, suffering nobly through the effects of a wicked hangover.

◆ ◆ ◆

One of Dr. Magavaro's nurses was taking Nilus for a walk when we reached Dr. Cade's house. Nilus dashed across the snow-covered front lawn and leapt up on me. A trio of crows sailed silently overhead, three black arrows against the clear sky.

Howie slept in his room while I packed my bags and made some chicken for myself. After lunch I called for a taxi and took it to campus. My room would be musty and cold but I didn't care. I didn't feel like staying at Professor Cade's anymore.

Chapter 10

I went to a party that night at the Cellar. It was organized by Nicole, as "a celebration of Dan's life, and a reminder that each day must be lived to the fullest," which translated into consuming as much liquor and drugs as one could stomach. I'd never been to the Cellar before, and found it true to its name. Low ceilings, dirty wooden plank floor, cramped bathroom with a single glaring lightbulb on which someone had drawn an anarchy sign in black marker. I danced among the drunken hordes of fellow students who treated me as the *cause célèbre*, the noble sufferer who needed solace and understanding. I danced and drank until numb, and then I left quietly, slipping out the back door.

I returned to my room and lay on my bed for how long I don't know—three, maybe four hours—before the phone rang.

"Dr. Cade wanted me to call you," Art said. "He needs your completed section by tomorrow morning."

"I can't come back to the house," I said. "I'll drop it off at his office."

"We're having a big dinner tonight," Art said. "And after, we're going for a hike. All of us. Howie and Ellen and maybe I can even convince Dr. Cade. We're going to Butternut Falls. We haven't taken you there, yet. You'll love it—there's a waterfall, and a little pool that you can ice-skate on, and huge, smooth boulders . . ."

"I can't," I said.

Art was quiet for what seemed like a long time.

"I can't stop, you know," he said. He sounded very tired.

I knew what he was talking about. "Yes, you can," I said. "Just walk away."

"Then Dan's death meant nothing," Art said.

"Death doesn't have any meaning," I said. "That's why we look for it."

I dropped the handset and pulled my pillow over my head.

A knock on my door before dawn. Another knock and then a familiar voice, drifting to me like a ghostly wail across a graveyard.

Eric.

I stumbled out of bed, and opened the door and there she was in a whir of perfume and shimmering skin.

Ellen floated past me. I felt as if I hadn't seen her in years. She wore faded jeans and a sweatshirt and sneakers. I looked around. My room was a mess. Sheets crumpled on the floor, papers scattered over my desk. The window was closed and the radiators were at full blast, rattling and hissing

I retreated back to bed.

"How are you," she asked, sadly.

"Tired," I said.

Ellen sighed. "I'm sorry I didn't make it to the funeral. I wasn't invited alone, only as Art's date. And you know what happened, I assume."

"I don't care," I said. "Really. I don't care at all." How impossible would it be, I imagined, to take her into my arms and kiss her, the two of us melting into bed, undressing languorously, making love in the light of dawn, silky blue covering our bodies in a delicate film.

"Eric, I'm worried about Art."

"Come here," I said. I felt deliciously giddy. I touched her hand.

"You're drunk," she said.

Perhaps I am, I thought. How, though . . . it had been hours since I'd gotten home. Or had it?

"Listen to me," Ellen said, grabbing my hand with surprising strength. "Art's still trying to make that elixir or whatever the hell it is.

We need"—she slapped my hand, rousing me—"we *need* to talk to him. And there's something else."

I stared at her.

"Tell me what happened to Dan," she said.

This is it, I thought. She moved closer to me. Her lips parted. *All you have to do is say a few words.*

"Art and I fought," I said, fumbling for the glass of water on my nightstand. "At the wake at Dan's mom's house. In the bathroom. We fought over you. But you love Howie so it doesn't matter, does it?"

Ellen drew back and started to say something but she stopped herself, and her expression suddenly changed.

"Are you mad at me?" she said.

I was going to ask her why she said that when I looked down at my hands and saw they were trembling.

"Don't you know," I said, "how much I hate all of you?"

"No," she said matter-of-factly. "I don't."

We sat there, silent, and then she left, closing the door behind her, leaving only a warm depression at the end of my bed and the lingering scent of sharp perfume.

As expected, I didn't sleep well. Muddied, murky dreams, and only one I remember:

I was walking Nilus along the edge of the pond on a chilly fall night, the sky a yawning chasm without any stars or moon, and yet a cold glow lit my path. Nilus was unusually fickle, taking his time, sniffing along the ground, rooting through the wet grass and cattails. I wasn't scared but I wasn't comfortable either, an ominous feeling particular to dreams when you seem to know something bad is going to happen before it actually does.

Nilus's breathing was unnaturally loud; blades of grass scratching against his wet nose sounded like metal against sandpaper. The damp earth gave slightly beneath my feet, and I remember thinking I was going to have to wipe Nilus's paws with a towel before letting him back inside. And then he stopped abruptly and raised his head, and looked out over the black water and everything fell silent. Something splashed in the pond.

I didn't want to look but I did. There was the canoe, skimming silently along, and seated in the center, paddling slowly, was Dan. I couldn't see his face but I knew it was him. He was wearing his plaid flannel coat and his short, straight hair ruffled in the wind even though no wind blew.

He floated past, looking straight ahead, off toward the forest behind Dr. Cade's house. I froze, praying he wouldn't see me, but Nilus barked and Dan suddenly stopped and turned. There was something wrong with his shadow-banded face . . . His skin was taut and bloated, and things moved in his hair, nasty, insectile shapes that scurried across his forehead, down his cheeks, dropping into the canoe with a hollow *plunk*.

Dan looked at me and smiled sadly. The canoe continued to drift, water lapping against its side. He turned away and resumed paddling. Clunk-swish. Clunk-swish.

I watched him dissolve into the darkness, past where the cold glow that lit my path stopped, and I lost sight of him as he made his way toward the middle of the pond. Nilus howled, suddenly, loud and mournful, and I woke up.

Sunlight streaming in through the window. Blankets kicked off and hanging over the side of my bed. Silence.

I stumbled over my crumpled shirts and scattered books, to my closet, where I had stored a "Welcome Pack" given to me the first day at school. In it were condoms and peanut butter crackers and various toiletries, and most importantly, two single foil packets of cold medicine. MAY CAUSE DROWSINESS read the warning label in the light of the bulb I'd clicked on. I ripped both packets open, dry-swallowed all four tablets, and staggered back to bed, hoping that whatever I'd just swallowed would do the job right and kill me.

That afternoon I went to Dr. Cade's office. I knocked on the door, waited, and knocked again, more firmly this time.

A moment later the door opened a crack. Deep blue eyes, like the first day I'd gone to his office. They widened in recognition this time, however, and the door swung open.

"Please, come in." Dr. Cade motioned to the single chair across from his desk. He was dressed well, but looked tired, and was putting on a false smile, obviously bothered by the intrusion.

The room was surprisingly large for a professor's office. The windows were draped in thick curtains, and heavy Oriental rugs covered most of the floor in layers of dense folds, brown and leafy green and deep purple and magenta. His desk was like the one he had at home, made of a dark wood, Shaker style. It was covered in stacks of papers.

"This is a rare visit," he said, leafing through one of the stacks. "I don't believe you've been in my office before."

I nodded, dumbly.

"Congratulations are in order, by the way," Professor Cade said. "Dr. Lang informed me this morning of your victory."

I had no idea what he was talking about.

"You haven't heard? Oh, well then, let me be the first to tell you. The Chester Ellis Award. The finalists were announced last week. You, Eric, are this year's recipient."

I tried to force a smile but couldn't. Dr. Cade didn't seem to notice.

"Art and Howie both turned in their work this morning," he said, marking one of the papers with a thick fountain pen. "I trust your section is almost completed . . . or are you having problems with it?" He looked up at me and stopped writing.

"Goodness, Eric, is something the matter?"

I took the envelope out of my pocket and placed it on his desk. Dan's letter was inside, creased and crinkled from the weeks it spent under my mattress. I told him the whole story, and when I finished I lowered my head and I cried silently, so hard and long the tears stopped and all I could do was inhale and exhale in heavy, hitching gasps.

PART III

—

Aberdeen, Departed

It has been said that the immortality of the soul is a "grand peut-être"—but still it is a *grand* one. Everybody clings to it—the stupidest, and dullest, and wickedest of human bipeds is still persuaded that he is immortal.

—LORD BYRON, *RAVENNA JOURNAL*

experiments on cats, and his gradual descent into madness. My suspicions about how Dan had died, whether or not he knew he was taking the formula, and what we did the night I came downstairs and found Dan lying on the foyer floor, face up, his skin pale and his eyes half-open. I told Dr. Cade that Art had confessed to writing the suicide note. I told him I had known this for quite some time.

Dr. Cade listened intently, his expression unchanging, and when I lost control and started to cry, he merely waited for me to finish. Five, maybe ten minutes passed, until I composed myself, and then he cleared his throat and set the letter down.

"This is a serious matter," he said, staring at me with hooded eyes. He looked down at the letter and pursed his lips.

"Most serious," he said. "Yes . . . yes, it is."

He folded the letter and put it into the top drawer of his desk.

"I will give it my full consideration," he said, and he uncapped his pen and smoothed his deep blue tie.

"Now then, I expect your completed section by 5 P.M., at the latest. I will be staying at my office until 10 this evening, should you need any more time, which I'm hoping you will not. I still have an enormous amount of work ahead of me, so if there's anything else . . ."

He went back to work, marking sheets of paper with his silver Mont Blanc. I waited for him to say something. The only sounds were the raspy scratch of his pen and the ticking of the radiator. Five minutes passed into ten, and still I waited, seated across from him, while he slowly worked through the pile of papers.

Finally I got up and walked out, not bothering to close the door.

I don't think Professor Cade believed in, or encouraged study of, the Philosopher's Stone. I do think he understood mortality more than any of us, and as a consequence I think Dr. Cade did succeed, on some level—despite Cornelius's insistence otherwise—at grasping the microscopic slice of immortality that's offered to us all. He was so acutely aware of his place in time that he never missed an opportunity to be remembered, and he was devoutly selfish, but he never claimed to be anything else. I was the one who created his image as that of a moral father, when in fact his decision to continue the cover-up of Dan's death was so in line with who he was—*I have chosen to view the world rationally,* he'd said, that one night during dinner, *and to my delight the world has presented itself as such*—that sometimes I feel a twinge of admiration for, if nothing else, his lack of hypocrisy. I know one can rationalize anything, but no matter what any of us did afterward, no matter how many lies we told or opportunities to choose differently we passed by, nothing changed the reality of Dan's death. That is what Dr. Cade understood, and that's the only consolation I've allowed myself.

◆ ◆ ◆

I fully expected Art to die that afternoon, poisoning himself accidentally in his lab and thereby recusing himself of any further guilt. But he was home when I called Dr. Cade's for the last time, and when I told him I had confessed everything, that I'd sat in Dr. Cade's office and admitted my role in covering up Dan's death, he kept silent for about a minute, and said he'd see me at dinner. *We're having lamb,* he said. *If you could pick up some sweet peppers on the way home that'd be great. And maybe a good Cabernet. Call me from the store if they give you a hard time.* In the background I heard Howie playing piano—his favorite Bach piece, The Air, from Suite in D Major—and Nilus whining to be let out. The illusions had been put back up, I remember thinking. Now I was the *memento mori.*

My last work for Dr. Cade I left unfinished, the end of the Carolingian empire, written in Nicole's dorm room while she was at class. I couldn't spend much time alone in my room for obvious reasons.

The idea of Charlemagne's empire did not die with him; to the contrary it flourished, reaching its conceptual apex nearly a half century after his death. But the most brilliant expressions of his ideal came long after the opportunity to realize them had passed—by the time of the Carolingian Renaissance the Empire was collapsing. Besieged on all sides—Vikings from the north and west, Hungarians from the east, and Saracens from the south—the end came swift and complete. Towns were burned to the ground, abbeys and churches were sacked and left abandoned. One order, the monks of St. Maiolus, long held as the shining example of Charlemagne's ideal, soon found themselves on the run from invaders. Vikings attacked their monastery on the island of Noirmoutier, and from there they fled to Deas, and then Cunauld, and after that to Messay, to St.-Pourcain-sur-Sioule, and finally to Tournus on the Saône, where they started construction of a magnificent cathedral. After forty years and six hundred miles they seemed to have at last found a safe haven. But their respite was short-lived. Hungarians attacked, burned the cathedral to its foundation, and the monks who survived were scattered. Charlemagne's ideal had taken its last breath.

I ended up leaving my unfinished section for Dr. Cade outside his office door, and I walked away from it all, as best I could.

That spring Cornelius Graves died in the library, at his desk, from a heart attack caused by the stress of radiation and chemotherapy treatments. His body was discovered by Josh Briggs, who, while returning an overdue book, found Cornelius slumped in his chair at the front desk, his cane lying on the floor beneath his dangling hand. I was the only person at Cornelius's funeral—aside from the priest and grave digger—and the church buried him in Forest Stream Cemetery, right off of Route 9, in Stanton Valley. Cornelius, unbeknownst to everyone at school (and perhaps even to himself), had lived in Fairwich County his entire life. The old priest told me this—his father had worked with Cornelius in the Stanton Valley paper mills, nearly seventy years ago. I like to think the pigeons breathed a collective sigh of relief when news of Cornelius's death reached them. I know I did. His death completed his mythology, and let the gods sear his constellation into the night sky.

I floated through the rest of the semester, doing well in my classes, enjoying dorm life, going to parties and dating a few girls. Throwing up in the broom closet because I couldn't make it back to my room in time, having sex with a freshman girl in Thorren's third-floor bathroom—"living the normal college experience," as Nicole said, puffing a joint while we sat together on the Paderborne fire escape on a warm April night.

I tried to stay at Aberdeen but found my sleep still restless and my waking hours overcast with a dark veil, despite some moments of true happiness. I toughed it out until my junior year and then I applied and was accepted into Aberdeen's Ivy League cousin, twenty miles south in New Haven. There were some parties thrown for me—another event at the Cellar, a small gathering at Jacob Blum's—and the requisite tears, mostly from Nicole, who said this time I was a goner, for certain. Before, she said, I was living in a house full of snobby elitists; now I was going to an entire *school* of them.

I saw both Ellen and Howie for the last time, on the same day. I was taking the bus to New Haven and had a few hours to kill so I decided to eat lunch at Edna's, and just as I sat down, Howie and Ellen walked in. Howie's hair was cut shorter, and he wore a black fitted sweater—something I never expected to see him in. Ellen had let her hair grow, past her shoulders, a flaxen rush contrasted starkly against her deep red sweater. I hadn't thought about her much in the previous year, not as much as I feared but more than I'd hoped, and seeing her—seeing them—brought back a sickening wave of nostalgia. *It was that fork-speared caper,* I thought, *that made me fall in love with you.*

I didn't want them to see me but they did, and to my surprise they asked me to join them, and again to my surprise, I accepted.

We fell into our old ways more easily than any of us expected (Howie gave me a brief lecture on the importance of starting an early-retirement fund, Ellen told him to leave me alone), and we discussed Ellen's new job opportunities in Chicago, how she was moving there within six months, and how Howie was going with her. Howie said he was sober, adding *at least for now,* and Ellen punched him in the arm. Also, he was proud to say, he'd summoned the courage to tell his dad he wasn't getting a degree—"the old man thinks I'm an indolent bum, of course"—but Beauford had finally relented. Only because he'd had a heart attack six months earlier, Howie said, and was now "putting things in perspective."

We talked about my future at Yale and how important it would be to keep in touch (which didn't happen, by the way—I wrote Howie a few times, care of Ellen's address, during my first semester at Yale, and he wrote back a few times, and then one day my letter got returned, with NO FORWARDING ADDRESS stamped crookedly across the front). We chatted for another thirty minutes while the usual cast of characters shuffled in and out of Edna's (including the heavy man who'd been so fond of Richard Chamberlain movies), and I waited as long as I could—through my BLT and my apple crumb pie—until finally asking them about Art. At the mention of Art's name Howie stiffened, and his smile faded.

Howie beckoned the waitress. "As far as I know," he said, "Art's still at Dr. Cade's."

"You're kidding."

"Nope . . ." Howie rubbed his eyes. "I think he's helping Professor Cade with another book. He didn't win the Pendleton, by the way. Did you know that? Linwood Thayers got it."

All that trouble, I thought.

"I can't see Art ever leaving Aberdeen," Ellen said. "He's thinking about getting his doctorate. At least he was when we last talked."

"When was that?" I said. The waitress brought the check and Howie promptly took it, despite my protests.

"Oh, let me think . . . six months ago, maybe. I ran into him at the new coffeehouse on Main and Tremont. What's that called—"

"Neely's," Howie said.

"That's right." Ellen smiled and rubbed the back of Howie's neck. "Art was sitting alone, as usual, big old book on the table, papers lying around. We talked briefly. He asked about you."

I sat up. "What'd he say?"

"He wanted to know what you were up to. Said if I ever see you to give you a big hug. And he also wanted me to thank you."

Howie and I both stared at her.

"For what?" I said.

Ellen shrugged. "He didn't say."

I already knew the answer.

"You never told me that story," Howie said.

Ellen smiled demurely. "It wasn't for you."

Some intimacies never go away—for a moment I saw Ellen as she'd been with Art, and he sat near her, a ghost, long arm draped over her shoulder, small glasses hooked behind his ears, scents of clove and tobacco.

Something gave and it came out of me. The way these things always do. Slipping past the guards. "The way Dan died . . ." I said, looking away. "No one really believes it. I mean how everyone says it happened. *You* don't believe it, do you?" I pinched my thigh, hard, to stop the tears, but it wasn't working.

Howie's hand shot across the table and grabbed my wrist.

I stared at him, then Ellen. She took his hand, gently sliding it off mine. Howie inhaled deeply, looked up, and shook his head. Art's ghost wisped away, mouth open in a silent scream, blown by spectral winds.

I didn't realize it at the time—we never do—but that was the most honest we'd ever been with each other, and none of us had said a thing.

We made our goodbyes, Ellen kissing me on the cheek, Howie nearly crushing me in a full-body hug, and then I sat in the booth and watched them leave.

Howie stood at the door of his Jag and searched his pockets, while Nilus barked at him from the backseat. Sun glinted off the car's sleek hood, bubbles of searing light, striking Edna's front window and shattering all over my table in cubes and beams, dappling my arms, my plate of half-eaten food, the cracked red Naugahyde booth. Howie looked up and saw me staring at him. He smiled, opened his arms to the sky, and got into his car.

And in that moment, I knew he'd forgiven me. *Ask, and ye shall receive.*

About the Author

Micah Nathan has been a radio talk show host, an amateur kickboxer, a motivational speaker, a filmmaker, and a strength and conditioning coach. He was in born in Hollywood, raised in western New York farm country, and now lives in Brookline, Massachusetts with his wife. This is his first novel.